Critical Praise for *The River Midnight*

"[A] mesmerizing first novel . . . *The River Midnight* is not simply remarkable as a historical text. Nattel's flair for the telling detail is just one treasure in her bag of writer's tricks."
—Natasha Stovall, *The Washington Post*

"As enchanting as a Chagall mural . . . Nattel writes with refreshing bawdiness."
—Roy Hoffman, *The New York Times Book Review*

"[Nattel's] supple narrative technique weds the discipline of scholarship with artistic license. *The River Midnight* is inspired matchmaking."
—R. Z. Sheppard, *Time*

"A magic-realist novel with equal attention to both magic and reality—not an easy line to walk. . . . Nattel weaves all the strands together in a visionary climax that unites the village and points across the generations to herself."
—Janice Pomerance Nimura, *Newsday*

"Readers who appreciate the magic of quality research wrapped in a well-told tale will find Blaszka worth a visit."
—Laura Rose, *USA Today*

"Lilian Nattel has written a first novel of wondrous mythical depth and rare spiritual beauty. . . . No doubt possessing prodigious literary gifts, Nattel's depth of study and passion for her subject also accounts for *The River Midnight*'s stunning originality."
—Paula Friedman, *The San Diego Union-Tribune*

"Like the mythical Polish shtetl of Blaszka in which it is set, *The River Midnight* is boisterous, tangled with secrets, and startlingly generous . . . with lush, scrupulous detail and an unerring eye for the tension between self-interest and benevolence."
—Ben Guterson, Amazon.com

"*The River Midnight* is a warm hearth to return to at the end of a chilly day."
—Rebecca Walker, *San Antonio Express-News*

"The novel's richly nuanced tapestry allows us to enter into a world that is at once familiar and lost forever."
—*Tikun*

"*The River Midnight* is a work of great ambition."
—Andrew Furman, *Forward*

THE RIVER MIDNIGHT

LILIAN NATTEL

SCRIBNER PAPERBACK FICTION
PUBLISHED BY SIMON & SCHUSTER

SCRIBNER PAPERBACK FICTION
Simon & Schuster, Inc.
Rockefeller Center
1230 Avenue of the Americas
New York, NY 10020

First Scribner Paperback Fiction edition 1999
SCRIBNER PAPERBACK FICTION and design are trademarks of Macmillan Library Reference USA, Inc., used under license by Simon & Schuster, the publisher of this work.

Designed by Brooke Zimmer
Set in Garamond
Manufactured in the United States of America

5 7 9 10 8 6 4

The Library of Congress has cataloged the Scribner edition
as follows:
Nattel, Lilian, date.
The River Midnight / Lilian Nattel.
p.   cm.
1. Jews—Poland—Fiction. I. Title.
PS3564.A8734R5   1999
813'.54—dc21   98-27773
CIP

ISBN 0-684-85303-5
0-684-85304-3 (Pbk)

Cover art (top): *A View of the River Volga* by Piotr Petrovitch Weretshchagin (1836–86), Phillips, The International Fine Art Auctioneers, UK/Bridgeman Art Library, London/New York.

For my mother,
who showed me the pleasure of being alive,
and for my father,
who taught me to look for beauty everywhere.

ACKNOWLEDGMENTS

I want to thank Jane Rosenman, my editor at Scribner for her excitement, keen insight and intelligent guidance, and her assistant Caroline Kim for her unflagging helpfulness; Marion Donaldson at Review in Great Britain for her enthusiasm and early interest; Louise Dennys at Knopf Canada for her belief in this book. Many thanks are due Helen Heller, agent par excellence and provider of delicious tea and sweets, for her calm sagacity and nerves of steel. I would like to express my gratitude to the Ontario Arts Council for financial support during the writing of this book. I am also grateful to The Writers' Union of Canada for its mentoring program, and to my mentor Rhea Tregebov, whose precise observations enabled me to fine-tune the final draft of the manuscript. My thanks go also to Jerry Silver and Susan Meisner, who introduced me to Helen. Many other people have been generously supportive of this project, and they have all earned my gratitude, especially Hope Dellon. Most of all, I would like to thank my husband, Allan, my greatest fan, who listened to me read the novel aloud to him scene by scene and draft by draft, and whose shining smile kept me going.

A NOTE ON SPELLING

There is a standard transliteration from Yiddish to English, established by the YIVO Institute, and used by scholars. I decided not to use this transliteration because it can lead to strange pronunciation by people unfamiliar with Yiddish. Instead, by approximating the Yiddish sound in words or names as they would be spelled by an English-speaking reader, I hope to ease the reader's entry into the shtetl world of Blaszka (pronounced "Blashka"). Polish words and names are generally spelled using Polish orthography. One exception is the city of Plotsk, the spelling used under Russian occupation; in Polish it is Płock. The only other exceptions are Warsaw and the Vistula River: I used the English names, which are familiar to many readers, just as the Polish Warszawa and Wisła would be to the men and women of Blaszka.

CONTENTS

PROLOGUE

ANGELS AND DEMONS

Time grows short at the end of a century, like winter days when night falls too soon. In the dusk, angels and demons walk. Who knows who they are? Or which is which. But there they are, sneaking their gifts into the crevices of change. Even in a place like Blaszka, less than a dot on the map of Russian-occupied Poland.

Someone might say that so-and-so is an angel or so-and-so a demon. But make no mistake, it's just a question of style. One sympathizes, the other provokes. But their mission is the same, and so is their destination.

It's a cold day, the short Friday of winter, the 20th of *Tevet* 5654, or you might call it the 29th of December 1893, according to the Christian calendar. Everyone's in a rush, anxious to finish their business before the sun sets. Once darkness falls, the Sabbath rules. Candlelight will have no other purpose than its beauty, and women and men will make love in honor of the Sabbath.

Listen. You can hear the excitement in the village square. "Fresh, hot, only two kopecks." Girls run through the crowd, carrying baskets of rolls, pretzels, pierogies, and herring cut into small rings. The herrings almost speak. Take your pick, the large smelly ones, horse herring, pickled, smoked, or packed in fat. Steam rises from the warm baskets in the winter air. The square smells of vinegar, yeast, and horse dung. Men and women blow into their cold hands to warm them, pinching this and sniffing that, bargaining as if for their souls, undeterred by the crash of a stall that collapses under its mountain of earthenware. This is what keeps Blaszka together, the flimsy stalls piled high with everything, where people lean toward each other, bargaining, touching what they need, shaking it, holding it up to the light.

Hurry, the villagers say, the Sabbath is coming. Everything has to close early today. Am I asking about money? Do I worry about money? I know that you, lady, will give it to me later, that you will pay. Look at this, straight from Plotsk, the best quality. A pity it should lie here, unused. Let me put it into your basket for you. Just a few kopecks. It costs less than air.

Fifty Jewish families and six Polish tenant farmers live in the village. But on market day, every Tuesday and Friday, dozens of Christian peasants, who farm the land along the Północna River, come down to Blaszka. In the village square they bargain and in Perlmutter's tavern, they drink vodka with beer and eat cheese and pickles and hard-boiled eggs.

A Jew can never be a peasant, even if he looks and acts like one, nor a gentleman either. Such categories apply only to Christians in Poland, each of them having a place on the land. But by law the Jews are townspeople. Even if they are farmers, they are townspeople borrowing the land; they have no right to it. Within their towns the Jews can make their own distinctions, so long as they service the people of the land. So in Blaszka, Jews buy the peasants' produce and sell goods from Plotsk. Jews are tinsmiths and blacksmiths and cobblers and tailors and wheelwrights and barrelmakers and butchers and bakers. They speak Yiddish and Polish and a smattering of Russian, on weekdays they bargain and on the Sabbath they rest.

The village square isn't paved. It's marked in one corner by the bridge, in another corner by the tavern, by the synagogue in the third corner, and where the square dips down toward the Północna River, by the house of Misha the midwife. Her house stands on stilts so that the spring floods flow under it, bringing a rich mud that makes the vegetables in her garden grow larger than anywhere else. If you stood on the doorstep of Misha's house, you could see the entire village, the river curling around it, the woods behind the river, the lanes leading out of the village square, the small houses, each with an eating room in front and sleeping rooms behind separated by a hallway where the hens roost in the winter. Across the river, in the new part of Blaszka, you could see the ruins of the mill and the woods overgrowing abandoned houses.

There is a legend about the Północna River. It's said that a saint was martyred in the river's waters at midnight, resulting in the conversion and baptism of the local tribe. *Północ* in Polish means midnight, and so the river was named. But others argue that *północ* also means north, the Północna so named because it enters the Vistula River from the north.

The Północna is frozen now, children sliding on its surface. In front of her house, Misha stands beside her stall, her hands on her hips. She's bigger than any man in Blaszka. Her table is crowded with jars and bottles, powders and ointments and liquids for women's troubles, and men's, too. "There's nothing to be afraid of," she says.

All right, the women say, but you'd better watch your behind or the Evil One will send someone to kick it while you're not paying attention.

"Well, let him just try to make some business with me." Misha holds out her hand, beckoning the invisible stranger. She grins, her gold tooth flashing in the thin winter light. "Don't worry," Misha says, "if someone comes from the other side, he'll soon be running out of Blaszka with his tail between his legs. You can be sure of it."

IN A SMALL house off the village square, an old woman is teaching the little girls their letters. Tell us about Misha, they beg. We want to hear the story about Misha and Manya again. Please, please. The old woman puts down her pencil. "Well, I knew Misha's mother very well. She was so happy when she had a daughter, but she had one fear. Do you know what that was?" The children shake their heads. "That her daughter would turn out like Manya. You've heard of Manya, haven't you?" Yes, yes, the little girls say, Manya the witch comes in the night to steal away wicked children. "But you're not wicked children, are you?" The girls shake their heads, no, no, no. "Now, listen carefully, children. Before Misha, there was Blema, her mother. Before Blema was Miriam, Misha's grandmother. And before Miriam was?" Who? the children ask. "Manya!" The old woman leans forward, wriggling her clawed fingers at the children until they squeal. "Oh, Manya was bigger than any man, and no one could tame her until they put her to death for casting spells. Blema was afraid that her baby should turn out like Manya, God forbid. So Blema named her baby Miriam after her own mother, who was a good woman. Modest and quiet. Like you girls, yes? But you can't cheat fate, children.

"Blema carried her baby in a shawl on her back when she went to the peasants' cottages. The peasants liked to play with the little one. They called her Marisha, you know that's Polish for Miriam. But the baby couldn't say Marisha or even Miriam. What came out was Misha. The peasants said it must be her true name, and that, since *misha* means bear in Polish, the girl would grow up to be as dangerous as a mother bear. And because Misha is a man's name among the Russians, she would also be as fierce as a Cossack. This is what came to be. I'm sure you heard your mothers say so. When a woman is in childbirth, even the Angel of Death is afraid of Misha."

In the village square, the watercarrier rushes by Misha's stall, his buckets swinging wildly on their yoke. As his foot knocks against a stone, he stumbles, holding onto her table for balance. And then he's gone toward the bridge.

Across the bridge is what used to be the wealthy part of Blaszka. There among the ruins of abandoned houses, you can see the village well and beside it the bathhouse with its marble columns, built with the miller's money, may he rest in peace. Beside it is the foundation of the new synagogue, never finished.

Inside the bathhouse, the old men sit naked on the benches, sweating in the steam that rises as the attendant pours water over the hot stones. At the end of the room is the sunken bath, the *mikva*, with its purifying water. Before the men leave, they'll dip in the *mikva* to make themselves ready for the Sabbath.

Why does the butcher get to sit in the second row of the synagogue so close to the Holy Ark? they complain. He's just a *proster*, a plain person, like us. A man should know his place. The *proster* do the work, the *baalebatim* make the money, and the *shayner* tell you what to do, either because they're rich enough or they're scholars.

Sure, that's how it is in most places, but you can't expect it here in Blaszka. Who would sit in the second row if not the butcher? In the days before the Russians blew up the mill, we had *shayner* in Blaszka. Fine people. But now? There's just *proster*. Anybody who was anybody left Blaszka. And why not? You can walk for two hours down the road and you're in Plotsk. The capital of the *gubernia*. Twenty-six thousand people. A theater. A Jewish hospital. Schools. Everything.

Tell me, what's a town when there's no fine people driving around in their carriages and telling you what's what? That's the kind of village Blaszka is. We have a rabbi whose greatest friends are unbelievers—I saw him get a letter from France myself—and he can't stand the sight of a lit match, either.

Never mind. It's good to be alive. A little schnapps, a little singing, something nice to eat on *Shabbas,* it's all right. I'm old, but I'm in no rush to leave. Tell me, if it's so good there in the next world, why doesn't anyone come back to tell us about it?

Outside the bathhouse, a lane leads to the bridge and across the bridge, the road from Blaszka leaves the village square, following the Północna River down to the Vistula where it meets the highway that runs from Plotsk to Warsaw. Here, at the juncture of the Vistula and the Północna Rivers, there is a shiny black carriage with THE GOLEM PLAYERS painted in yellow on the side. The horse snorts, flicking her tail, braided with a yellow ribbon. Crystals of breath have formed around her mouth, and the creature licks them off with her thirsty tongue.

The Director, in his top hat, sits aloft, puffing on his mahogany pipe, horns of smoke curling upward. He looks sideways at the landscape, the bare trees striped with snow like soft fur, the frozen river, the flat land. An open, unremarkable landscape. The Director's new partner is walking toward him, carrying a bag with rope handles—a young and very earnest sort of person, the Traveler. The Director smooths his copper mustache and waves. The Traveler's hair sticks up like rooster feathers. He wears a ragged black jacket with a drooping rose pinned to the lapel. His thin nose is crooked, bending a little to the left.

The Traveler climbs up beside the Director. Sighing, he tears a strip of paper from *The Israelite,* and lines his cracked boot with the headline, "December 29, 1893: More Refugees Fleeing from the East."

While the Director relights his pipe, the younger man leafs through a notebook. The notes are in a small, meticulous script that shines as if the ink were made of a green florescence. "So many people hurt and lonely, talents going to waste," the Traveler says, his voice hoarse with sympathy. "But what about this?" He frowns. "There must be a mistake. We can't be expected to waste time on an animal like that." The Traveler stabs the notebook with his finger.

"You have your orders and the fellow is on his way," the Director says, pointing to an approaching cart. The driver is a large man in a fur coat who is whipping his horse till she bleeds while he gnaws on a hunk of salami.

The Traveler shields his eyes with his hands, gazing up the road. "I'd just like to have a choice. Is that too much to ask?"

"It's the price you pay, my boy. You knew that when you came on board." The Director rubs the bowl of his pipe against his velvet vest. "You could resign. But then it's rebirth for you. You interested? I see not. You serious types are all the same." He draws an imaginary bow across an even more imaginary violin that nevertheless plays the opening notes to Tchaikovsky's violin concerto. Tchaikovsky has recently died of cholera. The Traveler looks from his notebook to the absent violin. He is impressed. "It's nothing, my friend," the Director says. "Anyone can do it. Even you."

"What's the trick?" the Traveler asks, looking around for a hidden music box.

"Nothing at all. Just a bit of magic."

"Magic," the Traveler says thoughtfully, studying his notebook again.

"Don't get any ideas. Let me tell you the facts. What's magic? A piece of chocolate. An almond torte. Delicious, and then it melts away. But all of this," the Director says waving his hand grandly, "is something else entirely. Open your eyes and look. Maybe you'll learn a secret or two. But you can't just sit there moping and letting the snow soak through the holes in your boots. No. You've got to look closely and pay attention. Then you'll see where you can give a little nudge and open a door. And who knows," he winks, "what you might find in there? Well, my friend, I can't sit here and talk all day. I have something to deliver in Blaszka. Would you like to join me?"

"No. I'd better wait here. You go on." The Traveler dismounts from the carriage, seating himself on a snowy log.

"Au revoir," the Director says. He picks up the reins and clucks to his fine black horse.

The Traveler pulls up the collar of his jacket as the snow trickles down his neck. "Have to get assigned here in the middle of winter," he grumbles. "Couldn't be Warsaw. Streetcars. Electricity. Unions. Oh, no. It's got to be where people still believe in witchcraft." He shakes his head. "They don't know what's coming to them." Studying his notebook, he taps his chin. "Could be an advantage, though. If you use it right." He looks down the road toward Warsaw, as if he can see the next century riding the train, trailing a line of smoke, the whistle blowing.

TIME IS a trickster in Poland. In Warsaw they have electric lights. On the farms, peasants make their own candles. And in Blaszka? There, time juggles fire, throwing off sparks that reach far into the past and spin toward the future.

BUT shh, we can't talk, now. The story is about to start.

PART ONE

THE WOMEN

1

MUSHROOM SOUP

THE SHORT FRIDAY IN DECEMBER

In the bathhouse, the old men sighed as they sat on a bench, steam rising from the hot stones. A Friday night was the time for certain things. All of them had fulfilled the mitzvah of being fruitful years ago, but that didn't relieve them of the obligation to satisfy their wives. No, that was sealed by the marriage contract. And it wasn't true that a woman lost interest after the change of life. No, they said, you know what's written about the marriage bed—it's a woman's right and a man's duty.

Across the bridge in the village square, the noise of women in a hurry was as loud as a dispute in the court of heaven. Everything had to finish by sundown. Darkness came early on the last Friday in December, and only the expectation of long hours of *Shabbas* pleasures got the women through the rush. Instead of the grainy dark bread of everyday with its smear of fat and the sweaty smell of tallow on a bare table, *Shabbas* came with the honey scent of beeswax candles. Syrupy red wine. Not one, but two braided loaves of white bread plummy with raisins. Carrots and sweet potatoes. Golden soup. Meat.

On a white cloth where brass candlesticks gleamed with a ruddy glow. The wine and the bread and the children would be blessed. There would be singing. And the leisurely pursuit of *Shabbas* mitzvos, particularly of the kind foreseen in the bathhouse.

It was no surprise, then, that Hanna-Leah, the butcher's wife, was more sharp tongued than usual, knowing that for her the early darkness would, unless a miracle occurred, remind her of her loneliness.

"Strangers. Every week someone else sleeping in the guest house," Hanna-Leah said, shaking her head at the women in their shawls and quilted coats dripping melted snow onto the sanded, earth floor of the butcher shop.

She herself was wearing only a shawl over her dress, though the shop was cold. Hanna-Leah was always warm, like a pot kept at boiling heat by a quick fire. Tall and curvaceous, blonde under her kerchief, self-conscious about her hawk nose, she scoffed at the women's envy of her beauty since it had no practical use. She was thirty-four years old, had been married to the butcher since she was nineteen, and was childless.

The women leaned toward her, elbows resting on the counter beside string, paper, and slabs of red meat.

"Strangers coming from who knows where and going to someplace worse," Hanna-Leah said. She pointed at the window. Outside in the village square, a horse and carriage were tied to the post in front of Perlmutter's tavern. "I heard that the Golem Players are running from the Tsar's police, and where are they leading them? Right to Blaszka. And if the pogroms start again?"

It's been more than ten years since the pogroms, the women said. When the old Tsar was assassinated, of course they blamed the Jews. Who else? But things are different now.

"You think what happened in '81 couldn't happen again? Don't you believe it. My Hershel still has a scar on his shoulder. And my father . . . "

Don't speak of it, the women said quickly. May God protect us from such a fate. Now tell us. Did you see the actors performing in front of Perlmutter's tavern? They've been there half the day already.

"Singing and juggling in the village square, who needs it? Beggars at least have a use," Hanna-Leah said as she wrapped some soup bones with a good bit of meat left on them for a woman whose coat was more patches than cloth. "How could you fulfil the mitzvah to have a beggar for *Shabbas* dinner without one? And who would you give alms to? You know what they say. Wine is stronger than fear, sleep is stronger than wine, the Angel of Death is stronger than sleep, but charity is stronger even than death."

"That's from the Talmud," Hershel the butcher called out from the back room.

"Listen to him. He can hardly write his name, but he thinks he's a sage. So tell me, Mister Genius," she called back, "What does it say in the Talmud about strangers?"

"Remember that you were also a stranger in a strange land."

"A stranger? Me? My family lived right here in Blaszka since the time of King Krak."

The woman in the patched coat reached into her pocket to take out some change for the bones. "Don't insult me. What am I going to do with leftover bones, bury them?" Hanna-Leah asked. "So, look who's coming with her nose in the air." Through the window they watched the women's prayer leader, the *zogerin,* approaching the butcher shop. "I heard she crossed the bridge."

Her? No, I don't believe it, the women said. In Blaszka when they talked about a woman crossing the bridge, they meant that she was carrying on with a man, and not her husband, either.

"Believe what you want. Just open your eyes."

The door swung open with a rush of wind and snow as the *zogerin,* with her fancy braided wig and her silver prayerbook, sauntered into the shop. So nobody should miss it, the young *zogerin* swung her gold chain with the double case watch on the end.

"Look what I have for you. The best," Hanna-Leah said, whipping out a two-kilo, purplish brisket crawling with fat. "For you, our *zogerin,* one ruble," she said, half-laughing at the ludicrous price.

"Very good. Wrap it." The *zogerin* wore a long string of pearls over her flat chest and it wasn't even *Shabbas* yet.

Hanna-Leah shook her head. "She doesn't even bargain. Like stealing milk from a blind cow."

"Should I bargain? Before *Shabbas?* I have to think of higher things."

"Oy, oy. The *zogerin* has to think of something higher than pearls. It isn't easy," Hanna-Leah said.

Well, she's still young. And no one makes a bargain like you, the women said. Not even Misha.

"Well, let me ask you." The women leaned forward as Hanna-Leah's eyes narrowed. Even the *zogerin,* taking the brisket from the counter, paused. "Did you hear that someone saw a pair of man's pants sticking out from under Misha's bed?"

Who do you think they belonged to? the women asked.

"Anyone she wants," Hanna-Leah said. "She wouldn't hesitate. You see her sitting at her stall with the women hanging onto her every word, peasants and Jews, too, like she knows the cure for death. Listen to me. A woman who's divorced and isn't ashamed of it must have plenty to hide. When I was young, we were friends. Misha danced at my wedding. Can you believe it?"

What about your other friend, the one who went to America? I remember how she could dance—like a feather. But now she's buried over there and who will visit her grave? Even her children are on their way back to Blaszka. You'll have them come to you for *Shabbas,* won't you, Hanna-Leah? A boy and a girl, I heard. But who knows what kind of children they make in America?

"They probably don't speak a word of the *mama-loshen,*" Hanna-Leah said. "They'll be trouble, you wait and see."

WHEN THE shop was quiet for a few minutes, Hanna-Leah put her shawl over her head and slipped out to the village square. The pressed earth was slick with melting snow, and in her hurry, Hanna-Leah fell, bruising her hip. I should have stayed in the shop, she thought as she got up and brushed the mud off her coat. But do I have a choice? A woman doesn't do what she wants, only what she has to. Not Misha, of course. No, never Misha.

When Hanna-Leah was a girl, there were four friends who played together, picked mushrooms and berries, told secrets, and walked arm-in-arm through the woods. The villagers called them the *vilda hayas,* the wild creatures. One of them was Hanna-Leah. She became the butcher's wife and had no children, though she was the best cook of all of them. The second was her best friend, Faygela, who was hungry for books and married the baker and had so many children that she had no time left for Hanna-Leah. The third friend was Zisa-Sara. She taught them to dance and never had a bad word to say about anyone. Zisa-Sara married a scholar and left them all to go with him to America, for which they could not forgive her. Zisa-Sara's best friend was Misha, the fourth of the *vilda hayas*. Misha swore that she would never marry, but just the same she did. Hanna-Leah had thought that marriage would straighten Misha out. A wife has to cover her head and know what it means to work. But Misha's husband had divorced her, and instead of moving away, she had grown her hair long again. It blew about in the wind like a living thing and Misha was a *vilda haya* still.

Now Misha stood behind a table laden with bottles and powders, creams and herbs, her head uncovered, black hair floating under a veil of snowflakes while she laughed with the women crowded around her stall. "And what about you?" she was saying to a young woman, the baker's oldest daughter. "When are you going to marry yourself off and have a proper *Shabbas* like the rest of the women?" The girl blushed. "And look who's here. Hanna-Leah. Listen to me, women, you'd better go to her shop before *Shabbas*. Get a nice piece of meat for your man to give him strength."

And you, Misha, when are you going under the wedding canopy again? the women asked.

"Never. There isn't a man who could tempt me. Not even the Evil One himself." Her large hands were busy, picking a pinch of this and a leaf of that, wrapping it all in a square of brown paper. "You know what I say? Have a little pleasure and don't worry about tomorrow. There's nothing to be afraid of."

Hanna-Leah frowned as Misha bantered with the women. Every month Misha made up a remedy for her. Every month it failed, and she had to come back for another. "You have something different?" Hanna-Leah asked.

"What I gave you before didn't help?" Misha spoke in a low voice, but Hanna-Leah looked around anyway, to see if anyone was listening.

Someone was laughing. Why was she laughing? Maybe Misha had said something. No, she wouldn't. Everyone knew that Misha could keep a secret. If she wanted to. But who could tell what a woman like

Misha wanted? Was she like anyone else? "Just give it to me," Hanna-Leah said. "I don't have time to stand here all day."

"Put it in the soup," Misha said.

"Fine. Good." Grabbing the package, Hanna-Leah thrust it into her pocket, slapping a few kopecks onto the table. As she returned to the butcher shop, she saw a cart crossing the square. Behind the driver, a boy and a girl held onto each other, pale from their journey. Strangers. Did they look at all like anyone Hanna-Leah had known?

IN THE afternoon, Hanna-Leah closed up the butcher shop and went home. The sun was setting, the *shammus* knocking on the shutters of the houses to let the women know that the candles should be lit and the men should be on their way to the synagogue. "Do you need more hot water?" Hanna-Leah asked her mother-in-law, who was sitting in the tin tub in the alcove off the kitchen.

"Don't you hear? *Shabbas* is coming," her mother-in-law said. "Hurry, get me out."

"There's no rush. The Holy One will wait for me to wash your back." Pulling up her sleeves, Hanna-Leah rubbed a bit of brown soap between her hands. As she knelt to massage her mother-in-law's brittle back, silk underthings nuzzled her hips beneath her *Shabbas* dress. She had ordered the fabric from Plotsk, a creamy silk embroidered with tiny blue stars.

"Not too hard?" Hanna-Leah asked.

"No, it's good, it's good," the old woman purred at the firm strokes on her back. "But it's enough, already." She pulled away. "Help me up. Hershel shouldn't come home to an unprepared table." Gripping Hanna-Leah's shoulders and leaning forward from her waist as she stood on her withered legs, the old woman said, "I asked the *zogerin* to say a prayer on your grandmother's grave that you should have a son."

"What business did you have to go to the *zogerin?*"

"She knows how to pray. When she opens her mouth, the angels above listen."

"I don't need her prayers."

"Well, you need someone's," her mother-in-law said. "You know what it says in the *Tzena-U-Rena.*" She pointed to a book on the sideboard. The biblical commentary for women, written in Yiddish. Every Jewish home had one, and Hanna-Leah's mother-in-law read it aloud every *Shabbas.* "The Matriarch Sarah died when she was a hundred and twenty-seven years old, but she only truly lived for thirty-seven years. And why? Because the years before her son's birth weren't any kind of life, 'for a person who is childless is compared to the dead.' You hear what I'm saying?"

Hanna-Leah's jaw tightened as she pulled a woolen dress over her mother-in-law's head, muffling her speech. Hanna-Leah considered leaving her to stand this way, with her head stuck between the shoulders of the dress, arms flailing. But instead she eased her mother-in-law's arms into the dress, tugging it maybe a little roughly over her head. As she popped through the neck opening, the old woman lifted her nose and sniffed. "What's that I smell? Mushrooms? You know mushrooms give me diarrhea. And I love mushroom soup. I can't resist it. Why did you make it? To torture me?"

Hershel also has a fondness for mushrooms, Hanna-Leah thought. But all she said was, "If the *zogerin* starts praying at Grandmother Rivka's grave, her spirit will thank the Holy One that she has a grave to protect her from the noise."

HANNA-LEAH's grandmother used to say that you have to see everything to pick mushrooms. Braiding Hanna-Leah's hair, thick and pale as ripe barley, Grandmother Rivka would say, "Behind a rotting log, child, you can find a prize, a king bolete. You must be like the Morning Star who lives deep in the woods. She picks mushrooms and she feeds the hungry wolf in the sky. It pulls at its leash to get to her basket. It could bite off your whole head. It wants to eat everything. But the Morning Star is big and wild, too. She just hits the wolf on the nose and says, 'Wait, doggie. Be good, you will get the mushrooms. But you have to wait for me to cook them.'" Then Grandmother Rivka would tug one of Hanna-Leah's braids and say, "So Hankela, you just watch me and you'll learn how to make a good mushroom soup." And there would be the flash of the knife chopping faster than Hanna-Leah could see.

"ARE YOU dreaming, Hanna-Leah? Button my dress. All right, now help me into my chair. Hershel will be here any minute," her mother-in-law said.

They waited, the table set with its white cloth, its braided hallahs and silver candlesticks. Wax dripped. The scent of mushroom soup wafted from the tiled oven. Hanna-Leah listened to her mother-in-law wheeze. More wax dripped, the flames reflected in the darkening window. The room was silent except for the gurgling of her mother-in-law's stomach. Hanna-Leah thought she would go mad. When she could wait no more, she threw a shawl over her head and pulled on her quilted coat, stamping through the snow across the village square.

In Perlmutter's tavern, her Hershel sat near the fire, legs sprawled, hat askew, raising a glass of schnapps to his new friend with the yellow hair and the forked beard flecked with crumbs. A middle-aged man, twice as big around as Hershel and half again as tall, his hairy belly bursting through the buttons of his shirt under the fur coat hanging open and trailing the floor on either side of his boots.

"Good Sabbath," Hanna-Leah said. "So you found another fool to entertain."

"He's a visitor." Hershel straightened his hat. He was a short balding man with a round face and graying beard. But under his caftan, his chest was massive and hard, his arms like iron pistons. Hershel hiccupped. "A visitor from Plotsk. His grandfather was a rich man in Blaszka once."

She looked from Hershel to the enormous man beside him, all hair and bristles and stomach, smelling of old onions. A pig standing on his hind legs, snout in the air, sniffing for something rotten. A *shayner?* One of the fine people with money that had left the village when the mill was blown up by the Russians? "Yes, sure. Everyone has a rich grandfather somewhere," she said. "And your friend is a very busy man, I hear. Yesterday a thief, today a peddler. I heard that all of Blaszka had the honor of watching this guest kill his horse in the village square this afternoon, and then he had a fight with our midwife. But I didn't have time to wait around and congratulate him because I was rushing home to make the house ready for *Shabbas*. Now I stand corrected. My husband, may the Holy One preserve him, is treating our esteemed guest right."

The guest swallowed his drink and refilled his glass, oblivious to everything but the bottle, while Hershel looked up at Hanna-Leah. "Maybe you want something?" he asked. "A cherry brandy?"

"You think money grows on trees?"

"Don't get aggravated, Hanna-Leah."

"Don't get aggravated, he says. While my hands get rough and red washing for his mother, the man entertains every stranger," she spat the word, "from here to Warsaw. An idiot. A know-nothing. Deaf to the world. Didn't you hear the *shammus* knocking on the shutters? It's almost dark. The synagogue is empty, the men have gone home already. You think *Shabbas* is waiting for you?"

Hershel shrugged and shook his head, but when she finished what she had to say, he picked himself up and followed her out.

HANNA-LEAH ladled steaming mushroom soup, with a generous dose of Misha's medicine, into the good blue bowl for him. The chipped one she took for herself. "Now eat before it gets cold. What are you waiting for? Go on, eat. *Shvyger,* for you I have a bowl of borscht," she said, but her mother-in-law had nodded off, again, in her chair.

Hershel sat without looking at Hanna-Leah. "Mushroom pierogies," he said, blowing gently on the soup. "The best in Blaszka. Such juicy little dumplings." He popped another into his mouth.

Hanna-Leah watched the tip of his tongue lick a speck off his lower lip. She thought of the wolf on its hind legs, crying at the mushrooms in the basket held just out of its reach.

HERSHEL snored. A galumph, followed by a snort, a half sneeze, and a galumph. Hanna-Leah moved closer to him, but as he felt her warmth, he pushed farther over to the edge of the bed, grumbling, then settling again: galumph, snort, sneeze.

In the village they said that if something's wrong, you should go to Misha. She'll know how to fix you up. And did Hanna-Leah ask for much? Just a simple remedy to give Hershel a little interest in his own wife. But no. Misha had just made a fool of her again.

Hanna-Leah knew that demons came in the night to women who were awake and hungry. Demons with curved horns, a cleft foot, and a red bigness that ruined a woman for any ordinary man, filling her and driving her wild. That would be her fate if she didn't take care, throat and belly kissed by demon lips. Massaging demon hands on her breasts, squeezing her backside. Insides stabbed with demon heat, again and again. A loose woman. Like Misha.

Sneeze. *Galumph.* Hershel snored. A curse on Misha's head, Hanna-Leah thought. A virtuous woman is worth more than rubies. Picking up her *Yiddish Book of Women's Prayers,* the *Tekhinas,* she crossed the room to the cot against the wall where Hershel slept when she had her period. She lay down, tucking her nightgown between her thighs, legs pressed together against the heat that rose up when there was nothing to distract her.

"*Father Dear, Ribono shel olam,*" she murmured, "*the soul that You breathed into me goes now to Your Throne of Glory. Keep it with You and send it to me at dawn. Blessed are you, Creator of seasons and times, darkness, and rest. Your servant, Hanna-Leah.*" But as she slipped into sleep, she touched her hawk nose, wondering, Am I so ugly he can't touch me? and the smallest groan escaped her.

THE DAY OF THE ICE STORM

In the woods behind the river, Hanna-Leah collected branches for firewood. A cold wind blew at her shawl, though it was March and the trees were budding. When she was a girl she liked to walk through the woods, especially when she picked mushrooms, looking behind rotting logs and in the dank places where delicious boletes lurked, treasures the size of her palm, caps smooth as the velvet crust of a perfectly baked honey cake, the underside like golden sponge.

But now it was different. She had to watch out. An unexpected branch could snag her, a stump trip her, a shadow startle her into spitting "thpoo thpoo thpoo" to avert the evil eye. Plants grew every which way, even on top of each other. It was never the same in the woods. Oh yes, the same trees, the same flowers, the same mushrooms and wind. But always different. The shapes never stayed the same for a moment. Where yesterday there was a tree, today there was a stump, yesterday a clump of grass, today violently trembling yellow flowers, tomorrow thistle down blowing. In the woods there was no order. But what could she do? The stove needed firewood. A horde of family and guests would be descending on her for Purim, not to mention the children of the village, who would be expecting something sweet from every house. So she had no choice but to walk with her head thrust forward, turning this way and that, peering into the afternoon shad-

THE RIVER MIDNIGHT • 33

ows as if wild beasts were hiding there, while she picked up fallen branches until her arms were loaded.

Turning toward home, Hanna-Leah cried out, her hand scratched by an unseen thorn.

"Are you all right?" a voice asked.

Hanna-Leah jumped, catching her sleeve on the thornbush, branches dropped and scattered. She saw a bundle of rags unfold into a scarecrow and then rise like a hungry man in pain.

"Who are you? What business do you have here?"

"Did I startle you, *mamala?*" Little mother, he called her, as if he were someone close to her, a brother or a cousin. "I'm sorry I frightened you," he said. He wasn't from around here. Not by that accent. And not by his voice. It was missing the hoarse edge that came from shouting above the din of market day. "I fell asleep and woke up when I heard you." The wind blew his shirt behind him like the wings of a ship. He held a ragged black jacket over his shoulder, a cloth rose hanging down from the collar. A traveling bag with rope handles lay at his feet. His hair stood up around his face like the copper pinfeathers of a rooster. He was young. But not a boy.

"Criminals hide in the woods. Do you think you scare me? Hah." She shook the twiggy end of a broken branch in his face.

He spoke slowly. "You're right, I am a criminal. Or next to one."

"I knew it. Those black eyes of yours, too small, too close together. You came here to rob good people in their beds. I can deal with your like, don't you fear." She showed him the point of her knife, the sharp little knife for trimming twigs. He didn't flinch.

"I ran away when it was time to register for the draft," he said calmly. "I came here from the East. No identification papers, so I can't stay too long anywhere. If an officer stops me, then I'll be sent back and you know where I'll end up."

It was true that he had an accent like her Grandmother Rivka's. It could be. She put the knife in her pocket, lowered the branch.

"A Jew in the army is lost," she said. "Beaten for saying a word of the *mama-loshen.* Made to eat *trayf.* Put in front of cannons like a dead crow for practice. It's not so stupid to run away."

"You are too kind, little mother."

"But what are you doing now? A person has to do something to eat." In Blaszka all the men were bearded, but he was clean-shaven. She was fascinated by the sight of his jaw, the sharp angle below his ear, the unobstructed line of his lips like Sabbath wine above the stubbly cream of his chin.

"I'm a traveler. There's plenty like me. Going here, going there, always looking for a little bit of work or some cheap goods to peddle."

"What do you have in that bag of yours? Maybe I need something."

"Not much, I'm afraid. I sold everything I had for less than I bought it. To tell you the truth, I could lose money selling vodka to soldiers."

"Never mind. We have too many peddlers, anyway. People always think somewhere else it's going to be better. Every market day we get peddlers from villages all the way from Plotsk to Warsaw. And in the meantime, our own men put their bags on their backs and walk to Warsaw, even farther, to make a few kopecks." He was standing close to her, so close she could see the curl of gold and red hairs inside his open collar. He smelled of spring mud, of nights in the woods, of sweat and sweet grass. Hanna-Leah stepped back too quickly, stumbling again. He held out his hand and she unthinkingly took it. In Blaszka, a man didn't touch a woman in public, not even his wife. But they weren't in the village. They were alone in the woods.

A woman shouldn't touch a man. Not a strange man. Not even if his hand is gripping hers warmly. Especially not. For something else to do, her hand retreated into her pocket and pulled out a chunk of dark bread. "Here," she said, thrusting it into the open palm of his hand. "I have to get ready for Purim, but even a criminal has to eat."

"Thank you, little mother," he said, slowly folding once more into a bundle of rags.

As she regathered the fallen branches, she had a plain talk with herself. What kind of a fool are you? A strange man in the woods, he says he ran from the draft, but who knows what he is? Maybe even a murderer. If you had any sense you would report him to the authorities. But her hand felt smooth from his touch. As if it were something apart from the rest of her.

IN THE evening Hanna-Leah walked to synagogue. Hershel went with the men and Hanna-Leah with the women. The synagogue was dug

THE RIVER MIDNIGHT • 35

deep into the earth so that the roof wouldn't rise higher than the abandoned and dilapidated church on the opposite side of the square. Stairs climbed up to the women's gallery and down to the men around the Holy Ark. It being the eve of Purim, everyone was dressed up to be someone else, swinging rattles, coats worn backward. The watercarrier was in satin like a rich man, the Rabbi in riding boots like a Russian cavalier, Hershel the butcher wearing a shawl over his caftan, stuffed with pillows so he stuck out like a pregnant woman. The children ran frantically upstairs and down, the boys in girls' clothing, the girls dressed as scholars.

Upstairs in the women's gallery, their mothers held pots and pans ready to clang when the evil Haman's name was read out, shouting, "May the earth cover him, may his bones fester, may his mother forget his name." Young women dressed like they were old and the old like they were young. Even the dairywoman, getting onto sixty, lost twenty years in her costume of shimmering veils. In the back row sat the midwife, Misha, resplendent in an old-fashioned dress, its bodice embroidered with gold thread, her red shawl waving as she vigorously swung a noisemaker.

Hanna-Leah sat in front with her sisters-in-law. Across the aisle Faygela, the baker's wife, held her youngest, a boy, on her lap, her five daughters in a row beside her. Dark-eyed and delicate, her head wrapped in a turban, Faygela glanced at Hanna-Leah but said nothing. Would anyone think that they had been the best of friends?

HANNA-LEAH lived across the lane from Faygela, and in good weather their doors used to be open so they could call to each other. Hanna-Leah would see Faygela among her children, braiding hair, knotting a broken shoelace, in one hand always a book. When good smells wafted across the lane from Hanna-Leah's house, the children would run to get a taste from her pot. In the winter, Faygela would warm herself in front of Hanna-Leah's oven and talk while Hanna-Leah did her mending. If a troupe of actors came through Blaszka, Faygela and Hanna-Leah would sit side by side, Hanna-Leah laughing at the funny songs and Faygela crying at the sad ones.

When Faygela was twenty-two and pregnant for the fifth time, it was to Hanna-Leah that she went to complain. "My Shmuel is going to Warsaw for business. And what about my business? I was supposed to go to school in Warsaw. But that's all forgotten now. Shmuel has to sell my grandmother's jewelery. She can't leave her bed anymore and she says we have to have something from her. Do I want her money, Hanna-Leah? She forgets what she's suffering when I read to her, but I'm alone with her and the girls. Who's going to help me in the bakery? I don't sleep because the middle one has nightmares. She wakes up screaming and then the other two start to cry. The little one still wants to nurse and she's already two, so how will I have enough milk for the new baby, Hanna-Leah? Yesterday I gave my Ruthie a smack and she just looked at me. What am I supposed to do? I have a cold and look what I have for my nose." Faygela held out a crusty old washrag.

"Here, you take this," Hanna-Leah said. She handed Faygela a clean, cotton rag. "It's from the nightdress I wore on my wedding night. Touch it, Faygela, you see how soft? And I'll take this other piece and sew under the edges and make you a real handkerchief."

Hanna-Leah took out her needles and thread while Faygela wiped her eyes and blew her nose. "I hate Blaszka," Faygela said, sitting down in the rocking chair. "The same faces. The same words. Even the same smells. The tanner's wife is making cabbage soup and Misha is cooking one of her potions and I'm nauseous. I want to go to Warsaw."

"And what's in Warsaw? Strangers."

"In Warsaw people can see a play any time they want in a real theater, not on a platform in the tavern. In the university there's a library with more books than you can count. And people who know what's going on in the world. They talk. They have ideas."

"Your father should never have taken you to see that school in Warsaw. It gave you too many ideas."

"Just try to imagine it, Hanna-Leah. A city like a marble palace with a thousand rooms and look at Blaszka, a hut with a mud floor."

"Don't be silly. Everything you need is here," Hanna-Leah said. "You should put away your books. Your head is always in another world and your girls look like orphans with holes in their shirts. If they were mine, I'd be ashamed."

Faygela's face reddened. "But they're not yours and you have nothing to do at home except to cook a little. If you had a couple of your own you'd have some sympathy."

But Hanna-Leah had none of her own. Not then and not later. So she closed her door and didn't call across the lane anymore.

IN THE women's gallery, the *zogerin* began to speak. "Listen to me, women," she said. "Remember the story of Esther the Queen. She saved our people from the wicked Haman, who ordered the killing of all the Jews of Persia. The King didn't know that Esther was Jewish. She could have hidden. Nothing would have happened to her. But instead she arranged a banquet for the King and his Minister, Haman. And then she revealed herself . . . "

Maybe I should have invited the stranger for dinner, Hanna-Leah thought. It's a religious duty, after all. The festival of Purim. A person should eat and drink. As the *zogerin's* voice mingled with the sound of the noisemakers, Hanna-Leah again felt the stranger's touch.

The last rattle was shaken, the last pot banged as the story ended. Benches pushed aside, the men danced in jubilation, a bottle passing from hand to hand as they clomped and stamped into the courtyard. Above, the women sang and swayed, Hanna-Leah standing aside, clapping her hands until the women made their way down the stairs and outside, their men following to go home and drink and sing until they didn't know the difference between Haman the wicked and Mordecai the righteous.

Behind the village square, the river gulped its banks, trees rustling as if to pull up their roots and take a stroll under the full moon. Hanna-Leah hurried to get home before her guests arrived. The wind was blowing storm clouds. Rain began to fall, and as if spring had forgotten itself, the rain turned into pellets of ice.

The next morning, her mother-in-law was cranky and Hershel hung over. Rocking in her chair beside the warm tile oven, Hanna-Leah listened to the wind, picturing the stranger cold and shivering. You're a fool, she told herself. A fool is more useless than a barren woman. He'll murder you in your bed and you'll deserve it. And while she cursed herself for her foolishness, she bundled herself into her quilted jacket and, covering her head with a shawl, headed into the woods with a pot and a blanket.

The Traveler, wrapped in Hanna-Leah's blanket, crouched against a linden tree, drinking the last drop of soup. He wiped the bowl with the last morsel of bread, and only then his hands, which had always been steady, began to shake. Yet when Hanna-Leah took the bowl from him, her fingers touching his, she felt as if he were the giver and not she.

"Don't expect any more from me," she said. "I don't hold with feeding layabouts. A man should work. He works, he eats."

"Yes, little mother," he said. "I expect no more from you."

He picked up a branch of linden by his feet and, whistling, began to trim the branch.

"I don't have time to throw away on a wastrel. I have a shop to run and a husband to feed." He nodded, but she stayed, watching him hold the branch with his knees as he carved with his left hand, curls of wood flying like maple seeds.

"It will be beautiful," he said. "A woman made from the tree. For her it's always Purim. You can dress her in anything. Who knows what's underneath? Only you and I."

She watched the wood, hot from the knife, taking shape. What are you thinking? she asked herself. But she wasn't thinking of anything, it was her body that blazed even though icicles hung from the trees. Sweat trickled along her neck. "I'm going," she said, not moving. Then she added, "I don't have time to waste standing here. But later I'm baking. The old bread, whatever's left over, I give to the birds. If I can trust Hershel to take care of the shop for a few minutes, I'll bring you some fresh bread. I always make too much."

BY AFTERNOON the sun was baking the path to the woods. Hanna-Leah carried a basket with the bread for the birds, a new loaf that was still warm, and some herring wrapped in paper. In the dark heart of the woods she faltered. No bundle of rags, no scarecrow. Only broken branches. As Hanna-Leah bent to pick them up for firewood, a dank and lonely coldness rose from the ground.

"Beggars," she muttered. "Drifters." She cut the twigs viciously. "Feathers, not men. A man knows where his head lies at night. A man works. His neighbors know him. He has a family."

Light steps behind her. A ragged shadow. Hanna-Leah jumped to her feet.

"You. I thought you left."

"I was over there, in that patch of light near the birches."

"Here, take this." She held out the loaf of bread and the herring.

He shook his head. "It's not necessary."

"It will go to waste. Take it." She put the bread in his hand, the left hand, calloused and square-fingered.

As he ate, he held a carving to the light, turning it this way and that. It was the figure of a woman, large, curvaceous, hawk-nosed. The wood shone like smooth skin in the sun. He caressed the doll, lightly touching the face, fingers brushing the neck, stroking the breasts, sliding across the tiny hard nipples, skimming the smoothness under the breasts, hovering on the round belly, gripping the legs, his thumb between the thighs.

"It's nearly finished, but here, you see there is a rough spot. I'll just smooth it, so. Now it's done. A small thing to remember me."

"You're leaving?" Good, she thought. Who needs a plague of beggars and strangers?

"Yes, but I want you to have this."

"You don't owe me anything. It's fine. Good riddance. Just go."

"Such a small thing. Take it. Please."

Her hand reached to his, their fingers intertwined across the doll, his touch warming her, again. But she was too warm. Always too warm. A woman has to cover her head, and under her dress, unless it's *Shabbas,* she should wear wool stockings and woolen underthings until she can hardly breathe. Because a woman doesn't do what she wants, only what she has to.

"Good-bye, little mother," the stranger said as he picked up his bag. "Thank you."

"Never mind. It was nothing," Hanna-Leah said, watching as he walked toward the river. When she came home, she put the doll in her bridal trunk, wrapped in Grandmother Rivka's shawl. Her Sabbath shawl of green satin.

SEASON OF RAINS

At the beginning of May, right after Passover, Hanna-Leah saw Faygela climb into Shmuel the baker's cart, her girls crowded around her, Faygela kissing them and saying it was impossible, she couldn't leave them, Shmuel saying not to worry, he would watch over their children, Misha handing Faygela a basket covered with a red shawl. "Hurry, you'll miss your train," Misha said.

Hanna-Leah was sweeping her doorstep though she'd already swept it that day. "So you're going to Warsaw after all, I hear," she said.

"I didn't want to go, but they're pushing me out the door."

"Shmuel's sister-in-law is sick and she's alone with her baby in Warsaw, so of course Faygela should go," Misha said, "but I think Warsaw isn't ready for Faygela. We should ask the postmaster in Plotsk to send a telegraph and warn someone. What do you say, Hanna-Leah?" The smallest girl was hanging onto Misha's leg, Faygela's youngest in Misha's arms, his hand on her cheek.

"Faygela should watch out that she doesn't get lost. Warsaw isn't like Blaszka where a person knows every corner," Hanna-Leah said.

"She'll be fine. It's not as easy to get lost as you think," Misha replied.

NINE DAYS after Faygela left for Warsaw, the women's gallery was full of whispers. Look at Misha, isn't she showing? Yes, I think she is. No, it couldn't be. And why not? You see how calm she is.

"So? That's Misha," Hanna-Leah said. "Her feet stick in the mud like everyone else's, but she laughs at everything, even the Evil One himself. I tell you, she won't be so cocky when the baby comes without a name." But as she spoke she remembered the Traveler holding up a figure to the sun, his fingers caressing the wood as smooth as skin and she fell silent while the women were still nodding.

Go on, you know what you're saying, the women murmured.

Hanna-Leah shook her head. "Never mind. Why should I waste my breath? You can't have a tiger without stripes. That's how it is."

IT HAD BEEN raining since Faygela went to Warsaw and it continued to rain. In another week, peasants reported they had seen a shower of frogs and people began to say that it might be time to build an ark. On market day, boards were placed across the mud of the village square. In the tavern men drank, steam rising from their woolen caps. Women took shelter in the shops, Polish and Yiddish mingling with the squawks of hens held by their feet. Children chased each other across the puddles, their boots, if they had any, tied around their necks.

In the butcher shop, the women said, Did you see Misha? She has no shame. Walking around with her belly out and no father for the child. The baker's oldest daughter is learning from her how to be a midwife. Maybe she's learning something else, too? If you ask me, the girl's mother should be at home watching out for her. What kind of mother lets her daughter do whatever she wants?

"If she was my daughter, I wouldn't let her out of my sight," Hanna-Leah said. "But Faygela's in Warsaw. Did she have a choice? If her sister-in-law is sick, someone had to go and take care of her. But listen to me. You can be sure that when Faygela comes back, I'll have something to say to her."

As the women nodded, Hanna-Leah pushed up her sleeves. Through the window, she could see Hershel bargaining with a farmer over a cow. It was a poor, rib-heaving animal, and when he sold the unkosher, sirloin and roast-ridden back half to the meat dealer from Plotsk, the remaining brisket, flank, shoulder roasts, tongue, and liver would be kosher, yes, but also shriveled and tough. "Look at that. Even a beggar wouldn't want it for *Shabbas*," Hanna-Leah said. "Let me go out to Hershel before he offers the farmer my grandmother's candlesticks for the old cow."

As she crossed the square, she let her shawl fall back a little so that the cool rain fell on her forehead.

"*Shoin*. My wife. And in a good hour. You see, Hankela, I was just making a price," Hershel said, the tense lines between his eyes relaxing as she came near. "But a man studies, he prays, it's a woman's job to bargain."

"Good day," she said to the farmer. "Your wife, she's feeling better?"

"Better than a corpse," the peasant answered, crossing himself.

Running her hand under the cow's flank, Hanna-Leah said, "I see you brought me a dried-up old milker. Her teats are older than Mother Poland's."

"You hear her? A woman knows business," Hershel said.

"Yes, sure. And I also know that there's half a cow lying in the back of the shop. What am I supposed to do with her? Sing her a lullaby?"

"Heaven forbid. The cow might wake up from the dead to beg

you to stop. I'd better go and save the poor cow from such a fate," Hershel said, blinking as he pulled his cap lower over his eyes to block out the rain.

IN THE evening, Hanna-Leah washed herself for the *mikva*. As she sat in the tin tub, she said to herself, So Misha the midwife is pregnant. Even though she insults everything proper, she's blessed with a child. Faygela has six children though she complains that they don't give her a moment's peace. Zisa-Sara had a son and a daughter. Now they're orphans, but still they have family in Blaszka. So what about Hanna-Leah? For her there's nothing.

How many times had she repeated the Woman's Prayer for Child-lessness: "*Where should I find offense, who should I blame? My mother? The midwife who delivered me? The angel who oversees pregnancies? No, they fulfilled their roles. It's me. Only me. It is God's will that I should have empty arms because of my many sins. I turn to You my Creator, with my hot tears. Deliver me from the harsh decree and shelter me under Your wing.*"

So many sins, Hanna-Leah thought. And what are they? The sin of taking care of my mother-in-law. Of giving charity. Of running my Hershel's shop and feeding him. Going to the *mikva* every month, though what for, I don't know. Such terrible sins.

HANNA-LEAH had immersed in the *mikva* for the first time before her wedding. When she was a girl, she'd known it was a married woman's religious duty to go to the ritual bath a week after her period, to purify herself for her husband's attentions. But what exactly were these attentions? she used to ask Faygela. They didn't quite know. It all had something to do with the *mikva* inside the bathhouse, a sunken pool lined with stone, four feet by six feet, filled with water. And not ordinary water. No, it was holy. Faygela said that free-running water dripped into it from a tank connected to the river, joining the *mikva* to the network of waters that cover the earth and flow to the sea, the earth's lifeblood.

Before Hanna-Leah went to the *mikva* for the first time, Grand-mother Rivka sent her to the outhouse to sit on the wooden slats. "*Pish*," her grandmother said, "and have a good *cack*. You have to be empty."

When Hanna-Leah came back to the house, Grandmother Rivka and Faygela were preparing the bath. Faygela poured kettle after kettle of hot water into the tub, insisting that it was too heavy for the grandmother to manage. It was just after Hanna-Leah's nineteenth birthday and Faygela was seventeen, already nursing her oldest daughter with another on the way. Into the water Faygela dropped lilies of the valley, while Grandmother rubbed hand cream into Hanna-Leah's skin. Misha had made it fresh for her, and it still smelled of the honeyed beeswax. Faygela trimmed her nails and scrubbed her hair with bought soap, lavender-scented. Hanna-Leah's mother, still lying in bed after a miscarriage, called out, "You have to wash good. Are you washing her good?" Yes, yes, Grandmother Rivka called back, don't worry yourself, Daughter-in-law. They dressed Hanna-Leah in a soft white shift, and then the women arrived.

All the married women came. Lighting candles, they led her across the bridge, a procession of floating flames in the darkness, singing from the Song of Songs, "*I am my beloved's and he is mine, who forages among the lilies. Let him kiss me with the kisses of his mouth, for his love is better than wine. His left hand is under my head, and his right hand embraces me.*" Among the married women, only Hanna-Leah walked with her head bare and her hair hanging loose like a shawl of sunlight, the warm wind ruffling her dress lightly against her bare skin. Around her everything was light. The candles flared. Threads of white smoke rose to the white moon, round in the sky and reflected on the water, bright and fat as a pregnant woman. From the bridge, she could see every house in its place, the village a single being, even with the broken lanes and overgrown bush surrounding the *mikva* on the other side of the bridge. The village was always the same, and she loved it with her whole heart, just as she expected she would one day love Hershel. "*Make haste, my beloved,*" the women sang. Hanna-Leah walked among them slowly, with dignity. The frogs sang, Grandmother Rivka cried softly. The air was redolent with lilies and apple blossoms. When they reached the bathhouse, Grandmother Rivka said, "*May the Holy One who let me live until this day be blessed,*" and she kissed Hanna-Leah's forehead.

In the bathhouse, the women sat Hanna-Leah down on a bench to hear what they had to tell her, each one interrupting the other. You came to this willingly, they said, and now your life isn't your own. You have to work. You're not a child. But on *Shabbas* after you light the candles, you're a queen in your house. Your husband will take you, but it's his duty to make sure that you're ready, that you enjoy it. Don't forget. Never mind, Hanna-Leah's a healthy girl, he won't be able to keep up with her. Better cook him some mushrooms, Hanna-Leah, to give him some strength on a Friday night. What are you telling her? Don't make it rosy. Listen to me, Hanna-Leah. The day after your wedding, when your mother cuts your hair off, that's your life falling on the floor. He'll want sons from you, and each one will drain your strength away until you have no teeth left. What a thing to tell a bride, you're scaring her. Listen, if your husband is a good man you don't have to be pregnant all the time. A considerate man knows not to spurt the water on the soil if you don't want flowers to grow. Depend on a man? No, don't pay attention to her. What you do is you go to the *mikva* a week late. You think he knows the time? Do that, and you're safe. One of the women shook her head at them all. My sister sent me something from Warsaw. Look. She pulled out a clear skin, rounded at the top, open at the end. What's it for, stuffing *kishka?* For stuffing something. She stuck her thumb into it. In Warsaw they call it a nightglove. And your husband will put it on? Well, to tell you the truth I didn't ask him, yet. Ah, the women said, ah.

Hanna-Leah didn't understand any of it. Faygela just sat beside her on the bench, patting her hand, and not saying a word of sense, either. "Don't worry, Hanna-Leah," she said, "it's not so bad." Bad? To marry her father's apprentice, whom she used to watch from the women's gallery? To raise children, the sons to study Torah and the girls to be modest and good? What else would she want? What else could she imagine?

The *mikva* attendant came over to them. "Women, please," she said, "let the girl alone. The stones aren't heated today and you see she's shivering. Let her dip, already. Come here, Hanna-Leah." She held up a sheet near the sunken pool at the end of the room, and Hanna-Leah stood behind it, throwing off her shift. Liba the attendant inspected Hanna-Leah, looking at her trimmed nails, pulling a few loose hairs off her skin. "Did you go to the outhouse? Did you brush your teeth?" she asked. Hanna-Leah nodded. "Good, then you can go in."

Hanna-Leah climbed down. The water was clear and pure, cold against her skin. It would enter every pore, changing her, preparing her to be a woman. As she dipped under the water, she thought to herself that she would have lots of sons, but daughters would be all right, too. She wouldn't push them away. Not like her mother, for whom only her little brothers lived.

"Again," the attendant said. "You have to go deep so your hair is covered. Open your legs. Good. Now repeat after me." Hanna-Leah repeated the blessing word for word, loudly. "Kosher," Liba said. "Now dip again. And once more. Mazel tov. May the Holy One grant that you'll be pregnant soon and I won't see you here until after the child is born, a son, God willing."

Later the women told Hanna-Leah that Faygela had moved heaven, earth, and the community council to have the water changed that day, so Hanna-Leah wouldn't have to immerse herself in greenish, slimy water her first time.

HANNA-LEAH had been to the *mikva* many times since then. And this evening after the rainstorm, the stone steps were as mildewed, the water as oily as ever. It seemed to her that a person should take a bath afterward and not before, but of course that wasn't the custom. The rain had stopped and the sky was clear when Hanna-Leah left the bathhouse. As she walked home, the air was sweet with lilies of the valley, and she took the long way through the woods along the bank of the river. The sun had set, no longer day, but not yet night, the sky in its depth of blue like the river's twin.

As she walked among the trees she knew from childhood, she thought it was strange that she didn't feel so different from when she was a girl. Grandmother Rivka could be standing next to her, carrying her shallow basket for picking mushrooms, telling her that this was God's market. "You can see things in the woods, Hankela. Some are good and some are poison. It's easy to get confused. But don't be afraid. Cut the stem of the mushroom. If it's pink like the palm of your hand, it's good. If it runs white and sticky like spider's milk, it's bad."

When Hanna-Leah came to the place where she'd seen the stranger, she paused. A wave of confusion swept through her, and then she shrugged, half-smiling. The moon was rising and in the moon she could see the silhouette of the hungry wolf. There's no reason to keep my silk underthings just for *Shabbas,* she thought. They're good for every day. Why not? Do I have to wear this scratchy wool and be so hot? Who's going to see?

Hanna-Leah began to hum a song that she used to sing with Faygela when they were young. And as she walked, she swung her arms, heedless of the kerchief falling back so that her hair showed golden against the night. When she came home, she put a fistful of purple and white flowers in a pickle jar on the table, and then she took the wooden doll out of her bridal trunk. Grandmother Rivka's satin shawl would make a nice dress for the doll.

It wasn't long before Hanna-Leah had cut the cloth and sat herself in the rocker to sew. Her mother-in-law was sitting in the armchair reading the *Tzena-U-Rena.* Hershel was at a meeting of the community council. Hanna-Leah hummed in time with the ticking of the clock on the cabinet. Above the clock was her father's portrait, drawn in charcoal just before her wedding. She held up the bodice of the doll's dress, the satin shimmering in the light from the kerosene lamp. A mushroom stew was baking in the oven. Hanna-Leah thought she might have a taste of it. She was hungry from her walk.

The door opened. Hershel. Taking off his muddy boots, he said, "You weren't here when I closed up the shop. Where did you go?"

"To the *mikva,*" she said, wondering that he should ask. But he was looking at her and rubbing his forehead as if something was bothering him. She cut and knotted the thread, held the little sleeves against the doll's arms to measure them, then began sewing the sleeves into the dress.

Hershel said, "They made me head of the council."

"Good." She looked at him. He wasn't the young man that had married her. He had no beard then, his hands smoother, unsure of themselves. Now his beard was graying. His hands were strong. Sure of what they did. He stood with his legs apart, feet planted on the floor like he was ready to swing an ax. He was looking at her as if he could see that she'd been walking in the woods, singing. She waited for him to speak. But he didn't. He only looked at her. Did he want her to say something more?

"Did you hear that Ruthie was arrested?" he asked at last.

"It can't be. Ruthie? No. What for? When?" Faygela's eldest daughter. It couldn't be. A good girl. Quiet.

But Hershel was explaining what had happened. Ruthie was caught carrying pamphlets. What kind of pamphlets? What did it matter? People said that she was following the lead of one of the other girls. And who was that? Zisa-Sara's daughter. Poor Zisa-Sara, the last of the *vilda hayas,* alone in her grave in America. She would turn over if she knew that her daughter had made friends with Ruthie and now Ruthie was arrested. Sitting in prison. And Faygela was in Warsaw, so far away. Hanna-Leah's needle ran in and out of the satin cloth. It didn't seem like such a long time ago that she had sewn baby's clothes for Faygela's daughters. They came one after another. Too many. After the fourth, Hanna-Leah didn't sew for them anymore. Why should she? Let Faygela take care of her own. If Faygela asked her, well, maybe. But she never did. Only now Hanna-Leah thought that Faygela might have been ashamed to ask.

THE LONG DAYS

Standing on the shelf above the fireplace, the wooden doll reminded Hanna-Leah of her Grandmother Rivka. The sun hovered in the sky, light glinting on the satin like a small fire as May came to an end and Faygela returned from Warsaw. The long days were too warm, Hershel's mother complained. Hanna-Leah bathed her face with cool water until the older woman settled back in her chair, snoring lightly. Hershel was busy mending his boots, sharpening his knife. So when Hanna-Leah finished what she had to do, she looked at the doll and heard her grandmother's voice.

"The hungry wolf used to follow a girl who had no mother to tell her what to do," the voice whispered. "All this poor orphan had was a little doll made out of wood. She carried it everywhere in the pocket of her apron. One day, her stepmother sent the girl far into the woods. She came to the house of the Morning Star. Just then she turned around and saw the wolf. Its jaws opened wide, its teeth were wet. But the doll called softly, 'Don't stop. Go to the river.' And so the girl did. She ran, the wolf running after her. And at the river she found the Morning Star. Oh, she was big and wild. Bigger than the wolf. But the doll said, 'Don't be afraid. Drink from the secret river. And then you'll know how to feed the hungry wolf.' "

ON HER wedding day, Hanna-Leah sat in the front room like a queen among the women, her hair long and loose around her for the last time. She'd been fasting all day and now she seemed to float above her chair, the bridal throne, waiting for the *bedecken*, the moment when her face would be hidden behind the veil. Soon she would be a married woman, her hair bound and covered forever. At Perlmutter's tavern, long tables were set with breasts of chicken, fish, honey cake, poppy seed cookies, braided bread, schnapps, and flowers.

"Flowers?" Grandmother Rivka had asked. "People need to eat and drink. For what do they want flowers?"

"A bride should be surrounded with beautiful things," Faygela had said. Despite the baby in her arms and her belly out to here with another, she had walked in the woods all morning, carrying Ruthie in a shawl on her back. When she'd returned, she'd held out her basket for Hanna-Leah to smell the vanilla-nutmeg scent of the gooseberry blooms. "When you feel faint, just close your eyes and smell the flowers," she'd said. "It will be just as if we were walking in the woods. I took the violets and the goldenheart to the tavern."

Hershel came from the river with the young men arm in arm, pushing, singing, and shouting. He walked steadily as if he were not hungry from fasting, shoulder to shoulder with his cousin Shmuel, Faygela's husband.

"Hurry," shouted Grandmother Rivka to the young men, "should the children starve?"

"What's the rush?" Papa asked. How could he know that he only had three years left? The wedding was in 1878, the pogroms wouldn't begin until '81. "I only have one daughter to marry off. The groom can wait a few minutes for his share in the butcher shop. Let the klezmer play and the wedding jester tell a few jokes."

Yekel the wedding jester wore a torn straw hat with bells and strings of garlic hanging from it. Red ribbons, pinned to the tail of his coat, streamed behind him as he gyrated among the company. Yekel was known from Blaszka to Plotsk as a mimic. One look at you and you were his forever. Now he leaped in front of Faygela. Clutching his belly, he squatted and groaned, "Oh, merciful God, don't tear me in two. I will never do this again. Please God, make it come quickly." She half-smiled, pretending to engross herself in juggling the baby.

"Who needs you here?" Grandmother Rivka said to Yekel, pulling him up by the sleeve and giving him a shove toward the hallway. "Go tell a few jokes to the men. We women need to stretch our feet. Play something fast, Mendel. Something for a *broygez tanz.*" She put a hand to Hanna-Leah's cheek. "That will make you smile. You look too serious, like it was the Day of Atonement. Come Faygela, give the baby to one of the girls. Dance with me."

The clarinet blew, the bass and fiddle joined in. Grandmother Rivka glided toward Faygela, cajoling with outstretched arms. The women clapped. *Why are you so angry without a reason,* they sang, *Why? Why?* Grandmother circled Faygela. As if furious, Faygela stamped her feet, snapping her fingers in Grandmother's face, flinging her chin at the ceiling. Grandmother sidled toward her, hands folded as if to implore her, motioning to the women who laughed, calling, *Make up now, there's no more time, the world is like a dream.*

"A dream," Hanna-Leah echoed, hunger forgotten, tears running down her face as Grandmother was jostled by Faygela's belly, first in the front, then behind. Faygela winked at Hanna-Leah, allowing Grandmother to take her hands and dance around the bride's chair.

Later the upstairs room at the tavern was too quiet, the last guest gone home, leaving crumbs for the mice. As Hershel snored, Hanna-Leah lay stiffly. So this was it? This was married life? She would never do it again. He could beg and plead. She would go to the Rabbi and tell him herself. Never again. She talked to herself this way for an hour while Hershel slept.

When the moon rose, she leaned on one elbow to look at him. Her husband. Such a husband. His nightshirt twisted around his stomach as he rolled onto his back, one leg half dangling over the edge of the bed. She glanced between his legs, looked quickly away, then turned toward him, a finger on her lips. Why shouldn't she look? Didn't she pay enough? It was small now, nestled like a mushroom on a tiny knoll. She poked. It jumped. She paused, looking intently. Hershel snored. Reaching out a finger, she stroked the top. How smooth it was, like a bolete mushroom. See how it rises like a twist of hallah dough, she thought. Her breath quickened. Carefully, she lifted the nightshirt, looking at Hershel's broad chest, lightly running her hand across the hair curling thick and soft like the moss where mushrooms grow. She rested her hand on the muscles in his thighs, her chest and neck warm as if her body was blushing.

"Hershel," she said, shaking him. "Wake up."

He half opened his eyes. "What? What?"

"I can't sleep. Can't we do something?"

"You want to play cards? Now?"

"Not cards." She shook her head, eyes modestly downcast.

"Then you must be hungry. Wait. I'll get you some honey cake."

"No," she said. "Don't you think it's hot in here?" She looked at him and he looked at her. Reaching toward her, he slowly lifted her nightgown, and as she smiled, he quickly drew it over her head, throwing it to the floor.

In the last evenings of May, Hanna-Leah heard Grandmother Rivka's voice again. At night she dreamed that Grandmother was making soup and talking to her about everyone in Blaszka. Then June began, and Hanna-Leah dressed herself as always, except that she wore her silk underthings, cool and smooth against her skin as she walked to the butcher shop.

The women who came to the butcher shop said, Misha is getting big, and only five months, too. But still she holds her head up like the Tsarina. She doesn't know what shame is.

"Let me ask you," Hanna-Leah said. "Who's going to take care of the pregnant women in the village when Misha can't get around anymore?"

The women looked at each other, shaking their heads. When you're right, you're right, they said. It could have been Ruthie. She was starting to learn with Misha. But now she's been sitting in prison more than a week. And her mother's in the bakery crying out her eyes until she can hardly see.

"A sea of tears won't water the vegetable garden," Hanna-Leah said. She remembered how Faygela could be. When Ruthie was just a year old, Faygela gave birth to her second child, a boy. He lived only a few days, and Faygela refused to nurse Ruthie, even though her breasts hurt because she was full of milk. The baby has a tooth, she said. Nursing hurts. Take her, Hanna-Leah. So Hanna-Leah took Ruthie, quieting her with a rag soaked in honey. It went on for a day, two days. Faygela wouldn't eat. And then it was enough. Hanna-Leah told Faygela what was what. I made you a soup, she said. From my only hen. A good soup. It's not going to waste, I'm telling you. So Faygela ate, and she nursed Ruthie again.

"How long can a mother cry? I'm going to her," Hanna-Leah now said to the women in the butcher shop.

SHE CROSSED the square through the hubbub of market day, sparks flying as the blacksmith hammered a shoe onto a horse's hoof, the cooper rolling barrels into a farmer's cart, the tanner's wife spreading out the sheepskins she'd treated with bran and chaff.

In the bakery, Hanna-Leah saw a knot of women huddled around Faygela, who sat at the table, her head in her hands. Behind her, the girls worked quietly, her little boy sitting on the floor, rocking and sucking his thumb. Shmuel was refilling the bins of flour.

Can't you see that she's upset? the women asked. You need something, go talk to Shmuel.

"This isn't your business," Hanna-Leah answered. "I have something to say to Faygela. Do you want to hear or not?" It wasn't any use to give Faygela sympathy. She'd had plenty, and it just helped her cry.

"I'm listening," Faygela replied. Rising, she came around the table to Hanna-Leah, pushing her way through the women. She stood straight though her eyes were swollen and red, her mouth trembling. She'd always been so small and fine.

"Grandmother Rivka came to me in a dream," Hanna-Leah said. "Your Ruthie will be safe."

"Thank you for telling me," Faygela said tonelessly, stroking Hanna-Leah's fingers the way she used to when she was sorry for something, as if her fingers could tap a message that her mouth had forgotten.

"Listen to me," Hanna-Leah whispered. "You always enjoyed a little too much drama when there was trouble. Think of someone else." Faygela's red eyes opened wide, and she put her fingers to her lips, but said nothing as Hanna-Leah left.

There used to be four of us, Hanna-Leah thought as she walked back to the butcher shop. The *vilda hayas*. Like the four corners of the village square. One became the baker's wife and her daughter is sitting in prison. One became the midwife and she's five months pregnant, in her mother's house by herself. Another, may she rest in peace, died in America and left her orphans to come home alone. And the fourth? The butcher's wife, who just turned thirty-five. Who should get back to the shop and never mind dreaming. A woman does what she has to. But why?

Is that a question? Hanna-Leah stopped in midstep. She looked around the village square. The tavern, the synagogue, Misha's house, the bridge, the beaten earth under her feet, the woods and the river. Everything familiar. It seemed to shiver for a minute, as if, without the butcher's wife to tell the women what was going on in Blaszka, it might disappear.

THREE WEEKS later, the wild strawberries were ripe. In the clearing near the birches, squatting on her heels, Hanna-Leah worked methodically, clearing a square of berries, then moving on. Her hands were red with juice, the basket slowly filling with the tiny berries. When she began, the sky was overcast. But now the sun beat down on her bent back. She stood, hands in the small of her back as she stretched. It was here that she had last seen the stranger. She stood where he had stood, picking up her basket of strawberries, turning her face to the sun, hot as the stranger's hand.

Grandmother Rivka used to say that in heaven they ate strawberries. Hanna-Leah was hungry. It wasn't easy picking strawberries. She should at least taste her work. She put a strawberry in her mouth. Was one enough? It was nothing. Just a morsel of sweetness. So she took another. And another. Why not? Didn't she pick them herself? Then a handful. So sweet. So juicy. More. And more. Until her basket was empty. All her work eaten. But how sweet it was. And how thirsty she'd become in the hot sun.

I'll go to the river, she thought, walking through the woods to the place where the river narrowed. The water was cold there, flowing quickly between the silver rocks. Hanna-Leah knelt, drinking greedily. Water ran between her cupped hands, down her throat, her chest. She drank again and again, until her thirst was quenched. Then she watched the river whirl around the silver rocks in white bubbles. She sat so still that a fox brushed his tail against her back and she saw the speckled scales of trout. Before she got up, she held a blade of grass between her thumbs, blowing into the opening, like a ram's horn blasting the silence. Enough hot sun. Off came her shoes and stockings. Up went her skirts, bunched around her waist. She waded into the river, cold water swirling between her thighs as she tore off her kerchief, shaking her hair loose.

WHEN SHE came home, Hershel was waiting. He sat in the rocking chair, but he wasn't rocking. He was holding the wooden doll in his hands.

"What is it?" she asked.

"You're different," he said. "I don't know you anymore."

"Well, you don't have to call the matchmaker. We're married already." She took the doll from him and put it on the shelf. Hershel's hands hung on his knees as if without the doll they didn't know what to hold onto.

"Did you eat?" she asked.

"You weren't here. How should I eat?"

She stood in front of the cold fireplace. "Where's your mother?"

"Asleep. I put her to bed," he said.

"Good. So we'll eat. There's soup on the stove." Hershel leaned back in his chair, fingers entwined over his chest. "But I'm going to sit, and you can serve it," she added.

"Me?" Hershel asked, sitting up.

She walked to the back of his chair, her hands on his shoulders, leaning over so that her hair fell over him, tickling his face. "Sure, you. Are your fingers broken?"

"All right, so I'll do it." He stood, taking her hands, pulling her. "You sit, Hankela. No, no. Not at the table. Here in the big chair." His fingers held onto hers so tightly she could feel the quick pulse of his blood. "You sit and I'll bring everything to you. Everything. Why not?"

Before they went to bed, Hanna-Leah threw out the rest of Misha's medicine. She undressed and lay down beside Hershel, but she didn't wait to see if he would roll toward her. She just went right to sleep, lying on her back, her hand in his. A woman has no appetite for potions when she can wade in the river and uncover her head and eat soup served by her husband.

NIGHTS OF THE SECRET RIVER

The raspberries were ripe and Hanna-Leah made preserves. On market day she crossed the village square to Misha's stall. There was the usual crowd of women, Misha's head high even though she was out to here. "I made too much," Hanna-Leah said, giving Misha a basket filled with jars of raspberry preserves. "Do me a favor. Take it."

Misha shaded her eyes against the sun, looking at Hanna-Leah. "You feel all right? You need something, Hanna-Leah?"

"What should I need?"

"Maybe a tonic."

"My grandmother used to say that what a person wants you can't buy in the market. When we went to pick mushrooms. Do you remember? She gave us each a basket. Me and Faygela. You and Zisa-Sara."

Misha nodded, her hand on her belly. "I remember."

"I'll save a nice piece of brisket for you," Hanna-Leah said. "Come before *Shabbas*. A pregnant woman needs to keep up her strength twice as much as any man." The women at Misha's stall laughed. "Am I right?"

"When you're not wrong, you're right," Misha said.

WHEN THE blueberries were ripe and Misha was seven months along, the women asked Hanna-Leah in the butcher shop, Who do you think the father is?

"It could be anyone. But I'll tell you." She leaned forward over the counter. "The baby's not a stranger. It's Misha's. Wasn't Misha born right here in Blaszka? There's nothing more to say about it."

ON A WARM day in the first week of August, Hanna-Leah watched Hershel in the back of the butcher shop. His sleeves were rolled up, muscles standing out on his arms as he swung the cleaver. "How is Zisa-Sara's daughter?" he asked.

"Not good. It's better that Zisa-Sara died so far away than that she should see her daughter buried here."

"Is Emma so bad, then?"

"It's typhus. What more is there to say?"

"Maybe children from America are stronger than ours."

"I haven't seen Zisa-Sara for ten years, she should rest in peace. Her children are practically strangers. But now they're here, at least we could take in the boy. God forbid that Izzie should fall sick, too."

"Where will he sleep?" Hershel asked.

"In the front room. We have an extra cot. What do we need it for?"

So Izzie came to them, his face pale, his small hands clutching the same canvas bag he'd brought with him on the ship from America. In the evening, after he fell asleep, Hanna-Leah complained that it was too warm in the house. "I need a breath of air. A walk. Watch over the boy, Hershel."

OUTSIDE there was a small breeze, but still she was warm. It'll be cooler by the river, she thought as she walked into the woods, taking off her kerchief. Night swallowed the last of the sun. The wind fingered her hair, the fruity perfume of summer darkness filling her lungs. When she came to the river, she took off her dress and hung it on a branch with her shoes and stockings as if she were a girl going to swim. How pleasant it was in her silken shift and her bare feet. She leaned against a willow, listening to the hoot of an owl, the rush of its wings, the squeak of a mouse. Clouds skimmed over the moon. Hanna-Leah sang:

> *"By the chimney birds are blinking,*
> *From the moon the birds are drinking,*
> *Not awake and not asleep,*
> *The night is long the river deep."*

As she sang, she heard music. A silhouette showed against the reappearing moon. A man playing the violin. The Traveler.

She lifted her arms as if she were dancing around the bride's chair, as if all the *vilda hayas* were dancing with her here in the woods where they'd once told secrets. She spun and her feet turned the earth. In the sky she patted the hungry wolf. Between her legs was the heat that eats time.

The music slowed, melted into silence, and she was alone again.

And hot. How cool the river looked, foaming white over the silver rocks. A goose flew across the moon, calling its mate. Why did they bring water from the river to the *mikva* instead of just going to the river itself? Hanna-Leah wondered. As she walked farther down the bank, the water lapped at her feet. Hanna-Leah waded in, her silk shift clinging to her like another skin. The river eddied around her legs, the current pulled her forward, sand sifting between her toes. She dipped under the water, deeply, as if she were in the *mikva* and had to make sure her hair was covered by water. Once, twice, and the third time, she stayed under, crouching, legs apart, water lapping her, rocking her, her eyes open to watch the reeds wave in the reflection of the moon and silver fish flicker between the reeds, from a great distance hearing the whisper of her name. Hanna-Leah rose from the river, looking up at the moon. "Kosher," she said.

She came into the house, her feet squelching in her shoes, her dress soaking, mud and water dripping onto the floor. "You're wet," Hershel said.

"Am I?"

"Where have you been?"

"The river. Near the silver rocks."

"There? The current is fast. The water's deep. You could have drowned."

"I didn't," she said, yawning and stretching and smiling as if she'd been to the River of the Messiah and back.

"You didn't," he said. "Thank God, you didn't. You're soaking, Hankela. You'll catch your death. Come into our room and let me help you take off the wet clothes."

They stood next to the bed, Hershel gently pulling the cotton dress over her head, and then the silk shift. "You could have drowned." He draped a towel around her back. A worn towel, rough, yellowed, frayed. "You should have a soft towel," he said, rubbing her shoulders, her spine, the small of her back. Her smooth strong shoulders. Her delicate spine. Curving into the large round rise of her full-moon bottom. Hanna-Leah sat on the bed. Hershel sat beside her. Then he began to take off his clothes.

*   *   *

ON THE eve of Tishah-b'Av, the boy sat with Hershel in the first row of the synagogue. The Holy Ark was draped in black while the village mourned for the destruction of the Holy Temple. They mourned their old losses, and they grieved because there was typhus in the village. Remember the cholera epidemic in '67, they said. So far only Zisa-Sara's daughter Emma was ill, but everyone knew how easy it was for the entire village to be brought down by sickness. And although Emma's brother was only ten, he prayed like a grown man, Hershel told Hanna-Leah when they came home.

How tired the boy looked, how small. "You see the doll on the shelf?" she asked as Izzie lay down on the cot.

"Over the fireplace?"

"Yes. That isn't any doll. She tells stories. It's true. And not any stories. Just my Grandmother Rivka's. Do you want to hear one?" The boy nodded, his pale hands folded over his chest. "All right. Once there was an orphan child that was afraid of a hungry wolf. Her granny used to tell her that there's never any reason to be afraid of a wolf. You only have to know what to do. You understand?"

"What happened to the orphan girl?" Izzie's eyes blinked as he struggled to stay awake.

"One day she ran from the wolf until she was lost. She ran so far, that she ran right into a deep river." The boy was asleep, curled on his side, his hands under his chin. Still Hanna-Leah continued the story, Hershel sitting in the rocking chair, looking at her and listening. "But the wolf followed her," Hanna-Leah said. "What was she to do? In the river she could drown and on the shore the wolf would eat her. But the Morning Star who was bigger and wilder even than the wolf said to the orphan child, 'Drink up the river.' So the child drank and drank until she'd swallowed the whole river and stood on dry land. And what do you think she found growing on the bottom? Mushrooms. Imagine, mushrooms growing underneath a river. So she picked the mushrooms and fed them to the wolf. 'Here, doggie,' she said. 'Eat.' And the wolf ate until it was full. After that, whenever the wolf was hungry, it came to the girl for mushrooms."

"She picked good mushrooms," Hershel said. "And her pierogies were the best."

THE DAYS OF AWE

Rosh Hashanah fell on the first of October, the ram's horn proclaiming the New Year. The men sat below, the watercarrier in the back, more important men, like the butcher, closer to the Holy Ark.

In the balcony above the women prayed in Yiddish, "*Dear God, You know what weighs heavily on my heart, things I cannot tell. You know every hidden thing. You know my wounds.*"

Below, the men chanted in Hebrew, the holy tongue, "*On Rosh Hashanah it is written and on Yom Kippur it is sealed. Who will live and who will die. Who will rest and who will wander.*"

Above the women cried with the *zogerin*, "*Do not let my children or grandchildren die while I live. Do not let my good friends bring me sorrow. On Yom Kippur, when we stand before you in our bare feet, weak from thirst, hardly able to say a word, accept our fast as atonement for our sins . . .*"

As THE days of awe mounted toward Yom Kippur, the Day of Judgment, the Day of Atonement, neighbor sought forgiveness of neighbor, resentments were cleared, debts canceled, and there was little bargaining in the village square on market day. Misha's time was near, her store of herbs replenished by the girls in the village. The Rabbi studied in the synagogue, preparing his sermon. In the bakery, Hanna-Leah was seen talking to Faygela.

"If I have done anything in the year to offend you, please forgive me," Hanna-Leah said. It was the custom to ask forgiveness in this way before Yom Kippur. To forgive willingly, in return, was a religious duty.

"Of course," said Faygela. "And I hope that you'll pardon me for anything I did to offend you." It seemed as if the words were having a little trouble finding their way out of her mouth. Hanna-Leah knew that Faygela didn't always hold with customs.

"You know what I say? Between you and me. Can someone be offended by a *vilda haya*? It only does what its nature tells it. Like your girls. And the little one, too. Look, I made a jacket for him. For *Shab-*

bas. It's nothing. I had the material from my grandmother's shawl," Hanna-Leah said.

"It's beautiful." Faygela held the green satin in her hands, turning it over and over. "I remember when your grandmother first wore the shawl. At your wedding."

"Well, that was then. And this is now. Another story."

"Will you sit with me in synagogue on Kol Nidrei?" Faygela asked.

"I shouldn't. My sisters-in-law might be offended."

"Then you can ask for their forgiveness next year," Faygela said. And she stood on her toes to whisper in Hanna-Leah's ear the way she always used to when she had a secret to tell.

IN THE butcher shop the women asked, Have you seen so many strangers in Blaszka? There isn't enough to feed them all. What are you talking? It's the same as always. A few Jews from the peasant villages upriver who come for the High Holy Days. A beggar or two trying his fortune some place new. A peddler making his way home. A student. A couple of wanderers. What about the Gypsy boy? I'm telling you, it's the same as always. So he hit his head in our river? It's the current and the rocks. Someone's always falling there. You can say what you like. I don't trust them. Strangers. Who knows what they want? Am I right, Hanna-Leah?

She was sweeping the earthen floor and sprinkling yellow sand over it. "Maybe. I'm not saying that you're wrong. But you remember what Hershel said? We were strangers in a strange land ourselves. It's hard to believe, but it happened. So should we let them sit by themselves? Listen to me, it's a mitzvah to feed a hungry person."

KOL NIDREI

The eve of Yom Kippur. Fathers and mothers cup their children's heads and bless them. The stones tremble. At this very moment, their life is under scrutiny, their fate written. Who among them can be sure to live another day? The Holy One sits on His throne in judgment over all the worlds. The stars hold their breath.

Over their *kittels,* their white burial robes, the men drape their prayer shawls as if it were morning. On Yom Kippur there is no night, though the sun is falling. The men and women of Blaszka walk to the synagogue, the women carrying the candles they made during the days of awe. Birds sit on the roof silently waiting. The Holy One lifts the seal of the Heavenly Court.

Inside the synagogue, the women's candles flash on the white garments of the congregation above and below. Outside the wind rises, blowing leaves through the cemetery, pulling at the walls of the synagogue, tearing at the loose shingles on the roof, crying through the window frames.

IN THE coming year, Hershel will go to Plotsk to find good towels. He will bring back five of them, the thickest, softest, biggest towels in the world for his Hanna-Leah.

In time she will sew the wedding dresses that Faygela's girls will wear under the bridal canopy. And for the one that's left sitting with no children of her own, Hanna-Leah will leave her Grandmother Rivka's silver candlesticks.

In a hundred years those candlesticks will grace the table of a house in London, where strangers will always find an open door.

2

MUD AND PEARLS

"Make it nice, Faygela. Please, don't upset him. It's not good to upset a new groom," the young woman said, looking for approval from the knot of married women who had come into the bakery to get warm. Faygela was writing a letter to the girl's husband in Germany, where he was looking for work. The married women stamped their feet, shaking the snow from their shawls. No one writes a letter like Faygela, they said. Pearls fall from her pen. When a man reads a letter like that, he wants to come home right away. Even the Tsar would have mercy on the Jews if he read one of Faygela's letters. The girl, hands folded over her slightly bulging belly, smiled tentatively.

Faygela's oldest daughter, Ruthie, was braiding round loaves of Sabbath hallahs while her sisters mixed the white flour, soft as silk, with eggs, sugar, oil, and water. Behind them the row of stone ovens glowed. The yeasty smell of baking bread hung in tendrils of steam around the doorway. From the finished batch of dough, Ruthie took a lump and threw it into the fire. As it blackened into a rock, she murmured in Hebrew, "*Blessed are you, Lord our God, King of the Universe, Who has made us holy in Your mitzvos, commanding us to separate a piece of dough for an offering.*"

The door swung open as the blacksmith's wife entered with a gust of snow. "Did you see the strangers?" she asked. "The carriage that stopped in front of Perlmutter's tavern."

"The actors?" Faygela asked.

"Yes, did you know that they were arrested in Minsk for performing in Yiddish?"

"They're not the first ones. The Tsar made it illegal to put on plays in Yiddish but Jews are too stubborn to close their mouths just like that. Instead they learn to change their costumes faster and run for the train."

It's just craziness, the women said. Does it cost the Tsar so much to let us have a little pleasure?

"It's not so simple," Faygela said. "The actors bring news that you can't get anywhere else. Not with the censors."

And you don't forget their songs, the women said. You feel them right here. They tapped their chests.

"The Russian authorities don't want us to know what's going on. That's why they shut down the Yiddish newspaper. And don't think we're the only ones to be denied our own language. It's illegal to teach Polish, too. But a Jew is always in the middle." Faygela sighed. "The Russians say that we're in bed with Polish rebels and the Poles accuse us of supporting the Russian oppressors. If you can read Russian . . ."

"I can write a plain letter in Yiddish like most people. But you won't catch me learning to read Russian or Polish. What for? Do the peasants read? Not a word," the blacksmith's wife said. "God forbid that we should have some dealings with the authorities, then it's the Rabbi's job to take care of it. Am I right?" The women nodded.

"You don't know what you're missing. There are wonderful books in Polish and in Russian, too. Listen to this." Faygela picked up a book protected by a covering of brown paper on which she had written, *Adam Mickiewicz, the Polish Prophet.* " 'In the beginning, there was belief in one God, and there was Freedom in the world. And there were no laws, only the will of God, and there were no lords and slaves.' Doesn't it make you think?" The women looked at her blankly. Stubbornly, Faygela went on. "If you ask me, I would say that there was always one law, that people should look for the truth."

Oh, yes, the women said. It's too easy to believe a liar. And when it comes to lying, the authorities are experts. You can't trust one of them. Hanna-Leah says that as long as there's a single Jew, someone will be aggravated. With the tax on kosher meat, it's hard to buy even a piece of flank for *Shabbas*. How will it end, Faygela?

"According to the Tsar's minister, one-third of us will leave the country, one-third will convert, and one third will starve to death. It's written right here." Faygela lifted *The Israelite*, a Jewish newspaper written in Polish and permitted by the authorities because it encouraged assimilation. "When my Shmuel goes to Plotsk, he sees hungry faces everywhere, and it's better here in Poland than around Minsk. The farther east you go, the worse it gets. That's why you see so many strangers these days. People have nothing, and they're looking for somewhere they can have a life."

It's true. Who ever saw so many strangers coming through Blaszka? Nobody knows where they're from and where they're going, the women said. You need eyes in the back of your head when there are strangers around. Beggars, peddlers, students, Gypsies. I say the worst are the Russian Jews. They're poor and they're dirty. And we're not poor? At least we have a home.

"Listen to me, women," Faygela said. "I'll tell you a story about strangers." She rested her chin on her two fists, looking off into the distance as if she were watching the story unfold in front of her. "It happened in the time of King Krak. A girl was going to give birth. It was her first baby and she was terrified. She was all alone. Her husband was away peddling. Her mother-in-law was visiting her relatives, because the baby was early. No one expected it. And, poor girl, she had no sisters. So she was alone, groaning. You know how it is."

The women nodded. She thought she'd die alone, they said.

"Yes, exactly. It was a winter day just like this, with the snow blowing and the wind tearing your skin off your bones. So what happens? There was a knock at the door. And who should come in, but the demon Lilith. It's true. Well, of course the girl fainted on the spot. She knew that Lilith must have come to steal her baby, and there was no one to protect her. Not even an amulet on the wall."

"How did Lilith look?" asked the young girl whose husband had gone away.

"Not like you'd expect. No horns. Not even a cloven foot. No, she had the prettiest, dainty feet, like a princess. Her hair was long and blonde, but she had strong hands. When the girl woke up from her faint, she thought that Lilith would strangle her with those hands. But instead she delivered the baby. And she blessed it, too. The baby grew up to be a scholar. In fact, he was an adviser to kings. So, who can tell about a stranger?"

That's as good as one of Shomer's stories, the women said. Write it down, Faygela. You'll be famous. When the book peddler comes, instead of calling out, "New romances by the Yiddish author Shomer, famous from Warsaw to Minsk," he'll say, "Faygela's stories, come and look, women, but don't damage the merchandise."

"Shomer's merchandise," Faygela sniffed, her delicate nostrils pinched as if she smelled rotten eggs. "With his silly stories of Jewish heiresses and knights in armor." Holding up a small, sharp-angled hand with an ink stain on the second finger, and flour under the nails, she said, "I swear before God—" The women shifted uncomfortably. It's a sin to make a vow, they said. Don't swear, please Faygela, no one meant anything, you might call down the evil eye on yourself. "I swear," she said insistently, "they should put Shomer on trial for writing lies. A real writer tells the truth, and that's how he changes the world. But what's the use of talking? Nothing ever changes in Blaszka."

The women looked at one another, eyebrows raised, hands busying themselves with arranging shawls and digging into bags as if suddenly reminded it was market day and there was work to be done. But the blacksmith's wife, undaunted, retorted, "What do you mean, nothing? I heard in the butcher shop that someone saw a pair of men's trousers under Misha's bed. Who do you think they belonged to?"

You can be sure it wasn't her former husband. The watercarrier only has one pair, the women laughed.

"You want to talk about Misha, I'll tell you about Misha," Faygela said. "Take a look at Berel." The little boy, hearing his name, poked his head out of the wooden crate he was playing in. He was a fat little bull, already nearly as strong as his next oldest sister, confident in the goodness of a world made of cinnamon and raisins. "After thirty hours of labor with him, I was so weak I could hardly breathe. I thought I was finished. When the doctor came from Plotsk, he said there was only one thing to do. He was going to cut me open to save the baby. I knew what that meant. He considered me dead already, because once they cut you open like that, every disease finds a home in the wound. But in walked Misha, like a queen. She threw out the doctor, turned the baby around inside me with her own hands. And you know what happened then?"

"Out came Berel, pop!" shouted Dina, who was six years old.

"Out I came, pop!" echoed Berel. He and Dina were playing Train to Warsaw on the floor of the bakery. Berel was the passenger in his wooden crate, Dina the driver who pulled him between the legs of her older sisters.

"But the *zogerin* always says it was her praying in the cemetery that did it," Leibela, the middle daughter protested.

Freydel, the second oldest, folded her hands over her chest and rolled her eyes at heaven. "May the *zogerin* pray for a good-looking boy to become Papa's apprentice," she said.

"Let me assure both of you that dead people aren't sitting in the cemetery waiting to talk to the *zogerin*. And they don't stand around in heaven arguing with God, either. A person lives, then he dies, and that's all. My father told me and I'm telling you. A grave is just for remembrance." Faygela shook her pen at the four older girls who were now loading the mounds of dough onto the long-handled shovels and sliding them into the ovens. "When a baby is coming out the wrong way, it's not a time to play patchie-patchie in the cemetery. No, you need a person who knows what's what. It was Misha who kept me in this world and only her."

Ruthie, the oldest, a slight girl of sixteen, dark-eyed like her mother, said nothing. At the mention of Misha's name, she blushed.

The sound of a horse and cart clattering up to the bakery distracted Faygela, and the girls rushed outside, Berel toddling behind them.

"What did you bring me, Papa?" and "Me, what about me," the younger children called out. "Candy? Did you bring us candy?"

"First the horse has to go into his stall, children. *Shabbas* is coming for him, too," Shmuel said. His cart was loaded with supplies from

Plotsk, rye flour, wheat flour, sugar, almonds, cinnamon, raisins, a pastry crimper, poppy seeds, and kerosene. Unhitching the horse, he carried the supplies out back, the younger children running after him, putting their hands in his pockets, shouting, "Good Papa," when they pulled out sticks of candy. The middle girls, waiting for Shmuel to give them their brightly colored ribbons, poked and elbowed one another until Faygela pushed them apart with an exasperated grunt, then held them close, her arms linked with theirs, while they snuggled against her. How patient Shmuel was with the children, she thought. And as she watched the feathery motion of his fingers touching their cheeks, she imagined the same light touch on her own body, later, when the children slept. And he would be just as patient when she braided his silvery beard after they made love, listening to everything she said, though he wouldn't understand half of it.

"I'm sorry, Ruthie," he was saying. "I couldn't get the herbal book you wanted. It was too expensive. But look at this. The bookseller gave it to me cheap because it's in English. And you see, Ruthie, there are drawings of plants." He patted her shoulder.

Thanking her father quietly, Ruthie slipped the book into her apron pocket, ignoring her sisters who were laughing and wrinkling their noses. "English, who wants a book in English?" they said.

"Don't tease your sister," Faygela said. "At least she can read a little German and Russian, which is more than either of you. If only my father was still alive, I might have educated daughters who respected their older sister. And who knows, maybe a little English might be useful someday. Ruthie could write a letter to your uncle in America. Well, once he learns to speak English. Yes, it could be quite useful. There are plenty of Jews in America. Plenty. Nearly as many as in Warsaw. It so happens that it was just lucky that your father found this book."

Shmuel gave her arm a quick squeeze as he handed her a package tied with string. "I found everything you wanted," he said. In the package was the latest issue of *The Israelite,* a book, two notebooks, and several pencils. Shmuel always made sure that Faygela had a few pencils and something to write in. Whenever she could spare a minute, she would sit on a low stool, using her bridal trunk as a desk. The notebooks were locked inside, and she wore the key around her neck. If she ran out of time or paper, she got cranky, and when Faygela was cranky her Friday nights with Shmuel lacked a certain enthusiasm.

As she cut the string, the book, sandwiched between the notebooks, fell into her hand. "Oh Shmuel, you brought it. And it wasn't too much?" She stroked the cloth cover of *Bakenta Bilder—Familiar Pictures—*by I. L. Peretz.

"Not too much," Shmuel said, rocking back and forth on his heels, hands clasped behind his back, his face alight as Faygela threw her arms around him.

"I don't know how an intelligent, cultured man like Peretz knows so much about life in a small village, but his last book could have been Blaszka itself. Every word was written on my heart. Look, girls," she said, opening the new book. "These are the words of a man who knows the truth about life. This is what I want you to read, not those cheap fantasies of Shomer's." She sighed. "If only I had time to teach you then you could read the books that belonged to my father. But a family of girls can't do what it wants. *Shabbas* is coming. We have work to do, and I want to visit Misha before it's time to light candles."

MADE OF half-planks with lichen still clinging to the bark, Misha's house perched on stilts above the floodline. The front door opened onto steps that climbed down to the village square, the back door opening directly onto the slope of the river bank. Faygela came toward Misha's house, not from the bakery, but from the woods, icy mud on her boots, a dried oak leaf caught in her shawl. Clattering up the stairs, she called out, "Misha, Misha," her face pale, her lips blue with a coldness that started in her bones.

Misha was standing at the stove, pouring melted beeswax into a pan, her broad back toward Faygela. "Sit," she said, "I'm making ointment."

"I can't sit. It's impossible. Not now," Faygela said.

Misha turned around. She took all of Faygela in, as if she were a book that Misha read from cover to cover in an instant. "If you have a behind, you can sit," Misha said. "And you can have a cup of tea."

Dropping onto the stool beside the pine table, Faygela took a deep breath as if the air of Misha's house were a shot of brandy distilled from the herbs hanging in baskets, the roots dangling in bunches from the beams, the loops of onions and garlic, the pots bubbling on the cooking grate, the honey smell of the melting beeswax. "I saw him again," she said. "My father."

Pouring the tea into two cups, Misha said, "So why shouldn't you? Aren't you his daughter?"

"But he's been dead for eighteen years."

"And?"

"He wouldn't talk to me. He ran away from me."

"Well, I would be upset, too. A father not talking to his daughter."

"Misha, my father is dead. Ghosts don't exist. That's just ignorance. My father would be the first one to say so."

"Well, then, he should tell you instead of running off."

"Misha, be serious. Let me tell you what happened."

"All right, all right. Tell me before you burst," Misha said.

"I could see him just as clear as you. His back was to me, but it was my father."

"Where was he?"

"Outside the bakery. I thought at first it was somebody who just looked like him, maybe one of the actors. But I had to follow and see. Just at the path between the synagogue and your house, where it goes into the woods, he half-turned. I'm telling you, it was my father and no one else. He was wearing his old apron with the torn strings and books in every pocket, just like when he was alive. I called out, 'Papa, Papa,' and I ran into the woods after him. I looked here and I looked there, but I couldn't see him anywhere. He disappeared. That's the way it always happens." Faygela's shoulders slumped. "I see him like that every few months. Each time I tell myself that it's just my imagination playing tricks because I miss him, and then I promise myself that the next time I won't pay any attention. But I can't help myself. I run after him, and then he disappears." She lifted the cup of tea, not drinking it, just warming her face in the steam.

AS FAR BACK as Faygela could remember there was just her father in the bakery, rolling dough, a book open on the table beside him, and her maternal grandmother praying in the cemetery. Faygela was two when her mother died. So how could she miss her? It was her father who taught her everything about the world.

"My life is cursed," Faygela's grandmother used to say. "I married Eber the grain merchant and our daughter could have had anyone. So who do I get for a son-in-law? Oh yes, the matchmaker told us that your father was a student in Zhitomir. All I heard from the matchmaker was Yekhiel this and Yekhiel that. A scholar. A prodigy. But did anyone tell us that he spent every waking hour poring over the books and letters of heathens and heretics? Your grandfather of blessed memory tried to turn him back to the right path. He said, 'Yekhiel, for the sake of my daughter I'll forget everything if you'll throw away those books of yours. You want to read philosophy? What for? It's lies. And that science of yours? It means nothing. The Holy One above gave us the Torah to study. If you devote yourself to it, then you and your wife will want for nothing while you're in my house. Otherwise, you're on your own, I won't have an apostate under my roof.' But did your father think of his wife's welfare? No. Stubborn as an ox. He chose to work as a plain baker instead of obeying your grandfather's wishes. And my husband, my dear Eber, was so upset he didn't even notice that his partner was stealing everything from under his nose. My daughter was a dutiful wife. She worked beside your father in the bakery and whenever you cried she ran to feed you. So small and a mouth like a sucker fish. You weakened her and your brother came too early. That was the end of the two of them. A boy, *nebekh*, to say the mourner's prayer when I'm gone. He would have been a scholar. But it wasn't to be. How she bled, how she suffered. My only daughter. You put her in the ground, you and your educated father."

Faygela learned Hebrew and German sitting beside her father at her grandmother's mahogany table. "At the yeshiva where I studied, we learned only Talmud. The teachers said it was a sin to read anything except Torah," he would tell her. "But plenty of the yeshiva students hid the books of Darwin and Goethe inside religious commentaries. Near the yeshiva, there was a Rabbinical Seminary. It was a Russian school where they learned philosophy and science, not just Talmud. I used to sneak into the classes and now your cousin Berekh is studying there. When he comes to visit you'll have something to talk to him about." Her father's hands, so much like Shmuel's with their cinnamon stains, would turn the pages of Goethe's essays, brushing the hair from her eyes while she strained over a new word. "Knowledge is freedom," he would say. "There's nothing I want more than for my daughter to be free. That, and to take a fresh raisin bun for each of her friends when she's done studying. Now read this paragraph for me, *mamala.*"

In the corner, her grandmother rocked her chair with a loud rap-rap, rap-rap as she slammed forward and backward, tsking and snapping her jaws, her long knitting needles spiking the meek wool. More often than not, when Papa went out, her grandmother pulled the book from Faygela's grasp. She was a long, thin woman in black, hard-boned and knobby. "Reading just fills a girl with the evil inclination," she would say, locking the book behind the glass doors of the cabinet. "You have no business with such things. Look what a mess your father made of his life. He could have been a Talmud genius. Instead he's just Yekhiel the baker, wasting his time on the books of unbelievers. And worse, he leads his daughter down the same path, God protect us."

"It's just a book," Faygela would protest.

"If you bring a piglet into your house, the next thing you know a wild boar is tearing out your throat with his tusks. A good Jewish girl marries when she's young and has plenty of children. Then she supports them. That's her learning."

As Faygela ran out of the house, her grandmother would shout after her, "And don't you go off into the woods with those *vilda hayas* of yours."

"WELL, I'LL tell you, Faygela," Misha said, taking a slurp of tea. "If you saw your father it probably means something good."

"Why something good?"

"Well, if it was bad news, he wouldn't be able to keep your grandmother's ghost from running to tell you."

"All right, who can argue with you?"

Misha poured another cup of tea. "I heard that Zisa-Sara's children came on the afternoon train. Did you see them?"

Faygela nodded. "The children look hungry. I thought at least in America Zisa-Sara would have plenty for her children."

"I wish I had gone with her to the train station when she left," Misha said.

"I went but I didn't give her anything to remember me by. And she was the one that held us together, the four of us. Whenever we had an argument, she could quiet us with just a few words."

"I remember that she had more patience than I did. You always wanted to recite poetry when we met in the woods. It put me to sleep."

"I remember."

FAYGELA WAS fourteen and it was late summer in the woods. "Listen to me, girls," she said, " 'Whatever you can dream, begin it. There is magic, power and genius in it.' " Hanna-Leah listened, because she was Faygela's best friend and that's what best friends must do, but Misha, sitting up in the tree, laughed and threw green apples at her. Misha refused to wear shoes, running barefoot like a peasant, as thin as the wind in those days. Sitting against the tree trunk, Zisa-Sara, her knees tucked under her dress, was braiding her hair, weaving a ribbon between the gold-brown strands. "You won't be so interested in poetry when it's time to get married. You'll have something better to think about," she said, her green eyes dark in the shadow of the apple tree.

"Oh, so you have your eye on someone," Hanna-Leah said, forgetting the mushrooms. "Tell us, who is it?"

But before Zisa-Sara could answer, Misha jumped down from the apple tree. "What do you want to get married for?" she said. "A woman doesn't own her own soul once she's in her husband's house. Let me tell you, no one's going to catch me."

"What makes you think anyone wants to?" asked Hanna-Leah.

Swinging her hips from side to side, Misha winked. "I know what I know," she said. "Don't you wish you did?"

"What do you know?" Hanna-Leah challenged. "Tell me one thing." But Misha only smiled as if she had made friends with the demons and had no price to pay for it.

"I have no intention of wasting my life in Blaszka, peddling rags to feed a bunch of children. My father is sending me to school in Warsaw," Faygela said. "And when I'm famous, you can come to visit me in my box at the opera."

"Well, in the meantime, Miss Famous, you won't be able to dance at anyone's wedding if you don't learn how," Zisa-Sara said. "And what about the rest of you?" She began to hum a wedding tune, and soon the girls' arms were linked as they danced while the sun glimmered through the leaves of the woods. Faygela was the youngest, Hanna-Leah two years older, Misha and Zisa-Sara a year older than Hanna-Leah. Faygela was the first to marry, Zisa-Sara the second. Then it was Hanna-Leah's turn and finally even Misha's.

After the pogroms in '81 and the May Laws in '82, which forced many Jews to move from their villages into already crowded towns, there were people who said that there was no future in Blaszka. No one thought that Zisa-Sara would leave them. Someone else, maybe, someone who was scared that what little she had would be taken away, not Zisa-Sara. She only asked that if she smiled a person smiled back, if she held out her hand it was taken.

But when her first child was close to four years old and she was pregnant with her second, she came to say good-bye to her friends.

They were sitting at the table in Misha's house, three of them in shawls and kerchiefs, Misha, who was divorced, with her hair falling around her shoulders.

"I want you to listen to me." Zisa-Sara's voice was low, as it always was, but her friends were surprised at the fierceness in her tone. "In America, my children can go to school and learn with everyone. Can you imagine it? My children, educated people. But here . . ."

Faygela nodded reluctantly. In Blaszka, Zisa-Sara's daughter would learn to read Yiddish in the kitchen of an old woman who could read and write and had no other way to earn a few kopecks but to teach the little she knew. Enough for prayers. Enough for a girl to write a letter. If Zisa-Sara had a son, he would learn Hebrew from a broken-down *melamud,* who slapped and pinched and made sure that by the time a boy was apprenticed at the age of ten, he knew his prayers and could follow in the Torah with a little understanding. Once in a while a boy went away to yeshiva. In the old days when people were better off, someone might hire a tutor for his daughter. But a good school where there was a chance to learn something about the world?

"Faygela, your father could think of sending you to school in Warsaw," Zisa-Sara continued. "But now with the quotas and the extra fees, what Jewish child can go to a higher school? You always said that you wish your girls were educated. Why don't you come with us? Then we won't be alone."

"Shmuel would never go." Faygela leaned forward on her elbows.

"Just tell me, why America? You could go to Vienna or Berlin and then we might see each other again. America is for rough people who wrestle with cows, not scholars like your husband."

"Leave my home? I wouldn't think of it," Hanna-Leah said. "If you go somewhere else you're always a stranger. Even the air isn't the same. Nothing smells right and you'll forget who you are. You listen to me, Zisa-Sara, and don't let your husband fill your head with nonsense."

"It's not for my Mikhal's sake that we're going. No one's begging for scholars in America. But if I have a son he could be taken into the army. They'll murder him there."

"Then wait at least until the child is born," Misha said. "You don't have an easy time with labor. The baby could come early if you travel so far by boat and another midwife won't know you like I do. It's safer for you here. I brought your little girl into the world, let me bring this child, too."

"I want him to be born there. Let him be an American. Then no one can make him leave his home. You understand, Misha?" Zisa-Sara held out her hands.

Misha stood up and turned her back to them as she walked to the stove. She put the kettle on the cooking grate. "You can have more children, but if something happens to you, I can't have another Zisa-Sara for my best friend."

"I SENT Ruthie to help with the trunk," Faygela said. "I wish we could take the children home, don't you? But we don't have room for them."

"I heard that their great-auntie isn't too happy."

"Why should she be? Alta-Fruma's a woman of sixty, alone, never had a child of her own. It won't be easy with a pair of orphans. But she wouldn't let anyone else take them."

"The children can help her in the dairyhouse. It would be good for them. I hear that in America you can't find a breath of good air."

"Air is air," Faygela said. "The problem is coal dust. Oh, I see how it is." Misha was suddenly engrossed in polishing her brass candlesticks. "You're trying to keep me busy talking. No, Misha, we have work to do." Misha screwed up her mouth as Faygela brought out

Familiar Pictures. "I have a new book. Let's see how many words you can pick out, and then I'll read you the news from *The Israelite.*"

"Now, so close to *Shabbas?* I don't have time. Just read me the news."

"No, no. I've heard that story before. You always had something better to do when we were girls than go to Old Mirrel to learn your Yiddish letters with the rest of us. It's not like in our grandmothers' time when half the women couldn't read a word."

"Girls still have to look after their mothers' babies and women still have to work. Not everyone has time for Old Mirrel's kitchen, even now. Not everyone reads."

"And I'm tired of my friend Misha being one of them. It reflects badly on me. Now take a look. What do you see here?" Faygela pointed her finger to *der kleiner boim,* the little tree.

"I'm surprised that such things are written in a book," Misha said. "My mother told me about it. But that any girl could read it, right here?"

"What are you talking?" Faygela asked, sure that Misha was making something up with that innocent expression and her eyes gleaming.

"Well, that's *der kleiner,* of course." The little thing. "Don't you remember how we used to wonder what *der kleiner* looked like? But you don't need to read a story about it. Not a married woman. After all, *Shabbas* is coming, and you'll have *der kleiner* all to yourself, and it's a good one, too, six children's worth. I should know since I brought every one of them into the world, and you weren't too quiet about it, either. Yes, one day I'll write a story, too. About all the 'little things' of Blaszka. Not such wonders, but they work hard. That's the way it is after the Garden of Eden. Let me tell you, you're not the only one. When a woman's giving birth, she has plenty to say about her husband's 'little thing.' And they don't get too many prizes. What do you think, Faygela, should I make a list?" But Faygela couldn't answer. She was laughing too hard, her father's ghost forgotten, tears running down her cheeks.

WHILE Faygela laughed, Hanna-Leah was bathing her mother-in-law. Ruthie was holding one end of a trunk and Zisa-Sara's daughter Emma was holding the other as they dragged it inside.

THE DAY OF THE ICE STORM

Faygela sat at her bridal trunk, writing in her notebook. In the corner was her father's cabinet with all his books to inspire her, and above it a charcoal portrait of him with his hands in the pockets of his apron, one foot raised as if he were walking somewhere in a hurry. The woods were sketched in the background, the river, high and wild, running through it.

Faygela frowned as she scratched out another line. The poem was titled, "Poland's Sons, The January Insurrection of 1863: An Elegy In Verse." Faygela wrote sometimes in German. Everything seemed to have more substance in German. At other times she wrote in Polish, but never in Yiddish. Yiddish? No, give the language its rightful name, the Jargon, she often said. It was the dialect of garlic, of villages sinking into mud, of half-starved peddlers, of women with their shabby romantic novels, of bawdy songs in taverns. She could barely forgive Peretz, her favorite author, for abandoning Polish in favor of Yiddish. "Can he lift the Jargon from the mud? I don't know," she would say to Shmuel. "But he has to try. How many educated Jews are there? A handful. Maybe two handfuls. There are millions who will never learn about the world unless they can read about it in Yiddish. Still, it's a pity. Peretz used to write Polish so beautifully."

Leaning her elbow on the bridal trunk, Faygela reread the first two lines of her elegy in its aristocratic Polish,

> *Come to me, for I am Freedom,*
> *Mother Poland summoned Thee.*

She tapped her pencil against the trunk, then quickly as if she might regret it, wrote another two lines.

> *Come to me, for I am Freedom,*
> *Mother Poland summoned Thee,*
> *To your sylvan printing press,*
> *So far from the bakery.*

Faygela groaned as she crossed out the last two lines and tried to block out the sound of her daughters arguing. There was always too much noise. She would never write anything tolerable. Kneading her forehead, she closed her eyes and tried to picture her father in the woods, printing the pamphlets calling for revolt against the Russian oppressors, clouds passing over the hut where the press was hidden. But into the vision strode her grandmother wagging a finger. You're wasting your life away, her grandmother said. And Faygela couldn't argue. After her father died there had been no more talk of school in Warsaw. Instead at the age of fifteen she had been married off to Shmuel, and Hanna-Leah had held her hand as her hair was cut off.

If she had gone to the girls' school in Warsaw, as her father had intended, she would have enrolled in the university and now she would be a teacher, attending concerts with her class, and reading works of literature to them. And what wouldn't she give for that privilege? Her own little finger, certainly, but her girls? Not one hair. Faygela looked around the crowded front room where her daughters jostled like shifting pieces of herself.

And yet it seems like just yesterday there were four of us dancing in the woods, she thought, and then Zisa-Sara left and we all argued and now I have only Misha. Whenever I walk past Hanna-Leah's house, I see her moving in the front room, but I don't dare say a thing. How did it happen that I became afraid to speak to her? But there was no more time to think. Faygela's daughters were yelling at one another like they were having a contest to see who could wake up the dead, and little Berel was wailing. A woman should have a minute to herself? God forbid.

"Girls, girls, what's the matter with you?" Faygela snapped. Rising from her stool, she grabbed the nearest daughter and gave her a little shake.

The youngest, holding out her hand, red and swollen where a week-old cut was healing, said, "Look, Mama. Devorah pulled my arm and my hand is hurting again."

Faygela took the hand and carefully kissed the sore spot, though it was common knowledge that you shouldn't kiss your children past five years old or they'd be spoiled. The girls began to shout again, each one trying to outdo the others. "Girls! Not another word. I don't want to know who started it. The table isn't even set and we have company after the *Megillah* reading. Freydel, don't stand there dreaming. Take down the dishes. God save me from a pack of useless girls. At least Berel will say the kaddish for me when I die, even if he turns out to be as lazy as the rest of you. Where is Ruthie? Just wait until she comes in, I'll give her what for. We have to leave for the synagogue, and nothing is done." As Faygela turned around, Ruthie came in, her face flushed from the cold spring air. "Where were you?"

"What is it, Mama?" Ruthie asked.

"I must be crazy to think my oldest daughter should be looking after her sisters and her brother. Were you paying attention when the little one cut her hand? No, you were talking to your friend. You and Emma whispering, your heads together like you're planning to overthrow the community council! So why should I expect you to remember that it's Purim tonight?"

Ruthie flinched, but she said nothing, her hands gripping the book she held against her chest.

"Should you remember that we have guests? Rabbi Berekh, who might expect some intelligent conversation, and his two children who are looking forward to an evening with their cousins? Not to mention that your father is sure to bring home another guest or two, and you're who knows where, running around like a *vilda haya*."

"Mama," Freydel said, "you sound just like *Alta-Bubbie*." Faygela's grandmother. Freydel was fourteen, and could still remember her. Leaning toward her two youngest sisters, Freydel grimaced and shook her hands. "Mama's possessed by a dybbuk," she hissed. The little girls' eyes widened.

"Freydel, stop if. Don't encourage the little ones to be superstitious," Faygela said. But she, too, had heard her grandmother's voice emerge from her mouth. It was not a pleasant feeling.

"Don't you remember?" Ruthie asked. "I was just showing Misha the plants in the book Papa brought me. You said I could go, Mama."

Faygela looked at Ruthie, who so much resembled her that it was like looking into a mirror of her childhood. "Yes, of course, I remember." Faygela linked her arm through Ruthie's. "Just go and change your clothes. You can take anything of mine you like, even your father's. How do you think Ruthie would look in Papa's fur hat, girls? Remember that tonight is Purim, and you can be anyone you want."

SEASON OF RAINS

The letter came when they were getting ready for Passover. The river flooded the bridge, throwing itself under the stilts of Misha's house with armfuls of purple-brown mud. Mattresses were airing in all the yards of Blaszka. Hayim the watercarrier ran from house to house with buckets of water so the women could wash every crevice where a crumb might hide. The villagers put in their orders for matzah, the community council making its purchase on behalf of the poor.

In the darkness before dawn to the darkness after dusk, Shmuel baked matzos, draping the flat dough over a pole, pushing it into the oven and out again quickly: from kneading to baking could not be more than eighteen minutes. The girls worked hard in the bakery and when *Shabbas* came, no one could hold them back, the younger ones shouting and running along the river, the older ones going off with their friends, arm-in-arm to walk in the woods. Ruthie was often seen with her friend Emma and Emma's cousin, Avram. People were starting to talk about a matchmaker, though Faygela told anyone who would listen that Ruthie was far too young yet.

ON PASSOVER, the Rabbi and his children were once again guests at the same mahogany table where Faygela had studied with her father. But now Shmuel sat at the head, and her cousin Berekh beside him, tall and thin, his red beard curling wild as a mountain fern speckled with gray spores.

"I brought you some books," he said to Faygela. "My old friend from yeshiva sent them to me from Paris. You remember Moyshe-Mendel. We were in yeshiva together and then in the rabbinical seminary."

"Moyshe-Mendel. Of course." She turned to Shmuel. "You know—at Berekh's wedding ten years ago—the one who's taken a French name. He calls himself Maurice LaFontaine now."

Nodding, Shmuel said, "A nice man. Polite. He kissed Berekh's bride on both cheeks and she blushed. Poor Hava, may she rest in peace." They were all silent for a moment, remembering Berekh's young wife. "Tell me, Berekh, how is your friend?"

"Not too well, I'm afraid. But let's not speak of it now. Here Faygela, take the books."

Her two oldest daughters leaned close on each side of her, Ruthie stroking the leather binding, Freydel pulling and saying, Give it to me, Ruthie, let me see.

"Sit down both of you and I'll show you what Cousin Berekh brought us. Look, girls. Pushkin. Part four of Nietzsche's *Zarathustra*. And a German translation of *The Debacle* by Émile Zola." Faygela opened the novel to the last page, reading silently for a moment, and silent still as she looked around the table at her cousin, his two small children, her husband, and their six. "Hope rising out of the ashes of war. How beautifully Zola writes of it. It's true that hope never dies. Even after the pogroms. Don't you agree, Berekh?"

"Perhaps it would be more accurate to say that we go on. A person must do what is right. The question is only, How does one know?"

Faygela and Berekh leaned toward each other, elbows on the table, chins resting on fists in their usual preargument stance. Shmuel shifted uneasily, though there was nothing improper, here. Nothing exactly improper.

"The Torah teaches us what is right," Shmuel said, his soft voice breaking the concentration of the two cousins.

"Ah. Yes," Berekh said. "And tonight we celebrate our freedom. Such as it is."

"And nobody leads a seder like my Shmuel," Faygela quickly added. "When he speaks you can see the fire of the Holy One leading the Jews out of Egypt. Now children, listen carefully and you might hear the footsteps of Elijah the Prophet coming to have a drink of wine at our table."

AFTER PASSOVER, Shmuel asked Faygela to read the letter to him again. "You have to go," he said. "My brother's wife Surala and her baby, alone in Warsaw, sick with no one to look after them? When my brother went to America, I promised that we would watch out for them. Should I break a promise?"

"If I go, I could be away for a month and the girls will run circles around you, Shmuel. You can never say no to them."

"I don't want you to go, Faygela, but we don't have a choice. Don't worry about the girls. Misha will look out for them. Just think of Surala. She has no one. We have everyone we know here in Blaszka."

Shmuel put his arm around Faygela, even though they were in the bakery and there were plenty of people to see. He kissed her quickly on the top of her head, and she squeezed his hand. "Why should I be so foolish?" she asked. "A chance to go to Warsaw and I should say no?" But it seemed to her that without her girls and her small son she would be left as shorn as the day after her wedding, hair cut off and falling to the floor in dark abandonment.

THE GIRLS dragged her into Shmuel's cart, extracting promises of gifts and stories to be brought back from Warsaw. Shmuel reassured her. Misha gave Faygela her favorite shawl for the journey, the red one that Misha wore to difficult births. Even Hanna-Leah came out and warned her not to get lost. So Hanna-Leah still remembered how Faygela used to wander off in the woods and lose herself. If only she had another minute she would have liked to say something, but there was no time. Shmuel was clicking at the horse and she was looking back at Misha, the younger children hanging onto her, Ruthie and Freydel waving.

Faygela sat on a bench in the third-class car. It was crowded with Russian soldiers and Polish peasants and Jewish men in caftans and women with hens and children who already made Faygela miss her own. With the elbow digging into her on one side and the chicken crate squeezing into her on the other, she could hardly breathe, which was a mercy because the smell of the hens' dreck and the unwashed hair and the sweaty greatcoats and the vodka breath would have smothered her if she breathed any deeper. Faygela pulled Misha's red shawl over her head and looked out the window past the grime to the Vistula, the queen of rivers, its water bluer, the trees along its banks greener, the ships like swans on its expanse. What was their own little Północna next to this river? The train rushed beside the river at thirty kilometers an hour, shaking Faygela as the fields flowed backward, giving way to peasant villages and shtetls with stops and starts, a soldier getting off, a woman with a crying baby on her back getting on.

When Faygela had gone to Warsaw with her father, they had ridden in his baker's cart and it took them several days, stopping

overnight at shtetls that seemed just like Blaszka, la
separate synagogues for the rich and the poor and th
ferent rebbes, but still not so different from hom
uncomfortable. But in Warsaw there were so many goyi.
in the streetcar that drove along the wide avenues, Faygela   ared
at the gentlemen in their top hats and the ladies with their bustles.
Afterward, Hanna-Leah had said that a woman who wears a bustle
might just as well have a pig on her behind, but Faygela had been
embarrassed by her plain dress. "We should at least have a corset-
maker in Blaszka. It's indecent to have my chest hanging and my waist
sticking out."

"You?" Hanna-Leah had laughed. "You have nothing to stick
out—not that little waist of yours and not your chest, either, so don't
worry."

The school was in the south of Warsaw on one of the grand streets
lined by lindens, but Faygela would live with her Aunt Esther, her
father had told her. She would take the horse-drawn streetcar to school
past the statue of Copernicus and the theater that could hold Blaszka's
entire village square behind its columns, and then she would return to
Aunt Esther and Auntie's cousin who lived together above a store in
one of the new buildings on Nalewki Street, where all the signs on the
stores were in Yiddish. But even Nalewki Street had seemed strange to
Faygela with its cobblestones and four-story buildings, the constant
noise, nothing but brick and stone as far as she could see, not a blade
of grass or a glimpse of the river anywhere. Aunt Esther had poured
tea for Faygela and her father, Aunt Esther's cousin standing with her
hands on Esther's shoulder, bending down to whisper in her ear. Aunt
Esther had smiled and shaken her head and said, "Faygela will be welcome to share our home as long as she wishes."

When they had returned to Blaszka, Faygela's grandmother had
said that if God was just, no granddaughter of hers would go live with
someone like that sister of Papa's. "People say she didn't want to get
married," Grandmother had said. "If a woman is left sitting because
she has no dowry or she's crippled, she deserves pity. But a woman
who goes to a city of goyim with no one but her female cousin to walk
with her? I could tell you . . ." But Papa had interrupted Grandmother
and Faygela heard no more.

ıfter Papa died, when it turned out there was going to be no War-saw, Hanna-Leah had walked with Faygela along the riverbank and had said, "I'm sorry you can't go to school, Faygela. I mean it. But now we can be friends always and I won't say I'm sorry for that."

"And when I have a baby, you'll be with me?" Faygela asked. "Every time?"

Hanna-Leah nodded, knowing that it was no light promise. She was old enough to realize that a woman in labor can easily die and Faygela had no mother or sister to help her. Hanna-Leah held out her hand. Faygela took it. Then they ran across the bridge, giggling, because only married women crossed the bridge to use the bathhouse on the other side of the river.

IN THE train, Faygela drank a little water from the bottle in her bas-ket, ate some bread, and watched as they passed the terraced hills descending to the river on the left bank, a covered bridge, a road blocked by sheep, a marsh, another bridge. It is ridiculous to think of that phrase of Grandmother's, the city of goyim, Faygela thought. In Warsaw one in three people are Jews, the same as Plotsk. In fact the anti-Semitic newspapers are complaining that if steps aren't taken, Warsaw will become a Jewish city. Imagine, the crown of Poland. There's nothing to be nervous about. Am I as provincial as Hanna-Leah?

The train was passing through woods and the window was dark. When it grew light again, she saw factories in a row, masses of brick and smoke and the train was curving, wheels screeching as they turned and they were on the railway bridge crossing to the left bank, her palms suddenly wet. There was Warsaw. The spires and the domes and the columns and the marble and the avenues as wide as a river and inside the third-class car the old woman snored and the woman with the crying baby took out a breast and pushed the nipple into the baby's mouth while she wiped her nose on her sleeve.

FAYGELA'S sister-in-law didn't live in the new tenements on Nalewki Street. She didn't even have a room in one of the windowless houses inhabited by the poorest Jewish tailors and carters near the Miła ceme-tery west of Nalewki. No, Surala was on the east side of the city, on the edge of the Old Town not far from Dung Gate, in a room above the Rooster Cafe. No coffee was served in the cafe.

Faygela sat on a wooden stool near the one window in Surala's room. If she put her head out the window and craned her neck she could see a little sky between the old walls of the buildings. Below, the street was so narrow that the prostitutes could lean their backs against one wall and brace their feet against the other while they conducted their business. From time to time, Faygela bathed her sister-in-law's face with a wet cloth, touched the back of her hand to the baby's red cheek, and returned to her seat.

There were two other rooms above the cafe, in each a family with a few children, a grandmother, an aunt and uncle, and a boarder or two shouting, crying, moaning.

"Do you hear that?" Surala asked. She was thin, her skin yellow, and the baby's head seemed too big for his neck. He was crying in a low voice. Surala had no milk. "It goes on day and night."

"I can't blame them. They live in each other's armpits and the smell is enough to hang you," Faygela said. "Too many people and not enough work. Every day more Litvaks come from the East, running from the Tsar and his program for the Jews. But you have to sleep, Surala. Don't listen to what's going on. Let me take the baby." Faygela lifted the baby from Surala's arms. Outside, the prostitutes were calling from beneath the window, Quick and cheap, special for soldiers. There wasn't an oven in the room or even a fireplace where Faygela could cook a little soup on a trivet or boil water for tea. She had to fetch water from the public pump several blocks away.

"It was good of Shmuel to let you come," Surala said as she closed her eyes. "I won't forget."

Faygela paced the tiny room, in one arm the baby, in her hand a newspaper from which she read aloud in the sing-song voice she had used with her own babies. "Another strike in the sugar works," she crooned. "The workers will be fined, including the man who lost his leg in the accident that precipitated," she swayed gently from side to side, "the strike." The baby rested his head in the crook of her neck. He smelled sour, not like a healthy baby, but he was asleep. She kissed his fist, the hot fingers tight around her thumb.

*　　*　　*

MOST DAYS before she shopped for Surala, Faygela walked down to the riverbank. There she would lean against a tree and watch the light play on the water and wonder if Shmuel was singing the lullaby that Berel liked and if Freydel was keeping her promise not to tease Ruthie. When she went home she would tell them about the city walls and the royal castle. The girls would like that, Faygela would think as she went to the market in the Old Town Square for bread and herring and a little sugar to mix with water for Surala's baby. At first she often lost her direction, peering this way and that, heart beating quickly, looking for something familiar while beggars accosted her. In Blaszka she wouldn't think of walking past a beggar, not when her father knew his father, not even if the beggar was a stranger. A Jew refuse charity? But here they frightened her, wrapping stumps of hands in her skirt, pleading and scolding. "You miser, have you no consideration for the future of your own soul? Look at my child," thrusting at her a baby tied around like a piece of fish in newspaper and string. Faygela would walk quickly, averting her eyes from the Russian soldiers, murmuring, Excuse me, until she recognized where she was.

AFTER A WEEK, Surala looked worse and the baby was too quiet. "I think I'm better," Surala said, trying to sit up. "I shouldn't keep you so long. You have to go home to Shmuel and the children. What would my husband think of my selfishness?"

"I can't leave you here. This room is impossible, Surala. Even poor Jews near the Miła cemetery have water and a fire."

"Yes, you're right. And as soon as I get a letter from my husband with some money, I'll go to a better place. An apartment on Nalewki Street." She put her hand on the baby's head. "And then we'll go to America, won't we, sweetie."

"When did you hear from him last?"

"I don't remember. He's working hard, Faygela. We'll hear soon."

Faygela could just imagine what Hanna-Leah would say about this. If the man's hands weren't broken, he could have written, and if he didn't, then the Messiah might come before the letter. And in the meantime? "I'll go home when it's time," Faygela said. "Now I have to go out. Herring is cheap but it's no good for someone who needs to get back her strength. Maybe I can get a little soup for you. And who knows? Maybe I'll find a better room, too. So don't expect me for some time, Surala. It could be a long walk."

Faygela threw Misha's red shawl over her shoulders and tied her kerchief firmly around her head. Surely, she could find her way to Nalewki Street. She only had to walk away from the river and keep going for an hour or two. Among the Jewish shops there would have to be someone who would know of a decent room for Surala.

As Faygela left the Old Town behind, the streets widened and she didn't have to squeeze herself against a wall when a cart drove by with its hard-breathing nag. Soon carts gave way to streetcars pulled by thickset horses, and after a while there were carriages pulled by thinner, taller horses with leather bags hanging from their backsides to catch their droppings. The men wore top hats, the women were in silk and Faygela realized that she'd turned the wrong way again. Leaning against a wall, she started to laugh, ignoring the passers-by staring at her. There, just across the square, was the Grand Theater that she'd seen with her father so long ago, more immense than she'd remembered, and yet she who was so small could take it in with her own two eyes.

As she continued through the square, she heard fragments of conversation in an elegant Polish, strange to her ear, used to the rough Polish of peasants. Did you see *The Queen of Sheba?* That voice. A genius. I wore a new chapeau. But that dress, my dear, the color. Emeralds and rubies together, how gauche.

Men and women walked together, promenading slowly in pairs, the women's gloved fingers resting on the arms of men who matched their stride to the women's. Faygela lifted her head to look up at the sky pierced by the roofs of palaces and churches and the statue of the saint with the sword. She didn't care that she was dizzy as long as she could go on walking, surrounded by this beauty. Here was Saxon Gardens, here the watertower like a temple, here the great willows. For a moment, despite her heavy boots and the coarse wool of her dress, the city was hers. And so she was unprepared for the fear that startled her when she bumped into the man with the copper mustache and the velvet vest.

"What is this?" he asked in an aristocratic Polish. Between his eyebrows, there was a small white scar.

"Pardon me, sir," she said. "Excuse me, pardon me. It was my fault. I didn't see where I was going." Her Polish was good, she knew it was good, and yet she was sure that her accent and her kerchief and the darkness of her eyes said Jewess, and what business did she have on this beautiful avenue? Perhaps this man would think she was a thief and he would call a policeman who would demand her papers and she had nothing with her but a few kopecks to get some soup for Surala.

The man answered her in Yiddish. "Are you lost, madam?"

This was a Jew? This beardless man in the top hat? "Yes, sir. I was looking for Nalewki Street."

"You have gone in quite the wrong direction. That is Marszałkowska Street. Many Jews live on that street, but only Polish is spoken there."

"Is it very far from Nalewki?"

"I own a bookstore cafe on Nalewki and I would not walk. It will take you quite some time."

"Then I had better start. Would you mind giving me directions, sir?"

"I have a better idea, madam. I must stop for a moment at my sister's house on Marszałkowska and then I will take a carriage to the cafe. Please be my guest." He held out his arm.

Faygela shook her head. "Thank you, no. I'll walk."

"But I cannot allow it. Are you not a fellow Jew?" She hesitated. "You see before you the director of a theater troupe. I know the villages. I may be unfamiliar to you, but your kind is quite familiar to me and it is far too easy for you to get lost again."

"Were you ever in Blaszka?" she asked. He looked like the director of the Golem Players. She couldn't be certain.

"Perhaps," he said. "But there were so many small villages . . ."

Faygela knew that Hanna-Leah would warn her away from this stranger. Even Misha, who was afraid of nothing, would say that she should stick to her purpose. But Faygela was curious about these Polish-speaking Jews that could live on a broad boulevard so close to the theater. And besides, her feet were already sore. Could she really walk to Nalewki Street if it was so far? "Very well," she said. The Director held out his arm and she put her hand in the crook of his elbow.

THE MAID came to the door. "Your wrap, madam?" she asked Faygela, looking her up and down.

"You mean my shawl? No, I'll keep it, thank you." It was silly the way she was clutching the shawl around herself, Misha's red shawl, to hide the drabness of her black dress. Faygela looked past the maid. In the room beyond, she could see men and women like those in Theater Square, silken and bright, their shadows thrown on the wall by the harsh light of an electric chandelier. Someone was playing the grand piano.

"Chopin's *Polonnaise*," the Director mumured. A woman separated herself from the crowd and came toward them. "Dear sister . . ."

"Here is your package. I don't know why the publisher cannot remember to send the books directly to the cafe. And who is your little friend?" The Director's sister was blonde, her hair in a crown of curls, her earrings Polish eagles with a ruby in each beak.

"She was lost, looking for Nalewki Street," the Director said. "One of our newcomers from the shtetl." Taking a pipe from his pocket, he flicked a match against his front teeth, the little flame causing the rubies in his sister's earrings to sparkle.

"You must come in for a minute," the Director's sister said. "My friends are just discussing the situation in the shtetls. They would be most interested to meet a person from—where did you say you were from?"

"Blaszka. My name is Faygela Shnir." The walls were lined from floor to ceiling with shelves of books. Books in German, French, Hebrew, Polish, Russian, English. Faygela moved toward them, forgetting Surala, forgetting Warsaw. What would she find here? Every thought she could think. Every question she could ask. Only to hold those books in her hands, to smell the leather.

"Come in then. This is my young friend from Krakow just returning from Paris, the painter and dramatist, Stanisław Wyspianski. And this is Isaac Goldman, a student of I. L. Peretz. Please meet Faygela Shnir from the shtetl."

"You know Mr. Peretz?" Faygela asked.

"Yes, personally," the young man said. He wore a fashionably cut coat, the other one, Stanisław Wyspianski, a cape. The two men nodded politely, each of them taking Faygela's arm as they walked up and down the salon. Soon they were shaking fingers at each other above Faygela's head while she looked from one to the other.

"But of what use is it to awaken your fellow Jews from their ignorance if they do not know their own land? Where is the spirit of Poland?" Wyspianski asked. "It is the national question that is of paramount importance. Our Israelite brothers must join us as they did during the insurrection of '63. By making our struggle their own, the Jews will earn emancipation."

Faygela nodded. Yes, her father used to say that very thing.

"No, dear sir," Goldman argued. "After the assassination of the Tsar in '81, a Jew cannot believe in brotherhood. Who can forget the pogroms?"

Indeed, Faygela remembered the mourning. Meyer, Hanna-Leah's father, dead. Killed during the pogrom in Warsaw—and how he died, unthinkable. Hershel was wounded. The Puks lost one of their sons.

"You cannot take that seriously," the young man in the cape said. "It was just a ploy. The people were whipped up by the authorities and the Jews made the scapegoats to break up resistance against tsarist oppression."

There was a time when many people in Blaszka wanted to learn to read Polish so they could prove their worthiness to be true Poles with the same rights as Christians. After the pogroms, no one cared about learning to read Polish anymore. They just wanted to live. That's all, just to live, she thought.

Goldman was shaking his head. "No," he said. "No, I cannot agree with you. My friend Peretz says that a Jew is not a Pole whether he wears a caftan or not. A man must be who he is. He can't escape it."

"Let us ask her," Wyspianski said, turning to stare at Faygela.

She flushed under his gaze. Men in Blaszka did not look at women like that. "I think," she said quietly, then louder, "I think . . ."

"What can she know of world affairs, tyrannized by the authorities in a stagnant backwater?" Goldman asked.

"Untainted by the false manners of this . . ." Soon they were wagging fingers again, voices fast and sharp.

"Excuse me," Faygela said. "I am not in another kingdom. I am right here, do you see?"

"Pardon me, have I offended you?" Goldman asked, taking Faygela's hand.

She pulled it away. "Pardon me, gentlemen. I will leave you to your great thoughts. Such a refined climate is not for me." The Director was standing near the doorway. Faygela made her way toward him. "Please let me by. I've decided to walk after all."

"But Mrs. Shnir, there are so many interesting people for you to meet here. You see my friends, Stefan and Albert?" the Director asked, pointing with his pipe to the two men sitting on a settee. One was lighting the other's cigarette, cupping the flame. As the first man thanked him, the other's hand brushed his cheek. "Charming people. What do you make of them?" The men were leaning toward each other, laughing quietly at a private joke.

"You think we hear about nothing in Blaszka? I read the German newspaper. In Berlin there are women who cut their hair short, put on men's dress clothes, and dance with each other. Does that make it something new? Believe me, it's not only in Berlin or Warsaw that such things go on. Only now all of a sudden someone decided that it has to have a name."

"For the sake of knowledge, madam," the Director said, stoking the tobacco in his pipe until the embers glowed.

She had the distinct, but unreasonable, impression that her own words were being thrown at her. "Let me by. I have to go."

"Just keep walking up Marszałkowska past the Karsiński Gardens and you'll come to Nalewki. If you want to return to the Old Town you will have to turn right and if you head left, you will eventually reach the Miła cemetery."

"Thank you," she murmured.

He bowed.

FAYGELA FOUND a room on Stawki, two blocks past Miła. The ramshackle house belonged to a Jewish family of wagoners. Poor people. Rough language. But there was a public kitchen, grass, even a cow or two, here at the northern edge of Warsaw. In another week Surala could help in the house and the baby smelled milky. On *Shabbas,* Faygela and Surala went to the wagoners' synagogue and Faygela began to look forward to sitting with her own girls soon.

THE LONG DAYS

On the 23rd of May, a Wednesday, Faygela came home. Bursting into the village square, she threw open the door to the bakery, ready to call out, *Sholom aleikhem,* children, In a good hour, Shmuel. But her words dried in her mouth. She saw a house of mourning, the girls with red eyes, Shmuel opening a sack of flour with trembling hands, and Berel sitting under the table, his thumb in his mouth, his little shirt stained with pee.

"Shmuel, what is it? Girls, what happened? Ruthie, Ruthie, where is my Ruthie?" Faygela cried, dropping her bag.

"Mama, you're home," the girls said, crowding around her, clutching her arm, her dress, her neck.

Faygela looked at Shmuel. His head was bowed in shame. "Ruthie was arrested yesterday," he said in a voice so low she thought she didn't hear him right.

"Shmuel, what did you say?"

"It's true," he said loudly. "She was carrying pamphlets. The young people, all of them were taking pamphlets to Plotsk. I don't understand it, Faygela. What did they want to do?"

"What are you talking about?" There was some mistake. Ruthie must be helping Misha pick herbs, that was all.

"It's true," he said. "I saw with my own eyes. They showed me one of the pamphlets."

"Who let this happen? Who? Didn't you know what she was doing? I said I shouldn't leave. You don't lift a finger to keep the girls in place. God in Heaven, what can you expect from a man? But Misha should have known. Ruthie looks up to her like a queen. If anything happened to Ruthie, it's her fault."

"Misha didn't know anything," Shmuel said.

"Didn't know, didn't know? And my Ruthie's in jail?"

"Faygela, Misha has her own problems. She's pregnant."

"That's impossible. She would have told me."

Shmuel looked down, embarrassed. "They say she just started to show after you left."

"So that's it? I'm gone for three weeks and everything's upside down. I trusted Misha to watch out for my girls. I thought she was the one woman in Blaszka who knew how to take care of herself. And now look. I'll never say a word to her again. Never."

"Faygela, the girls and boys did it all on their own. In the woods."

"Emma was the ringleader. Ruthie won't admit it, but it could only be Emma. Everyone says so," Freydel added. "They were using *Zayda*'s printing press."

Faygela held onto the girls tightly, sure that if she let go she would fall to the floor. "My father's old printing press? It can't be."

"They found it in the woods in the old hut."

Time seemed to collide: 1863—her father, a young man printing tracts calling the people to revolt; 1894—her daughter, her firstborn in the broken-down shed with the rusted press. "No, it's some mistake. Ruthie is so good, she wouldn't do anything wrong. We have to tell them." Faygela pushed the girls aside. "Shmuel, you have to tell them. They'll send her away from us. She'll die. Shmuel." She was shaking him by the shoulders and he was crying.

The justice system was a simple one. It consisted of flogging, hanging, and exile to Siberia, and the only proof of innocence was a bribe large enough to placate the Tsar's minions.

DURING THE preliminary investigation at the prison in Plotsk, the interrogators pinched Ruthie's breasts and slapped her till she cried, but they didn't break anything. She was a pretty girl and they had ideas for later. "Who are you protecting? Just tell us everything," the deputy warden said in Polish. To his assistant, he added in Russian, "The girl looks a little stupid, don't you think? But she's a nice little morsel."

Ruthie was doing her best to look stupid, fluttering and stuttering, signing her name with an X and coughing every so often, especially when the guards came near her, as if she had something catching. "I found the basket on my way home from Plotsk," she said. "It was so pretty with the blue ribbon woven into it. I never had one like that. And I thought the papers would be good for wrapping fish. I didn't know it was anything bad. I can't read. If I knew, well, you could cut my hand off before I'd touch it. I hope you catch those troublemakers from Plotsk." Then she coughed and hacked, spitting into her sleeve. "Blood," she said cheerfully. "Well, everyone spits a little blood, don't they?" she asked the deputy warden, who was wrinkling his nose. The guards, however, were not the least put off by Ruthie's display.

"You're from Blaszka," one of them said thoughtfully. "Didn't I hear of that?"

Afraid that someone would remember the insurrection of '63, the mill blown up, the printed pamphlets, Ruthie quickly said, "Everyone knows about Blaszka. It's famous for its cheese. Did you ever eat Alta-Fruma's cheese? It's like no one else's. My father will bring you some. With some vodka to wash it down."

This was the kind of thing that the interrogators liked to hear. "A little gift wouldn't be out of order either," the guard said, rubbing Ruthie's chin between his thumb and his forefinger. "And of course, something in appreciation of His Honor, the Governor." His hand smelled of fish and onions.

FOR SOMEONE in the Tsar's service, a posting far from the centers of power in Moscow and St. Petersburg was a rebuke. The farthest outpost was Poland, or Vistulaland as it was officially called, and unofficially Purgatory. But the empire was big, and the railway lines short, so that every administrator of the provinces could make up his own version of the Tsar's regulations. His Honour the Governor of Plotsk, in his villa on the hill, sighed extravagantly, removing his fat little legs from a velvet stool as his secretary brought him the latest communique from St. Petersburg. After reading it, the Governor ordered the public flogging of a woman who had been caught teaching Polish. This gave him a good appetite for his lunch, brought in on numerous silver serving dishes emblazoned with the crests of exiled Polish counts. His secretary threw a pile of silver rubles, a bribe from some distraught family, into a drawer, where it rattled among the other little piles of meaningless village life.

"What is that?" the Governor asked, his mouth full of honey and poppy-seed pastry.

"A gift on behalf of a young Jewess, requesting your clemency, sir."

"Ah. Well, I'm in a kindly spirit, today. Let someone from her family, her mother perhaps, have visiting privileges. Instruct the warden."

"And her release?"

The Governor laughed. "That's what I like about you, Josef. Your sense of humor."

"I won't write another page," Faygela said to Shmuel. "My grandmother was right, after all. It's from this selfishness," she waved her notebook, "that a woman forgets who she really is. I had my head in another world and that's why I didn't see Misha for what she is. How could I depend on her? She's just as helpless as any woman. But I promise you, Shmuel, things are going to be different. I'm getting rid of these. Into the fire." She began to take the notebooks out of the trunk, piling them up.

"Faygela, please. It's too warm for a fire." Shmuel took the notebooks from her. "Put them back in your trunk. It won't help Ruthie to make yourself miserable."

"You're right. It would be a waste. Better to burn them in the winter. In the meantime I'm going to speak with Emma's great-aunt. Imagine, letting the girl run wild, getting children into trouble. I'll give Alta-Fruma a piece of my mind. You can be sure of it."

"And Misha? Will you at least talk to her?"

Faygela slammed the lid of the trunk. "Never."

Shmuel winced. "You're nervous. You should write something. A nice poem. And I could make you a glass of tea. With lemon?"

"I told you from now on there's no more writing. Leave me alone." She grabbed her shawl and left for the dairyhouse, rehearsing what she would say to set the old woman straight.

RUTHIE SHARED her cell with four other women. The one with the streak of gray in her hair had murdered her husband in his sleep after he'd beaten her. The woman whose front teeth were broken was deaf and mute, so that no one knew who she was or how long she'd been there. The other two were whores from Avraham's Brothel in Plotsk, orange-haired, freckle-faced cousins, about fifteen years old. They had stolen the wallet from a Russian soldier, unaware that he was an officer.

"So you're from Blaszka," one of the cousins said to Ruthie. "A girl from the brothel got married in Blaszka. Years ago. She's dead now, but we always talk about it. Riva and the miller's son. We're neighbors, you might say. Sisters." Sisters, they both repeated, giggling as they leaned their orange heads against Ruthie's dark one. When she came back from the interrogation, they held her head as she vomited in the corner. Making soft hen noises over her, they sat her on the bench between them, linking arms behind her back, until the shuddering stopped. Then they painted her face with soot, blackened her teeth with a kohl pencil, packed straw under the left shoulder of her dress to create a hump, and, in a soft country Yiddish, advised her to drool when the jailers passed by. In contrast, the girls themselves laughed and flirted, twisting their thin shoulders and shaking their hips, sharp little tongues waving at the guards, so that when the deputy warden wanted some entertainment, no one gave Ruthie a second glance. In turn, Ruthie shared with them everything her mother brought to make her more comfortable. They piled their straw together under her sheet, slept under her blanket, ate her food, and peed in her chamber pot. Among the dangers they shared was the threat of typhus from the lice, which also passed between them.

FAYGELA'S HANDS were clenched on her lap as she sat on the edge of a bench in Ruthie's cell, breathing lightly so as not to inhale too much of the cell's odor. Ruthie, not meeting her mother's glance, also sat with her hands folded. They'd been this way for an hour. Every so often Faygela would ask a question, Ruthie would answer yes or no or perhaps, and silence would fall between them again while Ruthie picked at the scabs of dirt on her dress. What Faygela wanted to know was how the quiet daughter had joined with revolutionaries, and all she could think of was that she had shouted at Ruthie for coming home late on Purim. There were other times she'd been short-tempered with Ruthie. And don't forget that she had slapped Ruthie, too. Faygela had been pregnant with Devorah or maybe it was Dina and she couldn't find Leibela anywhere. Ruthie was supposed to be watching her but instead she had gone to the woods. Before Ruthie was able to say that it had been to find some herbs for Faygela's nausea, she had slapped her daughter and good. Was Ruthie paying her back now?

"How your father suffers," Faygela said. "He thinks of you every minute."

"Poor Papa," Ruthie said, her eyes welling.

"Devorah has nightmares. She can't sleep without you in the bed."

"And you, Mama? Did cousin Berekh bring you any more books?"

"Do you want books, Ruthie? I could bring them to you."

"It would be too dangerous if the guards saw me reading," Ruthie said in a low voice. "But the worst thing is that there's nothing to do here."

One of the orange-haired girls was squatting over the chamber pot. Faygela heard a thick splash followed by the rat-a-tat-plop of diarrhea, a new smell rising hot around them. Faygela turned her head, wrapping her shawl tighter around her shoulders. "You were saying?" she asked Ruthie.

"Nothing. Nothing important."

"For a girl to go from her parents' house to this. You would tell me if somebody interfered with you, Ruthie?"

"Yes, Mama."

"You know what I mean? A girl, here."

"Yes."

"Of course she wouldn't know what I mean," Faygela murmured. "Not Ruthie." And then louder. "Is there anything you want, *mamalu*? A message you want to send with me?"

"No, Mama." Ruthie gazed past her mother and silence fell between them again.

AT LEAST eat something, the women in the bakery said to Faygela. How can you walk to Plotsk if you're starving yourself?

She was sitting at the square table, the women around her. "If you saw what I did, you wouldn't think of food."

Don't speak of it. You'll just get more upset. Tell us about Warsaw. It'll take your mind off your troubles.

"Never mind Warsaw. It was just a dream. All I can see in front of my eyes is Ruthie's cell. The stone walls, the dirty straw stained with the blood from women. And the women, so ugly I nearly choke when I look at them. It's my fault that she's there. I should have taken her with me to Warsaw. No, I shouldn't have gone at all." Faygela put her head in her hands.

The door opened, but she didn't look up. One of the girls could take care of the customer. Or one of the women. Anyone. It didn't matter.

"*Sholom aleikhem.*" Hanna-Leah's voice. Faygela lifted her head. Hanna-Leah was staring at her, lips pursed, eyebrows drawn together. Faygela knew that look. It was the same look that Hanna-Leah gave her when she said she would run away to Warsaw. When she refused to eat after her first son died. When she said that if she had another child, she would go mad.

Can't you see that she's upset? the women asked Hanna-Leah. You need something, go talk to Shmuel.

"This isn't your business," Hanna-Leah answered. "I have something to say to Faygela. Do you want to hear or not?"

"I'm listening," Faygela replied. She stood up, walked around the table to Hanna-Leah.

"My grandmother came to me in a dream," Hanna-Leah said. "Your Ruthie will be safe."

Was this what Hanna-Leah came to say? No scolding? No advice? But when Faygela touched her hand in thanks, Hanna-Leah added in a low whisper that no one else could hear, "Listen to me. You always enjoyed a little too much drama when there was trouble. Think of someone else." Then she quickly left while the other women regrouped around Faygela.

Me? she wondered. But I think only of Ruthie. How it's my fault that she's in prison. Hanna-Leah's voice seemed to follow her as it did in Warsaw, asking her, And does your confession get rid of one louse on Ruthie's head?

THE NEXT DAY Faygela was in the prison at her normal time, the guards inspecting what she brought. She didn't walk this time. She had too much to carry. Fine white raisin bread and almond tortes for the guards, plain black bread and cheese for the women, boiled potatoes with dill and sour milk, also for the women, as well as buckets, rags, brushes, and lye. And for Ruthie she brought a roll of cloth, needles and thread, the brightest colors she could find in Plotsk.

While Faygela scrubbed the cell, she said, "Let me tell you a story to pass the time. It's a true story of course, about four wild girls who lived in the woods and never grew old because they drank from the secret river. One of them was clever, one was beautiful, the third was good, and the last had a gold tooth, and she was the queen of them all." When Faygela got to the part of the story where the girl with the gold tooth saved the King of Poland from drowning, the woman who was supposedly deaf and mute had picked up the pig-bristle brush and was working alongside her. And when the villainous Captain Ivan Ivanovich was bitten in the behind by the wild pig, she startled them all by falling into the bucket as she laughed. "That's a good one," she said.

Day by day as Faygela continued the saga of the wild girls, she noticed that the women in the cell across from Ruthie's had also begun to listen. Then the women began to use Faygela's fine-tooth comb on each other's heads, picking out the lice and untangling their hair, while she told them the story. If she paused for a moment, they would say eagerly, "And then what happened?" The next time she came, Faygela brought them ribbons to tie back their hair. The comb was passed from Ruthie's cell to the other one, and even the old hag, her white hair neatly combed, stroked the green ribbon that Faygela gave her. Her withered lips were fallen in. There was a goiter on her neck. But she smiled with as much pleasure as if she were a girl, and Faygela realized that she could tolerate the goiter without either anger or disgust for the sake of the old woman's pleasure. From one visit to the next, Faygela wouldn't allow herself to think of how long Ruthie might be imprisoned, or what would happen to her when she was sentenced at some indeterminate future time. It would take more than all the money in the village to obtain Ruthie's release. So Faygela cleaned, she brought food, she told stories, she combed Ruthie's hair.

"IT'S ALWAYS hardest on the oldest girl," Faygela said to Shmuel as she rolled out pastry dough. "With one child after another, you forget how much the first one has to do. Ruthie never complained the way Freydel does. But tell me, Shmuel, what does Ruthie think about, sitting day after day in that cell?" Eyes moist, he shook his head, refilling the flour bins as Faygela spread raisins and almond paste over the dough. "I tell the women my little stories and Ruthie sews," Faygela said. "Her hands are always busy." Except, she thought, when the story concerned the girl with the gold tooth who was as big as a man and knew every flower in the woods. Then Ruthie's hands were still. Her eyes would grow big and her skin flushed. I should know what it means, Faygela thought. Why don't I know what it means?

WHEN SHE came into the prison now, Faygela first took Ruthie over to a bench next to the wall. The other women retreated to the opposite side of the cell to give them privacy, stifling a ragged phlegmy cough, apologizing for the sound of pee splashing in the chamberpot. As she unraveled a tangled ball of yarn, Faygela would wind it around Ruthie's upheld hands, trying to draw her daughter out. Little by little, while Faygela waited, Ruthie began to speak to her. Every night, Faygela tangled up the ball of yarn for her next visit.

"Tell me, Ruthie, do you ever dream about anything?"

"Sometimes," Ruthie said shyly.

"I often used to sit on the silver rocks and dream about going to Warsaw. Do you ever do that?"

Ruthie nodded. Faygela waited for her to speak. Half of the ball of yarn was untangled before Ruthie said, "In *Zayda*'s books I read about women who travel. I'd like to see those places."

"You could," Faygela said.

"No, no." Ruthie shook her head. "I couldn't leave Blaszka."

"Why not?" Faygela asked.

"Everyone knows me in Blaszka. And besides . . ." Ruthie's voice trailed off. Faygela wound the yarn around her fingers, praying that the ball of yarn would be long enough.

"Some people have been telling me that you're old enough for the matchmaker. I said that sixteen is too young, but perhaps I'm wrong. When I was your age I had a baby already and there are some nice boys in the village. Emma's cousin, Avram, maybe?"

"Oh, Mama. I'm not interested in boys. I just want to learn from Misha."

"Don't talk to me about Misha. She should have watched out for you when I was gone. But of course she was too busy doing who knows what with her belly growing out to here," Faygela said. Ruthie fell silent, her eyes glazing as if shutters were closing over them. Faygela bit her tongue. "I shouldn't say a thing, Ruthie. Enough happens in the world that's nobody's fault. Who could expect Misha to look after you, when you already have a mother and a father?"

"Oh, but she does, Mama. There's so much I don't know about plants and she knows so much and she's seen everything about delivering babies and I just want . . ." Ruthie stopped speaking. Her face was hot and red. She looked confused. Her mother slipped the yarn off her hands and patted them.

"Never mind," Faygela said. "You have time to learn, and maybe you'll travel, too. Blaszka is such a small place. I feel more comfortable at home because I know every stone. But I think, Ruthie, there might be more for you somewhere else. Sha, don't interrupt. I'm not saying today or tomorrow, but soon. You'll see that there's something more to life than what the hens in Blaszka say. I didn't talk about it before because I was worried about you, but I saw some interesting things in Warsaw. When you come home I'll tell you everything. Believe me, *mamala,* you can go anywhere you want."

"Japan?" Ruthie asked, laughing.

"Well, I don't think I could bear to have my daughter so far away, but in Warsaw you could learn a lot. You wouldn't be alone. I know people there who could introduce you to students at the university, girls who are studying. What do you think of it?"

"I don't know," Ruthie said. "I'm more interested in people who know things because they do something than people who just sit inside and read about the world."

"Like Emma and her pamphlets?"

"Well, when she talks you really think something matters, even though she's hardly more than a child. She's been telling me everything that's going on in Blaszka when she comes to visit. It's almost like I'm home again. Oh, Mama, Emma meant no harm." Ruthie paused, looking down then up again, quickly, as if to catch her mother frowning, but Faygela only nodded. "Misha said that it's important to spend time with other girls, even if Emma is two years younger than me."

"You think Misha knows what's what?"

"Mama, I'll tell you," Ruthie said excitedly. Faygela leaned toward her, listening. Ruthie was usually so calm. "Misha knows a lot about plants, but she's always learning more. She tells me all the time that no one knows everything. You always have to watch and learn. You have to change your mind, she told me. One time using this herb could work, but with another person it might not. Oh, she's told me a lot, Mama. But I still have so much to find out."

Faygela saw that her eyes were clear, her face bright, and she was smiling like Shmuel did when *Shabbas* was coming. So this is how it is, like my Aunt Esther, Faygela thought. Sometimes a person chases after destiny, and sometimes destiny chases after a person. Now that she was just beginning to know her eldest child, now that she could make up for leaning on Ruthie too much, now that she wanted Ruthie close to her so that she could watch over her, she would have to send her daughter away. There would be no one like her in Blaszka. At home Ruthie's life would be one of hiding and making herself small and unnoticeable. But in Warsaw she might find friendship and happiness. "Just now you think that everything you need to know is in Blaszka," Faygela said. "But even Mother Eve got too big for the Garden of Eden and she had to go out into the world. You just think about it, and we'll see how it is when you come home."

And if she doesn't come home? Faygela asked herself. It's not to be considered. I can't bear it. But never mind. At least I'll be sleeping in my own bed tonight, let me give them a little pleasure now. "So ladies," she said. "Let's not forget where we were. Let me see. Yes. Remember that the King was looking everywhere for the beautiful girl he glimpsed in the woods. Meanwhile the queen of the wild girls fell into the hands of the villainous Captain Ivan Ivanovich. At this very moment he was tickling her throat with the point of his saber."

AT HOME, Faygela began writing in Yiddish. Instead of sitting at her bridal trunk, she sat at the table, the kerosene lamp on the sideboard, the shutters open to take in the evening light, the girls vying for the privilege of sitting near her and reading from *Zayda*'s books. "There are some things that can only be said in the *mama-loshen*," she told them. "An educated person should be able to read in German and Russian, of course. But don't give up the language of your childhood, girls. Nothing else has the same sound of truth as the *mama-loshen*."

On the evening of the summer solstice, Shmuel sat at the table, mending his apron, while Faygela wrote in her notebook, "June 21. Strawberries ripe. Cloudy in the morning, sunny afternoon. Saw Misha in the village square grabbing her belly. Baby must have given her a good kick. The queen of the wild girls brought low. She asked me to write a letter for her today. A letter to the Governor. As if it would help Ruthie. Does the Governor care about words? I wasn't talking to her, but when she came to me with this business about the letter, I couldn't help myself but tell her a thing or two. When a woman ruins her life and forgets that her friends depend on her, she should expect to hear something about it. There was only one woman in Blaszka, one who was free. And look what she had to go and do to herself. Shmuel says that it's better not to keep things inside." She smiled at him as she turned to a fresh page. At the top she wrote, *The True Tale of the Demon Lilith.*

The sky was still alight, the evening sticky and warm. The children were playing outside, except for nine-year-old Devorah, who wasn't feeling well. She was lying on the bed she shared with Ruthie and Leibela, calling out every few minutes, "Papa, I'm thirsty," and "Mama, my head hurts," then Papa again, then Mama again. "She's going to spend the night in the outhouse," Faygela said after the third glass of water. Shmuel shrugged unhappily. "She misses Ruthie," he said. From the bedroom another complaint floated on the string of a thin, high voice. "I'll go." he said. "I'll sit with her for a few minutes. Maybe she'll feel better." It was while he was in the other room that Misha knocked on the door, like a stranger. She was fanning herself with a swollen hand, dripping in the heat as she opened the door.

Faygela put down her mending. "In a good hour," she said politely. Misha was breathing heavily. The baby must be pressing on her diaphragm, Faygela thought. As she pulled out a chair for Misha, she said, "You look warm. Let me get you a glass of water."

"Thank you. That would be nice," Misha said.

Returning from the water barrel in the hallway with two glasses and a plate of honey cake with cherry preserves, Faygela said, "Do you want a cup of tea? I could boil the kettle."

"No thank you. Just some water is good."

"Maybe a little fruit then?"

"Sit down, Faygela. All your jumping around is making the baby nervous."

She sat. "So Misha?"

"So I brought you something."

"What is it?"

"Promise first that you won't ask any questions."

"Fine. I give my word."

Misha put a felt pouch on the table. Faygela looked at it. Misha pushed it toward her. "For Ruthie," she said.

Faygela opened the pouch, then upended it over her hand. A heap of gold imperials dropped into her cupped palm. One coin fell from her hand, glittering as it slid across the table. Misha pushed it back. "A gift for the Governor. Send the gold with the letter. It'll be enough to get Ruthie out of prison."

"But who? What? You didn't steal it?" Faygela asked.

"How could you suggest such a thing?" Shaking her head, Misha picked up her fork and dug into the cake.

"Well, it didn't come from one of our beggars or the beekeeper, surely."

"Faygela, you promised."

"I know, you got it from Alta-Fruma, didn't you? Her cow is *cacking* gold *dreck*." She watched as Misha wordlessly spooned the cherry preserves over the cake. Faygela put her hand over Misha's. "It's a miracle."

LATER, IN her notebook, Faygela wrote, "Everyone says if you want to keep a secret, give it to Misha. I have no idea how she did it. She didn't give a sign, the gold coins could have grown in her garden. Right this minute Shmuel is going to the Governor's palace with the money. Misha said he should take the letter with him, and he did. The girls are dancing on pins and I can barely hold myself together. They wanted to go of course, but I said no. This is for Shmuel to do. Let him come back with his daughter.

"It seems that even a woman trapped in the ordinary way, worn out from her pregnancy, with her feet swollen, isn't completely helpless. Is there anything more beautiful than Misha laughing at my surprise?"

NIGHTS OF THE SECRET RIVER

In the first week of August, when the blueberry bushes were full, Faygela made herself ready for the *mikva*. It had been three weeks since Shmuel had touched her, and she was restive. Her girls were all safe inside, Ruthie reading aloud to them, Berel sleeping on Shmuel's shoulder. "I'm going," she said to Shmuel. "Good, good," he answered. As he looked at her, her body became warm, and she hurried out.

Across the narrow lane, Hanna-Leah was leaving her house, too, following Faygela like a huge moon shadow as they made their way through the village square and across the bridge in a twilight blackening into night.

The bathhouse was on a small rise beside the foundation of the new synagogue, begun before the Russians blew up the mill, and never finished. From the steps Faygela could see the dark ruins of the mill on the upper bank where the river narrowed, silver rocks glinting in the last hint of daylight.

The bathhouse attendant for the women, old Liba, deaf, half-blind, and toothless, nodded dimly at Faygela and Hanna-Leah as they hung their clothes on a hook. Hanna-Leah walked down the slippery steps into the warm greenish water that smelled of mildew. Faygela stood at the edge, arms across her chest, waiting for her turn.

"Dip, dip," Liba yelled, motioning at Hanna-Leah to dunk under the water. Once, twice, three times she submerged, repeating the blessing for immersion. "Kosher," Liba pronounced.

Hanna-Leah pinched her nose between thumb and forefinger, blowing out water. "*Phew.* It would be better to go to the river."

"Outside where anyone could see? What happened to your modesty?" Faygela asked.

Hanna-Leah laughed. "And why not, here in the wild country? We're *proster* people, plain, not like the *shayner* in Warsaw. I hear that in Warsaw the bathhouse has tiles of gold. You must have seen plenty there, but you hardly said a thing to me about it. I never thought that you, Faygela, would be stingy."

Faygela's eyes narrowed. "You mean to tell me that you're criticizing me for not saying enough to you? Since when are we such good friends?"

"We used to be."

"That was before you stopped talking to me."

"Me?"

"Yes, you. Do you think I mean the Queen of Sheba? I'm talking about you, Hanna-Leah, who stopped talking to me after Devorah was born. I had four little ones and I wasn't even twenty-four years old. No mother, no sister to talk to. And who was left? If it wasn't for Misha, who would I turn to, tell me? Zisa-Sara went to America. And my best friend Hanna-Leah wouldn't look at me." She stamped her foot on the slimy edge. "So don't you dare call me stingy." She stamped her foot again, losing her balance. Yelping as her tailbone banged the wooden ledge, she tumbled into the water, sputtering and choking while Hanna-Leah steadied her.

"You were so busy with the children," Hanna-Leah said.

"They needed me every second and I was so lonely. How could you forget me when I had no mother, no father, no one?" Faygela asked.

"I didn't forget. Did I have a sister? A mother? A father? Or even one child?"

The women were silent, looking away from each other. Then Faygela tapped Hanna-Leah on the shoulder. "Do you remember how clumsy I was when we were picking mushrooms? I was always stepping on something you wanted."

"I remember how you used to spin around in a circle until you fell. You would sing that song of your father's. How did it go?"

"*By the chimneys birds are sleeping,*" Faygela began.

"Yes, yes. *Not awake and not asleep, the night is long, the river deep.* The river, like our river here in Blaszka." Hanna-Leah hummed, shaking her head so that her hair flew back and forth, sprinkling Faygela. Holding out her hands, Hanna-Leah beckoned as if there were a bride in the *mikva* and they were dancing around her. Faygela raised her arms. Humming, they swayed, circling the invisible bride. Above, the old bathhouse attendant nodded, smiling as if she could see them.

A FEW DAYS later, on the eve of Tishah-b'Av, while the village mourned for the destruction of the Temple, Hanna-Leah told Hershel the story of the orphan that drank up the river. At the far end of Blaszka in a small house under the willow trees, Zisa-Sara's daughter, Emma, floated between life and death. Her great-aunt cried while Faygela put an arm around her. "I know what it is to nearly lose a child," she said to Alta-Fruma.

THE DAYS OF AWE

The world was golden, the sun cast in the mold of sunflowers, barley, rye, and oats. In the woods, nightshade bloomed purple and mushrooms sprouted in the shadows. Birds flocked, preparing for migration. Squirrels gathered nuts, chittering protectively over their hollows.

From the peasant villages upriver, where there were no synagogues, the Jews who farmed or ran the local taverns came down to Blaszka. The ram's horn called in the New Year and in the synagogue, hot with the press of people crowded together, the villagers sang, "*O Lord, Judge of Compassion, You record and seal, count and measure; You remember even what we have forgotten.*"

Neighbor sought forgiveness of neighbor and every stranger had somewhere to eat, even the Gypsy boy, who hit his head in the river, finding shelter in the rabbi's house. Hanna-Leah was seen to embrace Faygela in the bakery and together they made up a basket for Misha.

After the Sabbath, Faygela took up a pen and wrote on a white sheet of fine paper,

The Village of Mud and Pearls

Let me tell you about three of the women in our village. Two are childhood friends: the midwife Misha and Hanna-Leah the butcher's wife. Misha, who is bigger than any man from Plotsk to Warsaw, was married to Hayim the watercarrier, a man who cannot speak without stammering, but who can draw anyone's likeness. Why they divorced is a mystery locked in the hidden places of our village.

Hanna-Leah, without whom many poor people would go hungry, is a tall and beautiful woman who hated Misha as only a childless woman can hate a midwife, suspecting her of many improper things, some of which turned out to be true. Nevertheless Misha returned my oldest daughter Ruthie to me and now I see that she is a child no longer. My firstborn, with her quiet dark eyes and her thick braids wound around her head, is no longer as good a girl as she once was and I thank the Holy One above. Goodness may be sweet in a child but knowledge will keep her safer. Now that my Ruthie has faced danger and passed through it, she may follow her Naomi, and wherever the road may take her, she will look with open eyes. It is my daughter who has taught me how to see.

Here in my village, as small as a yawn, angels grow from pearls thrown into the mud. The pearls sprout into strange and beautiful trees, which then turn into angels when you least expect it. This secret was revealed through the great benevolence of our Little Father in Moscow and the justice of his prisons . . .

On the eve of Yom Kippur, before it was time to go to the synagogue, Faygela picked mint from Misha's garden and brewed a pot of tea for her. Leaving *The Israelite* on the table, she said she would come back with something to brighten the room before she dressed for services. In the woods while she was gathering wildflowers, Faygela saw, as she had so many times before, her father's ghost walking along the riverbank. She ran after him, stumbling, calling. He stopped and turned. "Faygela, Faygela, there you are."

"Here I am, Papa. Here."

"Of course you are. And so am I," he said smiling at her tenderly as he faded away.

KOL NIDREI

In the balcony the women sit on the hard benches, waiting to rise for Kol Nidrei. There is no whispering, no gossip, no pointing of chins, no leaning together over delicious secrets. Mothers-in-law and daughters-in-law hold hands, sisters sit arm in arm, and even the babies are quiet. There is hardly room to breathe, the women sit so close together up here, near the roof of the synagogue. But who can breathe? Time is cracking open. The candles flare, sparks faintly snapping in the stillness.

*　　*　　*

IN THE coming year, the last Tsar of Russia will ascend the throne and wed the granddaughter of the Queen of England. Marie Skłodowska will marry Pierre Curie. A Jewish-French officer named Dreyfus will be court-martialed and sent to Devil's Island, witnessed by a reporter named Theodor Herzl who will write *Das Ghetto*. Freud will publish *Studies On Hysteria* and H. G. Wells will publish *The Time Machine*. The Lumière brothers will show the first movie to thirty-three people in the basement of a cafe in Paris, a two-minute clip of an oncoming train and the workers leaving the Lumière factory.

In six years, Stanisław Wyspianski will write an acclaimed drama called *The Wedding*, in which a Jewish woman will call forth the poetic spirit of Poland. She will wear a black dress and a red shawl.

Influenced by Wyspianski's work, I. L. Peretz will write a Yiddish play, *At Night In the Old Market*, published in 1907. Like *The Wedding*, it will be a symbolic drama in verse, blurring the line between the real and the unreal, the living and the dead. In the same year, Sholem Asch will publish a Yiddish play *The God of Vengeance*, in which a brothel-keeper comes to a bad end. A minor element of the play involves young Jewish lovers, both women, who tenderly kiss onstage.

In ninety years, the Polish director Andrzej Wajda will film *The Wedding*, its liberation themes resonating with the struggle between Poland and the Soviet Union. In it a Jewish woman with eyes like coals, a red shawl around her shoulders, will fling wide the shutters of a closed window.

But today, as the ram's horn brings in the New Year of 5655 along the banks of the Vistula River and its small tributaries, Warsaw is still Warsaw and Blaszka is Blaszka, less than a dot on the map. Yet in the new year, Faygela will show Hanna-Leah and Misha a story in *The Jewish Annual*, titled "The Village of Mud and Pearls" by Faygela Bas-Yckhiel. Faygela, the daughter of Yekhiel.

3

MIRACLE CLOAKS

mma floated in delirium. Above her was the Lower East Side of
New York, and below her was Blaszka. An angel of the revolution
with huge, shining red wings and a halo of burnished steel
floated beside her. Wearing a silver medallion of Karl Marx on a black
ribbon around his neck, he carried a placard that read CLOSED SHOP.
8 HOURS. IN UNITY IS STRENGTH.

In the nothingness where she floated, it wasn't day or night, not
dawn or dusk. She could hear and see clearly, though it all seemed far
away and yet amusing, like a drama about strangers. It wasn't wet, but
she swam. It wasn't cold, but she wore a patchwork of woolen garments. A piece of cloak, a bit of fur, a blue shirtwaist, a jacket sleeve.

From below her in Blaszka she heard a voice crying. It sounded
like her great-aunt but that couldn't be. Alta-Fruma didn't cry. "For
this the girl was sent back from America? They should be struck with
typhus themselves, the fine people from the United Hebrew Charities.
These are Jews? Murderers."

"I know what it is to nearly lose a child," Faygela said. "But there
was no choice. A pair of orphans, where were they to go? Emma and
Izzie are lucky you sent for them. How long would the boy last in a
workhouse?"

"He was the delicate one. I never gave a thought to her and now look. She's burning up."

"Has Emma been able to drink anything?" Ruthie asked.

"Not a thing. Every hour another girl or boy comes to the door. Little Henya the seamstress or Nahum the baker's apprentice, asking, How is Emma, is she any better? Did she eat the oranges? The young people collected every spare kopeck they had to buy Emma oranges. They know she has a passion for them. Who ever has a single orange in Blaszka? Now she has three and she can't even taste a slice of one."

"Then let her smell them. We'll put the oranges beside her bed. Squeeze a few drops onto the cloth and wet her lips."

EMMA FLOATED contentedly in her delirium, looking down beyond Alta-Fruma's house under the willow trees at the edge of Blaszka. Though it was night everything she saw shone as if it were burning with light. There was the dairyhouse near the river, and there the churn she'd knocked down when she fainted. The black cow was licking her calf under the chin. Emma looked across the green woods, past the clearing where the printing press had been dismantled, to the low roofs of Blaszka with their chimneys leaning toward each other like old men smoking in the warm August night. The men were just leaving the synagogue, draped in black for Tishah-b'Av. Beside the synagogue a beggar entered the guest house, settled himself on one of the straw pallets, scratched his neck, pinched a louse between thumb and forefinger, yawned, tore off a piece of bread begged from Hanna-Leah. Even the river flowed quietly. So different from up there, the Lower East Side, with everything and everyone Emma knew and loved.

She looked up to the Lower East Side. First Hester Street, with the school and the tenements six stories high, with its awnings and fire escapes, horse-drawn wagons, three-tiered pushcarts, fruit-laden stalls, the knife sharpener's bell, the whistling men with hands in their pockets, the bathhouse three steps down, two cents for two minutes, the boys with baskets—matches, fans, hairpins, baby rattles, dishpans, pails—the girls ladling milk into a pitcher for two cents, butter a bit sour you could get for five cents a pound, bread a cent a pound, potatoes, a fifty-pound sack for the winter, oranges by the crate. Down Hester Street to Essex, past the hokey-pokey man selling squares of ice cream from his cart. There on the second floor of the tenement, where she should be, was Emma's mother, a pile of finished piecework on the table. Her mother's eyes were red. Sure they were red, always red from sewing, but she was singing, "*A boy stands and thinks all night, who is the girl to catch his sight.*"

"MAMA, I'm coming," Emma called down, but her mother didn't seem to hear. She turned to the revolutionary angel. "Go and tell her. She'll be worried about where I am, and then she'll pretend that she has something in her eye and she'll cry." But the angel vanished and in its place appeared a hat, a brown fedora with silk daisies on the brim. Putting on the hat, Emma saw in front of her a square table and on the table a swath of white cloth and a pair of scissors. "Mama won't be upset when I tell her that I'm helping with the piecework." Humming, Emma cut the cloth. From time to time she looked down to Blaszka. There the seasons were running backward, from apples to pink buds, to green haze to bare branches lined with snow, like an ermine collar over charcoal wool. "An expensive cloak," Emma remarked.

ON THE short Friday in December, the river was frozen solid, around the silver rocks its eddies motionless as a painting. With a roar and puff of smoke, the train approached the river like a line of maverick tenements broken free of their foundations. In the third-class car, swinging his skinny feet, a greenish-faced boy sat with his sister, her face pressed to the window. First there had been the endless sea and now there was the endless land. Were there never going to be any more streets?

"I'm scared, Emma," the boy was saying. "What's it going to be like?"

"You remember what Mama used to tell us. There's a town and then there's woods."

He closed his eyes the way he used to when Papa asked him a question about the Talmud. "She said the woods smelled good in the spring." He opened his eyes and looked out the window again. "Oh, Em, it's so empty."

"Now you listen to me. You see out there? It's snow. Don't we get snow in New York? It's just a place, that's all. You'll go to school and

I'll make sure that nobody bothers you. Nothing's changed. They just have more cows here."

"I think I'm going to be sick."

"Here's the pail, Izzie. I'll hold your head. That's it. Okay. Let me wipe your forehead. You're a good kid. Curl up there and put your head in my lap. Don't worry about that lady's chickens. Let them squawk. Close your eyes and I'll sing. You go to sleep."

Stroking Izzie's hair, Emma sang, *"We swear our stalwart hate persists, Of those who rob and kill the poor; the Tsar, the masters, capitalists. Our vengeance will be swift and sure."*

"Not that one," Izzie said. "Please, Emma. I feel so weak. Sing something else."

"Are you getting feverish?" Emma touched Izzie's forehead. It seemed forever since the ground had been steady under their feet.

"Maybe. I could be."

"I won't let you get sick again," she said, poking his shoulder.

"Ow, not so hard. Sing something, Em. One of the ones I like."

"Okay, stop squirming. You have to lie quietly."

Emma looked left and right as if checking for informers. Then in a tone so low she had to bend toward Izzie's ear, she sang, *"Welcome among us, messengers of peace, angels of the Highest One, from deep within us, Majesty of majesties, the blessed Holy One."*

"Where's the town?" Emma asked as the driver took them through the village square. It looked a little familiar, but she'd always thought her vague memory of Blaszka must have been of some rural suburb like Coney Island, where her father had once taken her and Izzie for a day's holiday. They had rented bathing costumes, even Papa, his beard flapping, his knobby knees bare as he ran into the water, holding Emma's hand on one side and Izzie's on the other. Papa could swim. He told them he'd learned in the Północna River, though he looked like a frog when he swam. Laughing, Emma had told him so. Now she wished she hadn't.

"This is it," the driver said to Emma. In the village square she saw a crowd of strangers. Men in beards. Black coats. Women in shawls. They all looked alike.

*   *   *

INSIDE their great-aunt's house, Emma looked around at the front room with its green-tiled oven, the cooking grate over the fire beside it, the hen sleeping in the corner, the water barrel, the cooking benches, one for meat and one for dairy, the embroidered landscape of strange hills that marked the eastern wall for prayer. Emma had already argued with Great-aunt Alta-Fruma about waiting for Ruthie to help with the trunk and was now glaring while Ruthie sucked loudly on a lump of sugar, sipping her tea. Who ever saw sugar like that? Dark chunks of gravel.

"You must be tired," Ruthie said, "and it gets dark early on the short Friday. I should be going." Izzie was falling asleep at the table.

"No, no," Alta-Fruma said quickly. "I want to get something from the bakery for *Shabbas*. You stay and keep the children company."

After the door shut behind her, the two girls watched each other curiously over the head of the sleeping boy.

"My mother and your mother were good friends. Did you know that?" Ruthie asked.

"Sure," Emma said. "My mother told me stories about when they were girls. Boring stuff."

Ruthie tried again. "I remember when you left. You wouldn't get on the train. You ran along the track and your father ran after you. My mother and your mother were crying."

"Mothers always cry." Emma rubbed her eyes with the heels of her hands. "Got some dust in my eyes," she muttered, her voice trembling.

"Yes, it's quite dusty in here." Alta-Fruma's house was spotless. Emma looked at Ruthie to see if she were laughing at her, but Ruthie's face was serious. "I'll tell you a secret," Ruthie said. "I would love to see America. Are there many cowboys?"

"None on the Lower East Side." Emma smiled a little.

"I like to read about other places, but it's not the same as talking to someone who's been there. I've never been anywhere. Tell me about it. Please," Ruthie said.

The fire crackled, the tin roof banging in the wind. Emma leaned forward. "I'll tell you about my friend Dov," she said. "I met him in the Pig Market. That's on Hester Street and Essex. On one side you have the women buying fruits and fish for *Shabbas*. On the other are the men looking for work. Contractors come to the Pig Market and call out, 'I need a hand. Who's an operator?' Or maybe it's a puller or a turner he needs. Not a finisher, she works at home.

"Anyway, there wasn't much work that season. I was ten, so that would have been four years ago. In the Pig Market the crowd was big and ugly. My father was there and I was afraid that with all the cops he'd get clobbered."

"Your father in a place like that? A scholar? I don't understand, Emma."

"He only wanted to study Talmud. And to teach Izzie." Emma bit her lip, falling silent, Ruthie reaching out to take her hand. During the day her father had worked on the mezzanine, an extra floor built under the ceiling of the factory with scarcely enough room to stand. That didn't matter, though, because he was bent over his sewing machine from six in the morning until eight at night. There was no clock so he never knew how long he was working or how long he had left. No window. Just gas jets for light. Rush, rush, rush so fast that the needle sometimes went right through his finger.

When he came home, he sat at the table over a volume of the Talmud, swaying, chanting softly as he glanced at Emma and Izzie lying on their cot in the kitchen while he studied by candlelight, often falling asleep at the table. Mama would get up during the night and lead him to their bed, pulling off his boots and covering him with a blanket. Then she would sit at the table, spoiling her eyes with piecework in the dim light of the candle until it burned out. Sometimes Emma woke up, and her mother would tell her stories about Blaszka while Emma, wrapped in Papa's old coat that smelled of sewing machine oil, perched on a stool beside her.

My friends used to tell secrets in the woods, Mama would say, and Emma would think of fairy tales and castles where the King always had wine for *Shabbas* and the Queen's eyes didn't water. In the winter, Mama would say, When the river was frozen, we used to slide on the ice. How they teased me, especially Misha, because I wanted to marry a scholar like your papa. But why shouldn't I? For a man to study Torah and his wife to support him—there's nothing higher. That's what I was taught.

* * *

"PAPA WAS lucky," Emma said to Ruthie. "Scholars and rabbis ended up in the basement of the factory washing dirty old clothes with benzene, the fumes choking them. But my papa learned to be an operator on a sewing machine. At first he wouldn't work on the *Shabbas,* and no one would hire him. But then he said that he would pray over his sewing machine. Praying didn't help him much. In the slow season they let him go first because he didn't make a stink about it. Even in the busy season they'd take fifty cents to rent him the machine and so much off for fines and in the end they miscounted but said that Papa lost a dollar, he was so careless. All week he looked forward to the glass of wine he had on Friday night. Wine that's blessed for *Shabbas* is a taste of paradise, he said. When Papa was out of work, I carried finished cloaks from the contractor back to the factory. I could make thirty cents and it paid for the wine.

"That day when Papa was in the Pig Market, I had work for the day. Izzie was following me even though he should've been in school. I was carrying maybe thirty cloaks over my head and shoulders, all done except for the buttonholes, walking with my head bent on Hester Street. I didn't see the contractor hurrying to the Pig Market and I bumped into him. I fell onto the stone pavement in a pile of cloaks. I was lucky. Maybe if I didn't fall on a few coats I'd break an arm. But it so happened this was the same contractor who gave me the cloaks. He yelled, but that was nothing. He gave me a slap, too. Izzie started crying.

" 'Don't think I'm going to pay you a cent,' the contractor says. 'You're going to work off the cost of cleaning those cloaks.'

" 'You're going to pay me or I'll leave them right here and you can take them,' I say.

" 'So you think,' he says grabbing my arm. 'Stealing right from under my nose are you?'

"His fist was like iron. I just couldn't wriggle free even though I twisted this way and that. He piled all the cloaks on top of my head and was dragging me over to the cops. The cloaks were smothering me. I couldn't see a thing and all I could smell was the glue they used to fix the collars. Then I felt the cloaks lifted off my head. I saw this fellow, he wasn't so very old, maybe eighteen. And he wasn't so very big, either, but there was something different about him. Even though he was thin he didn't have the hungry look that everyone else had. Not the scared look either. Once I asked him about it and he said, 'I'm not alone. The brotherhood stands with me. If I fall, someone takes my place. They carry on.'" Here Emma turned her face from Ruthie, pressing her lips tight.

"What happened?" asked Ruthie, her voice softening.

"Well, he saved my behind, that's all. He put his face right up against the contractor's nose and growled about the workers' rights and strikes and the contractor put thirty cents in my hand and just ran off. He said, 'The boss. Look at him run, tail between his legs. A dog caught with his nose in dreck.' The wind was blowing against the contractor's back and his coat flapping between his legs was just like the tail of a scared dog. We all laughed. This fellow's name was Dov Baer and we became great friends. He wore a brown fedora, and he looked like a Russian with his long hair and his canvas shirt hanging out of his pants." Emma took a penny out of her pocket. A hole was punched in the center. "Dov gave it to me. You see this? No face in the middle. Just a hole to show that nobody should be the boss of you."

"My Grandfather Yekhiel used to say that a person has to live with his own conscience and that's all," Ruthie said. "I never met him but people still talk about him. He had a printing press in the woods. It was hidden in an old hut. He printed pamphlets there during the Polish insurrection."

"Insurrection?"

"A revolt. Against the Russians," Ruthie said. "The January insurrection in '63."

"You mean like the War of Independence?" Emma asked excitedly. Ruthie nodded. "Only it failed."

"Is it still there, the hut and the printing press?" Emma asked. "I'd like to see it."

"I don't know. That was another time. It's dangerous to hang around places like that."

"Living is dangerous," Emma said. "Show me? Promise." She held out her hand. The two girls stared at each other, eyes glittering. Ruthie stretched out her own hand in promise.

IN THE pleasant gray of nothingness, Emma took up the garment on the table, checking that the sides were evenly matched. When she was little, Emma loved to watch her mother sew. The fingers moving up and down, in and out so fast that Emma couldn't see the needle. Where's the needle, Mama? Emma would ask. And Mama would answer, You don't need to see something to know it's there, *mamala*. Only look what it does. Your *bubbie* didn't like to sew, she was too impatient, but my Auntie Fruma said that I had to learn. So she taught me and I've never been fined for spoiling a garment. You see, you can never know what will turn out to be useful in life. And Emma would watch how the stitches ran through the cloth like magic.

DOWN BELOW in Blaszka, it was the eve of both spring and Purim, and Emma was arguing with Great-aunt Alta-Fruma.

"Where were you?"

"Go ahead. Smack me." She wasn't going to tell Alta-Fruma, who was standing in front of Emma with her hand raised, a thing. Was it anyone's business that she and Ruthie were checking over the printing press hidden in the woods?

"God help me, what am I going to do with you?" Alta-Fruma's hand fell. She shook her head. "Never mind. Go get ready for synagogue."

"I'm not going." Emma crossed her arms. "And Izzie shouldn't either. His head is all muddled with superstition. He's got to learn that bosses run things, not his miracle-making rebbes. People have to fight for themselves."

"I don't want you filling his head with your ideas. He's a good boy."

"I never went to synagogue at home."

"That's fine for America but not Blaszka. Here everybody sees who and what you are."

"It's nobody's business."

"It's mine."

"As long as I'm working for my keep, you can't boss me around. The Klembas sisters were sick today and I did everything. Set the cheese. Put three rounds of butter to cool in the river."

"And?" Alta-Fruma asked, hands on her hips.

"So the butter floated downstream. It was an accident. You didn't have to pull my ear."

"We can dress up," Izzie said. "It'll be fun, Em. I always used to go with Papa."

She continued to scowl at her great-aunt. "I'm not going."

"Fine. Do what you want. Come, Izzie," Alta-Fruma said, turning her back on Emma.

Later when Alta-Fruma and Izzie came home, laughing and singing, Emma was sitting at the table, rereading *The Origin of Species*. Izzie was dressed in Emma's clothes, a pair of brown stockings twisted and pinned to his head for her braids. Alta-Fruma wore the veils of the disobedient, deposed Queen Vashti, her green eyes looking through Emma. My mother had green eyes, Emma thought.

"I wish you'd been there," Izzie said.

"Don't tell me about it. I'd rather be doused with ice water."

The wind rose, thunder crashed, and ice pellets pounded the roof. "It's a miracle," Izzie said, clapping his hands. Emma pinched him.

IN THE gray nothingness above, Emma floated from one side of the table to the other, abandoning the garment as she looked up at the Lower East Side. Past Essex Street, on Delancey, she could see the rag shop and above it the Anarchist Free Press with its notice on the door, LET THE VOICE OF THE PEOPLE BE HEARD. The door was open. Inside, Dov was painting a sign.

GRAND YOM KIPPUR BALL.
WITH THEATER.
*In the year 5651, after the invention of
the Jewish idols and 1890, after
the birth of the false Messiah.
Music, dancing, buffet, Marseillaise and
other hymns against Satan.*
BROOKLYN LABOR LYCEUM, MYRTLE AVENUE.

A ten-year-old girl sat on the printer's table, swinging her heels, sucking an orange, wiping her mouth with the back of her hand as she swallowed. "Nice hat," she said, pointing to a brown fedora on the window ledge. She belched and grinned. In the corner by the window, a black flag fluttered dustily in the breeze. The window was propped open on the three volumes of *Das Kapital*, relegated there to show the anarchists' distaste for the dry and authoritarian Mister Marx. The knife grinder's bell rang, a pushcart clattered over the cobblestones, a voice sang, "Genuine dirt from Jerusalem. Buy a piece of earth from the Holy Land. Only seventy-five cents."

A short woman in her early twenties heaved a bundle of newspapers onto the table. "So Dov, who's your guest?" she asked.

"Emma Goldman meet Emma Blau. I found her in front of the Pig Market. What a piece of luck. She can help me translate this pamphlet into Yiddish. I'll pay her five cents a paragraph, and she won't have to skip school to shlep cloaks from the workshop to the factory."

"You should get ten from him," the woman said. "Demonstrate before the palaces of the rich; demand work. Take your sacred right with your own hands."

"What?" young Emma asked.

"Ignore her," Dov said. "She's practicing her speech. Look, I'll give you ten cents a paragraph. It has to be clear so the ordinary man can understand. Women, too. Boys, girls, all workers. And my Yiddish is no good. In Vilna my father said we should only speak Russian, it was the gateway to the world. The ghetto jargon? Who needed it? But it's the language of the newcomers and you were born to it."

"Are you calling me a greenie?" Emma asked, jumping down from the table, fists ready. "Take it back. Nobody calls me a greenie. I'm an American."

"Of course you are. As much as anyone," Emma Goldman said, ruffling Dov's hair until it stood up in a cock's comb, slapping away his hands when he tried to smooth it straight. "They call him the *Maggid* of the Pig Market, but he hardly looks the part of a preacher, now does he, little Emma?"

Dov put down the paintbrush. "Five cents now. Five cents when you're done," he said. "You go to school tomorrow, you read this book. After school you come here. Work on the pamphlet. Meet some of the others, Sally, Ed. We talk." He handed her a red volume. *The Origin of Species* by Charles Darwin.

"All that for ten cents?"

"Okay. You can wear the hat, too."

"And I'll show you how to waltz," the woman said.

"Emma, we have work to do," Dov protested.

"So what? It's not my revolution if I can't dance." Emma Goldman laughed, lifting her hands for young Emma to take hold.

*   *   *

"MAMA, look what I have. Five cents just for translating a pamphlet into Yiddish for Dov. And a book about animals. Look how thick it is." Emma's mother was washing the boarder's laundry in a tin basin. Papa was sleeping.

"What kind of pamphlet?" Mama asked.

Emma shrugged. "Something about workers. Dov says they should get paid. What are we having for supper?"

"Potatoes and onions."

"Again?" I'll have to nick a bagel from the pushcart for Izzie, Emma thought.

"Papa didn't get work," Mama said.

"I got an orange from Dov. And one for Izzie, too." Emma held it out to her mother. Zisa-Sara put it on the shelf.

"Let me see the book." Zisa-Sara opened it. The pages were made of fine paper, the printing clear. "I want to meet this Dov that gave you five cents and an orange, Emma. Is he a nice person?"

"Sure, Mama. I'll bring him home. He's a writer."

"A writer, *nu,*" Papa said, sitting up. "That's good. A thinker. Where does he work?"

"The Anarchist Free Press."

Emma's father frowned. "Anarchists. Unbelievers."

But Mama said, "Don't worry what he believes. If he has a kind face then he's welcome at my table." Mama looked out the window. "There's Mrs. Agostino. Hello, Mrs. Agostino," she called out in English. Mrs. Agostino looked up with a smile, waving both her plump hands. "She's nearly due," Mama said, "and she can hardly walk up the stairs. I'm going to run down and help her. You sit and read, Emma. Do I want my daughter to be a pieceworker when she grows up?"

IN BLASZKA the woods were green and the swallows had returned to their nests. It was early May, a week after Passover. Through a hole in the roof, the sun formed a puddle of warmth on the earthen floor where Emma sat on her haunches. She looked contentedly at the walls freshly chinked with moss and mud, the wind yelping uselessly outside. Ruthie was scraping rust from the printing press. "If my mother finds out what I'm doing on *Shabbas,* I'll never hear the end of it," Ruthie said.

"How's she going to find out? She's in Warsaw," Emma said as Avram came in, throwing down his apron, stained with ink and marked M.P. for Mosaic Press. "Tell me. When did that blood-sucking exploiter let you go last night?" Emma asked.

"Eight," Avram yawned. "He let us off early for *Shabbas.* I walked from Plotsk first thing this morning. It was still dark when I left."

"He let you off early? Fourteen hours isn't enough?"

"Usually it's sixteen."

"In America they're fighting for eight hours."

"You always forget, Emma," Ruthie said quietly, "that this isn't America."

Avram stretched and cracked his knuckles. He was a sturdy boy about Ruthie's age, blunt-fingered and deep-voiced, with a few blond hairs trying to weave themselves into a beard over his Adam's apple. "I'd be happy with twelve hours," he said. "The bristleworkers struck for a shorter day, but they have a *kassa* with funds to help them out during the strike."

"What's a *kassa?*"

"Kind of a union."

"Good. Then form a *kassa.*"

"The printers don't want to leave the journeymen's guild. They say that real artisans don't belong in a *kassa* with common people who just want a few more kopecks to get drunk on. When the printers go on strike they swear on the Torah to stick together and that means something."

"Wake up," Emma said. "Religion's just superstition. Another way of bossing you around."

"But Emma, you have to be something. The peasants are Christians and you're a Jew," Ruthie said.

"Why does everyone keep saying, You're a Jew, Emma. Watch what you say, Emma. When the workers in a factory cough up blood, it doesn't matter what religion they are. In America, people know that it only matters if you're a boss or a worker."

"You think it's easy to be the boss?" Avram asked. "You should see the master. He's skinny as my finger and he works after we go to sleep.

We're not so different. Yankel the journeyman is leaving for Warsaw to open his own shop next year. One day I will, too."

"And that purple mark under your eye? You're going to give that to some poor apprentice, too, one day?"

"This? You should see what we gave the master. Yankel said, 'Boys, we stop working at seven.' And that's what we did. I didn't lift a letter of type. Yankel let the ink run dry. The others sat, too, until the master gave us our wages."

"How long since you got paid?"

"Let's see, he owed us for five weeks. That's why he gave me a smack. I wanted to give Mother my wages. She's upset that she had to borrow money from Great-aunt Alta-Fruma."

"You let yourself be knocked around because of Auntie? She's a witch."

"Did she turn you into a frog?" Emma swatted him.

"Alta-Fruma means well," Ruthie said. "She's just old-fashioned."

"I'm telling you she hates me. Do you know, my auntie sends me into the woods to get branches for the *pripichek,* practically every day. Just so she can boil a kettle for her tea, when I could be eaten by a bear!"

"Oh yes," Ruthie said. "Listen to your cousin, Avram. On our way here, today, I nearly jumped out of my skin. Emma was screaming, 'Bear! Bear!' I turned. I looked. I was scared, even though no one has ever seen a bear from here to Warsaw, and I was wondering if Emma would be able to climb a tree. And what was Emma's fine bear? The shadow of a cow. I had to take her by the hand, didn't I?"

"Well, I never went to cow school," Emma muttered. "Who can figure this place out?"

Ruthie put an arm around her shoulders. "Everything is still strange to you, isn't it?" she asked. "But what would we do for excitement without our Emma? Isn't it so, Avram?"

"You should have been there yesterday," Emma said. "Izzie was at the table studying some religious book. He wants to go to the yeshiva. Don't you think that's sick? And Auntie was going on about how her garden's dry. So I said, 'Well, if heaven really heard people's prayers, it would rain wouldn't it?' Then I yelled, 'Make it rain.' Just then the sky opened up and let down buckets. Izzie jumped up from the table, shouting, 'It's a miracle, a miracle.' Auntie went all pale, like I had anything to do with it, and she spit 'thpoo, thpoo, thpoo' to keep away the Evil Eye!"

"Well, if you're going be a socialist and make miracles, you have to watch what you say," Avram observed.

"I'm an anarchist, not a socialist," Emma said, affronted.

"Yes, of course. Just think, it'll be my fortune. Mine and Ruthie's. We'll be partners. 'Come see the socialist miracle worker. Only a dollar a peek!' What do you say, Ruthie?"

Ruthie paused in her polishing. "Yes," she said consideringly. "I think that would be a good idea."

"Oh you," Emma said, throwing herself at Ruthie. The girls tussled, hair springing from their braids, heels dug into the earth, their little breasts rising and falling with laughter as Emma pushed against Ruthie. Trying to pull Emma away, Avram found himself rolled between the two girls, who joined forces against him, until all three were breathless, red-faced, and suddenly awkward.

"Show me what you have there. I see it sticking out of your jacket," Emma said to Avram, breaking the silence. "What is it?"

"Oh, this. It's nothing much, but I thought you might be interested. A student from Vilna came through the shop. He wanted the master to print this up and for free, too. What a dreamer. No one's going to print it, not even for good money. He was on his way to Warsaw. I shared my lunch with him and he left this with me. Told me to pass it around."

Emma unrolled the handwritten sheet. "This is fabulous. And you waited until now to tell me?" She hit Avram in the shoulder. "Listen. 'Seven to seven is our requirement. A twelve-hour day—it is indeed legal from Catherine II's proclamation. Workers join together, we make it true . . .'He must be from the Russian schools, the Yiddish isn't very good. But we can fix that. Avram, you're a genius." She kissed him on the lips and, grabbing his hands, danced him around the hut until they fell in a dizzy pile.

"We'll print one for every worker in Plotsk," Emma shouted. "You'll get the letters from your shop, won't you, Avrameleh?" she asked. "Your boss won't miss a few extra pieces of type."

"And what about me?" Ruthie asked. "What will I do?"

"Everything," Emma said, pulling Ruthie down beside her.

*   *   *

A LEAFLET appeared on Emma's square table, beside the pieces of cut fabric. It was roughly printed, the letters uneven. "Seven to Seven" the title read.

"I hardly know my own children," Israel the printer says. "I leave for work when they are sleep. When I come home they sleep again. Only on Saturday can I hold my child. Can I even go to the synagogue for the evening prayers? No time to study or to learn."

SEVEN TO SEVEN is our demand. It is our LEGAL right. Catherine II ordered in 1785, "The working day of artisans is from 6:00 A.M. to 6:00 P.M. including half an hour for breakfast and one and one-half hours for dinner and rest."

Israel says, "The boss pays me when he wants. Sometimes in a week, sometimes two months. My children can't wait a month to eat."

MONEY EVERY WEEK is our demand. Do we have to bend to the boss's whim? Is he a KING? Are we SERFS? NO. We are FREE MEN.

No worker alone is in a position to carry on a struggle against his employer. None of us through his own efforts is able to attain a shorter workday and higher wages for his hard labor. Therefore we all unite in order to stand together and support each other.

We workers lament on the Day of Atonement not because we are Jews but because we are workers. The factory owners have their own God. Our God is unity. This is what we mean when we recite the morning prayer. "Hear oh Israel, the Lord our God, the Lord is one."

Now Israel is no longer concerned with legends. He is seeking another type of education. He gives up the belief in miracles that keeps his father enslaved. He is ready to struggle against his immediate enemy, the employer. Every day he comes into conflict with his boss. He needs the unity of all workers. Join the kassa. Pay your dues. Strike. SEVEN TO SEVEN. MONEY EVERY WEEK.

"Dov would like this," Emma said. "Yes, he should see it." She leaned back, waving her fedora, the daisies on the brim flip-flopping. "Dov, look at this," she called upward to the ghostly printshop on Delancey Street. "Do you see this? Why don't you answer? Oh. It's the garment. He's waiting for me to finish." A needle and thread appeared in her hands. As she began to sew, the stitches were perfect, her hands as quick as a machine, the fabric smooth and white. But the garment grew larger as she held it, the hem seeming endless. "I'm never going to finish this. Dov," she called, "take it away. Get someone else to finish it."

"He's not going to answer," a voice said. "He's got his job and you have yours."

A stranger was sitting at the table across from Emma, a young man with his chin resting on his fists. His face was thin, his hair cut ragged like copper pinfeathers. He wore a shabby jacket, the lining hanging below the hem, the cuffs frayed. A red rose was pinned to the collar. Pulling a notebook out of his breast pocket, he opened it to a page marked "Emma Blau" and nodded. His hands were calloused as if he knew what it meant to work. Putting the notebook back in his pocket, he took out a small piece of wood and a knife and began to carve. "I like to keep my hands busy," he said. "Think this would make a good whistle?"

"Who are you?" Emma asked.

"Mostly a traveler. Sometimes a peddler. I try to keep away from the authorities."

"In trouble?" Emma asked. The Traveler nodded. "I know what that's like," she said.

"You and me, we're in the same position. It isn't easy. Stuck in the middle between up there," he pointed, "and down below."

Emma looked down. It was raining in Blaszka, a muddy May rain. Ruthie's father was running toward the synagogue. She herself was in her great-aunt's house, sitting on her bed.

"Do you know what all the excitement's about?" the Traveler asked.

"It's Ruthie," Emma muttered. "She's been arrested."

"Poor child," the Traveler said and Emma wondered why he was looking at her as if she'd been the one to go to prison.

"How DID it happen?" Alta-Fruma asked. "I want the truth."

"I wasn't there." Emma wrapped her arms around her knees. "I didn't see what happened."

"Emma Blau, if Ruthie was arrested then I know you're mixed up in it. I want to know what's going on with you children. What about Avram? Does he have anything to do with this?"

Emma shrugged. Alta-Fruma sat on the bed beside her. "Emma, Ruthie could sit in that prison in Plotsk for a long time."

"What about—" Emma tried to think of the Yiddish word for bail. "Can't we give the lawyer some money to get her out until the trial? They can't prove anything."

"There's no lawyer and no trial, Emma. There's only the Governor's orders. And the Russian guards. They say a Jewish girl is like a chicken. The legs wiggle even if the head is gone. Do you understand now?"

Emma buried her face in her pillow.

Alta-Fruma put her hand on Emma's shoulder. "When you decide you have something to tell me, I'll be in the other room."

Don't tell, don't tell. Dov wouldn't tell, Emma said to herself, crying until she fell asleep.

THE NEXT morning Emma awoke to another May storm, rain pounding on the tin roof. Sitting up in the bed she shared with Alta-Fruma, she felt a wetness around her and wondered vaguely if the window was open. She yawned, pushed the quilt aside. A red blotch was spreading across her nightgown and drenching the bed. "Auntie, come quickly. I'm dying," Emma called.

Who would take care of Izzie after she was gone? She would never see him grow up. And Mama had told her that she had to watch out for Izzie. How often had she yelled at him to get his head out of the clouds? Would she have time to say good-bye to him? If only she could tell him that she was sorry for saying that God was a cabbage. Her chest constricted. The shutters rattled. It's the Angel of Death, Emma thought.

Alta-Fruma looked from Emma's eyes, wide and staring, to the bed. She slapped Emma on the left cheek. "Congratulations," she said, "you're a woman now."

"A woman? You mean I'm not dying? A woman?" So she would see Izzie grown up after all. She'd have time to make it up to Ruthie.

"Didn't your mother tell you? A woman bleeds monthly so she can have children." As Alta-Fruma spoke, she briskly tore strips from an old nightgown, rolled them, and handed them to Emma. "Pin this to your underthings."

"Of course she told me. I just, just wasn't expecting it. That's all. You didn't have to hit me." Emma's cheek stung.

"It's the custom. To keep away the evil eye when a girl becomes grown."

"And for that you hit me, old woman?"

"Watch your mouth or I'll give you a real smack."

"You see? It's not the evil eye that oppresses people."

"Emma, listen to me. You can't just yell out anything that's in your head. One word to the wrong person and your life is not your own. Look what happened to Ruthie. Do you want to be next? Never mind the bedding or your nightdress. Leave it to me."

"I'll take care of it," Emma said stiffly.

"I have something better for you to do. In fact, I have a very good idea. You won't get into trouble if you don't have the time. And you can help Ruthie, too."

"How?"

"You're going to help out in the bakery. Yes. And besides that, you're going to take in some piecework so you can give something to the community council. They're collecting money to give to the warden. To make Ruthie's life a little easier."

"I've got things to do," Emma protested.

"Do you think you're Hayim the watercarrier to be wandering in the woods? A girl should be too busy."

"I am busy."

"I have plenty for you to do here. When it stops raining, go tell Hayim to bring us water."

"I have to go out now. I'll let him know on my way."

"Not in this storm you're not. You couldn't see an inch in front of you. It's a flood."

"Rain, rain. That's all anyone talks about. Too much rain. Not enough rain. The world could explode and no one would notice. I wish it would stop raining till the earth turned to dust."

As Emma spoke, the shutters stopped their rattling, the pounding on the walls and roof sputtered and fell away. Alta-Fruma peered at Emma. "It's her monthly flow," she muttered. "When a girl begins, these things happen." Emma ran out before her great-aunt could start spitting into the wind or give her a smack. The wind slammed the door.

As she passed the synagogue she saw Izzie studying near the window. She knocked on the glass, once, twice. He looked up. She beckoned. The window lifted.

"What is it? I'm studying," he said.

"I'm a woman now."

"A woman? What?"

"You know. A woman."

"Oh. Yes." He nodded. "I know about that. I studied it."

"You know?"

"Yes. Move your hand away. You're not supposed to touch me now." He stroked his little-boy chin as if it bore a long beard. "This is something you need to know. Even a girl has to learn about separation. Man and woman. Milk and meat. Separate."

"God is a cabbage," Emma shouted, slamming down the window. Izzie pulled back his fingers just in time.

In the hut in the woods she first oiled the printing press, then counted the remaining pamphlets. "How can we go on now?" she asked herself.

"IT'S TOUGH to be a miracle-maker," the Traveler said in the haze of delirium between Blaszka and the Lower East Side. "Lucky for me all I can do is carve a little." He held up the whistle, now more than half done. "I'm not even a very good peddler. Making it rain, or stop, that's something special."

"So what good is it? Does a little rain teach the workers to stick together? To fight the real enemy? Not just once, but over and over? Oh, what's the use. My mother was a pieceworker and so am I."

"Rain is a sign of divine power. You know what it says in the Bible."

"Yeah, sure." Papa used to read aloud from the Yiddish Bible. On a hot day last summer he'd read them the story of Noah's flood—to cool them off, he said. Mama was heating coal for the iron. She'd taken in laundry, on top of the piecework, to pay for Izzie's schoolbooks. You see, it was a miracle that Noah was saved, Papa said. You call it a miracle when the whole world was drowned? Mama asked. I call that a tragedy. Mama burned her hand on the iron and she cried because even with the laundry there wouldn't be enough money in the slow season and Izzie would have to leave school. Emma said, Don't worry, Mama. I can finish the piecework and you can go to the factory with Papa. Mama said, I wanted something better for you, Emma. But she agreed just the same.

"You can tell my brother about divine power," Emma said to the Traveler. "All his favorite rabbis made miracles. But not one understood economics." She paused. "My brother belongs in Blaszka. Not me."

"A place for miracles, but not revolutions. Is that what you think?" the Traveler asked.

"No point in staying," she said.

RUTHIE WAS arrested on a Tuesday, her mother came home on Wednesday, and on Thursday Emma ran away. Wearing several layers of clothing, Emma carried a bundle of food and *The Origin of Species* on her back, a knife in her sash, and on a string around her neck, the penny with the hole punched in it that Dov had given her. The sky was a blue net between the trees in the woods as she sat on an oak stump, eating a piece of coarse bread and herring.

At the sound of cracking twigs, she turned to see Hayim the watercarrier walking with his hands in his pockets, gazing up at an owl in its roost. He looked a little like her father, broad-shouldered, the beard so dark it was a square of night. If only it was her father and if only she were back home. Fingering Dov's penny, Emma shook her head to clear it of sleepiness and dreams as Hayim took a small sketchbook from his pocket, a pencil from behind his ear and in the half-light began to draw the owl as it went to sleep. Gathering up her bundle, she moved quietly along the path, hoping that Hayim wouldn't notice her. If he caught her, he'd be sure to make her go back. From the corner of her eye, she saw him replace the sketchbook in his pocket. Now he was coming up beside her. Now he was matching her pace, whistling. What was the use? She couldn't run all the way to Warsaw.

"I'm going to Warsaw," Emma said.

Hayim nodded. She waited for him to say something. To scold her or reason with her. He was silent.

"I can't do anything here," she exploded. "Great-aunt Alta-Fruma is breathing down my neck every minute. The revolution will be over by the time I've satisfied her."

Hayim raised an eyebrow.

"Well, she hates me anyway. She won't miss me."

"And, and Izzie?" Hayim asked.

"Oh, he has his nose in his religious books all the time. He won't even know I'm gone." Emma's pace slowed. "Ruthie's mother came home yesterday. She's going to kill me and no one's ever going to speak to me again."

"No," Hayim said, looking at Emma with such certainty that she stopped walking. "No," he said, "no, no, no."

"No?" she asked.

He cupped her chin in his hand. "Just a, a, a little yelling, it could be. You, you're afraid of, of a little yelling? I don't believe it. No. Not a, a child of Blaszka."

She was close to tears. Why should she want to cry? It was ridiculous. She was on her way to Warsaw. To carry on the work of the revolution. But she suddenly felt very tired and wished she could go home. If only she knew where that was.

ON SATURDAY, Emma met her friends in the clearing near the hut in the woods. The ground was matted with old wet leaves and the gray sky pressed heavily on the tops of branches. A group of young men and women stood in a rough semicircle, most of them apprentices in Plotsk because there wasn't work for them in Blaszka. The girls wore their hair in braids looped below their ears and tied with bright ribbons, beaded pins breaking up the drabness of their plain, dark dresses. Slouched against the trees, hands in their pockets, the boys wore their caps low in the front, hiding their eyes like men with perilous secrets. When Emma arrived, they all stopped speaking, looking at one another furtively, then staring at their feet. The song of thrushes was violent in the stillness. Emma's belly ached.

"Well, say something," Emma said.

"I heard they've got Ruthie locked up in a cell with ten madwomen. She's never getting out unless they send her to Siberia," one of the girls murmured.

If that's all, she's lucky, the others added. Haven't you heard that the guards, each of them, have a turn at breaking in a new girl, and then they flog her by order of the Governor? After that she's good for pig food. Let the boys be revolutionaries.

So you want to leave it to us? All week I'm dragging lumber to the train station in Plotsk. On *Shabbas,* do I need to print pamphlets so that someone can get arrested and rot in jail? Who needs more trouble? A drunken peasant knocks you on the head, you're finished. An officer doesn't like the shape of your nose, you're finished. You have an accident in the factory, you're finished. You can't pay the Jews' tax, you're finished.

"In Plotsk kids sleep in the street. Where are they supposed to go? That's how it is," Avram said. "In America, it's another story. How would Emma know?"

"Is that what you think after everything I told you?" Emma asked, looking first at her cousin then at each of her friends in turn. "I held babies that died," she said, so quietly they leaned forward to hear her. "Their mothers so sick from work they had no milk. I saw kids that died, younger than me. Their heads bashed in by cops during a strike. Who knew their names?" she asked, her voice louder. "We're brothers and sisters. We watch out for one another. Have you forgotten how we all pitched in when our friend Henya was on strike? You didn't have to go begging to the community council for a *Shabbas* basket. Before you could ask we gave you." Her friends were looking at one another, nodding. "You said you wanted to dance, Rivka. Did anyone laugh at you? Did anyone say you don't deserve it? No, we danced together, right here. And soon we'll dance in Plotsk, even in Warsaw. Did you for-get?" Rivka smiled shyly, remembering one of the boys fiddling like a wild Gypsy, girls and boys tumbling in each other's arms, arms and legs flying with no sense of propriety.

"Put out your hands," Emma said. "Do it." The girls and boys stretched out their arms, opening their hands palms up. "Look at us. Don't we have the same hands? Red and hard from working by the clock? That's why we share what we have. Not one of us is alone, here." Emma reached out for Henya's hand on her right and Avram's on her left. "*May my right hand wither if I abandon thee, fellow workers shall know why, we swear our oath of blood and tears, together to live or die.*" The girls and boys took each other's hands. Joining Emma, they sang their oath.

"Fine words," said Lev, chewing on a birch twig. He was the old-est, a man of nineteen. "But fine words won't stop a peasant from beating you up or keep you warm in Siberia. I'm getting married soon and I've got a good job starting in Plotsk at the new saw mill." He stood up, breaking the circle, and sauntered back between the fir and birch trees. Emma looked up uneasily as if she could see herself above in the misty in-between.

IN MID-JUNE the days were long, and in the bakery the girls laughed as Emma, wrapped around in an apron, flour on her nose, her braids sweeping the table, struggled with a mound of sticky rye dough. Like this, they said, like this, patting and rolling the dough that in Emma's hands had been worked to a gray, gooey mass. The youngest was hug-ging her around the knees. "Tell me the story again, Emma."

"Which one?"

"The girl that was Dov's friend."

"You mean Emma Goldman?"

"No, no. The girl that had the red coat."

"Little Red Riding Hood?"

"Yes." Dina nodded, pulling on Emma's apron. "The one who tricked the Big Bad Boss and got her granny's pay."

"I'll tell you next time. Now I've got to go." Emma took off her apron. "I told Auntie that I'd bring these to Plotsk today." Emma waved at a bag on the bench. "I've got to pick up more piecework."

"It's a long walk," Ruthie's mother said. "If you go tomorrow Shmuel can take you."

"It's only two hours."

"Even with that big bag over your shoulder?"

"It isn't heavy."

"Buttonholes?" Faygela asked.

"No. Fake daisies for ladies' hats."

"How was the shop?"

"Hot and crowded," Emma said. "Plenty of lice. One of the girls fainted and when I told the boss she needed some air, he pushed me out the door." Slinging the bag over her shoulder, Emma asked, "Can I take some buns to Ruthie?"

THE TWO girls sat side by side on a bench in Ruthie's cell, chewing on the buns. "Don't have such a long face," Ruthie said. "I'll be home before you know it."

"Sure," Emma said with an effort. "You'll be dancing at Lev's wedding. After that, according to your sister Freydel, you're next. She's already making plans for her new dress."

"Oh, that Freydel. She shouldn't spend every *Shabbas* afternoon reading Shomer. Those romances fill her head with nonsense. Listen to me, Emma, I don't ever want to get married."

"You?"

"Don't look so surprised. I've got nothing to do here but think, and I've decided. I only have one life, only one Ruthie, and if I get out of here, I'm not going to waste it."

"You're right. Why should you get married? Back home, my friends just live with someone they love, and when their love finishes they part and no one is upset. Red Emma, she lived with two men and loved them both. Then Sasha went to prison and . . ."

"Enough already. It's always a man, even with you," Ruthie said. "One, two, what difference does it make? I don't want any of them."

The two young prostitutes sitting with their arms entwined on the other side of the cell giggled. "Of course, always it's a man," they said.

"I'm not selling my soul," Ruthie whispered to Emma, "not for a wedding canopy and not for free. One baby after another making me nervous and upset? No. I'm going to be independent like Misha was before she got herself into trouble. And who brought her down?" Ruthie asked agitatedly. "Nobody knows for sure, but it wasn't an angel, I can tell you. It was some man."

The cell was hot and the others had stripped down to their under-things. The murderess was darning her stockings, the lumpy woman who had been pretending to be deaf and mute was rocking herself back and forth, humming tunelessly. The two young prostitutes were tearing advertisements out of an old newspaper and laying them on the floor, creating paper dolls and a paper house, which they furnished amicably, arguing only over whether it was by the sea or in the Lazienki Gardens in Warsaw. The girls had grown pale. Their freckles stood out in dismay, their hair limp and colorless. They had welts on their arms and neck, marks of the guards' attentions. How could they ignore everything and play with their paper dolls, Emma wondered.

"You have to come home soon," she said to Ruthie. "We can't get organized without you. Avram loses pieces of type. Henya dropped half the new pamphlets in the river. We just keep falling over, like a cart with three wheels."

"So I'm a wheel, am I?" Ruthie asked, pretending to be offended, tossing her head and glancing at Emma out of the corner of her eye.

"Don't be mad, Ruthie. We miss you, that's all. Look here, look what I brought you." Emma thrust a tall, narrow book in Ruthie's face. It was the English herbal, and as Ruthie turned to look at it, she saw that someone had written between the lines in a painstakingly neat Yiddish. "You see, I started to translate it, but I don't know a lot of the plant words. You'll have to help me. I made Freydel sneak it out of the house and then I worked at it every spare minute."

"Emma, you're an angel," Ruthie said, hugging her friend. "I promise, when I get home, I'll show you every plant in the book."

"EMMA," the Traveler said in the grayness of her delirium. "Emma, you should be going home now."

"I have to finish this garment." She began to sew again, furiously, as if she had no time to lose. "My mama's expecting it."

"They miss you. Didn't you hear your auntie crying? Faygela's gone home and Ruthie went to get Misha. She's all alone."

"I don't know what you're talking about. Great-aunt Alta-Fruma just left the dairyhouse. Hayim is working for her. Can't you see him lifting the vat? There she is walking into the house. Oh, she's mad at me again."

The Traveler shook his head. "No, Emma. You're in bed. You're sick. She's crying."

"You have it all wrong. Just take a look."

Down below in Blaszka, Alta-Fruma was standing in front of Emma, shaking a finger at her. "Here comes Ruthie with a bucket full of raspberries and you want to walk to Plotsk in the hot sun," Alta-Fruma was saying. She stood between Emma and the door, holding onto Emma's bag of piecework. Sweat was beading on Emma's forehead. It was hot in July.

"I have to go."

"I don't understand you, Emma. You gave enough to the community council. I'm not so poor that I can't feed you. There's always work in the dairy if you have nothing to do. But more piecework? What for?"

"I just want to do it." Emma pulled on the bag her auntie was gripping with both hands.

"Then tell me. Just tell me why." Alta-Fruma put the bag behind her back.

"The girls in the prison don't have monthly cloths or blankets. I just want to get them some," Emma said.

Alta-Fruma sighed. "If it's for charity, then I'll help you."

"It's not charity. It's to free the workers from the oppression of the overseers."

"Fine. Good. You go and eat raspberry tarts with Ruthie and I promise that you can do some piecework afterward." She took one of Emma's hands and turned it over. "But not until these hands are not red anymore. I'll give you some old rags that you can cut up for monthly cloths. And I'm sure I have an extra blanket somewhere. Look, here's Ruthie. Go. I don't want to hear another word."

As they walked to the bakery, Ruthie and Emma swung the heavy bucket between them. "It's so dry. What I wouldn't give for a little rain," Ruthie said. "So, Emma rainmaker, would you oblige me?"

"Don't be silly. Clouds bring rain. I bring revolution."

"Misha's vegetables are wilting. Just a nice soft rain, Emma."

"All right." Lifting her left hand, Emma looked up at the sky and said, "Rain for the revolution!"

When they reached the bakery they were soaked, Ruthie laughing and shouting at her sisters, "Emma made it rain."

"Shh. It was just a joke."

"Could Dov make it rain?" the youngest sister asked.

"Even better, he could make a boss pay his employees," Emma answered.

IN THE gray haze, she watched the secret nights of August ripen the blueberries. Below in Blaszka she scratched at the bites of small insects.

RUTHIE, seating herself under the shade of a linden tree, pulled Emma down beside her. "All right, all right," Emma said, setting her bucket on a stump nearby. The girls leaned against the tree trunk, their heads bent over a book dappled with sun and the shadow shapes of leaves. Ruthie held a stalk of comfrey, its roots dangling, next to the book, pointing first to the parts on the plant, then to the diagram in the book. "You see, Emma? It's a common plant, one of the first ones that Misha told me about. It grows in wet fields like near the river. As a poultice, it's very good for wounds and bites, and for someone who's spitting up blood, you make an infusion of it for her to drink."

"You mean like the girls in the sweatshop?"

"Uh-huh," Ruthie said. Lying back on the ferns, Ruthie stretched her arms above her head and wriggled her toes inside her boots. "You don't know how good it is to be home."

"It's so hot. Let's go wading in the river. Come on, lazy." Emma kicked the sole of Ruthie's boots.

Where the river ran fast and white around the silver rocks, the girls held hands, balancing themselves precariously. On the shore, their dresses and boots were slung over a tree branch. They could see the ruins of the mill on the other bank, ancient under the dome of blue sky, a single swirl of cloud skirting the bridge. An orange cat, one ear tilted forward, the other half-chewed, was creeping across a mossy log that joined the bank to a rock in the river, where a pair of turtles were basking in the sun. Overhead a family of black ducks quacked, and the cat, torn between the turtles and the birds, leaped awkwardly, falling into the river. Ruthie laughed and Emma wasn't quite sure if she fell accidentally or on purpose, pulling Emma with her, but soon the girls were drenched, braids undone, their shifts transparent, water dripping like a fountain from their chins, and when Ruthie drank from Emma's fountain, she had to laugh and scream and push Ruthie away, her hands tingling strangely where they had touched Ruthie's chest.

Breathlessly the girls climbed up the bank. They put their dresses back on over wet shifts, pulling stockings and boots onto muddy feet, and as they squelched under the trees, they decided to check on the hut in the woods. A summer storm might have pulled off the roof and the type should be put in order. It was there that they found Hershel the butcher, head of the community council, in the process of dismantling the press.

INSIDE HER delirium Emma yelled at the Traveler, "It's not fair. The printing press didn't belong to the community council. We worked hard to fix it up. It wasn't anybody's business what we were doing. Hershel had no right to boss us around. I tried to stop him. Ruthie was trying to pull me away, but I stood right in front of the printing press. Hershel threw me aside like I was nothing. Nothing. Then he hacked at the press. All our hard work gone for nothing. I promised Dov I'd carry on. I promised."

DOWN BELOW, Emma was tossing her head from side to side in Alta-Fruma's bed. She moaned, tears running down her cheeks.

IN THE nothingness, the Traveler put an arm around her, but she shrugged him off, laying her head on her arms over the white garment on the table. He waited until, with a half-sob, Emma said, "Without the printing press, how will I carry on the work? I promised Dov I would. Before I left America. He was in the hospital and I held his hand and I told him I'd carry on. My mama said that somebody has to fight for a decent life for everyone. My mama told me. You understand? And that nurse said . . . she said that Dov couldn't understand a word. But I didn't believe her. He didn't have the bandages on his head anymore. He looked like he was just thinking with his eyes closed. The nurse said he was in a coma, he couldn't hear anything. But how did she know?" Emma waved at the Lower East Side floating above the grayness. "Don't you see?"

"No," the Traveler said.

"Why can't you see? Just look up there. You can see it all. Delancey Street. Elizabeth. Hester."

The Traveler took Emma's hands. "It's Tishah-b'Av, Emma. The Holy Ark in the synagogue is draped in black. It's time for you to go home."

"Just look up. Please. You have to see."

The Traveler looked up. "I don't see the hospital. I see you carrying cloaks. And it looks like there's a strike."

"I had to," she pleaded. "I had to work to keep Izzie in school. I swore I'd never break a strike again. But we needed the money. I did the finishing so my mother could work in the factory. The Miracle Cloaks factory. She made twice as much. And then she . . . it was all my fault. If she'd been working at home . . . Some days I can't even remember her face. It was a year ago. Exactly a year ago. Oh, just look."

ON THE Lower East Side of New York, Hester Street was thick with placards. WE WANT 8 HOURS WORK. IN UNITY IS OUR STRENGTH. FEREINIGUNG IZ MAHT. LUNIONE FO LA FORZA. CLOSED SHOP AND OPEN DOORS. Men and boys in dark coats, white shirts, ties, bowler hats, and woolen caps walked ten abreast between the tenements, arms linked, small American flags tucked under elbows. Behind them strode the women and girls, solemn and scrubbed and shawled, singing, *"We swear our stalwart hate persists, Of those who rob and kill the poor; The Tsar, the masters, capitalists. Our vengeance will be swift and sure."*

The sun was a moonlike disk in the west, burnishing the red jacket of the man walking beside Emma. He was a big-shouldered man and tall, his beard curling silver, around his neck a medallion of Karl Marx on a black ribbon. He nodded kindly at Emma even though she was obviously breaking the strike, her head and shoulders loaded with finished cloaks. Emma kept her head low as she hurried through the market toward Elizabeth Street.

Stumbling along Elizabeth Street, her vision blocked by the load of cloaks, Emma couldn't see what was going on when she heard the sound like a gunshot. "Cops," she yelled. "Run." Then a blast of heat lifted her and flung her against an iron fence. Something thick and sticky trickled into her mouth. Emma threw her arm over her face. There was a flash of red and green, like fireworks, the stench of tar, black smoke bursting like a tornado, the scream of a horse, running feet, rasping voices, "Where are you? This way!" A brick clanged against the metal bar above her left shoulder. Her eyes streaming. She squinted through the gritty, wavering air that juggled streetlamps. Fire wagons. Horses. Hoses. Water hissing in slow motion. The whole street seemed to be burning. Dear God, Emma prayed. Let it not be them. I'll go to synagogue every week, just let them be safe. One of the strikers squatted beside her. The man in the red jacket. "Get along, miss. It's not safe here."

"The factory. Which one is it?"

"Don't know. The whole street could go up. You've got to get out of here."

He pulled her to her feet. "No," Emma said. "I can help. It's a cold night. I have cloaks. Someone might be cold."

He slung an armful of cloaks over his shoulder. "We'll take them with us. Come to the strike office."

Emma clutched his hand like a little girl.

In Doc's Drugs on Chrystie Street, Emma sat on the counter, hanging onto a mug of coffee laced with brandy. Emma Goldman wrapped the girl in one of the cloaks, stroking her cheek with hands red and scraped from heaving bricks.

"Where's Dov?"

"The cops hit him on the head," Emma Goldman said. "He's in the hospital."

"Is he all right?"

"We don't know yet." She put an arm around the girl's shoulders. Young Emma was shivering. "Damn cops," Emma Goldman said.

"Did you hear where the fire started? My parents were working."

"On Elizabeth Street?"

Young Emma nodded. "In the Miracle Cloaks factory."

"Listen, I'll go out and find out what's going on. Don't you budge."

Every time the door swung open, Emma whispered, "Please,

please," fingers crossed, heart rapping. The last straggler was settled, wounds dressed, and still Emma waited.

She was slumped in a sleeping heap on the counter when Emma Goldman's voice woke her. "Little Emma Blau."

"Did you find out?"

The woman took one of Emma's hands in hers. "It was the Miracle Cloaks factory. An explosion in the basement. Probably the benzene from the cleaners."

"My parents? Did you see them?"

"No."

"Are they at the hospital? Can you take me there? You can say I'm sixteen. I'll visit Dov, too. Let's go right away." Young Emma jumped off the counter.

The woman held her back. "Wait a minute. Here, drink this." She held out a bottle and Emma took a swig, gasping at the bitterness of it. "The firemen couldn't get anyone out of the building," Emma Goldman said, her arm around young Emma's waist. "The doors were locked so the boss could inspect the workers for pilfering before they left. I'm sorry, dear."

"My mother?"

"No, Emma. Nobody got out."

THE GARMENT was finished. Emma looked at the *kittel* she had sewn. Her father used to wear a *kittel* at the seder and on Yom Kippur. "A simple and pure garment," he would say. "Unadorned. And so in this we greet God on the holiest days, and in this we shall greet Him when we are buried."

"So you're finished," the Traveler said.

"Yes." Emma leaned back in her chair. "Finally it's finished. And I'm going to wear it." She began to shed her woolen patchwork—the jacket sleeve, the blue shirtwaist. From below came crying and Misha's voice. "She's burning up."

"Ready to go then?"

"Yes." Emma reached for the *kittel.*

The Traveler snatched the white robe and held it behind his back. "Just a minute. I had a look up there at the old days. Now it's your turn Emma. Come on, now."

Emma tilted her face upward. "But that's our old apartment," she said. "We moved out when I was five."

A WOMAN in a cotton nightgown, the collar threaded with red ribbon, sat on a narrow, straight-backed chair, rocking a cradle with her left hand. Her hair was in two long brown braids flecked with gold, her lips quivering in a half-smile. Between her knees stood a little girl about five years old, with eyes like midnight, her hands balled into fists and her cheeks red with indignation.

"Next time Papa hits me, I hit him back," she said.

"A little girl should respect her papa. He was very sad to hit you. He only did it to teach you. How could you throw his holy book onto the floor and jump on it, Emma?"

"I wanted to see if God's in the book. God isn't. The book tore. It's just paper. I told Papa. If God was in the book it wouldn't tear."

The woman lifted her onto her lap. "I will tell you a secret if you promise not to aggravate your papa."

"What?"

"Do you promise?"

"Yes."

"Good, and I know my daughter will keep it. The secret is that miracles aren't as important as what you say."

Emma shook her head. "No, Mama. Papa says that God makes miracles."

"Do you know what a miracle is?"

"Uh-huh. It's a flood. When it rained for forty days and forty nights and everybody drowned except Noah."

Curling Emma's hair around her fingers, Mama sighed and kissed her forehead. "Just remember what I'm telling you, Emma. Words do more than miracles."

"More than magic?"

"Yes."

"Can you say magic words?"

Her mother laughed. "Put your head on my shoulder and I'll tell you a story about when I was a little girl in Blaszka. My mother and my Auntie Fruma went to the river to bathe. I followed them even though it was night and I was supposed to be asleep. And do you know what I saw there in the moonlight?"

Emma looked closely but she didn't see any magic words coming out of her mother's mouth and before the story ended, she fell asleep.

IN THE grayness below Emma clutched the fedora. "Will I see her when I go?"

The Traveler sighed. "You'll be assigned, but even up here you don't get what you want. It's the Boss's decision." He put the finished whistle in one pocket, his small carving knife in the other.

"You mean there's a boss up here?"

The Traveler patted Emma's hands. "It won't be so different, Emma. The Boss gives the orders and you carry them out. Just remember that there's no argument. All right, Emma. Take your *kittel*. We're ready, now."

Putting her arms into the sleeves of the white robe, Emma paused. "What do you mean, *no argument?*"

"When you come up here, you just carry out your orders."

"What about your opinion?"

"It won't be much use to you in your new assignment. You're just the messenger. There's no strikes or demands. No agitation."

"I've changed my mind." She began to take off the *kittel*.

"Now? It's too late, Emma. The deal's made."

"What do you mean, too late? I never said for sure. A person's entitled to change her mind."

"A person, yes. A dead person, no."

"Aren't I still alive?"

"Hmm." He looked down. "What'll you give me if I let you go back?"

"I've got nothing."

"That could be a problem. I might need a bribe for upstairs. Wait. I know. Let your brother have the miracles. The Boss would like that."

"There's got to be something else. It's too embarrassing. I can't do it. Can you just see the headline? 'Famous Rabbi Makes Rain': 'Due to his extraordinary piety, Rabbi Isidore Blau is reputed to bring rain to the parched fields of Poland. Daily his circle of disciples grows.' And his followers—praying when they could be joining the revolution."

"Well, you get the revolution. The Boss gets the miracles. That seems fair."

"Let me give you something else. Please. How about I start going to synagogue?"

"No. Miracles or nothing. And you can keep the hat. Deal?"

Emma nodded. The Traveler pulled the whistle out of his pocket and blew on it.

IN THE coming year, Josef Mill will be sent by the Vilna group of Jewish socialists to establish The Jewish Worker's Union of Warsaw. Izzie will go to study at the yeshiva in Kovno. In time they will call him The Rainmaker.

In a hundred years, in Los Angeles, there will be a strike of the Needleworkers' Union, protesting sweatshop conditions of new immigrants and illegal aliens. Among the picketers will be a man in a ragged jacket, his copper hair like rooster feathers. He will have a red rose pinned to his jacket, and he will be bareheaded.

4

A PLAGUE OF FROGS

In the village square the old women stood in a clump as the black carriage stopped in front of Perlmutter's tavern. Who is it, what is it? they asked, the frost of their breath mingling. The Director came down from his perch in the driver's seat, whip still in hand, tipping his top hat to the gathering crowd. The carriage door opened, the actors emerged. Such colors, such feathers, such a rollicking tumble of pushing and falling and singing about bodily functions. The old women, who had lived through everything there was to live through, laughed until the tears fell from their eyes. The juggler frolicked with his bottles and plates and the silver samovar flying up to heaven like a Hasidic rebbe. The crowd, swollen with amazement, clamored for more, stamping their feet, shouting, whistling, children shyly pressed against their fathers' coats or boldly climbing over the carriage with its fancy yellow lettering, THE GOLEM PLAYERS.

The Director held up his black-gloved hands for silence. The door to the inn opened and closed. There was the smell of schnapps. A girl and boy came out, plainly dressed, standing together without touching. And then, as the violin began to sob, the smell of yearning opened into song. Leaning against each other, remembering, the old women asked, Where is Alta-Fruma? She should only see this. Warm breath melted the ice on the edge of their shawls, they clasped hands and wept. The women were old and knotty and strong, and they counted on Alta-Fruma to remember them as they were when they were young.

She wasn't a big talker, Alta-Fruma, but she could tell you exactly how you looked on your wedding day. Too bad she missed the excitement, they said, throwing a few kopecks into the basket the actors were passing around. That's Alta-Fruma, she has no luck. She's the kind of person who always gets the smallest piece. What can you do? It's a nature. She was never one to push herself forward, not like her sister Rakhel, may she rest in peace. Do you remember how Rakhel always had an opinion about everything? She would look at you as if she were Devorah, the Judge of Ancient Israel. Rakhel's daughter was something else altogether—Zisa-Sara ran around with the *vilda hayas,* but she was goodness itself.

Did you hear that Zisa-Sara's children are coming back to Blaszka today? Of course, a brother and sister. Poor Alta-Fruma. She's used to living alone and having things her own way. What will she do with two strange children? Well, the boy will go to heder and the girl can work in the dairy. Maybe she'll learn something from her great-aunt. No one makes cheese like Alta-Fruma, not from here to Plotsk. And her floor—the Tsarina could eat from it.

It's a shame that Alta-Fruma had no children of her own. A shame? I don't know. You get no thanks from your children, they just break your heart. Maybe it's better for her. What are you talking? Alta-Fruma was only nineteen when her husband disappeared, and no one knew what became of him. An abandoned woman is a pitiable creature. By Jewish law she's not marriageable, an *aguna.* They say her husband could show up at any moment. She's not meat and not dairy. Nobody knows—is she *parev* like fish or potatoes that can go with anything? Or is she, God forbid, *trayf?* I'm telling you, there's nothing worse than to be alone.

ALTA-FRUMA was on the other side of the bridge, walking and talking to herself. She needed to be alone, to think things out, and so she walked in the ruins, blending with the shadows and meandering through the deserted lanes, her gray shawl frothing in the wind. What did she know about raising children? *The boy will listen to reason. But the girl, to be frank, is a handful,* it said in the letter.

This side of the village was a place of weeds and reeds, the river seeping into every crevice, broken houses falling over, saplings sprouted in the deserted houses of the *shayner,* poplar and birch cracking the cobblestones, nettles clustered thick around the bathhouse and the well, apple trees twisted as Warsaw beggars creaking in the wind near Hayim the watercarrier's hut.

As Alta-Fruma came around Hayim's hut, she saw someone emerging from between the alders. Who was this? Yes, the *zogerin,* her hand to her head, straightening her wig. Hayim stood outside his hut, watching expressionlessly. He wore a long unbleached shirt like a peasant, his shoulders broad and steady as if he stopped the wind. His hair was long and his beard was long, thick, black, smooth, blowing over his shoulder like a scarf. When he was a boy, women used to pinch his round red cheeks, but in his forties Hayim was not a smiling man. He had eyes like a cat, narrow, gold, and unreflecting. His eyebrows slanted upward toward his nose, meeting in the center quizzically as if the world were a sad and puzzling place. Other men in Blaszka avoided the glance of women, but not Hayim. He looked intensely at all he saw. Alta-Fruma, narrow and gray as a shadow camouflaged by a cluster of leafless trees, gazed at him equally intensely, remarking the proportions of Hayim's body while the *zogerin* hurried across the bridge.

So should I be surprised? Alta-Fruma asked herself. The *zogerin* might be the women's prayer leader, but she's still a young woman, given away by her family to a fat old man for a husband. And why? For honor, for family lineage, because her husband, the ritual slaughterer, has some rabbis among his ancestors. The *zogerin* doesn't owe anyone a thing and I won't tell anyone about her, either, but she's a fool. Someone else will see and then everyone will know. Who in this village can keep a secret? Just Misha and I. A midwife has to know how to keep things to herself. Otherwise no woman could trust her. And I learned from my sister. Whatever she did, I did the opposite.

As she walked back through the overgrown lanes, Alta-Fruma took the letter from her pocket, reading it yet again and muttering to herself. "If the girl were like her mother, Zisa-Sara, I would know what to do with her. Zisa-Sara was a sweet child. But it seems that this Emma takes after her Grandmother Rakhel."

Alta-Fruma could see her sister Rakhel as if she stood right in front of her, those blue eyes that darkened when she was excited, studying with the tutor until Papa found out what she was learning. The beautiful sister. Rebellious. Stubborn. A will of iron. She did whatever she wanted while Alta-Fruma milked the cows and made cheese and supported the whole family. The most sensible woman in Blaszka, people said.

Of course she was sensible. She kept her business to herself. Did anyone know how she made her cheese? Or how much money she had? Or what she did in Warsaw? No. And so there was no reason for anyone to make any trouble for her. But however sensible Alta-Fruma was, there was the matter of her little gift. A talent of no consequence. Something she had inherited from some unknown ancestress, maybe through a vague connection her family had with Misha's. People said that Misha's great-grandmother, Manya, had been a witch. And this little talent Alta-Fruma had—well, she could turn herself into a frog. A tiny treefrog whose skin shone green as her eyes when it was on a leaf and gray as her shawl when it clung to the trunk of a tree. When she was a girl, after she milked the cows and cleaned out their stall and sold her cheese in the village square and washed the floor in the front room of the house and prepared the soup and mended her sister's stockings, she might find herself in the woods, riding a leaf flung by the wind onto a shiny pool where snails roused each other to a wet frenzy of merging and mosquitos were born with the wings of seraphim. The smell of water, the sharp edge of a leaf, the sweeping wind. Could she forget?

Rakhel, whenever she wanted to unnerve Alta-Fruma, would whisper in her ear: Witch! Even later, when it had been so long since Alta-Fruma had exercised her gift that she wondered if she ever had or if it had been a dream, Rakhel could still prickle the skin on her neck by whispering, "Witch."

So now Rakhel's grandchildren were coming home. Two children in the house putting their noses into everything. Children from America? Who knew what they were like?

She'd had plenty of advice from all the mothers in Blaszka. Use your hand. Use a stick. Don't listen to nonsense. Wash out a bad mouth with soap. They only have you now. If the boy's to learn Torah and the girl to make a good match, you have to be strict.

The women probably knew what they were talking about, but Alta-Fruma remembered that all the beatings her father gave her sister Rakhel didn't stop her from reading the books of heathens and heretics.

Walking back across the icy bridge, Alta-Fruma still didn't know what she would do with the children, and she was sure that in the short time before they arrived, she wouldn't become any wiser.

THE BOY stood beside his sister, hanging onto the sleeve of her coat, one of his socks fallen in a sad crumple over his cracked boot. The girl twisted and turned, looking up at the flat gray sky and down at the flat white earth as if to find a place high enough to stand on and shout. Shayna-Perl, the cart driver, had brought the children from the train station, lifting the heavy trunk herself while her stout gray horse snorted and frosted the air with swirls of his breath. Leaving the trunk under the weeping willows beside the house, her sheepskin jacket opened to the cold and her pipe clenched between her teeth, the carter left without a thought for how the trunk would get into the house.

"So this is Emma and Izzie. Come in, children, get warm," Alta-Fruma said. The girl took after Zisa-Sara with her high slanted cheekbones, the mole like a tiny fingerprint above her mouth and the brown braids threaded with gold, but she carried herself like Rakhel, at the brink of a leap, and her blue eyes were Rakhel's eyes.

Emma picked up one end of the trunk, leaning back, her heels dug into the snowy earth as she tried to drag the trunk toward the door. "You'll hurt yourself," Alta-Fruma said. "Wait. Faygela said she would send one of her girls to help."

"I don't need any help. Me and Izzie, we can take care of ourselves." She turned toward her brother. "Right?" she added in English. The boy nodded, putting out a small hand toward Emma's tough, brown fist.

"Emma took care of me. She always takes care of me," he said in English, then repeated in Yiddish as his great-aunt shook her head uncomprehendingly.

"At least come inside for a minute. Get warm. You think I need sick children in my house?" Alta-Fruma spoke harshly, hiding the pity she felt at the sight of the motherless children in coats that were short in the sleeves and tight in the shoulders and not too warm, either. The boy was shivering. A person has to be firm with children, she reminded herself, noting the jut of Emma's chin. "I'm not asking you, I'm telling you. Get inside."

Emma shook her head. Only when the trunk caught against a stone, she paused, then slowly let her end drop. "Let Izzie go in. I'll wait over here," she said, "with the trunk."

"Come inside and dress for *Shabbas*. We have a guest coming," Alta-Fruma said. "Misha was your mother's best friend when they were girls. You want to know something about your mother? Just ask Misha."

The girl looked as if she might say something, but then she sat on the trunk, crossing her arms. Stubborn? Like a mule. Like a mule and a goat put together. Another Rakhel.

THE DAY OF THE ICE STORM

On the eve of spring, Alta-Fruma was in Warsaw, sitting decorously on the edge of a brocade wing chair in a lawyer's office. She had a ticket for the afternoon train so she could be home in time for Purim, but when a person came to Warsaw, who could tell what might delay her?

Mr. Hoffmann, the lawyer, hadn't moved from the building on Nalewki Street where Alta-Fruma first met him, but instead of an attic chamber, he now occupied half a floor, his office crammed with furniture from the time of Napoleon. His sleeves were rolled up and tied around with black binding, his round face beaming, his glasses slipping on his nose.

As always when she came to Warsaw, Alta-Fruma wore a green silk dress that brought out the radiance of her eyes. Even a sensible woman, when she goes away, is allowed some vanity, even a woman of sixty who, in Blaszka, wears a black shawl over her holiday dress.

People who live to be old have their characters written into their skin, smiles and frowns etched in wrinkles even when the face is at rest. And yet it isn't enough for age just to show what people are. No, age is a trickster. A willowy beauty hardens into spikes, an athlete falls into fat and an ugly young man, like Hoffmann's manservant, gawky and freckled with a potato of a nose, could, in old age, stand tall and straight, drawing people to him with his wry smile.

At rest, Alta-Fruma's face was smooth, revealing nothing, the lines only faint marks, the freckles of her girlhood faded into a scattering of gold dust across the bridge of her nose. This is what the villagers would have seen had anyone really looked. But they knew who she was without looking, didn't they? In Warsaw, where no one knew her, a person might see that Alta-Fruma moved with a lithe and agile grace, her breasts were still firm handfuls, her teeth were good, and when she smiled, which wasn't often, her tongue darted out to lick her lips as if she were about to taste something very, very good. Leaning back in Adam Hoffmann's plushy brocade chair, Alta-Fruma was smiling. Her eyes, fringed with dark lashes and green as the souls of leaves, were as arresting as when the lawyer had first seen them.

"It's so good to see you again. Please have a glass of tea, and some cherry preserves. Do you know," he said shyly, the morning sun forming a square of light across his shoulders and face and the painting of the gondolier behind him, "it's thirty-one years today that you came to my office. Purim, 1863. I remember it like yesterday. You were running down the stairs, do you recall? I think old Mr. Plutzer frightened you I could hear him shouting two floors below. Everyone had the windows open to hear the speeches and the singing outside. It was a cold day, more winter than spring, even though it was March."

"Cold?" Alta-Fruma said, tapping the side of her glass. "My lips were blue."

"And in my office? I didn't have a fire to keep it warm. Wood was too expensive. I was up in the attic, remember?"

"Yes, with the dressmaker's dummy in the corner."

"Do you remember the marching in the streets?" Mr. Hoffmann rapped his right fist on the table, humming "da, da, da," his left fist swinging as if he marched with the Polish nationalists, waving the flag of independence. "*Jeszcze Polska nie zginęła,*" he sang.

"*Poland is still ours forever as long as Poles are free,*" Alta-Fruma said. "It made me nervous. You know what happens when people get excited? Like the old story of the Polish counts arguing about who is the truer patriot. 'We'll settle it like men,' they say. 'I'll beat up your Jew and you beat up mine.' "

"There were Jews marching in the street, too."

"Not you, thank God. You always saw both sides of every question, so you sat quietly at your desk."

"Yes, with my scarf wrapped around my neck while I shivered from the cold. Then I heard a yelling so loud it blocked out the singing in the streets."

"He had a voice like a bullfrog, Mr. Plutzer."

"You wouldn't think he was a man of seventy-five years. I'll never forget it.'Witch,' he yelled. 'Whore. How dare you come to my office alone, with your hair hanging out of your kerchief, talking like a man. A Jewish wife, shame on you. Your husband missing for ten years? May God deliver him to teach his wife modesty. Get out before I teach you myself.' I ran down the stairs to look. I was a shy man, but I wasn't dead. It was a year since my wife died, and after all, I was only twenty-five years old. 'Witch, whore,' it sounded very interesting." He reached across the desk to take Alta-Fruma's hand. "You were running down the stairs, but you turned once to look up and I saw your eyes. Green lightning. I was struck." He put his hand over his heart.

"It was a cold Purim," Alta-Fruma said, pulling her hand away gently. "A late frost." Even thirty years ago his hair had been receding, his broad forehead and spectacles giving him a mild look. It was only this mildness that had caused her to pause on the stairs when he called after her. That and his lips. Red as beets. She had wanted to touch them to see if his lips were as smooth as they looked in the wiry nest of his beard. She wouldn't easily forget. Not that Purim or many others she spent in Warsaw.

They would walk together to the old synagogue to listen to the reading of the Scroll of Esther. Afterward he would take her to a Purim play. It wasn't like the children's plays in Blaszka, or the men's performances with the same jokes year after year in Perlmutter's tavern. These were professional actors that made her laugh until her sides ached. They cavorted, they sang, they fell on their behinds with innocent surprise, they spouted nonsense in imitation of scholars, and, gazing with astonishment at their uncooperative arms, they attempted to fly to heaven as the Hasidim claimed their rebbes did. "Unrepentant, stubborn as a wilful child, do you see these arms?" they would appeal to the audience. "Absolutely refusing to turn into wings."

After the play, she would walk with him. Some years there was a warm current of spring in the air. Other years there were still lumps of snow in the shadows of stone buildings. Matching his stride to hers, he would ask, "Did you enjoy yourself? Did you, Frumala?" He would look at her with so much anxiety and hope about this little thing, her enjoyment, which no one else in the world had ever been concerned with. She couldn't help herself but to slip her hand into the crook of his elbow with a reassuring squeeze. Then they would have wine in a cafe, and why not? On Purim it was a virtue to drink so much that you couldn't tell the difference between Haman the murderer and Mordecai the savior. And afterward, when they lay together in the darkness, Alta-Fruma remembered the smell of water and the pulsing of the wind and snails slowly merging on the surface of a tiny pool.

Yet they had to be careful. Always careful. Holding back so neither of them would forget what to do. When she got home, she bit her nails and was sleepless until her period came. Eventually her luck ran out and, as for all the women in Blaszka, in a crisis there was no one better to turn to than Blema Fliderblum, Misha's mother.

It was just after Passover, she remembered, and her period hadn't arrived in the punctual manner to which she was accustomed. Faygela, eight years old, was standing on the steps of Blema's little house built on stilts above the riverbank. "Why don't they wait for me?" she was crying. From the river below, laughter came, and a glimpse of Misha. She was thin as a reed then. She looked like a spirit from the river with weeds in her long dark hair and her borrowed dress trailing over bare feet. "They're playing 'wedding' without me," Faygela complained. Misha was singing:

> *"Who asked you to get married?*
> *Who asked you to be buried alive?*
> *You know that no one forced you.*
> *You took this madness on yourself."*

The *badkhan* had sung this song at Alta-Fruma's wedding and at Rakhel's, too. Rakhel's daughter, Zisa-Sara, was sitting on the bank, protesting, "No, Misha. Give me the doll. The baby has to be mine. You don't have a husband."

"I do so. I have two. A fat one and a rich one."

"Two," Zisa-Sara laughed.

"They're being silly, I'm going home," Faygela said just as Hanna-Leah emerged from the forest, calling to her, "The woods are full of greens. Get your basket, lazy." Alta-Fruma watched the child run off happily. How careless they were, how ignorant.

Inside the house, Blema was pouring vodka into a tincture of some herb. The room was neat, sunlight finding its way easily through the clean windows to the jars and bottles arranged on shelves in order of size, a braided rug centered on the floor, the eastern wall marked with an embroidered landscape, the *Tzena-U-Rena* between the candlesticks on the bridal trunk below. Misha's mother was a woman of average height, neither fat nor thin, calm-voiced and reserved, with nimble hands and serious eyes. She was as ordinary as a woman of her family could be, but she had refused to remarry after her husband died two years earlier, during the cholera epidemic. This was enough for people to talk. A widow alone with her unruly daughter in a house that shakes with the spring rains, what could be in her mind? Don't forget who she is. Manya's granddaughter.

Everyone knew that Manya had been tried as a witch by the Polish court. Only thirty-five and her hair had turned white. She'd left two little girls, no one even knew who their father was. Did an apple ever fall far from the tree?

"I need something to make my period regular again," Alta-Fruma said to Blema.

"How many times did you miss it?" she asked, looking at Alta-Fruma easily, without judgment and with no hunger for the shameful details, even though she was Rakhel's best friend, and so entitled to some curiosity about her friend's sister, the good sister, the modest sister, the always disapproving sister, coming to her with this.

"Once," Alta-Fruma said, her voice cracking. She felt old. Too old for this kind of problem.

"Once, that's good." Blema looked along the row of jars until she found what she wanted. "This will make you regular," she said, measuring out a dose. Alta-Fruma drank it. "And this will keep you from bleeding too heavily." She handed her a glass of something else. "If your belly hurts more than usual, that's to be expected after missing a period. But if the blood flows freely, like from a wound that can't be staunched, then you should send someone for me right away." Alta-Fruma nodded nervously.

Her period came with a terrible cramping, but the nausea vanished and so did the bloating. Alta-Fruma was grateful that her life was not ruined, though afterward she'd avoided Blema, who knew too much about her.

When she went to Warsaw after that, Adam still took her to Purim plays. Sometimes they drank wine. As the years passed, sometimes she found herself with him in the darkness again. But she was tense. When he began to think about marrying, she encouraged him.

She'd missed her period just before her thirty-sixth birthday. And now Blema's daughter Misha would be turning thirty-six. So young. So very young.

ADAM PUT his hand over hers, again. "Frumala, Frumala, how I've missed you," he said.

"It's not to be spoken of," she answered. "I'm here."

"Thank the Holy One above," he said.

"And I need you to take care of things. What if, God forbid, something happens to me? The children have to be provided for."

"But do you remember the cafe where we used to have tea?" he asked. "The bookstore in front, then the archway and the cafe in back."

She didn't resist him, allowing herself for a moment to enjoy, again, the sensation of his fingers stroking her skin. "You mean the one right here on Nalewki Street," she said. "With the damask curtains and the cherubs on pedestals?"

"Yes, that's it."

"Everyone called the owner Ginger Dybbuk because of his mustache. As red as fire."

"He let the place run down," Adam said. "But I heard that his son came back and took it over."

"Ginger Dybbuk had a son?"

"Who knew? But they say he did. And now the cafe is always crowded. Maybe you heard of the son? He was the Director of the Golem Players. It took their last kopeck to bribe the station master.

The troupe went to America, and the Director came to Warsaw to take over his father's business. What do you say, Frumala? Let's go to the Golem Cafe for a cup of tea like in the old days." He brought her hand to his still smooth lips, kissing the palm. "Your business can wait an hour."

Inside the doorway of the bookstore on Nalewki Street, six copper bells, the color of the Director's mustache, shimmied in the draft as the door opened and closed behind each new customer. Beyond the archway, Adam and Alta-Fruma sat in a corner of striped shadows, the red glow from a shaded kerosene lamp lighting the naked cherubs.

Adam looked at her and then away. "Don't go. Stay with me, tonight. I miss you."

"It can't be the way it was," she protested, but she didn't move his hand from its warm place on her knee. So many years, she thought, so many memories. A person needs a scribe to keep them in order. "Your wife?"

"She's not well." There was a change in him, she noticed, a plump quiveriness in his cheeks that had never been there before.

"Years ago the city was so exciting," she said, wondering when the mildness that had attracted her had turned into this jellyish something she couldn't quite name.

"It's still exciting. Stay with me," he pleaded.

"In Warsaw nobody but you knows me," Alta-Fruma said. "I used to think it was a dream. One can do anything in a dream." He had been so unlike the learned men of her childhood who tolerated no grays, only black and white, kosher and *trayf,* pure and impure, condemning her to the no-man's land of the *aguna,* the abandoned woman. Even a heretic can repent on Yom Kippur, but where is there redemption for an *aguna?*

"Yes, yes. A dream, exactly," he said.

"But for you, Adam, it's not a dream. You have a home. You have a wife now." But for him, the lines of every dispute were blurred. She had found it endearing that he wiped his spectacles compulsively as if he could never quite clear his vision. Now it irritated her.

"She's a sick woman. Half the time she doesn't even know me," Adam said, wiping his glasses. "In a big city like Warsaw, who's to know if I have a little pleasure?"

"Warsaw doesn't seem as big as it used to. I know it too well," she said. "I'm in this place or that place, it's all the same. Can I pretend that I'm someone else?" She shook her head.

"It was a mistake," Adam said. "At my age to marry a girl of twenty. I should have known something was wrong when the *shadkhen* was so eager for the match. Now I have my punishment." A tear welled up in the corner of his eye, a fat spider of a tear that climbed down his cheek and settled on his beard.

"There's no magic that can put the first Adam and our mother Eve back in *Gan Aeden*," she said, avoiding his eyes, giving him time to regain his dignity. "God gives a person his part and he has to play it."

"What does it matter if we're together?" He gripped her hand as if the pressure of his fingers could convince her.

The light flickered as the Director passed between the lamp and the table. "More tea?" he asked. "Another slice of babka? Or perhaps some news? I hear so much of interest from my patrons."

Alta-Fruma withdrew her hand from Adam's. "I don't hold with gossip. A human being is entitled to his secrets."

"Just between us, the three of us," the Director said, leaning toward her.

"Then let me tell you. Three people can keep a secret easily only if two of them are corpses."

The Director laughed, his mouth wide with gleaming white teeth in front and dark hollows behind. "Dear lady," he began, but his voice cracked. "Pardon the frog in my throat," he said, laughing again. "But you are right, of course. Silence is, shall we say, made of gold. And perhaps speech is nothing more than paper money. Wouldn't you agree?" He turned to Hoffmann.

"Maybe. But on the other hand . . . it's possible . . ." Adam murmured.

That was Adam. No opinion. "I don't agree with you at all," Alta-Fruma said. "Everyone knows that gold speaks louder than paper. If someone's in trouble, you need at least a few silver rubles in a pot. Or gold imperials even better."

NOT LIKE her parents who didn't have a kopeck to get her brother out of the draft. He was snatched by a *khapper*, kidnapped, a boy of thirteen sent into the army for thirty years, lost to them. Rakhel had begged Alta-Fruma to use her gift to find out where Ephraim was to be stationed. So when the *khapper* got drunk, he probably didn't notice the little frog under the table. And was that Alta-Fruma? Not on your life. Alta-Fruma just asked the barmaid to tell what she heard in exchange for some good cheese.

By morning, the family knew that the boy was going to the Crimea and they all mourned. Alta-Fruma's brother probably died in the Crimean War, but who could know for sure? Her husband ran away to avoid the draft, and whether he lived or died no one would ever know, either.

Alta-Fruma decided that since no one could do anything for her, she'd better manage on her own. When the Tsar began to print paper rubles to finance the Crimean War, Alta-Fruma said, "No one's going to trust Russian money if it's made from paper." Whatever she could save she took to Warsaw and bought gold. Then the Tsar took it into his head to build railways. Rakhel read in *The Israelite* that soon cotton would go from Turkistan to Łodz, and a regular person could buy a railway bond. "Good. At last the Tsar is getting a little smart," Alta-Fruma said. "He's learning from the English instead of sending Jewish boys to stand in front of their cannons." So she bought a few bonds. But a railway doesn't come from the angels. You need steel to build it. So she bought a little piece of South Russian Dnieper Metallurgical Company. This was how it went. A little of this and a little of that. "You think it's magic?" she'd asked Rakhel. "No. Just plain sense."

"BUT EVEN gold won't buy off a Cossack," the Director said, tapping his forehead. "You see this scar? It came from the tip of a Cossack's saber. He wanted to show that he could kill me if he chose."

"Why didn't he?" Adam asked.

"The Cossack let me go because I laughed. That's the only way to contend with Cossacks in this life. A good laugh. If you're too serious, they'll bury you."

"Some advice," Alta-Fruma said. "At my age I have a little experience of life and I'll tell you something about Cossacks. A pig is worse. A Cossack rides through the village how often? When there's a war or a rebellion. Maybe every twenty years. People write books and they talk about it for the next twenty years. But a person has to contend with pigs every day. This morning I got up before it was light to get the early train to Warsaw and I heard a terrible noise coming from the cellar. What do you suppose I saw? A pig ransacking my cellar. Worse than a Cossack. The watercarrier's pig ate half my potatoes and turnips. It's nothing to laugh about. But what can I do? When you live with people in a small village, you can't afford to upset anyone. Otherwise before you know it, half the village isn't speaking to you."

"And that's all?" the Director asked.

"Yes. God's will is God's will," Alta-Fruma answered virtuously, perhaps even smugly, since, at least in Warsaw, there was no Emma to contradict her.

The Director shook his head in disbelief. "Why, if it were me," he said, "I would not hesitate for an instant. I would proceed to this Hayim, that was what you called him, yes? I would inform him that he had best repay me for my trouble. A pig eating the fruit of your hard work. Potatoes and the turnips, too? The very least this Hayim could do is to plant your spring garden to replenish what his pig so rudely consumed. That's what I would do," he said, brandishing his pipe.

Alta-Fruma nodded. What kind of a Jew lives like a peasant in the woods with a pig for company? she thought. Everyone knows that the farmers' women, while their miserable men are looking for work in Warsaw or Łodz or Berlin, come to Hayim in the night. Any lonely woman within ten kilometers knows the way to Hayim's hut. Ten? No twenty. Fifty. Even the *zogerin*. But even so, it wasn't her business. Let every person mind his own house and leave others' alone. That's how you keep peace. Better to ignore the pig.

As the Director moved away to pour tea at other tables, Adam wiped his glasses again. "Frumala?" he asked. There was a sore starting in the corner of his mouth and the hand that was trying to hold onto hers was clammy with nervous sweat.

"It's no use," she said. "You're married and I have two children waiting for me in Blaszka. If I'm going to catch the afternoon train, we had better go back to the office and finish the business."

*   *   *

WHEN ALTA-FRUMA came home, only Izzie was inside studying at the table. The sky darkened and still Emma was out somewhere. What could she be up to? Alta-Fruma began to think of children falling into rivers and drunken peasants waylaying girls alone on the road. Wasn't there the story of Zelig the grain merchant's daughter who disappeared? She was just a few years older than Alta-Fruma. A pretty girl. He wanted to marry her off to someone and she ran away. No one knew what became of her. Ten years later he said he'd found out that she'd died, never mind how. Then he cheated his partner, Faygela's grandfather, of everything he had, and left the village. His daughter wasn't even buried in Blaszka.

The door slammed as Emma came walking in, her cheeks red from the wind.

"Where were you?" Alta-Fruma asked. "It's late."

"I had things to do."

"What kind of things?"

"That's my business."

"Your business is my business as long as you're in this house. Where were you?"

"Go ahead. Smack me." The girl lifted her chin. How Alta-Fruma wanted to slap her.

"God help me, what am I going to do with you?" Alta-Fruma's hand fell. She shook her head. "Never mind." What use was it? She would never be able to talk any sense into Emma, not any more than she'd been able to talk sense into Rakhel.

SEASON OF RAINS

Passover. Chicken soup bubbled on the cooking grate, the brisket was in the oven, a plate of egg noodles and a bowl of sweet glazed carrots waited on the sideboard. The table was set with its oddly matched Passover dishes and gleaming crystal, Alta-Fruma sitting with Emma on one side of the table and on the other Izzie and the guest he'd brought home from the synagogue. Hayim, his beard a rectangle of black silk against his white robe, looked away from Alta-Fruma and back again, his cat's eyes absorbing everything.

She knew all about Hayim, as everyone knows about everyone in a place like Blaszka. Who he was, that is, who his parents were, and what his position was in the village. His father was the miller, a rich man, and Hayim had an easy life, with private tutors. Then the mill was destroyed, his father died of a broken heart, and his impoverished mother remarried a man who, it turned out after the wedding night was celebrated, had no desire for a stepson. She moved to her new husband's home in a shtetl near Minsk, and Hayim was left to fend for himself in Blaszka, the mother sending him whatever she could, which wasn't a lot, until he grew up. When he was seventeen, the community council made a match for him with an older woman from Plotsk. A cracked boot, they called her, because so many men had worn her. But she didn't live long and then, when Hayim was twenty-eight, they married him off to Misha. She got a divorce from him before the year was out. No one knew why.

He had a gift for drawing a person's likeness. Half the houses, not only in Blaszka but also the villages upriver, had a charcoal portrait drawn by Hayim. But still, what was he? A watercarrier. Nothing was lower. His work was among the women, who bossed him around: Hayim, I need water. A turtle moves quicker. *Shabbas* is coming, can I cook with air? Hurry, Hayim, hurry. Among the men, his seat in the synagogue was in the shadowy corner farthest from the Holy Ark, the cabinet where the Torah scrolls rested in their velvet robes and silver crowns. In the back corner, Hayim was little seen and less heard. This was considered to be a good thing because he stammered when he spoke, and only God the Eternal had the patience to wait for Hayim to finish. Lucky for Hayim that women didn't want him to speak. Some said that the insatiable demon Lilith had come to Hayim in the night and had left, worn out and satisfied. Even though he was already forty-four, there wasn't a single gray hair in his beard. There you had proof that the demons protected him from the Evil Eye.

But on Passover it was a mitzvah to have a guest. And was it so bad to have a man there to pour the wine and chant the story of the Exodus and to look at Alta-Fruma from time to time with his cat's eyes as gold as honey? Izzie was listening with rapt attention, looking over Hayim's shoulder at the Haggadah, translating into Yiddish for the women while his sister fidgeted.

"Plagues," Emma said. "Is that the God you believe in? A magician turning water into blood."

"An unbeliever," Alta-Fruma apologized. "Don't pay any attention, Hayim. Please. Continue."

"N-no. It's, it's all right. A child should ask questions."

"Well, how can you read all that superstitious stuff?" Emma asked. "Blood, frogs, lice, hail."

"You made it hail, Emma," Izzie said.

"Don't be silly. It was just a coincidence. And what about the death of the firstborn? It was probably some kind of disease. That's what Dov told me."

Hayim was listening to the children, looking from one to the other, his eyes serious, until Emma and Izzie had said all they had to say and were quiet, waiting.

"You, you know what I wonder?" he asked. The children shook their heads. "Why did, did God harden Pharaoh's heart?"

"There," Emma said. "You see. Why do you want to believe in a God like that?"

"So I can ask questions," Hayim answered.

"Let me ask you a question, Hayim." Alta-Fruma smiled, the tip of her tongue touching her lips. She would ask him how he got his pig—a Jew with a pig! But see how he leaned forward, his hands clasped on the table, his shoulders straining the white robe, his whole body concentrating on what it was she might have to say. And suddenly she wanted to know something else, something entirely different, as if she were riding across a shiny pool, her eyes wide open. She had never seen a man naked. It had always been in the darkness. Always under a sheet. And she wanted to see. Before she died, she would like to see it all. Such thoughts. Not sensible at all. And Hayim was looking at her, waiting for the question that she couldn't ask. She had to say something. Anything.

"Did you ever hear the story of the frog princess?" she asked. Why she asked this particular thing, she couldn't say. But once she began she couldn't stop. "My sister read the story to me. It's Russian."

Alta-Fruma leaned forward, her hands flat on the holiday tablecloth, her eyes looking into Hayim's so that she could see the pupil of his eye dilating. "The Frog Princess was betrothed to the youngest son of a human king," she said, "and through her talents brought the boy a kingdom. And how did he treat her? When she appeared as a human bride, he found and burned her frog skin. Because of what he did, the Princess was captured by the old *Baba Yaga* who had turned her into a frog in the first place, and there were many trials until the Prince and Princess were reunited. What kind of a story is that? It doesn't make any sense."

Hayim nodded. "I see," he said.

"You see what?"

"It's the, the story of our Mother Sarah."

"What are you talking?" Alta-Fruma asked.

"Yes, it's true." Hayim became excited, forgetting to stammer. "Wasn't our Mother Sarah a prophet even wiser than Father Avraham? So it's written in the Talmud and the Midrash. She had to pretend to be his sister in Egypt to save his life. Was she his wife then? No, a frog. And then weren't there trials? Yes, many trials. And in the end, when Sarah was old, she was as beautiful as a young woman." The children were staring at Hayim and Alta-Fruma.

"Fairy tales," Emma sniffed. "Exactly what I said. Religion is just another fairy tale."

But Hayim said slowly, "You, you have to look, look hard to see what's there inside." Hayim looked at Alta-Fruma and she looked at him.

"Go on," Izzie said. And Hayim did. But by the end of the seder he had agreed to plant Alta-Fruma's garden in compensation for the damage his pig had done to her root cellar.

THE FIRST week of May. The Friday after Passover. While the children were still asleep, Alta-Fruma opened the door to watch the sky awaken. It was her favorite time of day, after she said her morning prayers, when the sun was still yawning, like a man coming from dream to wakefulness with slow pleasure, opening his eyes and smiling in a glow of welcome at the woman in his bed. Alta-Fruma stretched slowly to ease her morning stiffness, inhaling the smell of earth in spring as she walked, barefoot, into the yard. The hens scattered before her sweeping broom, loose pebbles and twigs flying. They squawked and scolded, making little runs at her toes as if they were plump worms, but never quite pecking. She stood for a moment, looking down the lane that on one side turned off into the woods and on the other continued on into the village square, obscured now by mist. The haze was soft and restful, like the tent of Sarah our Mother. Inside the tent Sarah had spoken directly to God and didn't have to veil her face.

Hayim, emerging from the fog, carried rake and hoe instead of buckets over his shoulders. Alta-Fruma waved, he nodded and set about his task of reparation in the garden at the side of the house.

Standing over the earth like a night watchman, Hayim scooped careful hollows, spilling seeds into the darkness. He worked in the earth steadily, unhurriedly, the same way he walked through the village square with the yoke balanced across his broad shoulders, lifting his head now and then to look at the sky or bending to watch the bird wrestle a worm out of the freshly turned earth. Wiping his forehead with his cap, Hayim said something Alta-Fruma couldn't make out, as if he were talking to himself, or perhaps to the bird, which cheeped and fluttered its wings in answer. She was curious about what Hayim, who spoke so seldom, would be saying now. I should see what he's doing, she said to herself, maybe he's thirsty, I should ask him if he wants a glass of water, I should ask him how long he'll be. Just then he turned to look at her, silently looking with his golden cat's eyes, taking in her stance, leaning on the broom, head tilted, shawl fallen over one shoulder leaving her head bare, a crown of gray curls that she rushed to cover. Dropping her broom, she was suddenly conscious of her bare feet and bare legs and how it would look if anyone walked by. "Put your eyes back in your head," she called out and stalked into the house.

Alta-Fruma broke up the branches lying in a neat pile beside the oven, thrusting them under the cooking grate. What hutzpah he had, this Hayim! She filled the kettle from the water barrel and set it onto the cooking grate. The quick fire burned high, spilling embers in a red-black fury. What was he? A nobody. Did he think he was still the miller's son? With a pair of tongs, she picked out a lump of coal from the fire, carrying it carefully to the samovar. It was part of her dowry, a simple brass samovar reflected in the polished pine of the sideboard on which it stood. What gave him the right to stare? Lifting the lid, she dropped the coal into the inner cylinder, then brought another ashy lump, and another. Didn't he know that a man isn't supposed to look at a woman? She touched her hand to the side of the samovar, feeling the warmth. Pouring the boiling water into the space around the tin tower of coals, she felt her back tingle as if someone were watching her, someone who wasn't fooled by the appearance of things. She dropped a handful of tea leaves into the water, a moat of tea to defend her from the day of children, cows, and watercarriers.

She could hear them stirring in the other room. The clump of Emma's boots, Izzie's familiar cough, the squeak of the cot as he rose, the rattle of the rod as he pushed the dividing curtain aside to roll his cot under the other bed.

His face looked pinched as he came into the front room. There were dark circles around his eyes, like the rings around a full moon forecasting storms.

"Did you have bad dreams again?" Alta-Fruma asked. He nodded. "Then have a cup of tea with bread and honey. You have to eat after a bad dream, it drives away the spirits." The boy is too thin, she thought, he should eat.

He sat at the table, chin in his hands, considering what she said. He took every word seriously, pondering its meaning as if an angel had spoken it, staring at the emptiness above the table as if the angels studied Torah there. "I don't want to drive away the spirits," he said finally. "A dream is a letter from God. It says so in the Talmud. It would be a terrible thing not to open a letter from God. No, Auntie, I won't have any bread with honey."

He looked, in his white nightshirt, with his thin white hands clasped under his pointed chin, as if he himself might soon float up to heaven. "Well, then, Izzie. You have your bread with jam. Spirits aren't at all bothered by jam, only honey. There's still some blackberry preserves left. It's your favorite, isn't it? Use it up so it won't go to waste." She looked approvingly as the boy smeared his bread thickly, eating while he read one of his Hebrew books.

"Don't fill his head with superstitions," Emma said as she came in, tearing off a chunk of bread.

"You sit down, too. If you eat running the food won't stick to you."

"I have to go out," Emma said. "I'm working on something with Ruthie."

"I need you in the dairy. And the garden is dry. You can bring some water from the river. Hayim is too busy."

"Well if heaven really heard people's prayers, it would rain, wouldn't it?" Emma asked Izzie. "Make it rain!" she shouted.

Izzie ran to the window. "It's a miracle. It's a miracle. Look Auntie!" Sheets of water poured down the window.

"Thpoo, thpoo, thpoo," Alta-Fruma said, automatically spitting to avert the evil eye. Could it be that Emma, too, had inherited a little gift, an annoying little talent from their mischievous ancestress? Alta-Fruma shook her head. Don't be silly, she said to herself, it's May. In May it rains. Through the window she saw Hayim running for cover. Rain beat the tin roof. Alta-Fruma wished that she were outside, her skin soaking in the spring rain. But that would be foolishness. Of course.

"Ruthie's waiting for me," Emma said as she flew out the door.

What could Alta-Fruma do? Hit Emma with a stick the way Alta-Fruma's father had hit Rakhel for reading Polish history in the woods on *Shabbas?* No, Alta-Fruma would just have to wait for Emma to come back.

On the second *Shabbas* in May, people began to notice that Misha was showing. By the third week of rain some peasants claimed they had seen a shower of frogs, indicating a fertile spring, but Alta-Fruma was working in the dairy at the time. And then, on May 22nd, a Tuesday, Ruthie was arrested.

After the farmers delivered their milk, Alta-Fruma set it to ripen overnight and went home. She checked the level of water in the water barrel, put some tea in the samovar, and went down to the root cellar to get some cabbage and potato for supper. It was while she was cutting up the cabbage for borscht that she heard the sound from the bedroom. A creaking, crying little noise. "Izzie? Emma?" No answer.

Alta-Fruma put down her knife, wiped her hands on her apron, and walked through the hallway where the hens roosted in the winter. In the back room, Emma was sitting on the bed she shared with her great-aunt, hands folded in her lap, blinking.

"Emma, what is it? Where's Izzie? Did something happen to him?"

"Izzie's all right. He's at the Rabbi's house. Studying."

"What is it, Emma? Tell me." The bed frame was iron, the white linen embroidered with red thread to keep away the evil eye, the feather pillows piled high behind Emma so that she looked as small as a little girl.

Emma looked up at her great-aunt, her face pinched, her eyes wet. "I can't tell you."

"What did you do, Emma?" The girl looked faint. "Is it so bad?" Alta-Fruma reached behind Emma, picking up the pillows one by one to plump them so the child wouldn't have to look at her.

"Ruthie was arrested."

Alta-Fruma's hands stilled. "Arrested? It can't be."

"On the road from Blaszka to Plotsk."

"What business did she have in Plotsk?" Emma just shook her head. "How did it happen?" Alta-Fruma asked. "I want the truth."

"I wasn't there." Emma wrapped her arms around her knees. "I didn't see what happened." The girl hid her face in her arms.

And what was Emma doing? Alta-Fruma thought. If Ruthie was arrested, then Emma must be mixed up in it. Was I too lenient? Did I let her run around too much on her own? I have to be stricter with her. Even if she hates me. Ruthie arrested. Dear God in Heaven, what if it had been Emma?

THE LONG DAYS

Wednesday morning. It rained. Emma got her period. She ran off while Alta-Fruma was trying to talk with her.

Wednesday afternoon. Hayim's pig tore up the garden. Then it got into the dairy and spoiled a vat of cheese. Alta-Fruma chased it home and Hayim offered to work off the damage.

Wednesday evening. Alta-Fruma threatened to send Emma to an orphanage unless she started to obey.

Thursday morning. Emma ran away. Alta-Fruma thought she would go out of her mind.

Hayim brought Emma home.

Emma was quiet, willingly helping Alta-Fruma in the dairy. It was unnerving.

The community council came around to collect money for a

bribe. It wouldn't be much, not enough to persuade the Governor to release Ruthie, but at least it would make her life a little easier. Alta-Fruma gave as much as anyone, but not any more. How could she? People would ask questions.

On Friday, Faygela left the bakery, marching across Blaszka to accost Alta-Fruma in the dairyhouse. The dairyhouse was cool, shaded by willows, and clean as a stone in the river. Not a strand of spiderweb dared cross the beams in the presence of Alta-Fruma's broom. Steel milk pans shone like silver. The air floated gently, dust motes softly spinning in the sweet-sour, pungent smell of butter, milk, and ripening cheese.

Emma was outside milking the cow. Her fingers were thin but she pulled thoroughly, not leaving a drop to block the teats. The two girls who worked in the dairyhouse had called Alta-Fruma to cut the curd. She always did it herself, carefully, so as not to bruise it. After she sharpened the knives on the blue-gray whetstone, she cut the curd lengthwise with the perpendicular knife and across with the horizontal knife until it was in squares the size of peas. The Klembas sisters were setting the vat on the fire, and Alta-Fruma was just in the midst of stirring the curd with her hands, when Faygela came in. Engrossed in the rubbery sensation of the curd bouncing into her cupped hands and falling between her fingers, Alta-Fruma didn't notice Faygela until she began to speak.

"Ruthie wouldn't say who gave her the pamphlets, but I know it wasn't her own idea. Not my Ruthie. She wouldn't put a foot in the wrong direction. It could only be Emma. How could you let her get involved in something so dangerous?"

"There's going to be no more of such foolishness," Alta-Fruma said. "I allowed Emma to run around too much, but she won't have time for it anymore. She'll help out in the bakery in Ruthie's place, and she's taking in some piecework, too."

"Well, at least in the bakery I can keep an eye on her. I hope that I can see what's in a child's heart before she leads all of the young people in Blaszka to the authorities." With that, Faygela left and Alta-Fruma could only shake her head and wipe her hands on her apron.

"What else does she expect me to do?" she asked Hayim, who had been silently cleaning out the curding vats. Hayim didn't say anything.

In his eyes she thought she saw a flicker of reproof. "You see what's going on, tell me," she said. "If I'm doing something wrong to the child . . ." She looked away, embarrassed, unable to bear his unflinching gaze.

"You, you're always saying she's like her grandmother. Another Rakhel." Alta-Fruma nodded, waiting for him to catch his thoughts in the precarious net of speech. He went on, "I remember her, Rakhel. She, she wasn't like Emma. Not really. Rakhel was always in the middle of the village square, talking about something." Alta-Fruma nodded. "But always something different. In '63 it was Polish independence. I remember even though I was just, just thirteen."

"She made a speech," Alta-Fruma said. "Like Emma."

"Not, not like Emma. Later Rakhel read poetry in the village square. And then she became the *zogerin*. For Emma there's only one thing. Justice. You have to look, look at Emma and see Emma, not Rakhel. The child has no mother to look at her."

"The cows are milked," Emma said as she came in. She spoke meekly, her face as solemn as her brother's. "What should I do now, Auntie?"

Alta-Fruma told herself that it was an improvement, this new meekness of Emma's. Remorse was good for her. It made her into a proper girl at last, as obedient as anyone could ask for. Why then, last night, did she find herself watching over Emma when she was asleep, touching her cheek and forehead, worrying that she was too warm, painfully listening to the tiny moans as the child tossed and turned?

"Auntie?" Emma asked. "Should I churn the butter?"

"No, you need stronger arms to make good butter. Why don't you go get one of your books? You can read something to us about this oppression of the workers that you're always going on about. To make the time pass."

After Emma left, Alta-Fruma turned to Hayim. "Do me a favor. Stay for *Shabbas* dinner." On her way to the butter churn, as she brushed by him, she thought perhaps he had reached for her, but it could only have been her imagination.

IN THE long days, *Shabbas* was slow to arrive, like a bride lingering in her girlhood. Children called to one another in the woods, men waited for the *shammus* to summon them to prayer, and women, preparing all things of pleasure, reveled in the long hours of evening sunshine. There were several *Shabbas* dinners with Hayim and when they worked together in the dairyhouse, Alta-Fruma found herself walking by Hayim just to be near him. Every day there was another sketch of Hayim's pinned to the wall. He began to lose his stammer. She began to think she was letting something get out of hand.

On the third Thursday in June, Hayim waited for his usual invitation for Friday dinner, but Alta-Fruma said nothing, no matter how he looked at her. It was hard to avoid his gaze, but she had a little business to take care of here and there, and tried to keep away from him. After the Klembas sisters went home and Hayim had left, she had a talk with herself while she swept out the dairyhouse. You have to say something to him, she thought. Tell him not to come to the dairyhouse anymore. She could smell Hayim's presence everywhere she turned, a shadow of pine needles and charcoal and sweet cream that clung to her. This isn't a business for an old *aguna,* not here, where anyone can see. No. There isn't any magic that can make a dog into a hen.

Satisfied, she left the dairyhouse, only to see Hayim waiting for her, his eyebrows lifted in a question. "Good. I want to talk to you," she said. He waited. But nothing more came out. She couldn't say a word. She could only stand with him under the willow trees outside the dairyhouse, watching the river, noticing the light and the smell of water and Hayim's deep, slow breathing. Leaves and twigs spun around in a whirlpool, frogs croaked from under the bank, Hayim chewed on a blade of grass while they stood side by side, each of them furtively glancing at the other.

"I can tell you why," she said at last.

"Why what?"

"The Pharaoh's heart was hardened."

"Yes?"

"The water turned into blood. So what? The frogs fell from the sky. What is that? Magic. A trick. It doesn't convince anyone. No, Hayim. You can trick someone into changing for a little while, but before you know it, everything will turn back to the way it was." As she spoke, she looked at him. There was nothing surreptitious about her gaze. She looked him in the eye, right into his golden eyes, taking in the movement of his hands as he thought over what she said, drawing his thoughts in the air, blue from the settling night. "A worm is a worm and it doesn't fly like a bird," she said.

"No? A caterpillar changes into a butterfly, Fruma. A tadpole becomes a frog. The Holy One made it a perfect, changing thing. People only think a creature that's first a tadpole and then a frog is two separate things because it has different names."

"No, Hayim. A name means everything." She turned from him, looking now at the river flowing indifferently between the old Blaszka and the new Blaszka. "When a woman marries, she takes her husband's name and covers her head so that everyone knows she belongs to him even if he disappears from the face of the earth."

From the corner of her eye, she saw Hayim shake his head. "That name is for the census takers. It's not her Hebrew name. You are your mother's daughter when a blessing is said for you in the synagogue. Fruma, the daughter of Gittel, they say. And your father's daughter when you're buried. Never your husband's. N-n-n-no. You belong only to the ones who made you. Mama. Papa. The Holy One above. You," and he touched her forehead, the first time he had ever touched her, with his fingers that smelled of sweet cream, that could capture anything with a pencil and a sheet of paper, "are Fruma. Just Fruma. Everything Fruma."

"When you live among people you have to watch yourself. You can't do anything you want. Not like my sister who didn't care what trouble fell on anyone."

"Your sister was beautiful," he said, "but, but, but . . ." Alta-Fruma waited. "You're not like anyone else."

"Me? How could you say that? I'm just like everyone else," but she spoke softly so as not to stop him from going on.

"No," he said firmly. "There's no one like you in Blaszka. I know. I see you."

"Are you sure you see everything?" she asked, smiling, her hand on his shoulder. "How do you know? Maybe I have a frog skin hidden in my bridal trunk."

"I'd like to see that. It would be very interesting," he said, his eyes closing to a narrow line of gold as he smiled back at her. She turned to face the river. They stood so close, she could feel the rise and fall of his shoulders as he breathed in and out. As they stood under the willows, night turned them into shadows, the wind carrying the smell of the river and the sound of nocturnal creatures calling to one another. "Tomorrow, after you go to synagogue, come to my house for dinner. You shouldn't expect an invitation anymore. Are you a stranger?"

WHILE THEY spoke, Shmuel the baker was on his way to Plotsk. He brought a pouch of gold coins and a note to the Governor, who ordered Ruthie's immediate release. Faygela was writing in her notebook. Hershel was serving Hanna-Leah soup, insisting that she sit in the big chair. Misha, coming into her seventh month, was walking along the river and so was the Rabbi, Berekh.

NIGHTS OF THE SECRET RIVER

In July when the raspberries were ripe, Hayim brought a bucketful of fresh berries to the dairy. Blaszka was quiet, market day past, the village square empty except for the wheelmaker, who was repairing the axle on a cart. Alta-Fruma was alone in the dairyhouse. The Klembas sisters were tending their sick father and Emma was in the bakery making raspberry tarts with Ruthie.

"Raspberries," Hayim said, presenting Alta-Fruma with the bucket.

"And I have fresh cream to go with it. Let me get bowls from the house. You sit right here." She pointed to the bench.

When she came back from the house, Hayim was sitting on the bench, his hands busy with charcoal and paper—a sketch of the dairyhouse, Alta-Fruma stirring the curd, Hayim's pig peeking through the window. The pig seemed to be smiling. While Alta-Fruma poured cream over the raspberries, Hayim pinned the sketch to the wall.

They sat side by side on the bench, eating, suddenly shy. The bench was made of soft pine, sloping where generations of Alta-Fruma's family had sat on it. She had to keep her feet square on the floor to hold herself in place so that she didn't slide into Hayim. Her feet were bare. Too warm for boots. If she were alone, she'd have tied her dress around her waist.

"Is Emma happy in the bakery?" Hayim asked.

"Why not? She talks as much as she works. The girls look up to her like to a queen. Emma says she's explaining the secrets of capitalism."

"People run after secrets." Hayim's lips were stained with juice.

"Secrets should be left alone," she said.

He shook his head. "A jewel that's hidden is nothing." He was breathing unevenly, his voice suddenly hoarse. Alta-Fruma looked at him intently.

A piece of straw was stuck in his beard. He swept with so much vigor that afterward there was always a bit of straw here and there about him. Alta-Fruma picked it out. "No," she said, her fingers lingering a moment longer than necessary in the softness of his beard. "An old jewel is better left in the box. Then no one can make trouble over it."

"But when it's hidden, it could just be a lump of coal." He put down his bowl, leaning toward her.

The light was dim in the dairyhouse, the stone floor cold under Alta-Fruma's feet. Outside a goose was honking over its nest. Hayim wore an apron over his caftan. A hair from his beard had fallen onto the bib, a black thread. She picked it off the apron, twisting it around her finger. "Maybe you're right," she said. "I won't say no." She lifted her feet onto the bench, rubbing them. "The floor is cold."

Hayim gently pushed her hands away. "Let me." He took one of her feet onto his lap. What if someone came in? What if someone should see them, her heel resting on the soft inside of his thigh? She looked at the door, a thin band of light around it, creaking with every small thrust of wind. But as he warmed her foot between his hands, rubbing each toe, the top of her foot, the sole, she forgot the door, she forgot the dairyhouse. There was only the bench, her foot, his hands lightly stroking, painting her foot with the tips of his fingers. "Other foot," he said. So she gave him her other foot and he took it between his hands, his square-tipped fingers, the nails gray just at the edge where he'd smudged the charcoal in the sketch of the dairyhouse.

When he bent his head, she saw the skin on his neck, smooth between his beard and his long hair, smooth and dark from the sun. She reached out. She touched him. It was the first time she had ever touched his naked skin, her fingers on the hot, smooth skin of his neck, tracing the shell of his ear as he looked at her, his hands stilled. His lips were as smooth as a shining pool, his apron stained with a single drop of raspberry juice. And under the apron? And under the caftan? And under his shirt? I should check the curd, she thought. He was sliding his hands along her leg. She should, she should . . . but how could she think? She was riding a leaf over a pool of water, his fingers sliding toward her thigh.

"Come with me," Alta-Fruma said, pulling him toward the door that opened into the cow shed.

Inside the cow shed, Hayim wrapped his arms around her. She wrapped herself in the smell of him, the cotton apron rough against her cheek as if it could peel away the lines and underneath would be new skin. But what did it matter? Hayim's lips on her neck were soft enough to remind the fragile skin of everything it knew.

"I want to see," she said, pushing him at arm's length. "Everything."

He nodded, his face serious, his eyes flashing.

The only light in the shed came from a small window, but it was enough. Standing in the shaft of sunlight, Hayim took off the apron, the black caftan, his cotton shirt, carefully, without any hurry, laying it all on a pile of hay, while Alta-Fruma watched him emerge from the layers of clothing. First the flatness of his belly as he pulled up his shirt, the ridge of muscle, the rows of dark hair, his chest, his nipples, red, pointed, not very different from her own, the thickness of his forearms, the narrowness of his wrists, hair like a line of fur on his square shoulders, his collarbones, a wing on each side of his throat, the hollow of his throat, exactly at the height of her lips. Smiling, he unbuttoned his trousers and let them fall. His thighs, the nest of hair, and there, there it was, thick and square-tipped like his fingers, darker than the skin on his neck, unfolding, rising as she looked and looked, her tongue darting out to lick her lips as if she were tasting something very, very good. And he was naked, shivering slightly. All naked. The whole of him. She looked and she saw while Hayim sat down on an upturned pail, his legs stretched out, smiling as she looked, holding his arms out to her. "You now," he said.

She took off her apron, untied the strings of her dress, reached back for the buttons, but it was too far, her fingers kept slipping on the buttons, the slight stiffness in her shoulders stopping her.

"Come here, Fruma," Hayim said. He stood behind her, his hands teasing into her dress as he unbuttoned her, sliding under her cotton pants as he untied the string. When she was naked, he held her against the length of him, holding her bones as if he held gold. They kissed, her hand behind his head, fingers entwined in his hair. His mouth tasted of raspberries, his tongue of cream. The odor of cow dung mingled with the husky sweet smell of entwined arms and legs as they lay on an old blanket thrown across a pile of straw. His hand traced the inside of her thigh reaching higher and higher and higher, his fingers teasing the edge, his lips on her nipples, tongue curving the underside of her breast. The mingling of moisture and sweat. No need to pull back. Not for a moment. Can a woman get pregnant after the change? No, she can touch here and here and here, her lips tasting everything. He pulled her on top and she sat where she liked to sit, her eyes open, his eyes widening, her eyes narrowing as they slid on the straw.

It seemed that an old witch and a man in his forties could, between them, produce a great heat.

Afterward, Alta-Fruma thought of a tune from *Hibbat Zion*, The Lovers of Zion:

> *Daughter dear, where do you lay?*
> *Oh mother, on a bale of hay,*
> *And oh what a pleasure that way.*

In the first week of August, Alta-Fruma began to show Emma how to make cheese. "You see? There's no magic in it. It's just a matter of knowing how long to let the milk ripen. You have to know when to separate the curd from the whey and when to add salt. And how do you know? Other cheesemakers put a bowl to float on top of the milk. They say the milk is set when the bowl lifts on one side. But I never liked that method. Imprecise. Unreliable."

Emma nodded. "Unscientific."

"That's right. Now my secret is the iron rod. I tried different things until I discovered this way of testing the curd. You take an iron rod. You stick it in the fire until it's black, not red, that's too hot. When the iron rod is just the right heat, you grip the curd tightly in your hand to squeeze out the whey, and then you hold it to the iron rod. If the milk is ripe enough, it will draw fine silky threads, a centimeter long. Then it's time to take out the curd. After the curd is cooled and cut and turned, again you make the iron black hot and hold the curd against it. If it draws velvety threads six centimeters long, soft and fat as butter, it's time to add salt."

Emma reached out to take the iron rod, then stopped. "It's red, Auntie. It must be too hot."

"That's right. We'll use the tongs to take it out, let it cool and I'll try again. In the meantime you can go get Ruthie from the bakery. You should be outside, you look a little pale. The blueberry bushes are full. Here, take a bucket."

Something wasn't right with Emma. She was walking, not running out the door. Maybe she just needs a little air, Alta-Fruma said to herself. But a few hours later, when Emma came home, leaning on Ruthie, her head aching, her face red, Alta-Fruma cursed herself for letting the child run around instead of putting her right to bed.

The doctor from Plotsk said it was typhus. He heard there was typhus in Plotsk near the docks. Alta-Fruma put her hand to her throat. "The piecework. She said that there was lice in the workshop and some of the girls had gotten sick. Why did I let her go there?"

Emma lay in the bed, her head propped up on pillows so she could breathe easier, her great-aunt in a chair beside her, keeping watch, bathing her hot face with water. Ruthie came every day with something from Misha, an herb or a tea, since Misha herself was so big it was hard for her to walk. Hanna-Leah took Izzie home with her to keep him from catching the typhus. Faygela brought soup, though no one could eat it. Emma's friends sent oranges. Emma asked for her mother. "I'm here," Alta-Fruma said, biting her lip.

Finally, on the eve of Tishah-b'Av, Alta-Fruma asked Ruthie to send for Misha, even though the midwife was in her eighth month and could lose her baby if she got sick, too.

Misha came and sat, uncomplaining, despite the discomfort of the hard wooden chair, looking over her basket of remedies while Alta-Fruma twisted her hands. "You're upset and tired," Misha said. "Here, all you can do is watch. But your sister was a *zogerin*. It must mean something. Go to the shul and pray. Maybe the Holy One above is listening and waiting for you."

Hayim was standing watch outside when Alta-Fruma left the house, watching as if the Angel of Death wouldn't dare to show himself while Hayim was looking.

"Misha says it's going to be soon," Alta-Fruma said to him. "I'm going to the shul to pray, although the Holy One knows that I have no merit." She leaned against him, her legs no longer able to hold her up. "Is heaven going to listen to an old *aguna* with no learning and no virtue?" she whispered.

Hayim held her tight. "Everything has merit to the Master of the Universe," he said. "Even a leaf. Even a frog. It's all from *Ein Sof.* So you, Fruma, have nothing to hide from the Holy One above. Not a thing."

She wanted to stay in the circle of his arms, breathing into the crook of his neck, listening to the murmur of his voice. Another minute, she said to herself, another minute. But Emma was waiting—and for how much longer? "I have to go," she whispered, pulling away. First walking, then running, she came to the courtyard of the synagogue. The moon was hidden behind a cloud, the night heavy and humid.

Opening the double doors of oak, Alta-Fruma climbed down the stairs to the sanctuary in a darkness made deeper by its depth in the earth. The eternal flame cast a faint light on the snuffed candles in their box of sand below. With shaking hands, Alta-Fruma kindled their wicks, and the Holy Ark, draped in black cloth for Tishah-b'Av, emerged from the shadows. Alta-Fruma pushed aside the cloth and opened the doors of the Ark, carved by Misha's father, Aba the carpenter, during the Polish insurrection of 1863. The doors were inscribed above, "And the Eternal heard our voice," and below, "From slavery to freedom, from anguish to joy," quoting the story of the Exodus. The crowned Polish eagle flew above lions, deer, and dolphins cavorting among the letters that rose to form waves and orchards, all green and gold, glinting in the eternal flame.

Alta-Fruma bowed to the curtain that shielded the Torah scrolls. "Dear God, I'm a simple woman. I have no merit. I only know one Hebrew prayer, the *Sh'ma.* Please accept this one prayer as if it were all of the blessings and prayers in the men's prayer book." Pulling her shawl over her head, as a man does with his tallis when deep in prayer, Alta-Fruma murmured, "*Sh'ma Israel, Adonai Elohenu, Adonai Ekhad.*" Hear O Israel, the Lord our God, the Lord is One. "*You shall love the*

Lord Your God with all your heart and all your soul and all your strength," she prayed.

Alta-Fruma swayed in front of the Holy Ark. "Master of the Universe, Dear God in heaven, what has this child done? Is this a child that has sinned? She has not done one thing for You to be angry with her. If You want someone to punish, I'm here. Don't hurt the child, Dear God, not my Rakhel's little Emma.

"Rakhel, do you hear me? Talk to Sarah, the Mother of our people. She was a great prophet, greater even than Avraham. Surely, she can plead with the Holy One. Let her talk to Him. Let her tell Him how it was to see her only child climb to the top of a mountain to be sacrificed. Tell Him not to let this girl suffer."

A gust of air blew out the candles. Alta-Fruma stood alone in the darkness of the synagogue. There were shapes in the darkness pressing toward her, teasing her, pulling at her skirt, leaping back into emptiness when she turned to look. Peering into the blackness, Alta-Fruma cried, "Is this Your answer? To send demons to laugh at me? Very good. Let them laugh. I'm a silly old woman, why not? What is my life worth? A round of cheese, a few rubles. But the child is an orphan. Aren't You then mother and father to her? For the sake of Your name, Dear God, let the child live." The wind rose, the walls squealing as if all the demons in hell laughed.

Alta-Fruma hurried back along the path, certain that she knew the cruel answer to her prayers, and yet she couldn't weep. She had to hurry home. She had to see for herself. Her eyes blurred, her mind in disarray as her feet followed a flicker of movement in the starlight. There's no hope, she thought, but hope wouldn't die. Instead a prayer went out into the night, a prayer to her mother, her sister, her grandmother, and her aunts, to Blema and her Grandmother Manya, to all of the women with their dangerous gifts. The darkness trailed her on either side, like a mother's skirts, and in between fireflies sparked here and here, always in the center of the path above the small frog leading Alta-Fruma home.

"Look," Misha said. "The fever has gone. She's asleep."

It was only then that Alta-Fruma wept brokenly.

THE DAYS OF AWE

Before dawn, when the souls of the dead hovered in the graying sky, the women gathered in the synagogue courtyard. They carried candles, the white shawls they wore over head and shoulders floating in the misty dawn like the souls of their grandmothers. The young *zogerin* didn't carry her double case watch or her silver prayer book, and no pearls swung against her flat chest. Unadorned, she led the women into the graveyard between the synagogue and the woods. They circled the cemetery seven times, soundlessly, stopping at Manya's grave. Once a year the women prayed at Manya's grave. During the days of awe, at the moment of judgment, all the women of Blaszka gathered at Manya's grave and prayed that their mothers and grandmothers and great-grandmothers would intercede for them with the Holy Court.

The rising sun was burning off the fog. Leaves drifted from the woods into the high grass and wildflowers that grew up and around the softly crumbling tombstones, the women's boots solid on the earth between the yellow blooms of butter and eggs. At this time of year, as at other times of life and death, dread and relief, danger and birth, the women stood together, arms linked, a net that gathered up their compassion, and let their grudges fall through. Only Misha, being close to her time, was not there among the women at her great-grandmother's grave. But Hanna-Leah was there. Faygela. Alta-Fruma. Even Emma, holding Ruthie's hand.

Facing Manya's tombstone, the *zogerin* made her confessional, praying slowly so that the women could repeat after her.

"*I beg mercy for my soul that I have damaged. I was unkind to others and I showed great anger. It was as though I bowed down to idols.*

"*I spread gossip about good people. It is worse than if I shed their blood. For this my soul will return in the mud of the river.*

"*When charity was asked, my hands were closed. For this my soul will enter a sow that eats its young.*

"*I have eaten* trayf. *I did not go to the* mikva. *I swore falsely. I thought of strange men when I had sex with my husband. I had sex with my husband in the light . . . for this my soul will be reborn in the leaves of a nettle.*

"Does it matter if I committed one or all of these? My sorrow alone is not enough to correct them. Only by Your will, Eternal One, can these transgressions be wiped out. Inscribe us for life. Grant each and every one of us a livelihood from Your gentle hand so that we may be able to give charity and never need to go to a stranger's table or depend on our children. Then we shall be able to serve You, dear God, with a happy heart. Amen. Sela."

Afterward the *zogerin* prayed at Misha's house and Alta-Fruma brought some feather pillows to Misha so that she would be able to sleep half-sitting, now that she was so big she found it hard to breathe when she lay down.

KOL NIDREI

Alta-Fruma and Emma walk along the narrow lane toward the village square. Izzie walks ahead of them, hands clasped in front of his narrow chest, looking up at the sky to catch the moment that the gates of heaven open. Along the village lanes, the men and women of Blaszka greet one another with open arms, falling on one another's necks with cries of forgiveness. "May you be inscribed in the Book of Life," they say, weeping unashamedly.

"I want to talk to you," Alta-Fruma says to Emma.

"What did I do?" she asks.

"I want to talk to you about your grandmother."

"Oh." Emma's voice falls unenthusiastically. "I suppose you're going to tell me again how I'm another Rakhel. 'So stubborn, like a mule, but she repented of her ways and became a *zogerin*. When she prayed the angels listened, and so on, and so on.'"

"That's all true, but I want to tell you something else. Even before your grandmother became the *zogerin*, she used to tell the women how to pray."

"Oh, I'm sure. She was probably a saint."

"She could have been. Maybe your kind of saint."

"Mine?" Emma looks at her aunt as if she's making fun of her, but Alta-Fruma's face is serious.

"Yes. Let me tell you what she used to say. It made the hairs on my neck stand up."

"What did she say?" Emma is interested now.

"She used to tell the women to scream and cry until they knocked down the gates of heaven and the Holy Court begged for mercy. Listen to me, women, she used to say, it's the angels above that should beg us for forgiveness. Who makes our children hungry and sick? Who takes away our sons into the army? Who makes us work until we drop? Cry out and ask the Holy One why they're not punished. Tell the Eternal One that if He doesn't see fit to bring justice to the world, we ourselves will take our brooms and our knives and we'll find our own justice."

"And they didn't throw her out of Blaszka?"

"Who pays attention to what goes on in the women's gallery?"

"Didn't people talk?"

"Oy, how they talked. I was afraid for her, just like I'm afraid for you. But she convinced them. Who do you think brought food to the rebels who were hiding in the woods in '63?"

"My grandmother?"

"All of the women. It wasn't any joke. Faygela's mother had her baby too early and she died from running around in the woods, and it was my sister who led her to it. Emma," Alta-Fruma takes the girl's hand in her own, "don't be so quick to think you know what's going on. Things aren't always how they look."

THE VILLAGERS are gathering in the synagogue courtyard, a host of light in the dusk, an escort of white prayer shawls and *kittels* and kerchiefs, the white of pure snow, of angels and death.

THROUGH THE window of the *mekhitzah*, the wall of the women's gallery that divides them from the men below, Alta-Fruma watches Hayim in the back corner. He smiles broadly, as if he can see her. They have lain together in the cow shed, under the willows, in Hayim's hut among the reeds, on the riverbank where moonlight glints on the silver rocks. Alta-Fruma stands with Emma, waiting for the Kol Nidrei prayer to clear the slate, for the door to open to her atonement. In front of them is Faygela, her daughters in a row on one side and Hanna-Leah beside her on the other.

A moan floats across the village square. There is a flutter in the women's gallery. Misha, it's her time, the women say. The *zogerin* peers through the window of the *mekhitzah*. "The Rabbi is just standing there," she says. "Why doesn't he sing Kol Nidrei?" The candles quiver. Another moan from Misha's house. The women look at one another uneasily. Their lives are in the balance. They have to pray for their children. But there, just across the square, is a woman in labor. Misha, who delivered all of their children. Alone.

Hanna-Leah leans toward Faygela. "How long must she suffer without anyone to give her a drink of water even?"

Alta-Fruma whispers to Emma, "Kol Nidrei or not, we can't leave her by herself."

"You're not afraid of what people will say?" Emma asks.

"When you were sick, Misha came. That's all I have to know. Let's go." She stands, Emma with her.

Hanna-Leah is covering her head with her shawl, Faygela following with her five daughters. Then Ettie the blacksmith's wife, Gittel the scholar's, Haia-Etel the ropemaker's. As Emma looks around, she sees they're all rising to go to Misha. The *mekhitzah* can't contain them, they are like the river in spring flooding the banks with wild excitement, carrying its rich mud to Misha's garden. The women flow from the gallery, all of them, so many women pouring down the stairs and across the square as if all the women that ever lived in Blaszka were flowing down to Misha.

And indeed as Emma follows Alta-Fruma, she sees a small green frog hop across the village square as if leading them. Who knows but that it isn't Misha's own great-grandmother Manya sent down from heaven to watch over the women?

IN THE coming year the villagers will become accustomed to seeing Hayim in the dairyhouse and Alta-Fruma crossing the bridge. They will shrug their shoulders and say, "If you have to ask, it's *trayf.* Better you shouldn't ask." And no one, except perhaps Hayim, will see a tiny tree frog camouflaged on a leaf in the woods.

Alta-Fruma will die in the fullness of years. Izzie will donate his half of the estate to the yeshiva in Kovno, and Emma will divide hers between the labor movement and Ruthie's orphanage in Berlin, where she has moved to be with Ruthie. In 1938 the two women will use the last of Alta-Fruma's savings to bring a group of Jewish children to London.

In 1945 Emma, stout and white-haired, will assist as a volunteer in processing refugees from Europe coming through London. She will ask everyone who comes through, "Did you see or hear of Rabbi Isidore Blau? Do you know what happened to him?"

"No," they will say. "No. No." Ruthie will beg her not to torture herself, but Emma can't help it. She asks and asks, until at last a young couple, Zev and Aidl-Mariam, hardly more than children, will say yes they heard of him. "A slight man with a limp?" they ask.

"Yes, yes. Where is he? What happened?"

Zev, the young man, heard that the Rabbi was seen in the Łodz ghetto crossing over to the Gypsy side during the typhus epidemic. Everyone heard him singing with the Gypsies as they died. An older man, overhearing Zev, says that he also heard of Rabbi Blau, but it wasn't in Łodz, he insists. No, it was in Buchenwald. The girl says, Neither of you remembers what happened. It was in Chełmno. But they all agree that on Simkhas Torah Isidore Blau danced with a Gyspy boy in his arms, singing. The Rabbi held the child toward heaven, saying, "This is your Torah, God." And the Rabbi died. How? They heard he was shot protecting the boy. They heard he caught the typhus from the Gypsies in Łodz. That he had a heart attack. That he died of hunger. It was in Theresienstadt, you know, added a middle-aged woman with a number tattooed on her arm.

"But did you see him yourselves? Were you there?" Emma will ask.

No, they weren't there. They only heard.

"Then you can't know for sure. He might still be alive. It could be."

In heaven the angels will turn to one another and whisper maybe. Maybe.

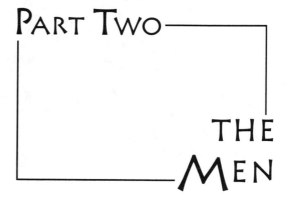

PART TWO

THE
MEN

5

GOLDEN EGGS

Hershel sat in the outhouse, contemplating his penis. It was an ordinary-looking one, wrinkled and red with a cap like a mushroom. An ordinary size, an ordinary shape. But it did not behave in an ordinary way. When he was alone, it jumped to attention at the strangest times and yet at home it receded into its nest while Hanna-Leah, so large and soft, lay waiting beside him. What kind of man was he? He couldn't even study like other men. He would open the prayer book and then, before he could blink, the letters would start to swim in front of his eyes. Of course he knew the prayers by heart, he didn't need the book. But a Jew is supposed to learn Torah. A man studies for the merit of his family. Take the ritual slaughterer. Hershel would buy a cow and bring it to the *shokhet* to slaughter according to Hebrew law. First Reb Pinkus made the proper benediction. Then he drew the knife across the throat, severing the windpipe, the jugular vein, and the carotid artery in one quick, merciful movement. A *shokhet* has to know exactly how to do it. If the knife gets stuck, if the throat is torn, even if he pauses for one second, the killing is cruel and the animal not kosher. Afterward, Reb Pinkus inspected the cow to ensure that everything inside her was kosher. No lumps. No sickness. He had to know each of the organs and how it should look. A man of learning. With a certificate. Who studied. And Hershel? After the cow was slaughtered, he would take it to his shop and butcher it into pieces.

Hershel looked at his hands. Large. The wrists hairy. Like his broad chest and his short sturdy legs. A Jew should be pale with dark hollows under his eyes from study. His mind on holy things. But Hershel's mind was always on what to do. The cow. The shop. The village. And Hanna-Leah. Could he approach her like she deserved, like something precious and delicate? No. He just wanted to grab her, hold her. . . . It didn't bear thinking about. She deserved better. A man had his place, a woman her place. And when a man couldn't give a woman her due . . .

The wind groaned against the cracked and rough planks of the outhouse as Hershel prayed, "Dear God, you know it's a mitzvah, a virtue to sanctify the Sabbath with the love between a man and his wife. I want to, you know I do. But when it comes to the point, my tail just lies there like a worm, no life. I don't look at another woman in Blaszka but my Hanna-Leah, a jewel among women. Yet there I am and nothing happens. So what am I to do, God? Give me a sign, a hint, something." As Hershel raised his hands to heaven, leaning forward on the rough plank of wood, a splinter caught him like a knife in his nether regions.

IT WAS past noon and in the village square, the Golem Players sang and juggled and somersaulted over barrels. In a quiet moment, Hanna-Leah walked over to Misha's stall for a remedy. Alta-Fruma crossed the bridge to walk among the ruined lanes of the new part of Blaszka. In the bathhouse, the old men were naked in the steam, pulverizing their reddened skin with bundles of willow twigs. Ah, they said, there's nothing like a *shvitz*. One of them paused, the willow branch drooping from his fist. You know what I saw just a few minutes ago? Hanna-Leah at Misha's stall again. So that's news? Everyone knows she goes every month for another remedy. But look, you can't raise a corpse. What's dead is dead. A man doesn't deserve such a fate. Listen to me, it's a warning from the Holy One. Hershel has fists like iron, and he uses them too often. Is that a Jew? Look, he was always like that. It isn't his fault that he doesn't have a head for study. Don't you remember when he was a boy and he beat up five other boys for teasing his cousin Shmuel? If Hershel had a son, maybe his son would study.

If, if, it's always if with you—if my grandmother had eggs, she'd be my grandfather. A man is nothing without children. Well, what's up comes down and what's down goes up. You heard of Eber the grain merchant? Yes, sure, Faygela's grandfather. Well, his partner cheated him, so Eber had to depend on his son-in-law the baker. You mean Faygela's father? Of course. Now you take Hershel's father, a shoe-maker, remember him? Sure, sure. Not even a shoemaker of uppers but of soles. Is there something lower? All right, maybe a cart driver or a watercarrier. But Hershel's a butcher and that's all. Other men can't be just one thing and still earn a living these days. The Hebrew teacher sweeps up the dreck in the village square and he brings his own shovel, too. So you look at Hershel and you see a man that works with his hands, a plain person, a *proster,* it's true, but the highest of the *proster.* Who should look down on him? Do we have so many fine people, *shayner,* in Blaszka? The rich left and we don't have too many scholars, either. Even our Rabbi is an unbeliever. Well, nearly. Anyway, never mind. Look who's coming in. Reb Pinkus, in a good hour. An old man with a young wife always looks healthy. So Reb Pinkus, how's your wife, the *zogerin* Tzipporah . . . ?

WHILE ALTA-FRUMA was watching the *zogerin* straighten her wig outside Hayim's hut, Reb Pinkus, the ritual slaughterer, was in the bathhouse, enjoying the steam as the other old men left and Hershel came in. "Reb Pinkus, may I ask you a question?" Hershel asked. They were alone on the benches of the bathhouse.

Pinkus folded his hands over the yellowing beard dangling above his naked belly, a wrinkled melon of a belly resting on his skinny legs. His slaughtering knife was known to be faultlessly sharp, without a nick or a dent anywhere. People said that when he examined the intestines of a cow to make sure it was clean and kosher, the angels themselves wouldn't argue with him. "Certainly, Hershel," he said. "What can I tell you?"

"Reb Pinkus, you're a learned man."

"Yes, I have some little learning."

"Well, I would also like to be learned. I wouldn't normally mention this. I have my position to think of, but I'll tell you in confidence that since I was a boy, when I look at the holy letters, they won't be still. They jump around. Did you ever hear of such a thing?" Hershel pulled on his ear. "I wouldn't mention it," he said, "only I heard that in Plotsk there are study circles, and the workers are learning. If even a plain tailor can learn, why not me? So what about it, Reb Pinkus?"

Reb Pinkus chewed on the end of his beard to hide a smile. Everyone knew that Hershel was a man of the hands, not of the head. Not much of a man at all. But a person of learning can draw on his well of compassion to bring light into the darkness. "The soul is like a beautiful woman, big and strong. You must cherish her, but never let her overtake you. She must have your guidance, your firm direction. You cannot let her wander like an aimless woman. A true man is in charge of his soul," Reb Pinkus said in the voice of a patriarch sitting outside his tent, beholding his dozen flocks. "And how? By study. Night and day. That is why we honor the man of learning. You must push away any earthly desires that distract you. Study in the morning before the sun rises, and in the evening after it sets. As it says in the Talmud . . ."

But even as Reb Pinkus droned on, Hershel, imagining the big beautiful soul, naked of course because what use does a soul have for clothes, felt a rising between his legs. He turned slightly, so that his back was toward the other bench. The steam lifting from the hot bricks seemed cold to his skin.

AFTER HERSHEL left the bathhouse, he crossed the icy bridge, slapping his hands on his shoulders to warm himself, thinking of a glass of schnapps at Perlmutter's tavern. Maybe two. Or three. But as he passed Misha's house on the other side, he hesitated and turned back. It could only be the evil eye that caused his tail to be so unreasonable. And who better to deal with the evil eye than this woman, whose great-grandmother had been a witch, one who knew it intimately?

Hershel stood in the open doorway. The house smelled of beeswax and vervain. Pots bubbled on the cooking grate. On the eastern wall was an embroidered landscape of elephants and golden mountains.

"I thought you might have a little something for me," Hershel said, twisting his ritual fringes around his fingers.

"Come in. What do you need?" Misha asked, no sign of surprise on her broad face at the sight of Hershel in her doorway. She was putting something in the oven, her red shawl fluttering in the draft as Hershel shut the door.

"I have a little weakness. It's nothing, just a sort of weakness," he said.

Misha looked at Hershel appraisingly. His eyes fell. "Where?" she asked.

"Where. Well, this weakness, it's in the area of my leg. My upper leg."

"Let me see how you walk."

Hershel walked from the door to the table, crossing the braided rug, turning around the bridal trunk with its brass candlesticks under the shelves of bottles and jars. He paused every few steps to shake his right leg. "You see?" he said.

"To me your leg looks fine. Are you sure that's the problem?" Again the deep scrutiny. Why did she have to look at him like that? As if there was something peculiar about him.

Hershel's voice rose. "Of course it's the problem. What else could be the problem?"

"Some men can have a weakness in other parts."

He couldn't stand to have her look at him like that. As if she knew everything. As if there was nothing private, nothing left to his dignity. What right did a woman have to know so much about a man, not even her own husband?

Misha casually added, "Not you of course, but when a man has a weakness in those other parts, the best thing to do is to forget about it. The man should remember that he has strong hands and soft lips. He should remember how it feels to touch his wife. These weaknesses aren't that important."

"I told you it's my leg. Of course you can't see anything wrong with my leg. What was I thinking? I should have my head examined. The *feldsher* would give me a leech or a good cupping and I'd be good as new. But you're a witch, not a doctor. God protect me from the evil eye," Hershel said. As the door slammed behind him, a piece of straw from the thatched roof fell onto his head and stuck in his hat. He punched the side of Misha's house, gouging his fist with splinters of bark.

* * *

IN THE tavern, Hershel waved for a bottle of schnapps. "What do the women want from her and her potions?" Hershel asked his cousin Shmuel, the baker. When they were boys, Hershel had protected the shy and timid Shmuel. But now that they were grown, Hershel often found himself confiding in his cousin, a good listener, calm, sympathetic. They sat at the best table, backs to the fire, right near the window so they could see what was going on in the village square. Shmuel's beard was still lightly dusted with flour. Hershel lowered his voice. "Hanna-Leah thinks I don't know she goes to Misha. But I have eyes. I see what she does. Am I stupid?"

"No, of course not," Shmuel said, "who says you're stupid?"

"Every market day, you can see the crowd of women at Misha's stall. What are they talking about?" Misha could be telling them anything. Even that a woman whose husband can't fulfill her needs can require the rabbinical court to force him to give her a *Get,* a religious divorce. And what was worse, it was true.

"When you're right, you're right," Shmuel said softly, flour drifting like snow from his beard. "But what can we do? My Faygela swears by Misha's remedies. And I'll tell you," he leaned toward Hershel, "after five girls, I had a son, and it was Misha who pulled him out. The big doctor from Plotsk told me that Faygela was too tired. He was ready to cut her open, but she begged me to get Misha. Could I deny her? I ran as fast as I could, and Misha came back with me. I told her what the doctor said. So what does Misha do? She marches into the house and to the doctor she says, 'And your wife, she cuts off a piece of your *shmeckel* when you get too tired? A little man like you, you'd have nothing left. Get out of here before I cut it off myself.'

"I pleaded with her, 'Misha, please. The doctor knows.' But he was shaking already, and she pushed him out the door. My boy is three years old, strong as a bull, and my Faygela still enjoys a Friday night, if you take my meaning. I heard that same doctor cut open a woman in Plotsk and made a mess of her." Shmuel hit the table with the flat of his hand. "She died and the baby, too."

"You know that doctor from Plotsk? I heard that Misha cursed him, the next day it turned black at the tip, and it just fell off," Hershel said.

"What, the whole thing?"

"No, just the tip, you idiot."

They sat in silence for a moment. "Misha's not a good influence on the women," Hershel said. "She's divorced. Her mother refused to remarry. Her great-grandmother . . ."

"It's true, yes," Shmuel said, "but . . ."

"When the women talk to her, they get excited. Who knows what kind of ideas she puts in their heads? A woman needs a husband. Doesn't it say so right in the Torah? Alone, she's like an animal, a wild wolf that doesn't know right from wrong. Like our Mother Eve in the Garden. She needs a man to take charge of her. I'm telling you, a husband would teach Misha what's what, and she wouldn't be so ready to mix into the women's business." From behind the stove slunk a ginger cat with one ear. Half purring, half growling, it twined itself around Hershel's ankles, rubbing the side of its head against his leg. Clicking his tongue, Hershel pulled some hen giblets from his pocket, placing them on the floor at the foot of his chair. The cat gobbled them up, pausing long enough to let Hershel scratch quickly beside her ear, then bolted.

"Look what's going on there," Shmuel said, pointing to the village square. Through the window they saw a crowd and in the midst of the crowd, like twin towers, Misha and Yarush, the peddler from Plotsk. He looked like a bear in the fur coat he wore summer and winter. Yarush was always hungry, they said, and was known to have bitten off the nose of a beggar who tried to sneak a salami from his cart. Yarush was as big as Misha, no, bigger. A good match for her. And why not make it a match? Didn't someone say that his grandfather was from Blaszka? Yes, it was an inspiration. It was destined. What better mitzvah than to bring together a man and a woman. Grabbing the bottle, Hershel ran outside.

"Leave the poor nag alone," Misha was saying.

Yarush was kicking his horse, which lay still on the packed earth just beyond the crowd. "What do you mean, ordering me around? Can you say what I should do with my own animal?"

"I told you once, and I'm telling you again. Leave the poor nag alone." Misha moved toward Yarush.

"I'll show you who's the master, here," he said.

The crowd pushed closer, excitedly urging Misha, no Yarush, no Misha, someone should teach her, what do you mean, her? what about him? a stranger, did you see? I don't believe . . .

Then Hershel could hear and see nothing, the crowd blocking his view as he pushed his way in. When he saw them again, Yarush's fist was halfway to Misha's mouth. "Try it," Misha was saying. "Just try it."

Hershel waved the bottle in front of Yarush. "Friend, friend, join me in a drink," Hershel said.

Slowly, Yarush turned, like a bear pulled on a chain.

"Schnapps?" he said in a gravelly voice. "*Mph.*"

"Ah. A man of few words. The best," Hershel said, leading him across the square to Perlmutter's tavern, where Shmuel sat at their table, tapping his glass nervously.

"She likes you," Hershel said.

Yarush flung his head back, his forked beard pointing to heaven while he swallowed a glassful of schnapps with one gulp. "She spit at me," he said as he slapped the glass onto the table.

Hershel refilled it. "A good match for you, no? Misha, the woman in the square. She just needs a little, what should I say? Encouragement. A woman appreciates a strong hand, especially a big woman. Just today, Reb Pinkus, the *shokhet,* said to me that a woman needs direction. Firm direction. Isn't that true, Shmuel?"

"I don't know," Shmuel said, dividing his beard into sections with cinnamon-stained fingers. "Women have moods like the river. When it's spring, it floods. What can you do but wait it out?"

"What does he know?" Hershel said. "He's as innocent as Adam in Eden. You listen to me, friend. I know what I'm saying. A woman is like a Sabbath brisket roasting with onions and potatoes. If you have no teeth, can you enjoy it? A big woman like Misha, she's a whole wedding feast, my friend, and you have the teeth to enjoy it."

Hershel watched Yarush greedily swallow another glassful, his eyes glazing. All right, not a refined man. But did Misha have so much to bring to a match? A woman of her age, her background, Hershel thought as he continued to impress her virtues on Yarush. The house. A dowry from the community council.

The door to the tavern flew open. "Good Sabbath," Hanna-Leah said, flapping her shawl and stamping her feet to shake off the snow. She had a few more words to say as she approached their table,

Shmuel looking away in embarrassment, murmuring Good Sabbath as he slipped away. "Deaf to the world," she said. "Didn't you hear the *shammus* knocking on the shutters? It's almost dark. The synagogue is empty, the men have gone home already. You think *Shabbas* is waiting for you?"

"We were busy," Hershel said, "with important matters. Village business."

"Of course, a glass of schnapps is important business. And a bottle, very important. With two bottles, you could call it the Tsar's business. Very good. Why should a Friday night be different than any other? But if I get home before you, don't expect to sleep in the house tonight."

"Hankela, don't get aggravated," Hershel said. "All right. I'm coming." Shrugging his shoulders, he followed her out.

HERSHEL WAS lying in bed beside a rigid Hanna-Leah, making snoring noises loud enough to annoy the dead when Yarush left the tavern. So how could Hershel see him lurch across the square in a gust of snow, a bear with a rock in his hand, moving toward Misha's house? No, Hershel was thinking of his own problems, drifting toward sleep half in dream, half in memory of Hanna-Leah with her hair like a cape of sunlight around her breasts, her wedding veil falling from the moon. He was walking toward her from the river. All around him were the trees of the woods. He knew every one of them, just as he knew every stone in the village and every person's face, everything arranged in the right way.

His half-dream was broken by a shifting in the bed. Hanna-Leah getting up and crossing over to the cot where he slept when she had her period. The sound of her skin whispering. Her thighs touched, parted, touched. What right did she have to take herself away from him, to leave the cold, teasing ghost of her shape in the hollow of the feather bed? But he knew, he knew. If she chose, she could leave him, and how would he live without her?

THE DAY OF THE ICE STORM

Hanna-Leah slapped a piece of brisket on the counter. "A beautiful piece of meat, an inch of fat on it," she said.

Old Mirrel, the girls' teacher, shook her head. "All gristle. It isn't worth anything." Beside her, Gittel the raisin-wine maker, a narrow-nosed woman, nodded approvingly. From the back room, the women heard the sound of whistling punctuated by the cleaver.

"All right, I'll give it to you for half."

"Half of what?" asked Old Mirrel. "Highway robbery?"

"Look, there's the *zogerin*, Tzipporah. You don't want it, I'm sure she'll take it for twice the price."

"Her? Strolling like a princess? The brisket will rot before she gets here."

Hanna-Leah leaned over the counter. "Did you hear about the pig?"

"What pig?" asked Gittel, pushing her bag of raisins to one side so she could lean forward on her patched elbows.

"What pig, she asks. As if there's another pig in Blaszka. Hayim the watercarrier's pig. Hayim with the cat's eyes. Hayim that looks at women. The *artiste*. Is there another Hayim or another pig in Blaszka? The one he found three months ago that he refuses to sell to the farmers. Offered good money but he won't part with it."

"The same pig that tripped Tzipporah on the bridge when she was coming back from the *mikva?*"

"The one. Yesterday it upset Tzipporah's stall. She screamed like she was attacked by Cossacks. The poor frightened pig went tearing off blind because it had got tangled up in one of her fancy tablecloths. Now she's telling everybody the pig is a nuisance and it's improper for a Jew to own a pig, and somebody should make Hayim sell it to Ambrose the beekeeper. But if you ask me," Hanna-Leah winked at Old Mirrel, "that pig is a particular friend to Tzipporah, the high and mighty *zogerin*. What I say is, if there is shmaltz on the face, someone's been eating *trayf.*"

"What would the pig want from Tzipporah?"

"Maybe it fancies her wig. After all, if she can make herself a fine lady just by waving her gold watch at us," Hanna-Leah said, "maybe the pig thinks he'll become a beauty by putting on her wig."

"I heard that the pig made a mess of Alta-Fruma's cellar this morning, before she went to Warsaw. If that pig mixes itself up with her again, it'll get the wrong end of her broom. You can be sure," Old Mirrel said.

"Don't worry, the community council is going to deal with it. Isn't that right, Hershel?" Hanna-Leah called through the open door behind her.

Hershel stood in the doorway, his hat angled back over his head, a bald gnome with a bushy brown beard, his apron blood-spattered. "Don't mix in council business," he said. "That's not for women."

"Can't a woman have an opinion?" asked Old Mirrel.

"If a woman is busy with her business, she has no time," Hershel said.

"Or if she's blessed with a scholar for a husband," said Gittel. "Someone has to earn a few kopecks. Thank God there are poor people who need a little wine for the Sabbath and never mind that I made it last week. Raisin wine is good enough for them. Still, it's not enough of a living to feed five hungry boys. Do I have time for opinions? When my feet are sore from walking up the river with my pack of needles and threads to sell to the peasants, I say to myself, Gittel, your Shloimeh is earning your merit in heaven. He studies the Talmud from morning to night and he should not be distracted by any complaints."

"Oh yes, a scholar's wife certainly shouldn't interrupt such holy work," said Hanna-Leah. "But a butcher's wife can have an opinion or two without disturbing heaven."

So he wasn't a scholar, was he? "Well, even a butcher knows that tonight is Purim," Hershel said. "And even a barren woman whose tongue is so long she'll come back as a frog in the next life must have something to do to get ready. Isn't that so, Hanna-Leah?"

She wrapped the brisket with shaking fingers. "Take it," she said to Old Mirrel. "We'll settle later. You heard the boss. The woman has to fetch firewood for the stove while the man gets ready for his labors in the bathhouse."

WHILE HANNA-LEAH was in the woods, dropping an armload of branches at the sight of the Traveler, Hershel was standing in the back room, his arms raised, the cleaver sharp and silver. Around his feet the sawdust was sprinkled with blood. In the corner the ginger cat with one ear chewed on a mouse. A shaft of light piercing the grimy window hit the ribs of the cow, fragile, separable, dotted with drops of blood like rubies. The cleaver struck precisely and cleanly with the solid, unfailing strength of Hershel's arms. Here he knew what he was doing. There was no worry about Hanna-Leah. No embarrassment at his failure to read even a line of Talmud. His concentration was sure, his blade accurate. He heard the thud of the cleaver striking the wooden block. There was the smell of blood, the green-black shimmer of flies. His skin was tight, his lungs swelling as he breathed large drafts of air, his hands firm around the shaft of the knife. Was he stupid? Not here. As the meat parted, a vision of the big, beautiful soul came into Hershel's mind, a soul lying open before him, vulnerable, penetrable. Why did he have to wait for Friday night, he thought as his body filled with its passions. Isn't Purim a time for festivity? The ginger cat stood on her hind legs, head high, staring at something in the air. "Here, puss puss," Hershel said, holding out a piece of liver. She came to him with her wary, graceful trot. She would allow no one else in the village to touch her. As Hershel scratched at the base of her tail, she purred, pushing her back end toward his hand.

HERSHEL OFTEN listed to himself Hanna-Leah's fine qualities. A woman like his Hanna-Leah deserved the best, and the best he couldn't offer. Not that he ever asked for her opinion on this subject, but he was certain that she longed for a husband like Gittel's Shloimeh. Why wouldn't she? She could support a dozen scholars, she was so clever with business. And she could feed a hundred on one pierogi and they would be as content as if they ate a feast, it was so good. And she was as beautiful as, as, well, as beautiful as a man could want. He often imagined how a scholar would approach her, his head full of holy thoughts, making love to her with a fragile, pale, and otherworldly air, while Hershel was overtaken with such violent passions that he was ashamed. This is a man? he would ask himself. No, a beast.

As he lay beside Hanna-Leah, dizzy with Purim merry-making and heavy with sweet wine, he tried to control himself. But what could he do? It was the same way each time. He wanted to grab her, to kiss her hard, to plunge into her hard and reach the root of her, his hands gripping the softness of her bottom. But was that right? To do that to his wife, his Hanna-Leah, beautiful and smart and good? His muscles ached with tension. If he touched her, they would explode uncontrollably, tearing into her like the worshippers of Baal who ripped living animals limb from limb and ate them raw. The smell of his sweat was the smell of the hungry wolf, and there is only one thing to do with a big, wild wolf that comes into your house. Shoot it. His "little thing" retreated backward into its nest, and nothing more he said to himself would coax it out.

SEASON OF RAINS

On the second Sabbath in May, Misha began to show. In the synagogue, her head held high, she stood among the women, with them repeating after the *zogerin* Tzipporah, "*Holy God, I am a blemished woman, a torn stalk, a broken pot, my heart full and my tears burning. For the sake of our foremothers' merits, give me the strength to turn away from the sinful people that walk in hidden ways, pulled by their lusts.*"

Below, the men shifted prayer shawls around their shoulders as they sat back on their benches. The most important (such as there were in Blaszka) sat closest to the ark. In the third row, the cooper and the blacksmith were arguing with the wedding jester. "Everyone knows it can only be Yarush from Plotsk," the *badkhan* said, pointing a finger at the women's gallery and moving his fist up and down in a rude gesture.

"Everyone? Who's everyone?" the blacksmith retorted, nodding at the corner in the last row where Hayim sat. "I'm telling you, a used pot makes better soup."

"What are you talking? One: Yarush comes to Blaszka the short Friday in December. Two: the inn is flowing with schnapps. Three: there's talk of a *shiddukh,* a match. A big man for a big woman. Four: Misha is showing and that's how many months since Yarush was here. Do you have fingers? Can you add?"

"Hayim," the cooper said. "He looks at women. And they look back, let me tell you. Each one says, 'Come first to me, I have to get ready for *Shabbas.*' We should dig a new well in the village square so the women can carry their own water."

"Not Hayim," Shmuel the baker said softly. "No, I don't believe it."

Hershel, in the second row, turned around. "Not Hayim," he

agreed. "When a man eats a meal does he sit down to eat again? He divorced her fifteen years ago."

"You think it's Yarush? Maybe someone should approach him on her behalf."

Hershel didn't like the turn the conversation was taking. So he'd tried to make a match. Did that make him responsible for Misha? "Listen," he said. "Yarush is a man like any other who steals a drink from the cow and doesn't care to buy her. There's nothing more to it."

A WEEK and a half later, as evening fell on market day, Hanna-Leah was at home preparing for the *mikva*. Hershel had taken Boryna's old milk cow to Reb Pinkus to slaughter and was back at the shop when a young man with a crooked nose and hair like soaked rooster feathers slid through the door of the butcher shop. Carrying a canvas bag with rope handles, the young man said in a friendly tone, "*Sholom aleikhem.*"

Hershel answered in kind, "*Aleikhem sholom. Vos makht a Yid?*"

"Not too bad," the young man said, "considering my head is in a different place every night."

A peddler? Not much of one with a small bag like that. A student maybe. Or someone who wasn't on good terms with the authorities. "Traveling?" Hershel asked.

The young man nodded. "You have it exactly," he said. Fastened to his jacket with a rusty pin, a silk rose drooped over the tattered collar, droplets of rainwater dripping onto the counter as he put down his bag. The rope handles slapped the counter.

"Is there something I can get you? I'm closing up," Hershel said.

The Traveler opened his bag. "Maybe I have something you could use." He pulled out a few small objects, laying them out on the counter in front of Hershel. A miniature cow and a tiny rocking chair carved out of wood. A packet of needles. A square of shiny cloth. "It's a torrent out there. I could stand to dry off," the Traveler said. Through the open door, Hershel could see the wooden planks laid over the mud in the village square shifting and quaking like flat tombstones.

"Look, I have to go," Hershel said. "And I don't need anything. But if you want to stay here until the rain stops, there's a bench in back where you can sleep."

"What's the rush?" the Traveler asked.

"The head of the community council went to Łodz to look for work. We're meeting to decide on a replacement."

"Oh, who do you think it will be?"

"Maybe Azriel the scribe, or the *shokhet,* Reb Pinkus."

"What about you?"

"Me? No. It should be someone educated."

"Sure, of course, I understand. Someone who can read Russian because he'll have to deal with the authorities, right? Like the scribe?"

"Well, no, Azriel doesn't read Russian. But if you put a pin through the Torah scroll, he could tell you without looking what verse it touched."

"I see." There was a long silence while Hershel tried to imagine what the scribe would do with an edict printed in Russian.

"But you see, we need someone with a head, not someone who works with his hands," Hershel explained.

"Like the Rabbi, maybe?"

"Yes, exactly. Berekh reads Russian. He's also the 'crown rabbi,' you know." *Crown rabbi* was the title of the local official responsible for registering births and deaths and reading the Tsar's decrees to the villagers. "So he has to deal with the authorities anyway. He should be the head of the community council."

"And he would be happy to do it, I'm sure."

"Well, not exactly happy. We can barely get him to come to a meeting. He always forgets. He's too busy reading, you see. And then he says we don't need him to decide how many matzos should be baked for the poor for Passover. And really, he's right. When he's there, it's hard to get anything done. He forgets what we're talking about and he goes on about war in China and how we're all clods of dirt under the Tsar's boots. I'll tell you the truth. If he weren't the rabbi and everything, I would think he was a revolutionary."

"Mmm," the Traveler said, looking around. "Nice shop. You do a good business?"

"Not bad, thank God. My wife knows how to put two kopecks together, and no one can cheat her."

"In a shop like this you probably hear everything about what goes on in the village."

"Oh yes, the women. Their tongues don't stop for a minute. And if you have a pair of eyes, you can easily see for yourself how everyone is doing. This one buys a brisket, that one just a few bones for soup. Hanna-Leah never says a word, but she puts in a little extra, and I see that, too. A person has to know his neighbors, doesn't he? It's not an easy world."

"You're right," the Traveler said. "It's just too bad that in most places the people who run the town council don't know what's going on under their noses. But why should they? The rich have servants, and scholars have their minds on higher matters."

"But you can't eat higher matters, can you?" Hershel asked.

"You're a wise man," the Traveler said. "Moses our Teacher couldn't have put it better. But I shouldn't keep you from your meeting." Sweeping the packet of needles, the square of cloth, the miniature cow, and the rocking chair back into his bag, the Traveler headed toward the bench in the back, unperturbed by the spots of blood in the straw or the buzzing flies. "Thanks for your hospitality," he added.

"It's nothing," Hershel replied. "Didn't Abraham our Father wash the angels' feet when they visited him in his tent?" Hershel left the shop, whistling as he crossed the muddy square.

THE COMMUNITY council met in the studyhouse, a large room at the far end of the synagogue. At the head of the table was Reb Pinkus the *shokhet* who had just lost a tooth and was feeling the hole with his tongue. To his right sat the Rabbi, Berekh, and to his left Azriel the scribe. Azriel, a youngish man with no prospects (after all, how many Torah scrolls are produced in a small village, maybe one in a hundred years), was scraping the dirt from under his nail using an obnoxious letter from his brother, a successful lawyer in Warsaw. Berekh's chair was tilted back against the shelves of biblical commentary, his red hair glinting in the candlelight, lanky legs stretched out as he read the latest article by his journalist friend, Moyshe-Mendel, now Maurice LaFontaine from Paris. The old *shammus* Nathan, who called the men to prayer morning and night, sat opposite Reb Pinkus. Nathan was a square-bearded, sincere man whose whole life was keeping the synagogue in order. Beside him, Gittel's Shloimeh, the scholar, was digging the wax out of his ear while trying to translate an obscure commentary from Aramaic. And to Shloimeh's left was Hershel the butcher and then Haykel the blacksmith, whose wife Ettie was a faithful devotee of Faygela's court in the bakery.

Reb Pinkus was speaking at length about the need to choose as head of the community council someone of learning, a person of venerated age, someone with respect in the community, and so on and on, while the Rabbi yawned, old Nathan nodded, Haykel the blacksmith rolled his eyes, Shloimeh chanted under his breath, Azriel the scribe considered moving to Warsaw, and Hershel tried, unsuccessfully, to get a word in.

Into this illustrious company burst Shmuel. He was hatless, breathless, still in his baker's apron, his face twisted in agony, his hand shaking so that the men were afraid he would drop the kerosene lamp he was holding and set them all on fire.

"What's happened? What is it?" they asked, each one praying that it wasn't his house, his wife, his child, not that it should be anyone else's, God forbid, but please *Ribono shel olam,* not mine. Shloimeh, the scholar, blinked rapidly as his mind descended from the heights. Reb Pinkus chewed nervously on the end of his yellowing beard. The Rabbi's chair slapped forward. Hershel rose to his feet, fists clenched.

"It's Ruthie. Faygela will never forgive me," Shmuel said. The lamp shivered in his hand, the light flickering wildly around the men.

"Someone get a brandy from the inn," Hershel said, his eyes still on his cousin as Berekh jumped to his feet and ran out for the bottle. With that look on Shmuel's face, it could only be one thing, Hershel thought, the worst. "Tell me who," he said, his muscles tensing. Shmuel shook his head, unable to speak. Who would dare to touch my cousin's daughter, Hershel thought. I'll find him and cut it off myself, with my cleaver. No, he said to himself, no, no. Is that going to help Ruthie? But what else could he do? I'll send her to Warsaw, he thought, to a nice house where no one knows her. And then I'll find him. Oh, then he'll have to answer to Hershel. He cracked his fingers.

Carefully, the old *shammus* took the lamp and set it on the table as Shmuel fell into a chair. "They're holding her in Plotsk. She's been arrested," he said, covering his face with his hands.

"Ruthie arrested? What for?" Hershel asked. It was impossible to imagine such a thing. Arrested. Not ruined by some young man, but in the hands of the authorities. His fists dangled helplessly.

Shmuel looked at the men with empty eyes as if he didn't care to know where he was. Now and then a tear rolled down his face, losing itself in his beard. The men watched him, eyeing each other, lifting an eyebrow, feebly pulling an ear. Berekh returned, his hat askew, a bottle in one hand, a glass in the other, clumps of mud plopping from his boots as he hurried to the back of the studyhouse and poured Shmuel a full glass.

After Shmuel drank, Hershel said, "Tell us what happened."

"Faygela will never forgive me. She goes to Warsaw and leaves the children in my charge and look what happens," Shmuel cried, covering his face again.

"Listen to me, Shmuel," Hershel said, putting a hand on his cousin's shoulder and shaking him. "Tell me exactly what happened. Slowly. Take another drink."

Shmuel's face took on a liquor glow as he drank. "Ruthie was gone in the afternoon," he said. "I thought she went to help Misha. But when it got dark I began to worry. So I went to Misha and Ruthie wasn't there. Then I thought she must be visiting Emma. But before I had a chance to go to her, there was a knock at the door. It's a terrible sound that knock." He paused, shaking his head. "So loud. 'Jew, open up!' The girls begged me not to go to the door. But what else could I do? There was just one man standing there. The soldier who caught Ruthie. She had some pamphlets in her basket. It's true. I don't know where she got them or why she was carrying them. Ruthie? But my girl is clever. She admitted nothing. She said she couldn't read, that she just found them. Yes of course, she can't read, I said. Does a girl need to read? But look here, take this bottle of vodka and thank you for telling me where she is, and don't worry, your friends will have a share, too. I'll bring a case to the prison tomorrow. I can't afford it but it doesn't matter. I'm telling you, Perlmutter will have to give it to me on credit, or I'll just take it from him." Shmuel spoke angrily, as if it was Perlmutter who had arrested Ruthie.

"Calm down," Hershel said. "No one is denying you anything. Our Ruthie isn't going to rot in prison."

"But how did it happen? What was she up to?" asked Reb Pinkus. "Don't forget what happened during the January insurrection. Maybe the authorities will take an interest in the whole village. Excuse me for saying so, Shmuel, but a man doesn't always know what his own child is up to."

"The insurrection was a long time ago," Berekh said. "There are no revolutionaries here. People are too busy working for their next meal. It's obviously a mistake."

"Do pamphlets grow on trees? Something's going on."

"As it is written," Shloimeh added in a sleepy scholarly voice, " 'Who prolongs his stay in a privy lengthens his days and years.' "

"What's he talking?" the blacksmith asked old Nathan.

"Who knows? But if you understood, you'd be wise."

"Listen to me," Hershel began, interrupted by the blacksmith and Reb Pinkus shouting over each other: "I think, no listen to me, how can you say that . . ." Someone had to take charge. The Rabbi. It was his duty. Hershel banged his fist on the table until there was silence. "Rabbi, what do you say?" he asked.

"I have to think about it. Maybe someone I know has some influence. I have an old friend in Paris who has good connections, but with the Polish gentry not the Russians . . ."

"Listen to him. Just because he went to a Russian school, he thinks he's above everyone. What the Old Rabbi forgot, he should rest in peace, this one won't find out in his whole life, Mister Crown Rabbi," Reb Pinkus said.

Soon they were all arguing again, and Shmuel was moaning, "She'll never forgive me. Never."

Dear God, Hershel thought to himself, it's worse than market day. Everyone shouts and no one hears anything. In the meantime the merchandise can rot. Someone should make them listen. Someone who can see what's under his nose. And who if not me? Hershel banged his fist on the table. "Is Ruthie a *shmata* that someone's buying?" he roared in his bass voice. "While you're arguing about who's the smartest, she's sitting alone in prison." The men looked at one another, sheepishly nodding and murmuring, yes, yes.

"We'll find out what's going on," Hershel said, rocking on the balls of his feet as he shook his finger at Reb Pinkus. "Of course, it's our village. We have to know what the children are up to. But one of them was stolen from us and we have to get her back. Plain and simple."

"What do you say, Hershel?" Shmuel asked, for the first time looking more like a man than a corpse, hope in his voice.

"You think the authorities want anything from her? What for?" Hershel asked, waving his hand dismissively. "No, they just want to beat out a little livelihood from the situation. I'm telling you, they just need a bribe, and we're going to give them one. That's what we have to do."

The men began to mutter, it's impossible, who has anything to spare, what does he think, you can milk a stone?

"I'm not going to argue while Ruthie sits in jail," Hershel said obstinately. "Whatever we can find, we'll take. If there isn't enough money to get Ruthie out, we'll collect at least enough to get Faygela in so she's not alone all the time, so she has something to eat and a pillow to put her head on. Just to start," he added as Shmuel's face fell. "Ruthie isn't an orphan without a home. No one is going to rest until she comes back to Blaszka. Do you hear me? You're all going to scrub the village for every spare kopeck."

The men looked at one another, silenced at last. Hershel leaned back in his chair, his two fists on the table, though he realized it wasn't his fists that convinced the others. It was only that he knew what was what. As simple as that.

"Hershel has the right idea," Berekh said. "But I propose one condition. He has to be the head of the community council. Are we agreed?" Yes, the others said, Hershel, yes.

"All right," Hershel said. "Then we start now. Who has something to give for Ruthie?"

"Here," Reb Pinkus said, "take my watch. You can sell it in Plotsk. Do I have to know the time? Nathan here tells us when it's time to pray. What else does a man need to know?"

HUMMING AS he opened the door, Hershel came home with a bag of coins and trinkets clinking satisfyingly. And what greeted him? Fragrant smells came from the oven, there was tea on the table, his mother was silently reading the *Tzena-U-Rena,* her lips moving softly, and Hanna-Leah's head was bent over her sewing. Something wasn't right. There was no pungency in the air, no sense of imminent strife.

"You weren't here when I closed up the shop. Where did you go?" he asked.

"To the *mikva*," she said.

Ah, at the *mikva*. So she was clean, and he could touch her. Couldn't he? Her skin was ruddy, and she seemed at once excited and content. Look there, on the table, in the pickle jar—flowers, purple and white flowers. Since when did Hanna-Leah pick wildflowers for the table? "They made me head of the council," he said.

"Good." She was looking at him, her hands still for a minute. What was she making out of that shining green cloth? Why was she smiling? What did she have to smile about?

Hershel threw himself down in a chair and stared at his wife. A damp cold crawled up his leg, shrinking him into himself. There was a clump of mud on the fringes of her shawl. A leaf clinging to the damp hem of her dress. Twigs in her hair. Where did she go? And worse, with whom? There was a wooden figure on the sidetable beside her chair. She was measuring the cloth against it. He could see the resemblance between the doll and his Hanna-Leah. Who gave it to her? Who?

"Did you hear that Ruthie was arrested?" he asked.

It can't be, the women said, Ruthie, no, what for, when?

"Shmuel told us. She was caught with pamphlets," he said.

His mother put a hand to her mouth, pulling out her teeth, as she always did when she wanted to concentrate on something. "You must mean the younger girl, Freydel," she said.

"No, it was Ruthie."

"You see, you never know in this world," she began in her tooth-less mumble, going on about daughters and mothers and Eve who brought misery into the world by making friends with a serpent, while Hershel ached for Hanna-Leah to throw in a sharp word, something, anything to let him know that she was in the room with them.

Finally, when his mother ran out of breath and put her teeth back in her mouth, Hanna-Leah said, "Poor Faygela."

"Poor Faygela?" his mother asked. "How can you feel sorry for her. She called it on herself, she did. Letting her daughters read and go around with anyone they want like *vilda hayas*."

"Yes, *vilda hayas*. The apple doesn't fall far from the tree, does it?" But there was no bite to her voice, only a wistful pause before she went back to her sewing. The hairs stood up on the back of Hershel's neck.

"Read out loud, Mama," he said. "I'm not feeling so well." He avoided Hanna-Leah's eye.

"No? What's wrong?" his mother asked, peering at him with alarm.

"Nothing to worry about. Just a little ache."

"A toothache?"

"Yes, a kind of one."

"Maybe you need a poultice. Hanna-Leah, pay attention to your husband." She was still sewing, oblivious to the conversation. "Hershel needs something from you," her mother-in-law pestered.

"Don't disturb yourself, Hankela," he said, though it was quite obvious that she wasn't moving. "Just read, Mama, it'll take my mind off it."

"All right, then. If that's what you want."

"Yes, yes," he said impatiently.

"*King Saul was of the tribe of Benjamin,*" she read, "*but was too shy to take a woman. One notable girl came and took him to dance, to indicate that she wanted him as her husband. He took this girl for a wife and she bore him a son, Jonathan, who was a devoted friend of David's. When Saul wanted to kill David it was Jonathan who argued with his father on David's behalf. Saul grew angry with him and said: 'You are the son of an impudent woman; you are like your mother, who showed her impudence by taking me to dance.'*"

He remembered how Hanna-Leah danced with him at their wedding, circling him, lightly holding onto her end of the handkerchief, her other hand lifting the folds of her dress, the flash of her calf. Then she sat in a chair. The men raised it above their shoulders and she was hanging onto the sides of the tilting chair, breathless with fright and laughter while Hershel's chair was hoisted high. Recklessly he held out both hands to Hanna-Leah. "Be careful, you'll fall," she cried, and he answered, "Then take hold of me quickly, Hankela."

Hershel felt an uncoiling against his thigh. "It's getting late," he said. "Maybe I'll go to bed."

"Go," said Hanna-Leah. "I'll finish my sewing."

He moved to stand behind her chair, looking over her shoulder, hoping that she would stop and look up at him. Her needle flashed. She took no notice of him. "What are you making?" he asked at last.

"Nothing," she said.

"It must be something."

"A little rag," she said. He saw it was her grandmother's satin shawl, and she was hemming a small, doll-size dress. Uneasily, he wondered again where Hanna-Leah had gotten the wooden figure and why she attended to it so carefully.

"Do you want to hear about the council meeting?" he asked tentatively.

"Me? Nooo, is it women's business?" she asked sarcastically.

That's my Hanna-Leah, Hershel thought, pulling a chair close beside her, seating himself, leaning toward her. "I decided that we're going to collect money for a bribe to help Ruthie. You see?" He showed her the bag. "*Nu*, what do you think of that?"

"In a good hour," she said. "I hope you're going to do something about Hayim's pig, too."

"The pig? Who cares about a pig? We have bigger problems."

"Oh yes, men always have such big problems," she said.

"And ever since *Gan Aeden*, where do men's problems come from?" he asked, wanting to take her two hands in his. He didn't quite know how to do it. He should know how, after all, she was his wife, wasn't she? But still, he didn't. Her hands, occupied with satin and a needle seemed very far from his, fiddling awkwardly with his beard. A man's beard is a good thing for hands when they don't know what to do with themselves. What do clean-shaven men do? Hershel wondered.

Later when he lay beside Hanna-Leah, his hand found a place on her belly as he put his arm around her. She didn't pull away, and when his tail began to pay attention, he said to it, Look you, in a minute you're going to make me want to grab her and then you're going to tell me no, it's not right, and you'll hide where I can't find you. So never mind. I'm lying with my Hanna-Leah. You know what we say on Passover. *Dayeinu.* It's enough. And Hershel went to sleep, Hanna-Leah pressed close to him.

THE LONG DAYS

The council, under Hershel's instruction, recruited the villagers not once but many times, until the last kopeck was found in the last corset, and people began to run away when they saw one of the councillors approaching. A bribe was assembled—a bag of silver coins sent to the warden, who took a commission for himself before sending the rest on to the Governor.

As the nights became shorter than the days, the weather was warm and dry, less cloud and more sky than anyone could remember. Nothing was the way it was supposed to be. The good girl had gone to prison. The bad girl was working in her place. The baker's wife refused to write letters. The butcher's wife wandered in the woods.

Look, people said, it happens to a childless woman sometimes. She goes a little crazy. Can you blame her? The world is upside down. Her arms are empty while the midwife is getting bigger by the minute.

In the strange evening light when the men went to pray, one would begin, Misha's baby could have any man for a father, don't you think? Or another would say, she's walking slowly these days. Maybe six months along, isn't she? And soon, someone would sigh and add, she's one of ours, after all.

Their wives had begun to worry. Who would come to Batia when she was near her time if Misha was too big? What if something happened to Misha? Pregnancy was a dangerous business, and giving birth worse than the draft. Some women were never the same afterward. Some died. Who's going to bring our babies safely into the world? the women asked. Where will I go when my mother coughs up blood?

They would run to her house for every little thing, Misha I need this and Misha I need that, just to make sure that she was still there making up her remedies and filling her shelves with rows of potent bottles. On market day, Misha was the first to fold up her stall these days, the empty corner of the village square like the hole after a tooth is pulled. Something has to be done, the women said. Misha's alone, how much money can she have? Is she able to get what she needs for herself? It's too hard for her.

Hershel, the villagers said, what are you going to do about Misha? Well, a woman alone isn't a good thing, he answered. So? they asked. So *nu,* Hershel, you're the head of the community council. You have to do something.

HERSHEL hired Shayna-Perl, the cart driver, to take him to Plotsk. The road followed the Północna River down to its mouth at the Vistula, then turned along the larger river toward the docks in Plotsk. As the cart approached Plotsk, small figures on the decks of ships turned into men loading hundred-pound sacks of salt onto the bowed backs of porters who staggered down onto the docks. Horses were backing up to the boats, the wagons opened to let loose a load of sugar beets, tumbling and rumbling into the hold.

Everyone around the docks knew of Yarush the thief and occasional peddler. "You're looking for the Bear? You're in luck. He must have had a good haul. He's drinking up the tavern on Whorehouse Row."

Where thirty years before the only brothel had been Avraham's house of pleasure, a virtual monopoly, now cheap brothels had multiplied like flies in the market place. Despite hard times there was one area of business, at least, that was expanding. The whorehouses were stacked one on top of the other, the street so narrow that two girls could lean out of opposite windows and shake hands—or at least pass over their customers' valuables. One could buy sex in Polish, Russian, Yiddish, Lithuanian, and Byelorussian. Only in Warsaw and America was the choice bigger. Of course you get what you pay for, and it was said that more *shmeckels* fell off after a visit to the docks in Plotsk than in a graveyard. It was a popular misconception that Jewish whores were cleaner, and there were always agents scouting for young Jewish girls newly arrived in the city. The Plotsker pimps complained that Warsaw got all the best workers. But that's how it is these days, they said. You just can't operate on a big enough scale in a small town.

The tavern occupied the main floor of one of the largest houses in the row. It was a safe place to drink as the owner had seven sons to keep order when they were done thieving for the night.

Shayna-Perl left her cart and horse tied up outside, got a bottle of something fumigatory, and joined her brother carters on the far side of the tavern. At the front of the room, eyes open for business, were the pimps, their favorite girls with them, and a few young sailors, newly tattooed. The older sailors sat at the back where no one could creep up on them. In the center were the thieves. Those who'd just finished a job were joking and roughhousing under watch of the seven sons. Those in preparation huddled together, speaking in low voices. On either side of the tavern sat the lowest of the low. Where their patches ended and their skin began was a mystery. Here drank the porters, permanently hunched from carrying hundredweights, the carters, and the beggars. All manner of crutches, eye patches, and lumps floated in the shifting smoke of bitter cigarettes.

In the back, alone, sat Yarush the Bear with a row of glasses in front of him. He slugged down each glass in turn, then refilled them all from the bottle of schnapps under his chair. Several ladies and pimps had attempted to share in his obvious bounty, but a little deep growling from Yarush put them straight.

Hershel put two bottles on the table before seating himself opposite Yarush. "You left some business in Blaszka," Hershel said. "Maybe you forgot."

"Business?"

"The woman, Misha, remember?" Hershel filled the row of glasses.

"I know lots of women." Yarush drank.

"This one is pregnant. People say she's around six months. You were in Blaszka six months ago."

"So?"

"So you want your baby to grow up without a name?"

"Who says it's mine?"

"Who else's would it be?"

"Anyone."

"I'm talking a match. There's a lot in it for you. A dowry. A strong woman. So why not? Since the child is yours anyway."

"Maybe. Maybe not. A man never knows, does he?"

"Weren't you with her?"

"What if I was? Women are dogs."

"You don't mean that. Our women? Daughters of Moses?"

"Dogs," Yarush said, nodding his head, vodka spilling into his beard. "Wild dogs. Bite the hand that feeds them. Take away your last bone. Bitches, all of them." Yarush burped, mouth wide, exhaling a fiery,desiccated breath.

Hershel squinted at him, scratching the inside of his ear as if he hadn't heard right. Then he grabbed the neck of Yarush's shirt. "Watch your mouth, you're talking about one of ours," he said.

Grunting, Yarush knocked Hershel's arm away. The seven sons began to rise. Hershel looked at them, gauging his chances, shoulders tensing as he got ready to kick over the table and grab Yarush by the eggs. He licked his upper lip, salty with excitement, eyes flicking from Yarush to the seven sons, to the sailors with their backs to the wall and their knives in their boots. When he was a boy, he wouldn't have hesitated, but now he paused as if watching himself from a distance, seeing himself as he would quickly be, gasping on the floor, swimming in a fertile mix of vodka and blood. Hershel relaxed into his chair and refilled the row of glasses. He took a swig from the second bottle himself. The seven sons slouched back against the wall.

"So, friend, I expect we won't be seeing you in Blaszka," Hershel said.

"Why not?" Yarush asked. "When I've got something to sell, I go through there on my way upriver."

"Well, sure, you used to," Hershel said. "But you know, all the peasants, they come to Blaszka on market day. People talk. It's too bad, but you know how people are. They're saying that Misha cursed the father of the baby. Well, it can't be true, of course, but the peasants are superstitious. They won't buy anything from a cursed man."

"I'm not the father, I told you," Yarush growled.

"Sure, I believe you. But the peasants, who can talk to them?"

Yarush peered at Hershel with eyes like eggs poached in vodka. "What kind of a curse?" he asked.

"Didn't you hear about the doctor from Plotsk?"

"You mean the one who—"

"It fell off," Hershel said solemnly.

Yarush scratched himself thoughtfully. Probably checking to see if his *shmeckel* was in place, Hershel thought.

"I'll tell you, though," Hershel said, "they say a little silver can remove a curse."

"Silver?" asked Yarush. "I have silver."

"Lucky you," Hershel said, taking another swig from the bottle as if Yarush's silver were of no interest to anyone.

Yarush opened his fur coat, retrieving a tin box from the gusty innards. He slapped it onto the table. "Here."

"What do you want me to do with this?" Hershel asked.

"Take it to the witch."

"Not me. I'm not anybody's messenger."

"Take it," Yarush said, half-rising. The seven sons were beginning to show an interest in them again.

"All right, if you insist," Hershel said, "then what can I do?"

As SOON AS he returned to Blaszka, Hershel stopped first at the shop, wanting to show Hanna-Leah the tin box full of silver coins. The shop was closed. It was a little unusual, but it wasn't market day and maybe she had something to do at home. "Hanna-Leah," he called as he went inside the house. She wasn't there, either. "Did you see Hanna-Leah?" he asked his mother.

"In the middle of the afternoon? She's in the shop, of course."

"Yes, you're right," Hershel mumbled. He looked up at the wooden doll on its shelf above the fireplace. Where did it come from? Ever since she made the dress for it, she was different. One day she would seem all right, sharp-eyed, a proper woman gossiping with the customers, making a good bargain, helping his mother into her chair, carrying a pot of soup to a sickhouse. The next day she would disappear, returning with the smell of the woods on her skin, and he'd wonder what she found there. Or who. She would fall asleep as soon as she got into bed, her hair unbraided like random rays of light across her pillow. She would sprawl across the bed, arms and legs flung wide.

Hershel sat in the rocking chair, waiting for Hanna-Leah.

When she came traipsing into the house, her hair was loose around her shoulders like an unmarried girl's, the hem of her dress wet. Hershel thought he had never seen her so beautiful. If there was someone else, he would . . . no, no. His hands clenched and unclenched. What was he thinking? She was here. She was standing behind his chair, her hands on his shoulders, leaning over him, her long hair on each side of his face a golden veil. She was laughing. Let her laugh. Let her be happy. "You sit, Hankela. No, no. Not at the table. Here in the big chair." His fingers held onto hers so tightly he could feel the quick pulse of her blood. "You sit and I'll bring everything to you. Everything. Why not?"

He brought her a bowl of soup and, sitting beside her on a stool, watched her eat. "Good, good," he said. "Your dress is wet. You have to get warm. When you're finished, you tell me what else I can bring you."

While Hanna-Leah drank her soup, Shmuel was on his way to Plotsk with a pouch of gold and a letter to the Governor, Hayim and Alta-Fruma were talking outside the dairyhouse, and Berekh the Rabbi was walking with Misha along the riverbank.

NIGHTS OF THE SECRET RIVER

Hershel spoke to the Rabbi's housekeeper, Maria, about getting the farmer Boryna's daughter to help Misha out. He entrusted the tin box to her, which she gave to the Rabbi, who went to his cousin Faygela to ask her what a woman requires during her confinement. Eventually the story came out: that Misha's mother, may she rest in peace, had interceded on her daughter's behalf in the Heavenly Court, and an angel had been sent down to bring her what she needed. You see, they said in the village square, it's just like in the days of the *Alter Rov*, the Old Rabbi. God in Heaven sends down angels to save the innocents. But of course in heaven they don't speak Polish, so they wouldn't be able to find their way 'round the docks, and they sent Hershel the butcher to handle the affair. You know, like in the old days, when a Polish count who didn't want to dirty his hands would hire a Jew to act as his agent. And if there was a biting edge to their voices, who could blame them? The Old Rabbi lived in a time when Poles and Jews thought they could be brothers and the Russian schools were open to anyone. Oh yes, they said in Blaszka, angels. My brother-in-law saw one in the factory in Łodz. It's true. Right before the saw cut off his hand.

THE RASPBERRIES ripened and then the blueberries. Misha and Berekh the Rabbi were seen walking along the river more than once. People talked, of course. But Hershel said, "I don't want to hear a thing. First you beg me to make sure that she has what she needs for the baby, now you're worried about who she's walking with. Let me tell you, she's walking slowly enough these days, as big as she is. She could use a little help. So? *Nu?* What are you going to do?" People still talked, but more than one also watered Misha's garden, brought her a honey cake for the Sabbath, took her washing to the river.

In the meantime Ruthie was home and Emma contrite, but the

young people of Blaszka were still congregating in the woods. Not as often since the Rabbi began holding classes for them in science and philosophy, but who knew what kind of trouble they might still be getting up to? What are you going to do about it? the villagers asked Hershel. "It's the press," he said. "Even after everything that's happened, they can't leave it alone."

In the first week of August, he took matters into his hands. Since it was the printing press that drew them, the printing press would have to go. He walked to the old hut in the woods, his ax over his shoulder. The air was sticky, his shirt clinging to his back, bees humming as they returned to their nest in the hollow of a beech tree.

As Hershel came to the clearing, he thought that this might be where his Hanna-Leah walked when she came to the woods. Perhaps here she met . . . no, he couldn't think such things. But as he strode into the hut, hot with jealousy, his hands sweating so that he had to wipe them on his caftan before he lifted the ax, he could almost see her, here with someone. Teeth gritted, he brought the ax down on the press with all his strength. Chopping first at the struts that held the printing press in place, he then broke the supports for the type, the brackets that held the rollers, the chill sound of falling metal pieces ringing so loud he didn't hear Emma come into the hut.

"You have no right," Emma was yelling as she ran in front of the press. Hershel grunted as she grabbed him around the waist, throwing him off balance, his ax striking the metal at an odd angle and nearly bouncing out of his hands.

"Emma! Stop. I could have hit you with the ax," Hershel said, flinging her aside.

Ruthie was right behind Emma, trying to pull her away. But she charged Hershel again, hitting his back with her fists. He tried to hold her but she was wild, and when she kicked him between the legs, he didn't think, he just threw her down.

He didn't mean for her to hit her head so hard. Afterward everyone assured him that you don't get the typhus from hitting your head on a dirt floor. Yet he couldn't help but think if she died, dear God Above, please protect her, it had something to do with him. When Hanna-Leah suggested they keep Izzie in their house so that the boy wouldn't catch his sister's sickness, Hershel was only too glad to agree.

He's either an idiot or very brave to risk bringing the typhus into his own house, people claimed. But in the bakery Faygela said to anyone who wanted to listen, and everyone who didn't, that Hershel had more sense in his little finger than a yeshiva full of scholars. "Do you know someone else who can milk money from a stone?" she asked. "And not for himself either, not a kopeck for himself, but only for the good of others. My Ruthie. And Misha." You call that sense, people said. But to outsiders they began to boast, Here in Blaszka we're not afraid of the authorities. Why should we be? Hershel the butcher takes care of everything.

In 1894, Tishah b'Av would be falling on Saturday, August 9th. Since it was forbidden to mourn on the Sabbath, the fast day would have to be observed after the Sabbath ended—from Saturday evening to Sunday evening.

That Sabbath was a solemn one, anticipating Tishah b'Av, the villagers anxious about the possibility of an epidemic, Alta-Fruma sleeplessly watching over Emma. After Hershel and Izzie returned from services on Friday evening, Hanna-Leah put the boy right to bed. "He's worn out with worry. He has to sleep," she said, wiping her face with a handkerchief. "It's too warm in the house. I need a breath of air. A walk. Watch over the boy, Hershel."

She left and he watched her go, chewing the inside of his cheek, worried that she might be getting sick and more worried, to his shame, that she might have another reason for going out at this time of night.

Hershel sat, arms flat on the table, looking at the carved figure in the green satin dress on its shelf above the fireplace. Where did she get the wooden doll? It couldn't be from anyone in Blaszka. If it was, he would have heard. Someone gave it to her. What kind of someone? Not a scholar. Not a person with holy thoughts who wouldn't lift his eyes to a woman. No. It had to be someone who worked with his hands. A *proster.* Not any better than Hershel himself. Looking at his Hanna-Leah. Touching her.

"Where is she?" he asked. "Who is she with?" He began to pace. Walking back and forth, he muttered, he groaned. "If I find her—them—I'll . . ." He couldn't hold himself back anymore. He was always trying to hold himself back. Enough. It would be a relief to let himself go. He would find them and he would give them what they deserved. He hit the wall with his fist. The wall cracked and the boy whimpered, tossing in his sleep. "Sha, sha," Hershel said, wiping away the blood on his knuckles. He sat down. He stood up. He sat down, his head in his hands. "Hankela, Hankela," he whispered, "what would I do without you?"

He remembered their wedding day, when he stood in front of her, weak with fasting, Shmuel at his side. He had a speech prepared, the injunction to the bride informing her of her duties and instructing her in her behavior. But in that moment, looking at her sitting tall in her bride's chair, wreathed with a veil and a crown of flowers, he thought only of how lucky he was. The same hands that could split a cow in half would soon lift her veil, and he saw himself falling into a bed of gold. The older men laughed at his speechlessness. It was something he would remember later. But then he didn't care. He only said, "Hankela, if you'll be a good wife for me, I'll be very happy."

But years had passed and now look what it all had come to. "Enough," he said. "I have to find her. I have to know. And if she wants a *Get?*" No. A man doesn't have to give his wife a divorce if he doesn't want. He would desert her first. Leave town. Let her find out how good it is to be an *aguna* like Alta-Fruma. "If she wants a *Get,* I'll, I'll . . ." There were tears in his eyes. "I'll let her go."

HERSHEL PEERED into the darkness, listening for footsteps, for a broken twig or a startled bird. A cool wind brought the smell of fall into the summer air. A goose flew across the moon, honking. At night it all looked strange. Charcoal, blue-black hazy shapes. Everything large merging with its shadow. Familiar landmarks missing. Where was the tree that he climbed with Shmuel to spy on the girls? He had pointed to Hanna-Leah and said, "That's the one I want. The big one. The one with the golden hair."

"What if her father doesn't want you? He's a butcher, and your father's not so much."

"He will. That's all. I'll make myself his apprentice."

"An apprentice doesn't count for anything."

"I will," he had said, pulling himself up to the next branch.

Hershel pushed his way deeper into the woods, tripping over logs, falling through nettles, tearing his caftan, cursing his clumsiness. When he heard singing, he stopped. A man's voice, a Polish drinking song. The man was stumbling through the undergrowth of the woods, singing and laughing as he fell to his knees and pulled himself up again, alone. Hershel continued on his way, the song growing fainter as he weaved through the trees like the drunk, without direction, without knowledge. When he broke through the underbrush, he blinked at the sudden light of the moon hovering above the river.

A figure stood in the water, her silken shift bright in the moonlight. Hanna-Leah. Alone. Thank God, alone. But in the water? What was she doing here, where the water ran so fast around the rocks? If she lost her footing for a minute she could trip. She could hit her head. She could drown. As Hershel opened his mouth to call her, she dipped under the water. Dear God, she was drowning. He began to tear off his boots, then stopped. She was rising from the water, standing. Not drowned. Maybe she was hot. All right, Hanna-Leah wasn't exactly herself these days. It didn't matter. She was his. Whatever she was. She dipped again and a third time, Hershel watching carefully, not wanting to disturb her, afraid that she might yet fall and hurt herself. The third time, when she didn't rise, he ran toward the water, calling "Hankela, Hankela, I'm coming," but then she was standing again, now walking toward the shore. Of course she didn't see him. Not in his caftan, as dark as the shore. When he saw that she was climbing up the river bank, he retreated to the bush, moving quickly into the woods. He would hurry home. She would never have to know that he followed her. Or why. Overhead a goose circled the moon seven times.

WHEN SHE came home, Hershel was sitting in his chair. "You're wet," he said.

"Am I?"

"Where have you been?"

"The river. Near the silver rocks."

"There? The current is fast. The water's deep. You could have drowned."

"I didn't," she said, yawning and smiling.

"You didn't," he said somberly, "Thank God, you didn't. You're soaking, Hankela. You'll catch your death. Come into our room and let me help you take off the wet clothes."

Standing next to the bed, he gently pulled first the sodden dress over her head and then her shift, wrapping her in a towel, his arms around her, arms like Moses. Not like Moses when he broke the clay tablets, but the Moses who met Tzipporah at the well and drove off her persecutors, helping her to fill her troughs and water her flock. Slowly, tenderly, Hershel dried Hanna-Leah, her shoulders, her breasts, her hips, her thighs, between her legs, with his hands warming every inch of cold skin until she glowed, her nipples hard under his hand, his body filled with the smell and the touch of her. As Hershel took off his clothes, he thought to himself, a butcher doesn't make a hacked-up mess of the animal. He cuts it carefully, knowing that people work hard for a little meat on the Sabbath. You need a good eye for that, and a strong arm. That was his last thought as he leaned toward Hanna-Leah, her lips soft against his, her legs open, her thighs gripping.

In the Hebrew month of Elul, while the harvest was gathered, the shofar was blown every morning in the synagogue, waking the people to the coming Days of Awe. The blackberries ripened as the Passages of Consolation were read from the prophets: "*Violence shall no more be heard in your land, neither desolation nor destruction within your borders. But you will call your walls Salvation, and your gates Praise. The sun will not go down, nor will the moon withdraw itself, for the Holy One will be an everlasting light, and the days of your mourning will be ended.*"

THE DAYS OF AWE

On the first day of the Hebrew month of Tishrei, the crescent moon was a sliver beside the setting sun, sitting like a red crown on a bank of clouds. The New Year was announced, and the children of Blaszka dipped apples in honey so that the coming year would be sweet.

In the morning Hershel asked his mother and his wife for their forgiveness, and they gave it before they left for the synagogue.

*   *   *

"THERE WAS a man of the hill country whose name was Elkanah," the reader chanted from the Prophets. Some of the men had fallen asleep, arms folded, heads nodding. Shmuel, who fired up the ovens in the darkness every morning, was half-smiling in a dream, but Hershel was awake and listening. "*He had two wives,*" the reader said, "*one named Hannah and the other Peninnah. Peninnah had children, but Hannah was childless. Whenever Elkanah offered sacrifices, he would give portions to his wife Peninnah and to all her sons and daughters; but he would give a double portion to Hannah, for he loved her, though God had made her childless. Her rival would taunt her severely because she was childless. This went on year after year. Whenever she went up to the house of God, Peninnah would so distress her that she wept and would not eat. Elkanah her husband would ask her: 'Hannah, why do you weep, and why do you not eat, and why is your heart so sad? Am I not better to you than ten sons?'*" Better than ten sons, Hershel repeated to himself. Hanna-Leah is more to me than ten sons.

KOL NIDREI

Near the Holy Ark, the Rabbi stands in a pool of light. In the front row are the scribe, the ritual slaughterer, the *shammus.* In the second row, Hershel, the head of the community council, stands with his cousin, Shmuel the baker. The poorest of Blaszka are in the back row. Hayim the watercarrier. Getzel the picklemaker. Their heads covered by prayer shawls.

A moan drifts across the village square. And another.

Hershel looks up to the gallery where the women are rustling like geese disturbed by a change of wind. Now there is the clatter of footsteps, the slam of a door. The men look at one another, confused, bereft as if while looking up for the heavens to open, the earth has opened instead. What's going on? they ask.

Hershel climbs the stairs to look out at the courtyard. "The women are leaving. They're going, they're just going, that's all. Come and look." He waves to the men, who follow him through the doorway of the synagogue where they look from the women to the darkening sky. On Rosh Hashanah their fate was written, on Yom Kippur the book will be closed. The sun itself is the red seal, coming lower, lower while the men crowd together in their white burial robes.

IN THE coming year, Hanna-Leah will say to Gittel the raisin-wine maker, "So what is a Friday night? Is it so special? What's wrong with Monday and Thursday, too. Tell me, did you hear that they say the *zogerin* Tzipporah has lost all her hair? It's true, I heard it straight from Liba, the bath attendant. That's what comes when you have an old husband. Some men have eggs of gold and others eggs of lead. You just have to have luck with the matchmaker."

Along the River Północna people will say, The governor of Plotsk might have eggs of steel, but the head of the community council in Blaszka has eggs of gold.

In five years, Hershel will arrange for the village square to be paved with cobblestones. When there is a resurgence of pogroms in Russia ten years from now, Hershel will institute self-defense groups. In fifteen years, he will organize the building of a school in Blaszka. During the First World War it will be used as a hospital where the Rabbi's son Adam and daughter Rayzel will nurse the injured and comfort the grieved.

6

THE WATERCARRIER

Just before sunset, the Director crossed the bridge, his top hat black against the fading sky, the tails of his coat flying behind him. The latch to Hayim's door lifted, the door banged open, and the Director, seeming to fill the entrance with a tall, gaunt shadow, held out a wriggling, crying little pig at arm's length. "Look what I found on the bridge. Do you know who this belongs to?"

"N-no," Hayim said. He was cooking his Sabbath dinner of potatoes on a tripod over the fire. His hips were bruised where the heavy buckets banged him, and there were grooves in his shoulders from the yoke. The well was beside the *mikva*, convenient to the fine homes of the wealthy, now in ruins. No one gave a thought to the convenience of the watercarrier who had to run back and forth across the bridge.

"I have no time to look for the owner of a pig," the Director said. "The troupe has to stay ahead of the authorities. You want him, or should I leave him with Ambrose the beekeeper for sausages? Tell me yes or no."

The piglet looked at Hayim appealingly, its coat dark brown with lighter stripes along its length. Probably not a farmer's pig with that coloring, but a wild one. Could he condemn a living thing, a child of God, to sausages, to *trayf?* "Give, give him to me," Hayim said.

"Take him, then." The Director handed the crying pig to Hayim and strode back into the dusk.

While the potatoes boiled, Hayim fed the piglet some goat's milk, dipping his finger into the bowl of milk and then giving it to the creature to suckle. "What will I do with you?" Hayim asked. "A Jew with a pig? Everyone will look at me." He didn't stammer. He never stammered when he spoke to his goat, or the birds, or his ax, or the night. Only with people.

He had begun to stammer when he was sent to school. In the stale, dim front room of the teacher's house, forty boys pushed and poked and shouted while the teacher cracked his ruler on their shoulders, the teacher's wife in the other room cooking potatoes with onions and garlic, her babies screaming over the sing-song chant of the boys. Hayim would sit in the far corner, praying, "Master of the Universe, make me invisible." Nine hours a day except for *Shabbas.* At night, Hayim would see the teacher's face, as huge and pale as a bearded moon with its mouth open to swallow him. Only when he jumped up from the bed and with a stub of a pencil drew a picture of the teacher in the margin of his scribbler did the trembling leave him. In the morning, he would carefully black out the sketch and the teacher would beat him on the knuckles for marking up his notebook.

Hayim's father, Ari the miller, was determined to lift up his son among the fine people, the *shayner.* First he'd built the bathhouse with its marble columns. Then he dressed Hayim in satin and velvet, like the sons of the *shayner.* And finally he hired tutors for Hayim so that after his nine hours of heder, he was shut into a snug windowless room, where Hayim could hardly breathe, never mind speak when the tutors ordered him to recite Torah. All of this so that Hayim would someday be matched up with a girl from a good family. The best, his father would say. Full of rabbis.

On *Shabbas* in the synagogue they sat in the second row, behind the scribe, the cantor, and the two grain merchants, Eber and his partner, Zelig. "You'll see, Hayim. You'll be a fine scholar," his father would say. "Thin, pale, your head full of the Holy Word. Not grain, flour, taxes, and bribes. Hey, what do you say, my friends?" The miller would lean forward and slap the shoulders of the grain merchants. "My son the scholar. Maybe he'll learn to chant and the cantor will be out of a job. He'll be in the back row and Hayim here will sit among the *shayner* beside the Holy Ark. Good seed from old apples." The miller would pat the inside of his thigh and wink while the cantor coughed and turned away. But as Hayim, red-faced, turned his eyes to the ceiling, he would hear one of the grain merchants say, "A rich apple full of worms."

Hayim would look up at the umbrella-shaped ceiling of the synagogue, with its ribs of oak, painted in 1622 by a man known as Ari the Eggs, the many times-great-grandfather of Hayim's own Papa, who was named Ari after him. Mama said their ancestor was called Eggs because he was bald, but when the miller took Hayim to immerse in the ritual bath before the Sabbath, he winked and nudged, pointing to the other men's nakedness, and said, "Him, no one would call Eggs, with those shriveled peanuts, but that one, there, you see? He has a couple big ones. He could father a dozen, let me tell you. That's why they call a man "Eggs." Ari the Eggs—you understand, Hayim?"

On *Shabbas,* Hayim looked at Ari's ceiling, drinking in the vividness of color, the elephants and monkeys, the huge bright flowers, the hot blue sky. How did Ari the Eggs see so far? All the way across the Sambyaton, the river beyond which the ten lost tribes of Israel waited for the Messiah. Hayim thought about it for a long time. When he was finished thinking, he had decided that Ari the Eggs so revered the Master of the Universe that he practiced looking at the Holy One's creations, gazing deeper and farther until his vision was unmatched. A man like that would look at everything. If it was foreign or forbidden, he would have to look harder until he knew it by heart; there was not a thing that didn't contain the spark of the Holy One.

After the Russians blew up the mill, the family lost everything. They lived on the charity of the community council. Instead of becoming *shayner,* they had fallen to the lowest of the *proster* and Ari's heart gave out. What could Hayim's mother do? She was a rich man's wife. She had no skills, no livelihood. What choice did she have? She remarried. Her new husband took her away, leaving Hayim behind, ignoring her tears and pleas, even though she went down on her knees and kissed his hands. And Hayim, who was fourteen years old, went to live with the watercarrier, Asher the Hasid, an old man who had no children of his own. People said that if Ari wasn't dead already, he would have died to see his son sleeping in a shack on a bed of straw. But Hayim was happy cutting wood for a few kopecks. There were no more tutors yelling at him. No teacher cracking a ruler over his head. No airless classroom. Only Asher, who put a bowl in front of Hayim and told him that everything is a child of the Holy One, even a blade of grass, even a pig. Hayim didn't have much to eat, but when he was done cutting wood for the Old Rabbi or the scribe's house, he could wander among the trees and look as long as he wanted at anything he liked, breathing the cool, sweet air while he sketched the world into being.

HAYIM WAS seventeen when the cholera swept through Plotsk in '67. It came along the river to the edge of Blaszka, taking first the women weak from childbirth, then the children. It was spring and the river rose high with the melting snows of a hard winter. On market day, the village square was frenetic, men and women running before the Angel of Death, who didn't care whether someone was Jewish or Christian or even human. Our pigs are dying, the peasants said, they have the cholera, too. The village men were working with grim concentration, caps screening their eyes from rain, black caftans tucked into their belts. The farmers' wives, gripping grey hens by the feet, talked in loud voices with the village women, who slapped their merchandise onto stalls more vigorously and noisier than usual, as if to defy the evil eye. The farmers crossed themselves. The villagers whispered Hebrew blessings. In the wet gray air, their faces were white, the cholera epidemic swallowing all color, their sweat smelling of fear. Only now and again a sudden silence would fall. A woman's voice would be heard crying, "Not my Shayndel. Dear God, have pity!" as she ran across the square to pray in front of the Holy Ark in the synagogue. Then the hubbub resumed. The sound of the blacksmith's hammer, the carpenter's saw, the thump of clay on the potter's table, the clatter of a cart, the curses, the shouts.

The women made candles, placed in the sand box beside the Holy Ark and lit while the villagers recited psalms, men and boys below, elderly women in the balcony above. Peasants came to the Old Rabbi, asking him to bless their holy relics. So what if he was a Jew? It was said among them that he had once fought the Angel of Death for the life of a child, and the child had lived.

The *feldsher* was busy letting blood, using glass cups heated to create a vacuum and then applying them to cuts made in the skin of his patient's back. When cupping didn't work, he tried leeches. When leeches failed, he used enemas. Meanwhile the midwife, Misha's mother, Blema, was walking in the woods looking for larch trees. Five drops of larch resin mixed with honey would dry up a blood-spotted diarrhea, but larch trees were uncommon around Blaszka. Hayim, who had taken over carrying water when Asher the Hasid became blind, ran back and forth across the bridge from the well to the sick-houses. More water, the villagers called, the children are thirsty, they're drying up. So Hayim ran, his buckets swinging, and his only rest was to roll a cigarette for Asher, who couldn't eat a thing, but smiled at Hayim through the smoke of his cigarette.

The men of the village met in the studyhouse. The back wall was lined with shelves of biblical commentaries from Hananiah, the martyr of Galilee, to Dov Baer the *Maggid* of Mezhirech, filling the air with the ancient smell of musty leather. Over each of the study tables, a brass candelabra lit with tallow candles cast gaunt shadows of the men onto the walls of the studyhouse. The Old Rabbi sat at the head of the first table, the *shayner* near him, the *proster* at the back, kneading their beards with stained fingers. Why did the Holy One above send us a plague? they asked. What did we do? If we set it right, then maybe the Holy One will forgive us and our children will get better. Didn't you hear? It's a punishment for the way the Hasidim treated the rabbi in Plotsk. He doesn't like Hasidim, so they drove him out of town and then the cholera came. Now they're begging him to come back. But what about us? We only have one Hasid, Asher the water-carrier, and they buried him this morning. I'll tell you whose fault it is. Yekhiel the baker. Everyone knows he's an unbeliever. It's his sin. No, no, it's Blema the midwife. Don't you remember her grandmother was burned for a witch?

"Friends, friends, listen to me," the Old Rabbi said, rapping the floor with his oak staff. Someone had thrown a rock through the baker's window. It had to be stopped. "The sin is all of ours and we can rectify it together. It is written that arranging the marriage of orphans and conducting the ceremony in the cemetery at midnight will stop a plague, even the cholera. This should tell you what a great mitzvah it is. Right here among us we have a boy of marriageable age without father or mother to arrange his destiny. No family, no money—who would marry him? But we'll find a bride for Hayim, everyone will witness his happiness, and the Holy One in His infinite mercy will withdraw the punishment that we brought upon ourselves, even if we don't know how. As for the Hasidim, it's too bad they're misguided, but each of them is a mother's child, just like each of you. They even have a few scholars among them. As it is written, 'There is no limit to the practice of benevolence and the study of Torah.' "

In the women's gallery there was much excitement when a match was found for Hayim. God has compassion, we are saved, they said. She's a pearl. How lucky our Hayim is. She's not so good-looking, but you can only see the scar on one side. And if she's not so young, well, he needs to learn a thing or two. And if they found her in the brothel near the docks in Plotsk, what then? Did anybody see her do anything wrong? It's God's will that the match will rescue her from a life of sin. And who is Hayim, anyway, a Talmud genius? He should just be thankful that he has a warm place to put his body on a Friday night.

AVRAHAM'S BROTHEL stood at the edge of Plotsk where it dipped below the waterline, soaking the houses with mud in the spring. Here lived the poorest and meanest Jews, the carter with her skinny horse stabled in back, the tailor working at the table while his children slept head to foot on the floor, cooking over an open fire on a trivet, smoke blackening their lungs. Sewage ran in the street and flies died in the thatched roofs of one-room houses.

The brothel had three rooms and two floors. On the upper floor lived the owner Avraham and his wife, Devorah. She no longer worked in the trade, but wore a fancy wig and pleaded with her daughter to stay upstairs and read to her the weekly lesson of scripture from the *Tzena-U-Rena*. The prostitutes stayed in the basement. Two of them had come to the brothel because they had no other way to keep themselves alive. The other two had been married in false ceremonies to the freelance pimp employed by the brothel. After the wedding night, they were told that the rabbi was no rabbi and the marriage contract invalid. Ruined, there was no option but to work in the brothel.

From the baker's cart, Hayim watched the barges and riverboats on the Vistula. He had a boy's narrow shoulders, thin wrists hanging out of his caftan, and three hairs attempting to sprout from his chin. Beside Hayim sat the Old Rabbi. "You have to understand how things are with you, now" he was saying to Hayim. "You're not the miller's son anymore. But still, I don't want you to worry. I made all the arrangements when I went to Plotsk last week. Riva is a good match for you. She's a grown woman, but still young enough. She can work hard. And since you insist on meeting her . . ."

"Of course, he insists," said Yekhiel the baker with a worried frown. He had left his little daughter, Faygela, with his mother-in-law, who could be too stern sometimes. They were riding in the baker's cart to save money. It took everything the community council had to pay off the brothel keeper. "Don't think you have to do this," he added. "When you see her, you can decide if you want to marry her. We're not living in the dark ages. No one can force you to act against your principles if you know your own mind."

Hayim wished that they would both keep quiet. He only wanted to look at the sky and think of nothing. Though it had been more than a week since old Asher the watercarrier had died, for some reason tears kept coming to his eyes as he gazed at the hill above Plotsk where the cathedral, with its spires and dome and the tombs of kings, overlooked its domain, peacefully unmoved by the small speck of the cart, with its smaller speck of Hayim, rolling forward.

When they arrived, the Old Rabbi, who of course wouldn't set foot into the brothel below, went upstairs to settle with Avraham, while Hayim and Yekhiel walked down to the basement. The room was divided into cubicles, but all the curtains were pulled open so that the girls could enjoy the little bit of sun coming through the cracked window. They sat in their underthings, mending stockings and writing letters, looking up curiously when Yekhiel knocked on the open door. "Come in, don't be shy," the oldest said, a woman in her forties who looked sixty, one shoulder higher than the other. "We've been expecting you," she said. "You're from Blaszka, right?"

Yekhiel nodded. "This is the groom, Hayim, and I'm Yekhiel, usually a baker, but today the driver. And you are . . .?"

"Lipsha. And these girls are like my own." She pointed to the
youngest, sitting on her narrow bed and staring at a stain on the wall,
then to the next-youngest, a plump, round-faced girl with a friendly
smile, and last to a woman she introduced as Riva, Hayim's intended.
Riva, a woman of great, golden earrings and red cheeks, marked on
one side by a scar, wore a shawl of many colors, draped low on her
arms to reveal her shoulders and breasts. The scent of her perfume
overlaid the sweat steaming off unwashed bedding and the fishy,
sewage odor of the street. Against the wall of her cubicle, Riva had
tacked the postcards her younger brothers had sent her from Berlin.
"So Riva, tell me. What do you think of your groom?" Lipsha asked.

"What should I think? Every month my mother writes to me,"
Riva said. "She thinks I'm a fishmonger. When are you getting married? she asks. You're not getting any younger, she says. My mother's a
sick woman. Who knows how long she'll last?"

"I thought you were an orphan," Yekhiel said.

"They wanted an orphan, so they have an orphan. I'll be one soon
enough." She laughed and snapped her fingers, but Hayim saw that
she grimaced as she laughed, her eyes slanted down, her lips drawn
back as if in anger. "Let my mother's last days be happy. I'll send her a
letter about my husband. Even a photograph. My mother will be very
happy."

"Hayim's just a boy," Yekhiel snapped. "He's too young for a wife
he doesn't even know. Why not take the photograph and forget the
wedding?"

"What? Lie to my mother on her deathbed? A pig doesn't deserve
such a fate." Her fingers twisted the fringes of her shawl. Her fingers
were long, the nails split, the tips of her fingers raw from scrubbing as
if she couldn't get her hands clean enough. "So have you ever been
with a woman?" Hayim shook his head. "How old are you anyway?"
she asked.

"Seventeen," Hayim said.

"Not much older than Yarush there." Riva pointed to the oldest
prostitute's son, standing in the doorway, eyeing the newcomers suspiciously, hefting a knife from hand to hand as he crossed over to his
mother's side.

"You see yourself," Yekhiel said, "this isn't right."

Riva touched Hayim's head lightly. "So young." She sighed. "Is it fair to keep a boy stuck with someone like me? Does he deserve it, an orphan?"

Lipsha, the oldest prostitute, wincing as she stood up, shook her head. "Look at me, a crooked back, I can hardly stand. Do you want to end up like me? No, Riva. You're still a young woman. You're beautiful. You're smart. So he's a boy? He should consider himself lucky. No one can be sad with you. If the world was on fire, you could still make a person laugh till he cried. I don't know what I'll do without you. But you have to take your chance."

Yekhiel sputtered, but Riva held up her hand and he kept silent. "No," she said. "I've changed my mind. I'm not interested in getting stuck in some tiny *shtetl* in the armpit of nowhere."

"Blaszka's not such a bad place," Lipsha said. "And what about your mother?"

"She has two sons. She can forget her daughter. What difference does it make anyway?" Riva asked. Hayim noticed the vein in her neck pulsating as she looked around the dirty room, her eyes dimming. He'd never seen anything sadder.

"The *Alter Rov* made the match. Let, let it be," Hayim said. "It's a sin to break a betrothal." He looked at Riva boldly, not like a religious man at all, and she laughed. This time there was no grimace in her laughter.

THEY WERE married at midnight in the cemetery, standing among the tombstones of scholars and holy men. In the darkness the men of Blaszka led Hayim to the wedding canopy. The women led Riva, whose veil was made by the Old Rabbi's wife and trailed five feet behind her like moonlight on the river. The peasants, a row of dark stones, stood at the edge of the cemetery, watching the bride circle the groom seven times.

Afterward Riva and Hayim were escorted to the inn with horns and the clash of ladles against tin pots. When the guests sat down to their feast, Riva and Hayim retired to the back room. She undressed by the light of a candle, sitting naked on the bed while Hayim looked. She leaned back on the pillows, one foot tucked against the opposite thigh, the other leg falling wide so that nothing was blocked from his view. She wasn't wearing any perfume, and a musky smell rose between them while Hayim looked. He studied her face, half light, half dark, the triangular shadow under her chin, the skin of her angular breasts shining like white stones, the puckered aureoles, the nipples like blackberries, the quick rise and fall of her belly as she watched him looking at her, the thin arrow of dark fuzz from her belly button to her mound, where the hair curled against the heel tucked into her thigh, the long second toe, the high arch, which he brushed with his finger. Only then did she remove his wedding garb, speaking softly as she touched his body, guiding him to hers.

FOR A WEEK, there was little water to be had in Blaszka unless the villagers went to the well to fetch it themselves. Riva showed Hayim everything she knew and he was happy to learn it all. At night they lay naked in the hut, looking up through the loose thatching to the stars in the sky. Riva told Hayim about her younger brothers and how they would be educated and make something of themselves. Hayim said little, but he drew pictures of Riva while she talked. "That's not me," she would protest. "Look, she's beautiful. Don't you see this?" She would point to the scar on her cheek.

"Yes, yes," Hayim would say, drawing the scar and the earrings and the shawl draped over one shoulder, and Riva laughed to see how beautiful she still was. Neither of them had any thought that many years later, in the prison in Plotsk, a pair of young, orange-haired prostitutes from Avraham's Brothel would defend a daughter of Blaszka for the sake of Riva's memory.

After a week with Hayim, Riva said she had to go back to Plotsk, briefly, just to pawn her earrings. She would hire a photographer, she said, and would then return to Blaszka to take the pictures for her mother. "Don't sell your, your earrings," Hayim said. "I can draw a picture. A proper picture. With you cooking. You can send it to your mother." The gold earrings were all that Riva owned and she was proud of them.

"No, I want her to have a photograph, so she'll believe that I'm really married. I don't need these." She fingered the earrings. "I'll be back soon, Hayim. You'll hardly notice I'm gone. It's just a two-hour walk to Plotsk. I'll be back tomorrow."

Three days later she was still gone. And the day after that, too. In the village square people said, What do you expect? Can you make a pig kosher by putting a wedding veil on it? The Old Rabbi offered to take Hayim back to Plotsk so that he could find Riva and bring her to the rabbinical court for a divorce, but Hayim shook his head. "No. Riva didn't do anything wrong. I don't, don't, don't believe it," he said. But he kept tripping, spilling all the water in his buckets and had to go back to the well, again and again.

It was Lipsha, the oldest prostitute, who sent word to Hayim that Riva was dead. When she came to the brothel with presents for the girls, the pimp asked her for the rest of the money she got for the earrings. They fought and she came out the worse. They buried Riva in the Jewish cemetery in Plotsk. Hayim mourned, sitting shivah on a stool in his hut, barefoot and unkempt for the full week. The cholera moved away from Blaszka after taking a few more villagers with it, including Aba the carpenter, Blema's husband, who had carved the doors of the Holy Ark. You see, they said in the village square, Heaven had mercy on us, just as the Old Rabbi said.

When Hayim got up from the shivah, he went to a small clearing in the woods outside the hut where the printing press was rusting. He often went there to think, but now, sitting on a stump, he put a board on his lap and a notebook on the board. In the notebook were sketches of Riva in her wedding veil, himself with his yoke and buckets, the river and the bridge, Riva standing beside his hut, Riva cooking over the trivet. When the notebook was full, it would go to Riva's mother.

While he was drawing, a peasant carrying a bundle of wood on his back and an ax over his shoulder, stopped in the clearing to watch Hayim. The pencil moved in slow steady strokes until, from seemingly disconnected lines and shadings, the farmer saw the village square appear all at once, like magic. "That's the blacksmith's," he said excitedly pointing. "And there, the cartwright. He makes a strong axle. Good wood. You have it exactly right." Then the farmer began to speak so quickly and in such a thick Polish that Hayim couldn't follow. Dropping his bundle of wood, the farmer pulled Hayim urgently, shouting, not as if he were angry, but as if Hayim might understand if only he spoke loudly enough. Hayim stared at the man, who was clearly not one of the poor tenant farmers that lived near the abandoned church, but someone who owned his own land, a man who didn't have to share his boots. His face looked familiar, the fist-flattened nose, the ears sticking out under the cap with the fur band. "Yanek?" he asked, remembering a man bringing grain to the mill when his father was alive. The man nodded excitedly and continued in his rapid Polish. Hayim smiled and nodded, following him. The only word he could make out was "Maria."

Maria was the man's little girl, who had fallen and died. She lay with her hands crossed over a picture of Saint Mary, blue ribbons tying up her yellow braids, candles at her head and feet. Yanek's wife was afraid they would forget what she looked like. In his clumsy Polish, Hayim asked for charcoal and a board. He soon had it and when the portrait was done, Yanek and his wife gazed at it with wonder and tears, thanking him over and over again, *"Dziekuje, dziekuje."* Hayim wouldn't take their money, though they pressed it on him.

Over the years, there were many more drawings of sons and daughters, mothers and husbands in cottages along the Północna River. In Blaszka the charcoal portrait of Faygela's father, Yekhiel the baker, hung above his books, and the Old Rabbi's portrait hung in the studyhouse. Although Hayim refused any payment, he was the best-fed watercarrier in the district of Plotsk. Baskets of potatoes, cabbages, apples, pears, the odd hen, flour, onions, carrots, and lately a goat were left outside his hut. Sometimes a woman came inside. But no one had ever offered him a pig. A Jew with a pig—it was unthinkable. Except, of course, for the Director.

THE DAY OF THE ICE STORM

The air smelled of winter, though there were catkins on the willows and poplars, and the birches were budding. Hazzer, the pig, ate his afternoon meal of turnips and was rooting behind Hayim's hut for worms. He'd lost his baby coloring, his coat now a brick red with bands of brown, and when he got stuck under a fence in his curious wanderings, the village children would pull out his bristles while he squeaked in protest. As Hayim hurried over the bridge, Hazzer trotting behind and bumping Hayim's knees with his snout, the buckets swung on their yoke, spilling water and drenching his pants. "Hazzer, Hazzer," Hayim said soberly, shaking his head, "what will become of you if you can't learn to conduct yourself like a good Jew?" But the pig, like a wilful child, pushed between Hayim's legs and rushed over the bridge pell-mell in search of adventure.

In the bathhouse, the men were getting ready for the feast of Purim. As the steam rose around them, and the subject turned to Hayim, they said, Did you hear that the Countess of Volhynia once came to him? No, not really. Yes, it's true. And not only her but a camp of Gypsy women. My cousin's brother-in-law heard it straight from the peasants, I swear it. Hayim isn't like other men. Drawing pictures? Who does that? But you know what people say. If not for Hayim's picture, who would remember the face of the Old Rabbi? That's true, but still, he's more like one of them than one of us. You can see for yourself, a Jew with a pig. Yesterday, it follows him into the synagogue, jumps onto his lap squealing like there's a murder. Everyone starts to shout, and the pig runs under the benches. A pig in the synagogue? It was the Romans defiling the Holy Temple all over again. But the more they shouted, the faster the pig ran. Hayim turned red, then white. I thought he was going to faint from embarrassment. The Old Rabbi, of blessed memory, did his best to make Hayim like other men. He arranged a match for him, not one but two. A father couldn't have done any better by Hayim. I'll tell you all about it, but first pour another bucket of hot water on the stones. *Ahh,* when the steam rises like ghosts in a cemetery, then you have a good *shvitz.*

EVERYONE IN Blaszka was invited to Hanna-Leah's wedding. The feast was held in Perlmutter's tavern, at two long tables that ran the length of the room, women at one, men at the other, crowded together in their finery, lifting the roof with their singing and dancing—the men with the men shoulder to shoulder and women with women, arms around one another's waists. The most important women sat near the bride and her grandmother, the most important men near the groom and his new partner in the butcher business, his father-in-law, Meyer. Hayim the watercarrier sat at the farthest end of the men's table, near the hallway where the hens were scratching. He was no longer the boy who'd lain with Riva, but a man of twenty-eight with broad shoulders and a smooth, black beard. Still stiff and sore from emptying out the *mikva* bucket by bucket at the order of the community council, so that the water might be replenished for Hanna-Leah's first immersion, he half-dozed in the warmth of the room. The Old Rabbi sat near the groom's father, of course, and a few chairs down from him was Berekh, the "crown rabbi," the younger cousin of poor Yekhiel the baker, who had died three years earlier.

The villagers called Berekh *der Yunger Rov,* the Young Rabbi, with a wink to indicate he was no rabbi at all, but just the local official who registered births and deaths and represented the community to the Tsar's ministry, which had fooled itself into thinking that anyone would believe a "rabbi" appointed by the crown meant a thing. In a few years, when the Old Rabbi would die, the village would decide that a "crown rabbi" could be a real rabbi, after all. But at Hanna-Leah's wedding, Berekh sat somewhere in the middle of the men's table, watching the festivities with a cynical eye, his red beard already untameable. His little cousin, Faygela, sat at Hanna-Leah's right side, her belly swollen to bursting with her second child.

The four *vilda hayas* sat together like a clump of violets in the woods. First came Hanna-Leah, who was nineteen, then Faygela, seventeen, Misha and Zisa-Sara who were both twenty years old. Zisa-Sara had eyes only for her new husband, Mikhal, sitting at the men's table, engaged in scholarly debate. "In the Talmud," he began.

"Yes of course, in the Talmud," said Berekh. "Do you see there something pertinent to the war between the Tsar and the Sultan of Turkey? Was it the express wish of the Holy One that Bosnia and Herzegovina should be transferred to Austrian administration? Tell me, friend Mikhal, was it the Eternal One's aim to establish the Principality of Bulgaria? Yes, yes, it must be written. God on High desires that Pinye the foot soldier should die in Herzegovina this very year, 1878 as calculated by the Christian calendar. Not any Pinye, you understand, but Pinye the brother of Berekh the 'crown rabbi,' authorized by the Tsar's ministry to register births, deaths, and marriages. Show me, dear Mikhal, where is it written?"

"Who am I to answer you?" asked Mikhal, who had no idea, then, that he would have a daughter named Emma and a son born in America. "Do I know anything about either the Tsar or the Sultan? I don't read a word of Russian." Mikhal paused, looking at the women's table with a besotted smile, and then continued. "But in the Talmud it says that the sword comes into the world because of the delay and perversion of justice, and on account of those who misrepresent the Holy Word." Mikhal looked again at his beloved Zisa-Sara, with her dimpled chin and the beauty spot like the touch of an angel's finger above her lip. His face alight, he missed the reply of the "crown rabbi," who rolled his eyes at heaven.

"Enough Talmud," Hanna-Leah's grandmother said in a loud voice. "Let's have another dance."

Berekh rose from his chair and bowed. To the musicians he said, "Give us something for the Angel of Death dance."

The women clapped their hands, hooting. Berekh looked the part, they said, so tall and gaunt. He chose Hayim to play the dying victim. Hayim shook his head unwillingly, but Berekh pulled him into the center of the room, and what could he do? Obligingly, he pretended to die, but he was so large and vital that the women couldn't help but laugh until they hiccuped. Such a fragile Angel of Death, they said, such a lively corpse. It should only be this way. The klezmer played their instruments accordingly, the violin as the weak and weeping Angel of Death, the clarinet as the lively, uncooperative corpse. The men banged the table with their cups, some shouting, "Take him to heaven," and others, "Don't let Death get you," while the women's hands stung from clapping and their throats grew hoarse from screams of laughter. Only Misha, who was in mourning for her mother, watched the dancers with a serious expression. Finally Hanna-Leah's grandmother pleaded, "Enough, no more, we're choking," and Berekh subsided. Hayim, however, completely surprising himself, held out a handkerchief to Misha for the kosher dance.

She was in no mood for dancing until Faygela's grandmother grimaced and said, "Is she the bride? It's not right for her to dance with the men. Has she no shame?" At that, Misha sprang from behind the women's table. Taking hold of the handkerchief, she looked Hayim full in the face, challenging him to take her on while everyone watched. He was embarrassed, but she stamped from side to side, pulling on the handkerchief like an impatient horse, strong, unruly and reckless, flinging back her head, her dark hair rolling across her shoulders like the night.

"Are you waiting for the Messiah?" she asked him. She was as tall as Hayim, but not yet as big as she would become. Mourning had thinned her cheeks and purpled shadows under her eyes.

He shook his head sheepishly. "Come on. Let's make a show for the old woman," she said, winking. She laughed, her gold tooth flashing as she jutted her chin at Faygela's sour-faced grandmother. "You musicians," she shouted. "Did you die while my back was turned? It's a wedding. How fast can you play?"

The klezmer stopped. There was silence. The guests paused, forkfuls of chicken and kasha stalled in midair. There was a long blast from the horn, like the final, breath draining summons on the Day of Atonement. Then the violin joined it, wild and searing, and the clarinet rattled the roof with staccato bursts. Hayim twisted the handkerchief around his wrist, swinging Misha with a surge of energy, and when her feet hit the floor, she pulled back full force. As they careened around the room, Hayim hung on dizzily, his feet pounding the floor, the music pounding in his chest, the room spinning out of sight, the guests small and far away.

When he came around opposite the hallway where the chickens pecked, he caught sight of someone he didn't recognize. A youngish woman stood with her hands on her hips. She was tall and broad, dressed like the women in his grandmother's time, with a *kupka* instead of a kerchief on her head, the cap embroidered with moons and stars that caught the light, gold ribbons dangling from the cap over her long, loose hair, as white as candles. Over her dress she wore a *vestel,* a black bodice with red and gold threads like flames between the braided borders. She nodded at Hayim. When he spun around again, she was gone.

A FEW DAYS later the Old Rabbi sent for Hayim. "I think of you like a kind of son, Hayim. It's not good for a man to be alone. The evil inclination gets the better of him. And it's time that Misha was matched up, too. It's been a year since her mother died. There's no reason to hold it off. Neither of you has anyone to approach the matchmaker on your behalf, so I'll do it. After all, what's there to arrange? It's an easy matter. All right, Hayim, you can go. Leave it to me." The Old Rabbi turned back to the volume he was studying at the front table in the studyhouse.

"But, but, what does Misha say?"

"Say?" the Old Rabbi asked, turning a puzzled face to Hayim. "A woman has to marry. Is there someone else for her in the village?" Hayim shrugged. How would he know? "I watched you and Misha dancing," the Rabbi continued. "It's good. You'll see, Hayim. After marriage, the babies come, you work for them and you grow together."

A baby. A son. That would be something. He'd always assumed that he wasn't going to have children. Who would marry him, a water-carrier? He liked Misha. He liked the way she cared nothing for what people said. He liked the way she'd danced with him. He liked her long black hair. And if she was willing . . . "All right," Hayim said.

They didn't talk to each other before the wedding. That was the custom and Hayim had decided that from now on everything in his life would be done in the usual way, no more weddings at midnight. He was going to be a man with a family. As was traditional, Hayim went to the cemetery and prayed at the grave of his father, inviting him to the wedding.

They were married at dusk in the synagogue courtyard. As the men led Hayim to the wedding canopy, he thought of how tender he would be with Misha. How he would tell their babies everything that Asher the Hasid had told him and they would look at him with Misha's dark eyes. His first son would be named Ari after his father. When Passover came, Hayim would throw open his door to invite the needy stranger to eat with his family. And on the Sabbath he would recite "A Woman of Virtue" to Misha. As she approached, led by the women with their lit candles, she smiled at Hayim, and if her eyes looked sad, that was only natural since her mother couldn't be with her. When they went up to her house, Hayim took his time, sitting with Misha, stroking her hands, waiting until she was ready to undress and then attending to her until she told him that if he didn't hurry, she would pull his ears. Afterward she seemed content and her sleep was easy. She lay on her side, her full breasts under the light touch of Hayim's hand.

But before long, Hayim could see that something wasn't right. He carried water, Misha made up her remedies and sold them on market day. In the evening they ate together. In the morning he prayed. But Misha sighed. Every once in a while, she looked away from Hayim and her sigh ended with a little groan. A month passed. Two months. When they made love, she would seem happy, but then the next day she would mutter to herself, biting her lip. He asked her over and over what he could do for her, but she said there was nothing. She couldn't sleep. She said there wasn't enough air in the house. So Hayim opened the front door and the back door to let the summer wind blow through with the smell of the coming harvest. But still she tossed and turned. So he lay on the floor, leaving the bed to her. "Just tell me," he pleaded. "What, what is it?" She would shake her head or she would turn her back to him and once, to his surprise, she climbed out of bed, threw her arms around him and kissed him deeply, pulling him to her. Afterward she said only that he shouldn't think it was something he'd done wrong. But what else could he think? Misha, who'd danced with him so that he could hardly keep up with her, who laughed like a dozen, who knew what to do for every ailment, was growing thin. In the village people said she looked more dead than alive.

One day in late fall, when the fields were cleared and the trees bare, Hayim climbed the steps to Misha's house as usual. He couldn't think of it as his house. No, it was all hers, and he was a guest who slept on the floor more often than not. He dropped his yoke and buckets in the corner, beside the bridal trunk. The room was in its usual disarray, the table a clutter of jars and herbs in the process of being sorted. On the tile oven there was half-crushed bark in the mortar. Pots bubbled on the cooking grate. The nauseating smell of ergot rose from some indeterminate corner. His wife was sitting, not looking too well. She gripped a cup of tansy tea between her hands.

"Maybe you should lie down a little. You're pale," he said.

"I'm not sick," she answered hoarsely, as if she'd been crying. "I'm pregnant."

"Misha, Misha," he said, seating himself opposite her at the table, surprised at the awe and tenderness that overwhelmed him. Now we'll come to know each other, he thought, now we'll come to love each other with this new life, this precious soul between us.

"I want a *Get*," she said abruptly.

A rabbinical divorce? "What did I do?" he asked in astonishment, wondering how he could drive her to such a thing without even noticing. And in her condition yet. In his mind he reviewed all the grounds for a *Get:* impotence, infidelity, revulsion, cruelty. What did he do to hurt her so terribly?

"Nothing. I just want a *Get,*" she said.

"Nothing? No. It, it must be something. Tell me," he said gently. "Let me make, make it up to you."

"Are you an idiot?" she asked harshly. "I said you didn't do anything. I just want a divorce. That's all. You can say whatever you want to the Rabbi. Tell him that I'm a hag, that you can't live with me. I don't care. I need a *Get.*"

She shivered. It was getting cold, and he heard the geese honking as they flew toward Egypt, but he had no sympathy for her drawn, pale face. Did she think he was a stick of wood with no feelings that she could just throw onto the fire and burn into ashes? He had a wife, he had a child, and she wanted him to have nothing but his yoke. "We have a child coming into the world and you want a divorce? A child without a father? No. You, you, go to hell." He kicked the water bucket across the room. It banged into the eastern wall underneath the embroidered landscape, which he faced every morning for prayer.

She yelled at him until she couldn't yell anymore, then she begged him for the *Get.* He stammered angry replies, pacing from the table to the eastern wall to the tile stove to the table again, stamping his feet and twisting his hands. For the first time in his life he wanted to hit a living thing. "Dear God," he shouted, pounding the table until the jars crashed to the floor, shattering ground glass into his heart, "Show this woman your justice!" Then he walked out, following the river bank beyond the woods to barren fields, gray with oncoming winter, thinking his terrible angry thoughts.

When he came home a few hours later, Misha was calling for her mother. Her legs were drawn up in her agony. "Misha?" he asked, his anger drained. A pulpy, bloody mass was spreading along the bed. "Misha, what should I do? Tell me." She didn't answer, her face twisted as she rolled onto her side, groaning. Hayim ran for the *feldsher.* While the barber-surgeon tended Misha, Hayim waited outside. His legs shook. Unable to stand, he fell to his knees in the mud beside the river, covering his face in shame. "Master of the Universe, forget what I said. Am I a person to listen to? All right, she's having a miscarriage. The baby is gone. Just don't take her, too. Let her have the divorce if that's what she wants. Only let her live." Dead leaves floated on the river.

The *feldsher*, with his leeches, did more harm than good, but Misha managed to survive his ministrations.

ALL THROUGH the divorce proceedings, Misha refused Hayim an explanation. She told him once, she told him twice, she told him ten times, even with a kiss on his cheek, "It's not your fault." Yet her face shone with relief when he handed her the parchment that cancelled the marriage contract. As she carried it under her arm, walking around the table in the Rabbi's study to show that she had received the document with full knowledge of its meaning, she paused for a moment. There seemed to be a look of regret on her face. The Old Rabbi saw it, too, and stopped her, saying that he could tear up the *Get* and it would be as if nothing had occurred. But she said, "No. Let's finish this." They left the Rabbi's study side by side. It was hard to realize that they were now strangers. He had tried many times to draw Misha, but had never gotten her quite right. Now he never would. Misha whispered to him, "You give a woman great pleasure, Hayim. Don't forget it. But I have to live alone. It's just meant to be that way."

So ON THE eve of Purim in 1894, Hayim filled the water barrel in Misha's house without any pain. He'd been with many women, all of them content to seek him out in the thatched hut that let in the stars. But as he lifted his bucket, he sniffed. The smell coming from the stove, how familiar it was. Yes, that aromatic odor of tansy tea mingling with the nauseous skin-penetrating stench of ergot. He'd never forget it. The day she miscarried, that same smell. The sense of loss was returning as if it had all just happened. Hayim stared at Misha.

She was sitting at the old table, the pine slab on the maple stump. It had been the table of Blema the midwife and Aba the carpenter. Then Blema the widow and her daughter Misha. Then Misha the orphan and Hayim the watercarrier. And now it was her table alone. She sat with her knees apart, feet flat on the floor, her red shawl billowing over her shoulders and chest. Her eyes were glazed as if she could only see inside herself, as if she had absorbed the world, and outside was a starless, moonless night. It was the same expression she had had fifteen years earlier.

Misha blinked, slowly focusing on Hayim's presence. Steam rose from the cup in her hands.

"A mazel tov, Misha," he said. She dropped the cup. It rolled off the table onto the floor. Tea soaked into the braided rug.

"How did you find out?" she asked. "Does everybody in Blaszka know?"

Crouching, Hayim retrieved the cup. Replacing it on the table, he bit his lip and shook his head. God forgive me, he thought, I have no sense. An idiot like me should stick with talking to animals.

"Who's talking?" she asked tensely. "Tell me. How did you know?"

"Why, I, why . . ."

" 'Why not?' Is that an answer?"

"Shouldn't I know? I was, I was . . ."

"My husband? Only for eight months."

"Long enough. I see. In your eyes, I see it."

"My eyes? What's wrong with them?"

Hayim felt as though his tongue was swelling up. The more clearly he saw, the less he could speak. His head was emptying itself of words as it filled up with memory. There she was the night she miscarried, and there on the day they were married, and there when she first looked at him at Hanna-Leah's wedding.

Water trickled from his jacket. His ritual fringes, slapping against his pants, dripped into his boots. "If you know, the whole world will be pointing fingers at me," Misha said.

"It's not. Don't, don't trouble yourself, Misha. I can't put two words together when I want to."

She wasn't looking at him now, but at the dried herbs hanging above his head. Hayim waited, dripping. "Happy Purim," he said at last.

Hayim was the first person in Blaszka, other than Misha, to realize that she was pregnant. It was the day that Hanna-Leah found the stranger hiding in the woods. The day that the Director poured tea for Alta-Fruma and Mr. Hoffmann.

SEASON OF RAINS

It was the boy who brought Hayim to Alta-Fruma's house on Passover. Izzie slid up to Hayim in the courtyard of the synagogue, saying to him, "We should have a guest for the seder. Would you come?" Taking hold of Hayim's arm, he continued, "There aren't any strangers in Blaszka today. Did you notice? And there aren't enough beggars for everybody to have one. If you don't eat with us, we won't be able to fulfil the mitzvah." The boy sighed as if contemplating a great sorrow, looking up at Hayim, one hand on his cap so that it shouldn't fall away and bare his head before heaven. Hayim joined him with a deep sigh of his own. Side by side they exhaled their profound contemplation, the boy in his knickers and stockings, the man robed in his white *kittel*. Darkness was falling, the moon fought with the clouds for a place in the sky, and Hayim weighed the emptiness of his hut against a debt of gratitude. Alta-Fruma might be uncommonly attractive for her age. Hayim wasn't as blind to this as others in Blaszka. But she was such a good woman, such an unremittingly good woman, an intimidatingly, even boringly good woman. What would she say to him? The Jew with a pig. And not any pig. But the particular pig that had eaten half the turnips in her root cellar. Of all the houses that might accommodate Hayim for the Passover seder, hers was one of the last he would choose, but he had nowhere else to go, and the boy's trusting hand was slipping into his.

As they came into the house, leaving behind the cold wind and spring drizzle and whipping trees, Hayim saw Emma, her back to the door, putting the kerosene lamp on the sideboard. The room was warm. Chicken soup bubbled on the cooking grate. A plate of egg noodles and a bowl of glazed carrots waited on the sideboard. The fragrance of roasting brisket drifted toward the flames in the candelabra. Alta-Fruma stood in the circle of its light, blessing the table with its Passover dishes, unmatched remnants of fine china and oddly shaped, glaze-streaked clay bowls around the holiday candles.

Shimmering in the candlelight, her black lace shawl draped over her head and shoulders, she recited in Yiddish, *"Dear God, I thank and bless Your holy Name for permitting me the sweet* mitzvah *of candlelighting. May the effort of preparing for the Passover and cleaning the house of all leavened food be for the merit of these children. Help us to sweep out the evil inclination that leavens our heart like yeast."* Alta-Fruma cast Emma a quick glance. "Amen."

As she saw Hayim and Izzie standing in the doorway, she said, "Come and sit," her hands beckoning as if she were pulling light to the table. *"Gut Yom Tov"* Hayim said, entering the room hesitantly, Izzie pulling him by the hand and settling him on the chair beside him. The warmth, the richness of food smells, the gleam of the green-tiled oven, the brass samovar, and the crystal goblet full of sweet red wine unsettled him.

"Please begin," Alta-Fruma said, seating herself beside Emma.

Almost inaudibly, Hayim chanted the kiddush, but as the ritual of the Passover seder took hold of him, he began to relax in its familiar rites. Lifting the plate of matzah, Hayim recited from his father's Hagaddah, *"This is the bread of affliction which our ancestors ate in the land of* Mitzrayim. *All who are hungry, let them come and eat. All who are needy, let them come and celebrate the Passover with us. Now we are here, next year may we be in the land of Israel. Now we are slaves, next year may we be free."*

When Hayim put down the plate, he leaned back against the feather pillows on his chair like a man of leisure. Izzie also stretched out his legs and inclined, as one should on this night when everyone remembers what it is to be free. Leaning over to look at Hayim's Hagaddah, illustrated by Ari the Eggs, the boy rested his head on Hayim's shoulder, as his own son might have done had he lived to be born.

Alta-Fruma looked at Hayim over the head of the boy, a direct unswerving gaze that startled Hayim. *"Nu,* Hayim, isn't the boy the picture of his father? An angel, not a human being," she said.

Hayim nodded. The boy did remind him of Mikhal. There was the same innocence about him.

"Not like Emma," Alta-Fruma added, pinching the girl who was fidgeting and making faces. "But what can we do? We come from the earth and we go to the earth. Like Adam *Harishon,* we have to make a living. Then we turn to go back to the Garden of Eden, but what happened in the meantime? God locked the gates. Can anyone get in? No. But they can't help themselves. They try anyway." She shook her fists in the air like someone rattling the gates to paradise. For a moment her whole body tensed as if she were standing at the fence, peering between the bars with an intensity of desire that fell from her like sparks. And then it was gone. She relaxed so quickly that Hayim blinked. Only someone who by habit watched as closely as he did would have caught that expression, and had he been looking the other way, as he often was when it came to Alta-Fruma, the good and thrifty dairywoman, he would have missed it.

"So Izzie, are you going to sing or do you intend for us to go hungry all night?" she asked. As the youngest child, it was Izzie's job to recite the four questions that introduce the Passover story recited before the meal.

"*Why is this night different from all other nights?*" Izzie chanted. "*Why on other nights do we eat bread but on this night we eat only matzah? Why on all other nights do we eat herbs of any kind, but on this night only bitter herbs?*" Izzie asked, repeating the question in Yiddish for the women, and pausing as if waiting for an answer.

"Well, if you ask me," his aunt said, "it's because on other nights a *pig* came into my cellar and tore up my herbs, but pigs, you know, have no interest in what is bitter. That they leave to human beings who drink a bitter cup every day. Isn't it true, Hayim?" He noticed the flicker of mischief in her green eyes. "Go on, Izzie," she said, "hurry up and finish the *Ma Nishtanah* or we won't eat until the Messiah comes."

Reciting the long answer to Izzie's questions, Hayim didn't stammer. The words weren't his but his ancestors'. The melody wasn't his but his father's. His thoughts remained his alone, while he chanted flawlessly.

They ate slices of horseradish on matzah until the tears ran from their eyes in memory of the slaves' bitterness, then comforted their mouths with sweet *haroses* and the second cup of wine. Alta-Fruma rose to bring in the soup, pulling Emma with her.

"My favorite part," Izzie said excitedly, "is where it says, '*For more than once have they risen against us to destroy us; in every generation they rise against us and seek our destruction. But the Holy One, blessed be He, saves us from their hands.*' "

"It's not any God but our own hands that save us," Emma said.

"*Ha-ra,*" Alta-Fruma observed to Hayim, shaking her head. "Our fathers, who wrote the Hagaddah, were thinking of Emma when they described the wicked child who thinks she knows everything but doesn't want to hear anything. Don't interrupt, Emma. We have a guest." As she spoke, Alta-Fruma was preparing plates of food for the children, meticulously cutting away the fat on Emma's brisket because the girl didn't like it, all the while scolding her for leaving the best part.

A good woman, Hayim thought when she rushed to him with a clean rag, mopping up his spilled soup, clucking over his wet *kittel.* But why was it that she allowed her hands to linger on him as she pulled away the damp edge of his sleeve, a mix of something in her eyes that didn't quite belong to a virtuous and predictable woman? And as Hayim watched her, he realized to his surprise that she was eyeing him with equal interest and equal stealth.

Casting around for something to bring her into conversation, Hayim said, "Your, your cow, it's well?"

"Yes," she said. "And your pig is healthy?"

"Y-y-yes," he answered, ducking his head in embarrassment. But one of the merits of a worthy and virtuous woman is her patience. Alta-Fruma waited without speaking until Hayim looked at her again, unable to contain his curiosity. She was holding out the bowl of glazed carrots in both hands, at arms length, like a food offering in the Holy Temple. She smiled, and as she smiled, her tongue slipped out and quickly touched her upper lip.

After the meal, by the third cup of wine, Hayim was singing and drumming on the table with Izzie joining him enthusiastically, translating into Yiddish for the edification of his yawning sister.

> *Of old, the wonders You did perform at night.*
> *It happened at midnight!*
> *And Israel wrestled with God and prevailed at night.*
> *It happened at midnight!*
> *To Daniel you revealed Your mysteries at night.*
> *It happened at midnight!*
> *Haman wrote his edicts of hate at night.*
> *It happened at midnight!*
> *Make bright like the day the darkness of night.*
> *It will happen at midnight!*

"At midnight," Hayim echoed Izzie, "at midnight." Darkness and light played over Alta-Fruma's face, her eyes gazing out of the shadows in a gleam of mystery. Darkness wrapped around the house as Hayim poured the mandatory fourth cup of wine. Darkness held the children in their tender half-sleep, as Alta-Fruma drank it down.

"At midnight," she proclaimed, "if a person should walk in the graveyard he'll see the spirits of the dead and they'll try to enter his living body because they miss being in the world."

"Is it so wonderful, then, to deal with all the *tzuris* and turmoils of life?" Hayim asked, the wine and the quiet and the leaping shadows loosening his voice.

"A person's spirit hungers for life always," Alta-Fruma replied.

Sleepily, Izzie said, "The sages wrote that without the evil inclination the human race would die out. What does that mean, Auntie? Why wouldn't there be any more people?"

"Just like Hayim's pig," she said. "An instinct to get into everything. You know what they say about a pig? She lies down and sticks out her hooves that are split like a cow's and wiggles them at you as if to say, 'You see, I'm kosher.' And if a person looks too hard, then he's seduced and before you know it, the pig is deep in your cellar eating everything you have."

Her eyes glittered. Was she talking about pigs, Hayim wondered, or something else? And all the while, he was noticing the graceful lines of her body and the spicy smell of her skin as she leaned toward him. Before he finished the fourth cup of wine, he had agreed to plant her garden to atone for his pig. Later, when he lay on his straw bed, looking up through the holes in his thatched roof at the black night, he thought that of all the women who had come to him, there wasn't one that he had chosen for himself. Yet.

CARRYING A rake and a hoe, Hayim walked along the path through the woods, undisturbed by the darkness and fog. As he walked, he thought of Asher the Hasid, whose hut near the well was Hayim's home now, whose yoke was Hayim's yoke, and his buckets Hayim's, too. When he first went to live with Asher, Hayim would come back at night, exhausted from a day of carrying wood on his shoulders to the farmers along the river. Asher would say, "Hayim, don't think because you're a woodcutter and not sitting in a yeshiva studying the Torah that you've fallen in the world. I'm telling you plain, everything is God. Are you looking, Hayim? Are you using your eyes? The *Ba'al Shem Tov,* of blessed memory, spent days in the fields and the woods, and there he saw the Holy One arising from every living thing and also the stones."

Later Asher would say to Hayim, "Come back and tell me what you see." This was when Asher had become blind, before the cholera epidemic, and Hayim carried his buckets and was his eyes. Hayim was seventeen. He would sit on a stool, Asher reclining on his cot as if it were Passover, lifting a cigarette to his mouth with shaking hand, inhaling and coughing, nodding at every point as if he, too, saw it. The little boys were in the apple tree, the one that always blooms first even though it was cracked in half by lightning, Hayim would say. They were throwing apples at the girls. Hershel it was, the cobbler's boy, and his cousin Shmuel. The girls screamed and gathered up the apples. Faygela pulled Hanna-Leah by the hand and told her to ignore them, but Hanna-Leah looked up into the tree. She said if you throw an apple at a girl you have to marry her. The barley is ripe. It looked like a field of light under the blue sky. That's what I saw, Hayim would say, and Asher would say, "That's good, that's good. And what else did you see?" I saw wasps making their paper nest, I saw them flying from the dead log to the eaves over Yekhiel's old printing press in the woods. I climbed onto the roof and I saw the wasps spitting paper into the nest. The wasps were humming, like this, Hayim said. Gray clouds were running across the sky. I saw Yekhiel standing in the doorway of the hut. He was wearing his apron, and holding a book. And then Yekhiel walked away like he was a giant, not a thin little baker. I'm drawing a picture of him, Hayim said. "I see it," Asher said, staring into the darkness as if he did. "But tell me, Hayim, did you see anything else?" I saw a tree frog sitting on a leaf. I nearly missed it, but I saw it when it moved its head, as small as my finger, like a green star on the leaf. The clouds broke and the tree was so bright like it was on fire but nothing burned, and I looked at just this branch and just this leaf with the tiny green frog shining in the sun. Do you think, Hayim asked hesitantly, I saw the Holy Presence? "Don't stop looking, Hayim," Asher said, putting his hands on the boy's head in blessing as if it were *Shabbas.*

But although Hayim continued to look deeply, it never occurred to him that someone else might look at him and see anything except the stammering hauler of water who couldn't keep a wife.

"Do you see her?" Hayim asked the bird perched on a branch of the willow tree. He was scattering seeds in Alta-Fruma's garden, the smell of rich spring earth intoxicating him with delight in God's beauty. Alta-Fruma was leaning on her broom, barefoot and bareheaded with enticing carelessness, watching him. "Do you think she's watching to see if I'm doing it right?" He paused. "Why else would she be looking?" And as he gazed at her, he wished that she was looking because she wanted to see him. But that was a ridiculous thought for a man whose life-long ambition was to be invisible.

"Put your eyes back in your head," she shouted at him, throwing down her broom. "Are you here to look or to work?"

Hayim didn't answer, but he thought stubbornly, I'm here to look. He plunged his hands deep into the earth, snorting like Hazzer the pig.

SINCE THE early spring when Hayim's pig had grown big enough to break into a cellar, Hayim had tried to keep it penned up. Still, it managed to escape too often, and had been gradually working its way from house to house in the village. That pig is a menace, people said in the village square, Hayim should sell the pig and the community council should make him do it. But then Ruthie was arrested, Tuesday May 22, two weeks and four days after Hayim dug Alta-Fruma's garden, and the community council had no time to worry about a pig.

THE LONG DAYS

On Wednesday, in the house under the willows, Alta-Fruma slapped Emma and said, "Congratulations, you're a woman now," while a clap of thunder sent Hayim's pig squealing and scurrying into the dairyhouse, a carrot hanging from its mouth. At the other end of Blaszka, Hayim was looking up at the sky, hoping he'd get the wood under cover before the rain began.

He was cutting wood for Misha. Wasn't she his wife before the

Get? Should she have to bend down and carry in her condition? No. Someone should get it for her. He owed her that at least. He wouldn't say anything to her about it. He would just leave it behind her house.

When the rain stopped, Hayim stood in the doorway of his hut. He stretched, inhaling the electric grassy scent of May storms. The wind riffled the tablet of paper on his stool, page after page of eyes. Almond-shaped eyes surrounded by a flagrant thickness of lashes. "You see?" Hayim turned to the goat, who had clambered onto the low thatched roof to munch on the sod. "I still don't have her eyes right. What's the use? I have wood to chop."

Hayim had just lifted his ax when the pig came charging at him, its snout white with dried curd, and close behind it, Alta-Fruma with a stick in her hand. She gave the pig a loud whack on the behind, and then another as the pig ran into the goat shed.

"Your pig is a Cossack," she said. "A whole vat of curd spilled. *Vilda haya*," she called to the pig, shaking the stick. It quivered in the straw. "The farmer could make good sausages out of you, pig, and then this *shlemiel* of yours could pay for the damage you made." She turned back to Hayim, leaning toward him as if to leap from the ground and fly over the treetops. "What good is it that you planted my garden? It's ruined. There's not a stem the size of my little finger left."

"I can replant it," Hayim said.

"And the cheese?"

"I can work in the dairy."

"And the carrots?"

"I'll work for that, too."

"How long?"

"Whatever you want."

She chewed the inside of her lip, nodding. "A person couldn't ask for more than that. It's a bargain. Do you hear, pig? I won't hand you over to the draft." The pig's snout lifted above the straw while Alta-Fruma held out her hand to Hayim. He took it, a warm firm hand pressing into his decisively, not caring that men and women shouldn't touch in public. "You're an honest man, Hayim," she said looking him in the eye. "Your father was an honest man, too. He would be happy to know that he raised a mensch." If he had his pencil, Hayim thought, he could get her eyes down just so, the yellow glints in the iris swirling, the lines curving under her eye like a waterfall drawn in soft pencil over her cheekbone. He wanted to touch the lines, to feel the texture of the skin, to study it with his charcoal. "Don't move," he said. "I, I." His tongue swelled. "I . . ."

She waited while he stammered and stumbled toward the door, returning with a wildly waving tablet of paper and a pencil tucked behind each ear. He seated himself on the tree stump, the tablet on his lap, his pencil moving quickly. That was better. Yes. Her eyes exactly. But how could he draw the way his heart beat faster as she looked at him?

THE NEXT morning, while he was walking in the woods, Hayim saw Emma. She was running away. So much was evident. She wore traditional running-away garb, several layers of clothing, a precious trinket on a string around her neck, a bundle tied onto her back, a knife hanging from her waist and a startled, guilty expression at the sight of Hayim. Wordlessly, Hayim matched her pace until finally, discomforted with the silence, Emma said, "I'm going to Warsaw."

Hayim nodded, walking alongside her without further comment.

"I can't do anything here," she exploded. "My great-aunt is breathing down my neck every minute. The revolution will be over by the time I've satisfied her."

Hayim raised an eyebrow.

"Well, she hates me anyway. She won't miss me."

"And, and Izzie?" Hayim asked.

"Oh, he has his nose in his religious books all the time. He won't even know I'm gone."

As they walked the woods thinned, the path widened, and below the rising sun, the road appeared. On either side fields of rye and barley tossed in the wind like a green sea. The peasants were busy with their hoes weeding around the rosettes of cabbages and the endless rows of potatoes. Pushing his hat back under the warming sky, Hayim hummed, "*On Monday we eat potatoes, on Tuesday potatoes, on Wednesday potatoes again, and on* Shabbas *potato pudding.*"

Emma's pace slowed. Head bent, in a low voice she said, "Ruthie's mother came home yesterday. She's going to kill me and no one's ever going to speak to me again."

"No," Hayim said. "No, no, no, no."

"No?" she asked.

He cupped her chin in his hand. "Just a, a, a little yelling, it could be. You, you're afraid of, of a little yelling? I don't believe it. No. Not a, a child of Blaszka. You heard of the rebellion of '63."

"Ruthie told me," she said.

"Many, many people in Blaszka were involved. Even my father. He, he, supplied coats and boots to the young people hiding in the woods. That's why the Russians blew up the mill."

Emma shifted her weight from foot to foot. "I wouldn't be able to visit Ruthie in prison if I went so far away," she said. "But it's too late." She took her bundle from her shoulder, swinging it back and forth. "My aunt will know I'm gone by now. I can't go back." She squinted at Hayim, the sun now directly behind him. "Unless," she said, "oh, Hayim, would you talk to her for me?"

"Me, me?" he asked in surprise.

"She would listen to you. She likes you."

He shook his head. "She, she wouldn't listen to . . ."

"She would. I know she would. She's always saying to Izzie that he should grow up to be a mensch like you. Please, Hayim," she pleaded.

"I don't know. Maybe. What, what do you want me, me to tell her?" he asked.

"Oh, you know what to say. Something about how it's her religious duty, you know, as a good Jewish woman. Something like it's just proper for her to leave me alone."

"And you'll go home?" he asked.

She nodded. "If you come with me," she said.

ASHER ALWAYS used to tell the young Hayim that he shouldn't be self-conscious about his stammering. "Every word is a prayer if you say it with all of your heart," he used to say, rolling a cigarette from the coarse strong tobacco he kept in a wooden box. It smelled like the end of days, Hayim thought, but Asher insisted the sharp taste reminded his tongue that it was still alive. "Let me tell you the story of the village that was suffering from a drought," Asher would say after taking a long drag. "It was terrible. The fields withered to nothing. No one had a *groschen* to buy a needle. The synagogue was full of scholars and worthy men who prayed and fasted and recited psalms day and night. But still it didn't rain. They tore their clothes and smeared their faces with ash. Still God had no mercy. Everything was closed. Even the tavern. One day Shloimeh, the village drunk, raised his hands to heaven and cried out with more sincerity than all the righteous in the synagogue. '*Gotteniu,*' he cried, 'I need a drink. Let it rain so the tavern can reopen.' And so it rained."

A drunk, yes, Hayim would tell Asher. But no one has the patience to listen to someone that stammers. Better not to say too much than to watch people turn away. In the village square they said that Hayim hoarded words like a miser hoards gold.

ALTA-FRUMA was in the dairyhouse churning butter, her shoulders hunched like an old woman's when Hayim and Emma arrived. Hayim was carrying Emma's bundle, and Emma dragged her feet like a calf coming to the *shokhet.* As they entered the dairyhouse, Alta-Fruma straightened up with a start, her arms stretched out to greet them, her face caught between relief and anger. "In a good hour," she said. "You didn't cause enough aggravation already? You had to run off and scare your brother half to death?"

"Didn't he get my note?" Emma asked sullenly.

"Yes, sure, but he didn't believe it. He thought the Gypsies kidnapped you and made you write the note. I assured him that the Gypsies have plenty of their own children and have no use for anyone else's, never mind a troublesome Jewish girl who doesn't know what's good for her and doesn't give a thought to anyone else. He ran off to find someone with a cart to go and look for you, but I see you decided to come back. Or did you lose your way?"

Emma began to turn around, quite prepared to march back down the road, but Hayim held her by the shoulder. "No, no," he said. "She, she wasn't running away."

"No, she was maybe baking matzos in the woods?" Alta-Fruma asked.

Murmuring a quick apology to the Holy One above, Hayim took a deep breath. "Emma was going to Plotsk to get work," he said. "Piecework. You said she should help out with the bribe for Ruthie's warden, didn't you?" Emma's protest turned into a squeak as Hayim jabbed her in the ribs with his elbow.

"Is that what you were up to?" Alta-Fruma asked.

"Hayim met me and . . ." she looked at him. He nodded encouragingly. "I realized I forgot to say in the note where I was going, so I . . ."

"You didn't eat, Emma. Go inside and have some tea and bread. You can help me in the dairyhouse today. There's enough time for you to go to Plotsk next week."

After Emma went inside, Alta-Fruma said to Hayim, "I'll have to stop her brother from raising the whole village to look for her."

She knew, Hayim thought. How could she not? No one needs to wear three dresses to walk to Plotsk. She wouldn't think he was such a mensch anymore, not a man who tells lies. No she would think he was an idiot who imagined that she would be fooled by such an obvious fabrication. May God put it to his merit that he sacrificed his character so that Emma could come home. Well, is the character of a water-carrier worth so much anyway?

Hayim turned to go. He had water to haul. "Wait a minute," Alta-Fruma said. "You know, Hayim, the sages write that even God lies to protect peace in the home. Avraham heard Sarah laughing in the tent when the angels told him he would have a child. She laughed at the idea—imagine, at his age. 'Do you hear how my wife laughs at me?' he asked the Holy One. But God said, 'No, you have it all wrong. She's laughing because she thinks that she herself is too old.' It's true, Hayim. I'm not making it up. The *zogerin* told the women in synagogue." She left the butter churn standing as it was. But as she passed Hayim, she said, "Thank you for bringing Emma home. You'll see, I won't forget it." Her hand was on his arm, and he could feel her heat through the sleeve burning into him.

The next day she asked him to stay for *Shabbas* dinner.

The following week she asked him to stay for *Shabbas* dinner.

The next week, again.

The week after that, on the day that Ruthie came home from prison, Alta-Fruma told him that he didn't need an invitation anymore. "Are you a stranger?" she asked.

They were standing under the willow trees outside the dairyhouse, looking at the red sun fall into the river. "I hope not," he said.

"Of course not." She turned toward him, looking as if in the half-dark she could see everything about him.

NIGHTS OF THE SECRET RIVER

When the raspberries were ripe, Hayim left a stack of wood behind Misha's house, and, with his yoke, walked along the path to a sunny spot near the birches in the woods. There the biggest, sweetest raspberries grew and he whistled as he picked them. The day was warm and muggy, the bucket big. By the time he got to the dairyhouse a thin line of sweat was trickling along his neck.

Alta-Fruma stood with her back to him, a straight and narrow back, the shoulders working as she stirred the curd in the big vat. Hayim could see a single gray curl under her ear, freed from the confines of her kerchief, the ends of the kerchief trailing along her neck. Picking up one of the ends, Hayim pulled gently, as if to untie the kerchief. Alta-Fruma spun around. "You," she said. "Stop it." But her voice was soft and she was smiling.

"Raspberries," Hayim said, presenting Alta-Fruma with the bucket.

"And I have fresh cream to go with it. Let me get bowls from the house. You sit right here." She pointed to the bench.

While she was gone, Hayim took a tablet of paper from the corner and a piece of charcoal from his pocket. A number of his sketches were pinned to the walls of the dairyhouse. Emma and Izzie and Alta-Fruma and even Hazzer the pig in every characteristic pose, Emma arguing, Izzie studying, Alta-Fruma working and Hazzer trying to get into whatever was forbidden to him. There was not a single sketch of Hayim, though Alta-Fruma had asked him for one many times. "How can I draw it for you?" he'd asked. "Can I see myself?"

When Alta-Fruma came back with the bowls, she sat beside him on the bench while they ate and when they were done, still they sat. Could he say what they talked about? He moved toward her and pulled away a dozen times, muttering madly about jewels and secrets. How could he keep himself from her? The sages were right to put a *mekhitzah* between men and women. A man wasn't to be trusted. Even her bare feet on the floor attracted him. She was so close. Just a hair's breadth away from the touch of his hands. No, he just imagined she

was so near. If she was across the room she would seem close, so conscious was he of her presence. If he reached for her she would back
away, and he would have to leave. Maybe he should leave. How could
he insult her with these thoughts? And yet, see how she leaned toward
him, picking a hair from his apron, twisting it around her finger.

"Maybe you're right," she was saying, "I won't say no." She spoke
quietly, leaning so close he could feel the small puffs of her quick
breath. "The floor is cold," she said as she lifted her feet onto the
bench, rubbing them. Narrow feet. Calloused around the heel. Plump
toes. Sweet round pink toes.

Without a thought, like Hazzer the pig facing the door to a cellar,
Hayim pushed her hands away. "Let me," he said, taking her foot. She
didn't pull away. She only looked at him, her head tilted, eyes narrow,
little sighs escaping from between her lips as he warmed her feet
between his hands. Delicate bones under his fingers. Plump toes that
could fill his mouth. He couldn't meet her gaze. Hayim who saw
everything, Hayim who looked at women, bent his head. It was then
that he felt her cool fingers on his neck, reaching upward, tickling the
edge of his ear, touching his lips. Her leg began to tremble, his hands
slid along her calf. Lifting his head, he saw her looking at him with a
half-smile.

"Come with me," Alta-Fruma said, pulling him toward the door
that opened into the cow shed.

In the cow shed he wrapped his arms around her. She was so light
in his arms. A bird with her head bent, the trailing ends of her kerchief
feathers on each side of her neck. He kissed her neck, his lips gentle on
the fragile skin, his heart beating against her breasts until she pushed
herself away with a strong arm, saying, "I want to see." She was looking at him, nodding. "Everything."

"Why not everything," he said, taking off his apron. His caftan.
His shirt. The undershirt with his ritual fringes. His buttoned
trousers. Unbuttoned. And he opened his arms to her as she looked at
him.

WHEN EMMA fell sick with typhus, the whole village was afraid there
would be an epidemic. They wore garlic in pouches around their
necks as they recounted the deaths of the cholera epidemic. Mothers

cut off their daughters' braids and scoured their children's heads for lice. The *zogerin* prayed at the grave of the Old Rabbi. People asked Berekh, still the "Young Rabbi" though he was forty, to bless their homes. Disease is caused by germs, not the evil eye, he explained. But the villagers said, Tishah-b'Av is coming, you know how many terrible things have happened on that day. And still Emma shook with fever.

On Tishah-b'Av bittersweet nightshade was blooming around the edge of the cemetery, tiny purple stars shining above the tombstones. It was the ninth day of the Hebrew month, the lunar month, of Av, a day of mourning and fasting in memory of the first Temple, destroyed in 586 B.C.E., and the second destroyed in 70 C.E. It was the day that the Talmud was burned in Paris in 1242. The day the Jews were expelled from England in 1290 and from Spain in 1492.

The evening meal before the fast was meager. They ate soup, some dry bread, an egg with ashes on it. The synagogue was dim, lit by only a few candles. The Torah was draped in black. The congregation recited dirges, sitting on the floor in their torn garments as if in mourning. The Scroll of Lamentations was chanted and the Book of Job studied for the meaning of pain. In the courtyard, children threw seed burrs at one another.

The doctor from Plotsk had come and gone, offering little hope. Alta-Fruma begged Misha to take a look at Emma, even though the midwife was so far along, even though it was Tishah-b'Av. Hayim waited outside under the willow trees, standing vigil as he had the day that Misha had miscarried.

When the door opened, he could see Misha bending over Emma. I have to tell Misha that she shouldn't worry, he thought. As long as I'm around she'll have wood for her fire and her child will be warm. Misha looked tired, but his eyes followed Alta-Fruma, her shawl over her head, as she emerged.

"Misha says it's going to be soon," Alta-Fruma said. "I'm going to the shul to pray, although the Holy One knows that I have no merit. Is Heaven going to listen to an old *aguna* with no learning and no virtue?"

He held her tight. "Everything has merit to the Master of the Universe," he said. "Even a leaf. Even a frog. It's all from *Ein Sof.*" The Endless One. "So you, Fruma, have nothing to hide. Not a thing. Merit? You without merit?" He shook his head in wonder. "It's impossible. Don't you hear how I'm talking? If a poor watercarrier can speak so easily for your sake, then what about the Holy One above? Let me tell you. I heard about a village where there was a drought. And it was only the prayer of the town drunk who brought rain, because his prayer was the most sincere. Can you believe it? But it's true. Not even the wisest scholars could do what the town drunk did."

"I have to go," she whispered, tearing herself from his arms. He watched her walk, then run, into the darkness.

IT IS WRITTEN that the Messiah will be born on Tishah-b'Av. In the afternoon of the fast day, while the women swept out their houses in honor of his coming, Emma was sitting up and sipping a little soup.

A FEW DAYS later, Alta-Fruma and Hayim sat on the river bank watching the light of the full moon play on the water. He kissed each of her fingers, with their sweet milky scent like the breath of cows.

In the Talmud it says of the full moon of Av, "There are no days as festive to Israel as those of Yom Kippur and the fifteenth of Av. The daughters of Israel used to dress in white and go out to the fields to dance and young men would follow after them."

THE DAYS OF AWE

In the afternoon of the first day of Rosh Hashanah, the birthday of the world, Hayim joined the parade of villagers who walked in solemn procession to the River Północna. They crowded onto the bridge. They lined the shore. The "Young Rabbi," Berekh, stood in the middle of the bridge, his red beard curling skyward like the shofar, the ram's horn, as he recited slowly in a loud, firm voice, *"Cast away from yourselves all your transgressions and create within yourselves a new heart and a new spirit." Tashlikh:* cast off. And so they emptied their pockets of crumbs and dust, throwing their sins into the river. Once upon a time, their ancestors sent the goat Azzazel into the desert, carrying the people's iniquities on his poor head. Now, running excitedly along the banks of the Północna, their children tore up small pieces of bread, flinging them onto the water with glee, asking for more as the ducks paddled over to their sins and ate them up.

The Rabbi raised his arms. The congregation began to sing, *"My Lord, my Lord . . . "* Hayim was watching the trees. They shook down their yellow leaves onto the river in a singing rustle, a windy rush of unclothing their adornment, their bare forms, crooked or straight, revealed. The leaves floated down river, lightly floating, a river of gold, the golden calf melting into the earth's veins. The *Tashlikh* of trees, Hayim thought. The trees were alight, and Hayim smiled as he saw the Holy Presence. "Adonai *is ever-present,*" he sang, joining the rest, *"all-merciful, gracious, compassionate, patient, abounding in kindness and faithfulness, treasuring up love for a thousand generations, forgiving iniquity, transgression, and sin, and pardoning the penitent."* The acrid smell of Asher's strong tobacco wafted past Hayim, though of course there would be no one smoking on this holy day.

KOL NIDREI

Trees burn red in the lowering sun of Kol Nidrei eve. From his seat in the back corner of the synagogue, Hayim looks up in a half-smile as if he can see through the window of the gallery high above to Alta-Fruma in her white dress among the women. In the dusk the ceiling of Ari the Eggs is a blur of colors melding into darkness. Candelabra, hung on triple chains, burn among the tallow candles, dipped and formed by the women of Blaszka. The sanctuary is bright with flames. The candles dance around the ark, on the reader's platform, along ledges on the walls above the benches.

Hayim stands in the back row with the beggar, the picklemaker, the dung sweeper. Behind him, leaning against the wall are strangers who have come to pray on this holiest of days. Visitors from outlying Polish villages where there are no synagogues. A peddler—Yarush from Plotsk. Others whose names Hayim doesn't know. No one will ask them why they are here. It is their right. Shoulder to shoulder, the men wait for Kol Nidrei.

IN THE coming year, Hayim will sketch a self-portrait, using a mirror that Alta-Fruma will hold for him. She will bring back colored pencils from Warsaw, and Hayim will draw the red pig, with his bands of earthen brown, galloping under the sky toward the silver rocks and the narrowed river where the ruins of the mill lie. At the bottom of the portrait he will write, "Hazzer escapes *Mitzrayim,*" the narrow place.

Eventually a boar will be sighted snuffling mushrooms among the beech trees and pines of the forest, and in time there will be an unusual number of piglets bearing his wild coloring, born behind the cottages along the river.

7

THE DANCING BEAR

Yarush was driving his cart toward Blaszka, snow melting on his fur coat, a half-eaten hunk of salami in his hand. He took another bite. "May all his teeth fall out except for one, and that one should rot until the pain makes him take a hammer to his head," he muttered to himself. It was his mother's worst curse. He was invoking it on Andrei Gulbas, owner of the tavern on Whorehouse Row in Plotsk and leader of a gang of thieves that included his seven sons as well as Yarush. " 'Get out,' Andrei says to me. Me, who's been as good as his own brother. He said so many times himself. I just got a little mad. All right, I hit Matthias, but I never drew a knife." Already he'd forgotten the pallor of Andrei's youngest son as his head hit the cobblestones. Yarush had fallen to his knees and bent over the boy, a giant weeping, "I killed him, I killed him," until Andrei's sons pulled him away.

They'd brought Matthias into the house, laid him on the bed, and covered him first with a sheepskin, then with straw. The boy was so warm he'd turned bright red, as if he had a fever. "Andrei's boy,"

Yarush had moaned. "Your papa took me off the docks and brought me to his own mother."

Look, he's still breathing, they said, but Yarush wouldn't be consoled.

ON A Friday night when Yarush was seven years old, in the basement of Avraham's brothel there were only two prostitutes, the pimp and Yarush, who was dazed and breathing painfully. His mother, the older of the two prostitutes, was slumped against the wall where Dovidel the pimp had thrown her. "I'm begging you. Leave the new girl alone," his mother cried. "Riva doesn't know anything yet."

"And she's going to learn." Dovidel swung the buckle end of his belt. "The slut holds back a kopeck from me?"

"It wasn't for me," Riva said, sidling toward the door. "Just my brothers."

"Please, Dovidel. Don't," Yarush's mother said. The pimp turned and snapped the belt against her legs.

Yarush rushed at him. "You don't hit my mother," he yelled. He yelled loud so Dovidel wouldn't see that he was scared. But Dovidel just snickered and slapped his face, right where his nose was broken. Yarush screamed, covering his face with his hands.

"Get out. Or you'll have to run to the other side of the moon to stay alive," Dovidel said.

"Go, son," his mother said. "Please." On the rickety table, the Sabbath candles flickered.

Yarush slept on the docks. The next morning, while Dovidel the pimp went to the gang's synagogue to pray for a good week, Yarush was sneaking his hand into a barrel to steal a beet for his breakfast. He hardly had a bite out of it when an old man caught hold of his wrist and twisted it. "Get away from here," he shouted. The boy stumbled against a stone wall, head aching as he got up, tripped over a beggar, hit his head again, fainted, came awake to find his jacket stolen but it didn't matter, he was so hungry he didn't feel the cold. He found some moldy potato skins but he ate too fast and threw up. Then he was so thirsty, he begged the sailors for a drink, though it burned at first. "I'm not afraid," he said. "I've had my nose broken before. And my arm, too." The sailors laughed, saying, This little Yarush is a man, practically a Cossack. When Yarush woke up, he was lying on a pile of rope, his head hurting more than his nose and his throat all sticky. It was hours before he was hungry again, but then he began to dream about food even though his eyes were open.

When Andrei found him, Yarush was digging a fish head out of the garbage.

"This will make you sick," Andrei said, taking it from him.

"Give it back. It's mine. You can't have it," Yarush said, kicking and hitting with his fists though Andrei was so much bigger. Sweat poured into Yarush's eyes. He had to get it back. He had to. It wasn't just a fish head anymore. It was a whole fish. A fish with potatoes. And sour cabbage. And . . .

"Come with me. Mama will feed you something better," Andrei said.

"No. Leave me alone," Yarush said as Andrei picked him up. He wailed against Andrei's shoulder, then struggled to get away, but Andrei only laughed, saying, "So you're a tough one," as he carried him off.

In Andrei's house, Yarush had five helpings of onions and potatoes lathered in cream, not rusted and rotting like he got at the brothel, but beautiful white potatoes. He fell asleep, the fork still in his fist and someone carried him to Andrei's straw bed.

His mother's left shoulder healed higher than the right and Dovidel the pimp called her the Hunchback after that. Sometimes she laughed. "You see me, son?" she would ask Yarush. "I was once beautiful. The daughter of Zelig the grain merchant. You can say that your grandfather was a rich man in Blaszka, but don't say his name. I'm dead to him, and how can a dead person have a father?" Then she would laugh. It was worse than when Dovidel hit her.

On Passover, his mother would tell him to be a good boy and not eat any bread. Yarush would nod and pat her hand before going off to Andrei's family. There he would eat *sweicone,* holy food, pork and pastry blessed by the priest for Easter. Andrei's father sometimes grumbled about feeding Jews at Easter when it was more appropriate to beat them up. But Andrei's mother, crunching on the piece of *matzah* Yarush had brought her, would say, "Never you mind, he's our Jew."

When he was thirteen, Yarush went to prison for a while and the guards called him the Bear, because of his fur coat. One night, for fun, the guards put a rope around his neck and poked him with bayonets and shouted, "Dance for us." And Yarush did, clumsily, while they laughed and threw him some meat, which he ate.

THE ROAD from Plotsk followed the Vistula River until it joined its small tributary, the Północna. There the road divided. Straight ahead, it continued on to Warsaw, and to the left it twisted toward Blaszka. It was quiet on the road. Too quiet. There was just the sound of the wheels grating and it got on Yarush's nerves. There was always someone to have a drink with on Whorehouse Row. A tip about a job. A game of dice. And if you wanted to be left to yourself, all right, you sat at your table and drank alone. The noise around you let you know you were alive. In his cart he had a load of stolen goods to sell to the farms upriver, but the old wheezing nag was pulling the cart like she was taking a Sabbath stroll. Didn't she feel the whip? Yarush flicked it again and again until, bleeding, she began to trot.

At the bend in the road, he saw someone sitting on a log, looking at a notebook. Hatless. Red hair sticking up. Torn jacket. Poor and young. But he had a traveling bag with rope handles. Might be something in it. The Traveler waved at Yarush. "Can I get a ride?" he called.

"If you got money," Yarush said. The Traveler looked him up and down like Yarush was the one begging a ride and the young man a somebody. I know the type, Yarush thought. A proper Jew, thinks the mud in his village square is something finer than the mud on Whorehouse Row.

"Money, no. But something in trade," the Traveler said, his face twisting as he forced a smile.

"What have you got?"

The Traveler held up a rock.

"You want a ride for a rock?"

"What if it was blessed?"

"Blessed? You mean a lucky rock. My boss has a lucky pig's foot that he carries with him on every job." As he spoke, Yarush eyed the traveling bag.

"Well, I'll tell you," the Traveler said. "You keep this rock in your pocket for a hundred and twenty years, guaranteed you'll have a long life."

"Where you going?" Yarush asked, as if he hadn't noticed the Traveler's scornful tone. He'd just let that stranger get into the cart so he could give the bag a kick and see how heavy it was. Then he'd show the young man the point of his knife.

"Oh, just that ways a while." The Traveler waved in the direction of Blaszka.

"All right." Yarush moved over to make room. As the Traveler climbed into the cart, his nostrils fluttered. Yarush smiled. The smell of his fur coat was a powerful thing, lunging at strangers like a *Rusalka,* the fish women who lurked in swamps and tormented unwary travelers at night. Yarush gave the bag a kick. It shifted easily. Worthless. Still, the stranger might have a rich relative somewhere.

"Where you from?" Yarush asked as the cart rollicked along the ice hard dirt between last year's nettles and the hunched willows with their golden branches praying over the frozen river.

"Around," the Traveler answered.

"No place special? Just around."

"Right."

Not so proper then. A man from nowhere is on the run. Has to sneak out of places. Wanting nobody to know he's gone. "Everyone says there's nothing like a corpse's hand for keeping a house asleep," Yarush said. "You want one? I can get you one for a good price. Works like magic."

"Like magic?" the Traveler asked.

"Magic," Yarush said.

"Well, what do you think I've got in my hands? It's a magic rock. Take it."

In the Traveler's hands, the rock had a reddish tinge. Maybe it was lucky. The young man should hope so. Yarush was getting itchy.

"Who knows what could happen if you have this?" the Traveler insisted. "What do you want? A nice house, maybe a wife?"

"I had a wife," Yarush said. "She left me." He was hungry again. Where did he have that salami?

"Ran off?"

"Yeah and for nothing. Didn't even use a belt on her. I just gave her a slap with the back of my hand and she fell down the stairs. Took my little girls away. I couldn't find them anywhere." Andrei's wife never complained. Not a word. Never a word about anything. And sometimes he knocked her around anyway, just to remind her. "A man has to let the woman know he's the boss, doesn't he? It wasn't half of anything my mother got," Yarush said.

"You miss your girls?" the Traveler asked, his voice suddenly warm with pity like Yarush was some soft old man that anyone could knife when his back was turned.

Yarush spit over the side of the cart. "It's not like they were sons," he said. "If they were sons, my wife wouldn't dare take them. I'll tell you something about women. You go with a woman and you think you're having a good time. But afterward you're still hungry, know what I mean? Like you've had nothing. And she's just whining and crying over every little thing. Driving you crazy so you can't get any sleep. You've got to sleep after a job. Drink up and sleep it off. But there she is crying and pulling on you and complaining. She's cold, the baby's cold, where'd the money go? Women? There's not a good one among them."

"The rock works. Good women will come to you. Even a flock of them. Believe me, I wouldn't cheat you," the Traveler said, the scorn back in his voice.

Yarush shrugged. He was always too generous after Andrei threw him out. Missing the boys. Maybe he could use a lucky rock. "I won't break your neck this time," he said to the Traveler.

It was late afternoon by the time Yarush reached Blaszka. Hungry, he searched through his cart, amazed at the absence of all the cheese and bread and meat he'd loaded behind the stolen goods for sale. Inside the pots, between the coils of wire, within the barrels of nails, unraveling the bolts of cloth. Nothing. The village square was empty, the stalls dismantled for *Shabbas*. The low wooden buildings were gray against the gray sky, shops closed, blinds drawn. Even the Director's carriage was heading out of Blaszka, minus one piglet now asleep in Hayim's arms.

So it was nearly *Shabbas*. What did Yarush care about that? He was angry at the shuttered stores. At his slow horse and at the setting winter sun for cheating him out of a chance to buy a piece of bread before the Sabbath. Yarush was monstrously hungry. Red and black spots

confused his eyes, obscuring the village square as he heard the sound
of wood breaking, a thump as the nag hit the ground, the broken shaft
of the wagon like the mast of a drowned ship on top of her.

Yarush jumped down from the cart. "Stand up!" he shouted in a
frenzy. "You good for nothing horse, get up!" he shouted again,
punching her for good measure.

"Take your hand off the horse," a woman called out. Yarush
looked up to see a big woman with wild black hair coming to him,
storming across the village square. A crowd had appeared, from
nowhere it seemed. One minute the square was empty, the next it was
filled with a flock of women, a milling mob making way for the big
woman.

"You talking to me?" Yarush asked. Now the men were joining the
crowd, nudging one another, eyeing Yarush suspiciously.

"Who do you think I'm talking to? God in Heaven?" the big
woman asked.

People were laughing. *Shabbas* is coming, they said, who's going to
take the peddler home for dinner? Not me. I'm not ashamed to say
that I'm afraid of him. Let him get going and eat with the peasants.
He's more one of them than one of us.

Yarush scowled. All of them with their shops closed and locked
against him, with their Sabbath breads and soups hidden from him.
Smoke was rising from their chimneys, from the tiled ovens cooking
good meat and potatoes. Yarush smelled it, yes, with his nose in the
air, thick nostrils inhaling the wafting odor of Sabbath food for everyone except him. "Go back inside, woman," he said as she approached.
"Mind your own business."

"If it happens in Blaszka, it's my business."

"You think you're something, don't you?"

"Leave the poor nag alone."

Yarush kicked the horse. "What do you mean, ordering me
around? Can you say what I should do with my own animal?"

"I told you once, and I'm telling you again. Leave the poor nag
alone." The woman moved closer.

"I'll show you who's the master here," he said, grabbing her shoulder. A heavy round shoulder that fit his hand nicely.

"Master? Of me? The Pope will marry our blind Hindela first."
The woman laughed, her head back, her gold tooth gleaming.

"I'll give you something to laugh for." She was trying to get out from under his grasp. He could feel her pulling back, straining. A big woman. It wasn't easy to hold onto her, but he would. He'd show her.

"You'll show me some respect," she said. She kicked him. Right in his calf. There's a woman for you. Blink and she's at you. Keeping you from your business. Making a scene. But he didn't move. He wouldn't give her the satisfaction. Instead he pulled her closer, squeezing her shoulder, pressing into her collarbone with his thumb. She winced. So, she didn't like this? Wait. He had more for her.

And then she turned her head and spit into his beard. She spat at him!

"Go to hell," she said.

Now she was going to get it.

From within the crowd, a bass voice was calling, Let me through, let me through. Like water swirling around a tossed stone, the crowd's attention shifted toward the new voice. What is it, they asked. Who's getting mixed up in this business? Hershel, they cried, this is a good joke. Does he think he's King David sent to fight Goliath?

Yarush's fist was midway to Misha's mouth when he was distracted by the sight of the bottle in the raised hand of a short, balding man, his hat slipping over one ear.

"Friend, friend, join me in a drink," the gnomish man said. Yarush slowly turned. Where there was drink, there was food, and if not food, at least the hot fire of a schnapps. What was a woman compared to that?

"Schnapps?" Yarush asked.

"Ah. A man of few words. The best." Hershel took Yarush by the arm and gently drew him across the square, the crowd parting like the Red Sea.

In the tavern Yarush gulped down three quick tumblers of vodka. His hunger burnt up in the fire, the outlines of the men wobbly in its smoke.

"She likes you," his benefactor, Hershel the butcher, was saying.

"She spit at me." For nothing. Just like a woman, Yarush thought.

"A good match for you, no? Misha, the woman in the square. She just needs a little, what should I say? Encouragement."

A match, a match, it went around in Yarush's head like a drinking song.

"A big woman like Misha, she's a whole wedding feast, my friend, and you have the teeth to enjoy it," said Hershel, pouring another glass.

Yarush drank. A big woman for a big man. Her shoulder in his hand. Meaty. Nice. He leaned back, digging his hands into his pockets, imagining Andrei patting him on the shoulder, winking and flicking his thumb under his chin in the go-ahead sign.

In his pocket he felt the rock rolling into his right hand and his thoughts turned to a hazy dream of his ride with the Traveler. "Like magic," Yarush said aloud.

"Yes, yes," Hershel replied. "You're absolutely right. It's meant to be. Of course the community council will provide a dowry for our esteemed midwife. With silver, all right maybe brass, candlesticks. And you'll have a house, too. A small house but right on the village square. You can see it through the window. The one on the stilts above the river." The door to the inn flew open. "And look who's here, may Heaven bless her. My wife, Hanna-Leah."

A dowry. A house. A big woman like a feast. Through a haze Yarush saw Hershel arguing with the woman who had come in to haul him out of the tavern. Let her go, Yarush wanted to say, women just tease you and keep what you need for themselves. But the words fell into the glass of vodka as he drank it down. Hershel's friend, the baker, left and soon after Hershel followed his wife. The innkeeper put another bottle on the table, and he went, too.

Yarush sat alone. The inside of the tavern turned red with the setting sun, and then black with a darkness lit fitfully by the fire. With his second bottle in hand, he found his way into Perlmutter's cupboard. Pushing bread and shmaltz herring into his mouth, he remembered Misha's abundance. Not like the other women he'd lain with. Stringy bits of meat such as poor men boil to nothing in their Sabbath soup just to give it a little flavor. This Misha would be firm. She would be warm. She would wrap herself around him like a feather bed. He would plunge into her over and over until he was finished, and then he would know what he'd had. She wasn't a ghost, that one. She had substance. A proper woman.

As Yarush toyed with the empty bottle, he imagined sitting at her table. The cloth was white. Candles were lit. There were two braided hallahs. A whole roasted hen with gravy crackling through the skin. She would speak to him, call him "my Bear," stroking his head, and, and . . . his imagination failed him. And? She would turn against him. No, he could hear her say. No. You can't have that. What? Not any? No. Nothing. The cupboards were closed. The door was locked against him. Even though she was his. Yes, his. She was promised to him. And what did she do? Shout at him. Kick him. Spit on him in front of the whole village.

Pulling himself to his feet and nearly falling out the door, he lurched across the square to Misha's house. There he climbed the steps that rose up from the river bank, glinting as the moon skidded across the frozen river. He held the rock in his hand. He raised it high, seeing already the crack in the feeble wood of the door. When dawn came, Yarush was gone, the rock left on Misha's step. It had split in two and between the two halves a red drop glinted in the morning light. The broken door swung weakly on its hinges.

THE DAY OF THE ICE STORM

In the yard behind the tavern, Andrei's sons were throwing knives at Yarush. The storm had passed and the muddy yard was pocked by melting ice pellets. In the fenced-off corner, the sow was suckling her piglets. The rooster was trying to ruffle his bedraggled feathers. "Come on, you dogs," Yarush called. "We've hardly started." His coat lay on the ground. His pants were tucked into his boots. His shirt, the sleeves cut off, hung to his knees. He used first his right then his left hand to catch the knives, the tattoos on his arms shivering, the Angel of Death on one and a mermaid on the other. He'd gotten the tattoos when he was drunk, and he was sure they meant he'd die by water. He was afraid of water. And darkness. And hunger.

"Is that your best? You'd better go back to ploughing fields," he said, "and sucking the landlord's asshole."

"Forget it," Matthias said. "Take your twenty rubles."

He threw the money down on the woodpile beside Yarush, who pulled on his coat, hiding the slight shaking of his arms, his back to Matthias and his brothers. They'd bet that if Yarush could last for ten throws, either Matthias would try it or forfeit twice the number of rubles. As Yarush pocketed the money, he thought it was a good thing Matthias decided to pay up. Andrei wouldn't take kindly to Yarush throwing knives at the hands of his favorite son, the lock picker, even though Matthias himself had put Yarush up to it. But you have to let people know you can give as good as you get, especially when you're not so young anymore. Otherwise they'll tear you to pieces. Yarush put half the money in each pocket. One side was for drinking and cards. The other side was put-up money for Andrei, who got half of everything. It's not cheap to pay for bribes, supplies, and church candles.

Inside the tavern, Yarush bought drinks for everyone. To Yarush, they said. To Yarush. To Yarush. The pimps at the front of the tavern, the old sailors at the back, the thieves sprawled in the center, the hunched porters and the beggars with their crutches leaning against the side wall lifted their cups calling, Luck and health to Yarush. Yes, yes, to Yarush, a young sailor said, though Yarush had never seen him before. He was paying over his wages to one of the pimps, taking hold of the freckle-faced, orange-haired cousins, fifteen years old, who, the sailor was solemnly promised, were twins. One under each arm, his hands crawling down their dresses, the sailor began to sing, "*Poland is still ours forever as long as Poles are free.*"

Yarush hadn't been with a woman since the winter, when he'd found out that lying with a big woman wasn't better than any other. As far as he was concerned, the young sailor was wasting his money.

"Where's Antek?" Yarush asked the barmaid. "I want to pay his tab." She looked at him. "For luck," he added. Antek was blind and legless and the chief of the beggars' guild.

"He died," she said. "Didn't you hear?"

Yarush shook his head. "His turn today, mine tomorrow." Then he took his bottle to the back and drank himself under the table.

THE SEASON OF RAINS

In the stable, Andrei's sons joked quietly to keep the horses calm while they saddled them. They pulled knit caps low over their brows, buttoned dark coats below their knees, laced their high boots tight. The animals were pawing their straw, hooves wrapped in rags, snorting as if they'd forgotten they'd been gelded. The bottle was passed around and each of the brothers took a drink, but only one. Andrei would whip anyone who got drunk before a job. Yarush handed out the revolvers. The seven brothers tucked them into waistbands front and back, pockets, saddlebags. Yarush didn't like guns, but the Jewish gang had them, the Russian soldiers had them, and so must Andrei's boys.

Yarush slipped his knife into his boot and an iron rod up the sleeve of his coat and he stayed close to Matthias, whose sensitive fingers could pick the lock of a saint's halo.

THE FIRST TIME Yarush had seen a revolver had been in his grandfather's hands. It was after the grain merchant had moved away from Blaszka. Somehow his mother had heard that he was in Bezoyn, and she took Yarush with her to see him. "You have some hutzpah," the old man had said, "pretending to be my daughter. Was my daughter a hunchback? If you want to beg, go to the community council. You'll get nothing out of me."

"I don't want your partner's money," Yarush's mother had said. "Just take my boy. He's your grandson, for pity's sake."

"My daughter's dead, I'm telling you. Get out." He'd pulled a revolver out of his cabinet and pointed it at them, his hand shaking.

IT WAS dark and wet on the docks. The watchman's hut was unlit, as agreed on payment of his price. Three ships rocked in the river. Yarush counted them. Just three, he said to himself. Same as in the morning. Nothing to worry about. The darkness of the sky clouded over the thin moon, and the darkness of the water licked at the docks. The ships were taller than they should be, as if they'd grown. Everything grows in the darkness. But still, it was just three ships, and the strange shapes were just pylons, and the fishy smell was just herring, same as by daylight, he thought, but his skin prickled and his boots skidded on the slick surface of an oily spot. As he caught his balance, he thought, There could be something in the water reaching out to grab the legs of someone walking by, and that person wouldn't notice if he wasn't looking, would he? No, there'd just be a splash as he went under, and not even a stone to mark where he lay. He stopped, peering into the darkness. "What you looking at?" Matthias asked.

"Shut up," Yarush hissed, cuffing Matthias. The other boys were approaching the warehouse from different directions, Andrei waiting outside with the oldest, ready to load up the carts. Yarush moved on, rocking from side to side like a sailor. The rhythm kept him walking steady, his right fist tight around the iron bar in his sleeve.

"Now," he said to Matthias, and they ran down the length of the dock to the warehouse. They didn't have to run. The guards were drinking up a case of Andrei's offerings in the guardhouse, where it was dry and warm. But running worked off the edge of excitement, so you could do your job right. And it got you out of the darkness faster.

The warehouse was full. Lighting the kerosene lamp, Matthias whistled. "Look at that," he said as three of his brothers wandered between the rows of stuff just lying there, waiting for the taking. Barrels and crates piled from floor to ceiling. Tea. Fine cloth. Sugar. Gunpowder. Silver. Vodka. Fur hats. Each box a fistful of gold imperials. Their footsteps echoed as the boys raced between the rows, punching one another and hooting, I'll be a dog if I don't take this and that, too. It's my fortune. I'll be a landlord. You? You can't piss straight. Hey, suck my black hole, this is the big haul. "Yarush, you're gonna retire," Matthias said, "like a rich Jew."

When Yarush had been eighteen, he couldn't stand still inside a full warehouse, either. But now he just wanted to get the job done. "Here," he said. "Move." He pulled the iron bar from his sleeve, cracking it on the side of a beam. The boys began to stack the shipment from Hamburg, marked with chalk by the watchman they'd bribed.

"The vodka's just sitting there," Matthias said.

"No. Wasn't arranged."

"So? Leave it to me." Grunting, Matthias pulled the crate out from the middle of the stack. He grinned, turning his back on the unbalanced stack of crates. As Yarush pulled the boy out of the way, the crates toppled around them. Bottles broke, Yarush fell, the iron rod clanging as it dropped, a stinging liquid splashing into his eyes. Blearily he saw the warehouse door open. "Andrei," he yelled, "get your sheep-screwing sons out of here."

"What's going on? Who's in there?" a voice called.

Matthias's brothers scrambled through the debris, jumping over Yarush and Matthias, who was lying stunned under a pile of crates.

The back door slammed open. The horses neighed. Andrei's oldest yelled, "Nix." There was the squeal of heavily loaded carts jerked from a standstill, and then silence.

Rising to his feet, Yarush waved his arms at the figure in the doorway, shouting, "Thieves. Catch them." While the man ran outside, Yarush threw crates aside, pulling Matthias to his feet. "This way," he said, grabbing a solid hunk of board out of the wreckage, but before they'd reached the back door, a kerosene lamp was flashing at them, and the same voice as before said, "Halt! I'm warning you, I'm armed." It was a gentleman's voice speaking Polish with a Russian accent. Matthias reached for his revolver. Yarush tried to knock it out of his hand, but he was still dizzy, and Matthias hit off a shot first. It went wide. Of course it went wide. You can't rely on a gun. And the gentleman got off a shot, too. It went wide, but not wide enough. Yarush felt a burning in his thigh. He didn't think the bullet went in, just grazed him, but there wasn't time to take notice of the blood oozing through his fur coat.

The coat had once belonged to Dovidel the pimp. He used to stroke the smooth fur of the coat as he never stroked any of the women he brought into the brothel. He had been passionate about the coat, stylish, dark, and lush. A Russian coat. A conqueror's coat. Yarush had been just a boy when he removed the coat from Dovidel, but he'd been very enthusiastic about it. I'll wear the coat until the fat rots off your bones, he'd promised. And he kept his promise, wearing the coat summer and winter, as if the wearing of it avenged his mother's grief.

"Save me, sir," Yarush whined, while to Matthias, he hissed, "Get out." Yarush moved into the pool of light. "They run me over, sir," he said. "Just look at me. The young dog got away and look at me, wounded, just doing my duty. It's hard to be a watchman, just a few kopecks and your life isn't safe these days."

The gentleman wasn't an officer. What was he doing here? Yarush kept up his patter as he moved closer, the wooden board tucked under his arm.

"So you're in here. That's why the watchman's hut was dark," the gentleman said.

"I was just doing my rounds when they came on me," Yarush said.

"Thanks be to Mother Mary, Queen of Poland, that you chased them off."

"Well, it was just fortunate that I was going by. I have an appointment with the captain of the *Maiden*." Yarush was close enough now to see a girl cowering behind the gentleman. A Gypsy girl, by the look of her, dressed up like a lady. So you're going out to see the captain in the middle of the night? Well, the fiddlings of the rich aren't anything to me, Yarush thought, but that gentleman's starting to look at me funny. "Thank you, sir," he said. As he touched his right hand to his cap, his left hand swung around with the board and smashed it against the side of the gentleman's head. The Gypsy girl ran off in one direction, and Yarush in the other.

Yarush lay low for a while, but no one came asking after the gentleman or the Gypsy girl, either.

THE LONG DAYS

In the tavern on Whorehouse Row, Andrei glowered over the tables flung aside like drunks in the gutter. "What's the matter with you?" he shouted at Yarush. "First you give up your share of the job to a pipsqueak stranger moaning about some woman in a Jew village who's gone and got herself knocked-up, and then you pull a knife on Matthias. What's the matter with you?"

Cracked bottles were leaking vodka. Andrei's sons, grumbling, shoveled the broken glass. "It's nothing. Just a scratch," Matthias said.

Yarush was breathing heavily, trying hard to stay on his feet though he'd drunk enough to knock another man unconscious for a week. "He said I was stupid," Yarush muttered.

"Get out. I don't want to see your face," Andrei said.

"All right. Who wants to stay in this stinking hole with a bunch of stomachless dogs anyway." Yarush went outside and hitched up his cart to a nag just as bony and tired as the one that died on the short Friday. As they rode along the familiar road toward Blaszka, he muttered to himself, "Every tooth in his head should rot . . ."

Just where the road opened into the lanes of Blaszka, the way was blocked by a fallen pine. Swearing in Polish, Russian, and Yiddish, Yarush dropped down from the cart. He strained at the tree, the branches scratching his hands and face, but he couldn't move it. To his left the woods were eating up the road with young saplings growing like weeds. Down by the river, he could see a dairyhouse. A broad-shouldered man swinging a bucket was walking up from it. Yarush waved, calling, "You. Come here." As the man approached, Yarush saw that he carried a round of cheese under his arm. There was good cheese in Blaszka.

"What is it?" the man asked.

"Help me move the tree."

The watercarrier put the cheese down on the grassy verge, joining Yarush. Tucking his caftan up into his belt, he said, "You haven't been around since winter."

Yarush grunted.

"People say that, that you left something in Blaszka. With the midwife, Misha."

"People say lots of things," Yarush said.

"It's not yours, then?"

"You think I'm stupid? I don't like people who think I'm stupid. You know what I do to them?"

"What?" the watercarrier asked. He was looking at Yarush curiously with those cat's eyes that didn't blink.

Yarush burped. " 'A burp goes out, a little health goes in,' " he said in Yiddish. "My mother used to say that." Weaving slightly, he nearly fell over the tree. "Got to move that," he said.

The watercarrier gripped the tree at its base, Yarush at its midsection. With some effort, much cursing on Yarush's part, and a few stammered replies on the other's, the tree was moved. Yarush picked up the round of cheese and was tucking it into his cart, when the watercarrier said, "That's, that's mine."

"What of it?" Yarush asked.

The villager planted himself in front of Yarush. He was just a little shorter, though not half as wide as Yarush, but he looked him over as if he were memorizing Yarush's bushy brows, the forked beard sticking out above his Adam's apple, the knotted scar under his ear, the twitching fingers, the matted tangles in his fur coat. The smell of the coat didn't seem to bother the watercarrier at all. "Get out of my way," Yarush said.

"I'll, I'll take the cheese first," Hayim said.

Yarush stepped back and squinted at him. The way this man

stared, the way he stammered, it was familiar somehow. "I know you. Your voice, it reminded me. Don't you remember me?"

"Yes, sure. You come through Blaszka sometimes. Everyone knows, knows who you are. Yarush from Plotsk. The Bear. The hungry man."

"No, I mean from before. When we were boys." Yarush tried to fix the memory in his mind. It was there, between the smell of cheese and Matthias sneering, "Stupid idiot." Yarush could see it moving closer, wavering in his drunkenness. Yes, a stammering boy with the same golden eyes as this man, there in the basement of Avraham's Brothel. "We're practically brothers, you and me," Yarush said.

"Brothers?"

"You married Riva, didn't you?"

"Yes. How did you know?"

"She worked in the same house with my mother. Don't you remember? My mama was the one with the crooked shoulder."

"Yes, yes," Hayim said. "She had black hair."

"Dyed fresh every week. And it didn't get messed. She used the water from fava beans to keep it in place. All the girls called her Mama. Riva, too. My mother took care of them like they were her own. So you're my brother, kind of. Right?"

"I guess so."

"You could've been my papa," Yarush said, hitting Hayim in the shoulder. "The owner of the brothel, Avraham, he wanted my mother to marry you."

"Me?" Hayim asked. "What do you mean? How do you know?" He looked surprised.

"I know a thing or two," Yarush said. "I was there when your Old Rabbi came looking for orphans. 'The *Alter Rov* is coming,' Avraham said. 'Watch out. Clean up. Make up the fire. Brush off the chair.' I heard the whole thing because I was carrying the missus's baskets into the house. I fell and spilled everything and she knocked me one under the ear and I was cleaning up, y'know when the Rabbi came in. He sat beside the table in the best chair with the velvet back and the fringes."

"STUPID BOY," the missus was hissing. "You'll be lucky to eat dirt when you grow up. We have an important guest here. Didn't Avraham warn you? If you make him ashamed, he's selling you off to be a ship's boy and your ass is going to be split wider than the Red Sea. He meant it. Don't think he didn't."

The Rabbi had a long white beard. Yarush, glancing at him from the corner of his eye as he swept up, could swear that the beard practically touched the ground. A real rabbi, he thought. The old man's hands rested on the top of a walking stick. Not a fancy cane, like he'd imagined a rabbi would have, just an ordinary staff of oak, knobby like his hands.

"The matchmaker told me you have someone suitable," the Rabbi was saying.

"It'd break my heart," Avraham said, clutching his chest, his fingers heavy with rings, the fingernails long and dirty. "Lipsha was my first girl. I started out with just her and now look, I have a fine house of girls and my own man to bring in the customers and give a little something to the police. How could I let her go? No, no. Lipsha's worth a fortune to me."

Behind him, his wife was preparing a tray of tea and cake, her face pinched below the blonde wig, stiff as a helmet. "A fortune," she repeated. As she nodded, tiny flakes of rouge fell from her cheeks onto the tray.

Yarush, kneeling on the floor, stared at them. A fortune? His favorite? His best? But Avraham was always telling Lipsha that she wasn't any more use than a toothless dog. It's just the goodness of my heart that I keep you, he'd say to her. Your brat eats up all my profits.

"And what about her boy?" Avraham was saying. "He's like my own son. Come here, Yarush." Warily, the boy approached the table. Avraham pinched his cheek between his knuckles, giving it a little twist in warning.

The Rabbi didn't seem to notice the red mark, but called Yarush to come closer to him. "Do you *daven* every morning, *yingeleh?*" he asked. No one had ever called Yarush "little boy," but it didn't sound like an insult. The Rabbi was looking at him kindly. He had big soft pouches of skin under his blue eyes.

"I don't pray," Yarush answered. He didn't add that he couldn't read the prayers even if he wanted to.

"Oh," the Rabbi said. "On *Shabbas,* you go to synagogue?"

"No."

"But you don't eat any *trayf?*"

The boy shrugged. Food is food, he thought.

The Rabbi was sitting on the edge of the chair, like maybe if he leaned back he'd catch some lice. He tapped the stick impatiently on the floor between his feet, while Avraham wiped his eyes and blew his nose on his sleeve, saying, "No, I can't give up my dear Lipsha."

Leaning on the staff, the Rabbi rose to his feet. "All right," he said, "so there's no match."

Avraham stopped wiping his eyes, a slightly panicked expression on his face. "Don't be so hasty," he said. "I have a big heart. For a little commission I might be willing to let her go to Blaszka. Devorah," he commanded his wife, "call her up. We'll talk."

When Lipsha appeared, Yarush placed himself at her side, as he always did, ready to protect her even against the Rabbi. But at the sight of Lipsha, the old man said, "This is the orphan? This, this . . . no. Not even for the cholera. I'm not going to match up a boy with this worked-over, crippled hen."

Lipsha made a small choking noise.

Yarush grabbed the Rabbi's caftan, twisting it at the neck. "You take it back!" he shouted. "My mother is good enough to marry anybody. Her father was a rich man."

"Sha, Yarush. Don't say anything," his mother pleaded.

"Zelig the grain merchant. And he came from your stinking little *shtetl,* too."

The Old Rabbi looked at her. "You're Zelig's girl, Lipsha?" he asked.

She didn't answer.

"I don't believe it. He didn't know what happened to you. He mourned like you died."

"He knew," she said. "He found me."

The Old Rabbi shook his head. "How could you do it to him?"

"You want to blame me?" Lipsha asked. "Be my guest."

"Listen to me. What's past is past," the brothel owner said. "Let's talk business. The match."

Lipsha laughed. "Do you think I want to get married? No. Never. And to a boy of how old?"

"Seventeen," the Old Rabbi said.

"Only four years older than my son, Yarush. Ridiculous. But I have an idea," Lipsha said. "You should take little Dina. A girl from the country. Hardly worked."

Avraham was aghast. The youngest? The newest? She had years of usefulness ahead of her, not to mention that she could be passed off as a virgin for a premium price at least another few times. "I won't hear of it," he said.

Finally they settled on Riva. The Rabbi would have to cough up a good price for her. She didn't come cheap. The Rabbi said he'd see what he could do. He went away and when he came back a week later, he wasn't alone but brought the prospective groom. The Rabbi went upstairs to deal with Avraham while the groom and his driver went to meet the bride-to-be.

Yarush came home to see a couple of strangers talking to Riva and his mother. The younger one was a boy with golden eyes, the other looked to be ten years older. Yarush crossed the room to stand beside his mother. "That's Hayim, the groom. The other one drove him to Plotsk. Yekhiel's his name. A baker," his mother whispered.

Riva was saying she wouldn't do it. "Is it fair to keep a boy stuck with someone like me? Does he deserve it, an orphan?"

His mother winced as she rose from her bed. Her shoulder must be hurting her. She had that look on her face, the one she used to get when Dovidel the pimp started to unbuckle his belt. "Look at me, a crooked back, I can hardly stand. Do you want to end up like me? No, Riva. You're still a young woman. You're beautiful. You're smart. So he's a boy? He should consider himself lucky. No one can be sad with you." Yarush nodded. No one could mimic Avraham and his fat wife like Riva. "If the world was on fire, you could still make a person laugh till he cried," his mother said. "I don't know what I'll do without you. But you have to take your chance."

The baker, Yekhiel, frowned and shook his head, while the young groom was watching Riva and blinking, his eyes moist.

They argued some more, but it was all settled the way it began. Riva was going to marry Hayim in Blaszka. After the visitors left, his mother told Riva, "Your new husband will be good to you. He's a fine person, this Hayim, refined. A *shayner.*"

The younger girls laughed. What's his fortune, a couple of buckets? they asked.

"Pay no attention," Lipsha said. "He'll treat you right, Rivala, and won't mind whatever happened before."

Avraham appeared in the doorway. "Yarush. The Rabbi wants to see you. Go. They're waiting outside for you."

Hayim and Yekhiel were in the cart, the Rabbi leaning on his staff in the shadow of the brothel. "It's a shame that a Jewish boy doesn't know kosher from *trayf*," the old man said to Yarush. "Aren't you a mother's son? Don't you deserve something in life? Look, I'll take you with me to Blaszka. I can use a sturdy boy to help in the synagogue. I'll teach you the letters. You can have as many potatoes as you can eat. Fresh bread every day, a whole loaf if you want, two even. All right, *yingela?*"

"But I wouldn't go," Yarush said to Hayim.

"Why not?" Hayim asked. He was leaning against a beech tree, Yarush seated on an oak stump, his legs stretched out like thick roots, a half-smile on his face as he recalled the Old Rabbi.

"I couldn't leave my mother, could I? The *Alter Rov*, he said I was a good boy. He patted my cheek. Afterward I found two rubles in my pocket. Well, I wouldn't leave her, not even if she slapped me a hundred times to make me go. I was getting big enough so the pimp wouldn't dare lift a hand to her if I was around. My mother wasn't just anyone, you know. She came from a good family. It's true. Her father was a rich man in Blaszka. A grain merchant."

"Who?" Hayim asked.

"Zelig. Did you know him?"

"He was in business with Eber?" The two of them used to sit in the front row of the synagogue. Zelig and Eber, Faygela's grandfather, who was cheated out of his share of the business by his partner.

"All I know is that he wanted to marry my mother off to a rich old widower that promised to get him out of debt. Mama didn't want it, and he beat her with a poker. Left her with a scar, but not on her face, not so it showed. So she ran away."

As if seeing the other man for the first time, Hayim said excitedly, "I do remember you. You were standing beside your mother in the brothel. And then when Riva died, you came to Blaszka. You were maybe thirteen, right?"

Yarush nodded. "It broke Mama's heart when Riva died. She

jumped on Dovidel the pimp and tried to rip out his mustache with both hands. He threw her against the wall. Hurt her back where it was broken before. She kept crying, 'Riva, Riva, why did you come back? You should have forgotten us.' She was shaking when she told me to go to Blaszka. She didn't want you to think that Riva went back to work in the brothel. You shouldn't think anything bad about her, she said. She told me to tell you everything. You see this fur coat? I took it off Dovidel so he'd remember me. I didn't want to leave my mother alone. But I had to, didn't I? I promised."

Hayim nodded, looking away from Yarush's twisted face. "It's because I'm so stupid. Who hits a Russian officer for nothing?" Yarush said, smacking the trunk of the beech tree with his fist, hitting it hard again and again. "I was walking home from Blaszka and this Russian officer said something to me. Asked me for my papers maybe. I wasn't even mad at him, but I hit him, and they sent me to Warsaw. Why did they take me to Warsaw? Why?" Yarush shook Hayim by the shoulders. "Everyone knows me in Plotsk. They would have told my mother where I was. But in Warsaw? I disappeared. Invisible. A ghost. She waited and waited for me and I never came back to her." Then he dropped his hands and said, "So she never knew I went to Blaszka like she told me. Andrei couldn't find me. Maybe she thought I ran away. When I got out of jail she was dead. My mama never knew I just did what I promised."

"She knows," Hayim said. "I'm sure of it."

"Really. You think so?"

"Would a brother lie? Look, we'll split the cheese."

"Here. I have some salami in the cart." Yarush put his arm around Hayim's shoulder. "And how about a drink?"

"Just, just the cheese. That's enough," Hayim said.

But Yarush pressed the salami on him, and Hayim took it. Yarush got into his cart and let the old nag walk at her own pace while he drank and dreamed.

HAYIM walked back to the dairyhouse where he stood outside under the willow trees, waiting for Alta-Fruma. Farther up the road, Shmuel the baker harnessed his horse. He was on his way to Plotsk with the gold that would release Yekhiel's granddaughter, Ruthie, from prison.

NIGHTS OF THE SECRET RIVER

On the day that Hayim and Alta-Fruma gazed at each other in the cow shed, the Traveler and the Director were holding a meeting in the woods near the Północna River. The younger man was sitting on a log, whittling a small branch, while the Director paced. A pigeon flying overhead considered aiming his industrial waste at the Director's top hat, a marvelous circle of black, a smooth and silky target, but one glare from the Director sent him spinning politely over the river.

"I interceded on your behalf," the Director was saying. "I told them that you're new to the position and it's not an easy assignment. But the best I could get you was an extension. You have to fix the mess you made of the job with Yarush. Are you listening?"

"My instructions said to give Yarush the rock. So I did," the Traveler said.

"And you had a talk with him."

"Well, yes."

"About?"

"You can't expect me to remember."

"But I do, indeed," the Director said.

The Traveler shrugged. "What can you talk about with a man like that? Some dreck."

"I see. Can you be more specific about the particular dreck that you discussed with him?"

"Something about women. He doesn't like women. A man like that doesn't like much. But that's all right because not much likes him either." The Traveler dug into the branch of pine, splinters flying.

"Did you take a good look at the rock?"

"It was a rock. What was I supposed to look at?"

"Of everyone in the universe I had to get you assigned as my part-ner—someone upstairs must have taken a dislike to me. My dear young friend, it wasn't *just* a rock. No, it was a crust of blue earth with red amber embedded in it. The Egyptians imported Baltic amber from Poland five thousand years ago. You can still see it in Egyptian tombs. And had you cared to look, you would have known what you had in your hand. You could have nudged Yarush in a particular direction; he might have given the amber away. Do you understand? A gift freely given. A gift received with kindness. Might have made all the difference." He poked the Traveler in the shoulder.

"Does a man like that give anything away?" the Traveler asked, his eyes on the carving as it became an angry face with a forked beard. "He just wants to take what he can get. So I made it a magic rock, and he took it. I followed orders."

"My righteous young partner, have you forgotten that your 'magic' rock broke down a door?"

The Traveler looked up from his carving, face crestfallen, his knife unmoving.

"This is magic," the Director said, snapping his fingers. There was a flash of fire, then a hint of sulphur in the air. "It doesn't cook an egg, my friend." The Director took the carving from the younger man's loose grip and threw it onto a pile of driftwood in the river. "Couldn't you spare a little thought to do the job right? Have a talk—like one person to another?"

"There are plenty of human beings for him to talk with if he wants to."

"Brilliant. Brilliant boy, you figured it out. Maybe they don't need us. So you want the Boss to realize it? You want to be sent into oblivion, or worse, rebirth? Fine. But let me tell you, my fine young friend. You have until the end of the year to finish the job with Yarush. Otherwise . . ." he snapped his fingers. This time the small flame grew into a ball of fire that fell into the center of an eddy in the river, hissing as it burned through a mass of branches and leaves. The eddy swirled, and the network of green and wood re-formed as if it had never burned. "Magic." The Director blew on the tip of his finger. "It only works on angels," he said. And smiled. The smell of cooking raspberries drifted across the water from the village. A flock of crows chased a hawk above the woods.

THE DAYS OF AWE

The Traveler sat on the log where the Vistula and the Północna met, looking at the yellow fields, the snail-shaped clouds streaming overhead, the peasant standing thigh deep in the water, fishing and teasing the girls in red petticoats who were running along the bank. Their thick-armed mothers, scrubbing linen, called after the girls to come back if they knew what was good for them. The Traveler could hear the distant honk of ships coming up from Warsaw, and nearby the sad tune of a brown-skinned boy, whistling as he led a bear on a chain. The Traveler stood up, walked toward the boy, and pushed him into the river.

Just behind them, on the road from Plotsk, Yarush drove up in his loaded cart.

THE BOY splashed and flailed his arms, crying out as his head hit a rock. Gypsies have silver, Yarush thought as he jumped out of the cart. The boy's hat bobbed on the river, three-cornered with a peacock feather for good luck. Beside it floated the photograph of a young girl with golden imperials woven into her braids. Yarush reached under the water to pull out the boy. The Gypsy's face was greenish brown with cold, a trickle of blood beginning to ooze from a cut on his brow. As Yarush knocked on his back, water spouted from his lips and his eyes fluttered. On his chin there was a tattoo of triangles, one inside the other. Yarush pulled off the boy's water-logged jacket, the photograph of the girl with gold in her hair sailing downstream.

"WHAT TREASURE did you fish out of the water, Master Peddler?" called one of the women twisting and wringing their linen like hens' necks.

"He's got himself a drowned Gypsy," answered the peasant.

"That little fish will steal you blind," the woman said, "better throw him back."

"Shush, woman, don't give the Jew such good advice. Let the boy take from him what he squeezes from us."

Yarush dropped the boy at the foot of an alder, where he lay moaning in Russian, "Saint Sara, help me," while Yarush examined his jacket. There were four rows of silver coins for buttons. As he snipped them off with his knife, the bear huddled behind a clump of birch trees.

The boy was shivering. "Here," Yarush said in Polish, tossing down the buttonless jacket. "Drink." He forced the tip of a bottle between the boy's chittering teeth. "Cigarette?" the boy asked. Yarush rolled a cigarette for him. With trembling fingers, the boy raised it to his mouth and took a deep drag, tilting his head back against the tree trunk as he slowly exhaled. Yarush walked along the riverbank. The boy might have something else. But there was nothing except a bow and an instrument shaped like a flat violin. "My *gudulka*," the boy called as Yarush picked it up.

"Then play something to drink to," Yarush ordered.

Eyes closed, the boy held the *gudulka* upright between his knees, drawing the bow slowly across the strings. At the sound of the music, the bear poked his head through the trees, loping forward until the end of his chain fell into the boy's lap. Winking at Yarush, the boy took up the chain, hooking it around his wrist as he plucked a few wild notes. The bear shuffled from foot to foot without any sense of rhythm, a whining sound deep in his throat as if he was remembering the hot steel sheet on which he was trained to hop around as a cub. The boy crossed his eyes and threw down the *gudulka* in disgust, the bear flopping onto his bottom with relief.

"Mirga," the boy said, tapping his chest. His face had lost its greenish tinge. "Pyotr Mirga." The boy looked at the pouch, filled with his silver coins, hanging from a string around Yarush's neck.

The boy wasn't stupid, Yarush thought. "Yarush," he said, pointing to himself. The bear was standing at the edge of the river, catching fish with a sweep of his paw. I could bring them back to the tavern on Whorehouse Row, Yarush thought. Make a few kopecks. Split it with Andrei.

"You find picture?" Pyotr asked.

"The one of the girl?" Yarush asked. Pytor nodded. "Sank in the river."

"Everything gone," the boy said, reaching for Yarush's bottle. He took a long drink and stood up, though he was still unsteady. "I go look girl. I find her. My Pasha. Mine."

"Tell you what, Pytor. You come back with me to Plotsk."

"I look Plotsk. Nothing. Now, I look Warsaw. You go Warsaw?"

There was something hungry in the boy's look. What's it to you? he asked himself. But he wasn't in any rush to go peddling. And he might make something from the boy. "What're you doing here?" he asked. "Gypsies don't come this way much."

"Ah." Pyotr sat down and sighed. In his sigh, all the great tragedies of the world seemed to find their home. "Speak Russian?" he asked.

Yarush shook his head. "Polish. Yiddish. No Russian."

"Only Polish. All right." The boy knocked on his chest as if he was reciting the confessional on the Day of Atonement. "I from Moscow," he said. "In Moscow Gypsies sing, speak Russian. Papa sing Rachmaninov *Aleko*. You know?" Yarush shook his head. "Uncle have horses. Beautiful horses." The boy looked at Yarush's nag, curling his lip. "I had horse. Horse gone. Now I walk. To find my Pasha. Pasha is wife. Wife, you know?" Yarush nodded. The boy's face twisted. He spit. "*Guliaka* steal wife. You know *guliaka?*"

"No," Yarush said, taking a swig from his bottle.

"Russian gentry." The boy rolled the word on his tongue as if it was something *mahrime,* polluted, he was trying not to swallow. "Young man. He like Gypsy cafe. Like singing. Like drinking. Like Pasha. Now Pasha gone. I find Pasha. Walk up mountains. Find Gypsies, speak Romany. Train bears. Very poor. They say, Pyotr, don't go Romania. Romania Gypsies slaves before. Now no slaves. So burn Gypsies. They say, no Poland. Gentlemans hunt Gypsies for money. Stay here. Stick with Gypsies. Stay away from *gadje.*"

"*Gadje?* What's that?" Yarush asked. He liked this story. It was the kind of story a man might tell in the tavern while he ordered drinks for everyone.

"*Gadje* is not-Gypsy. But Pasha with *gadje.* I look Pasha."

"For a woman? Waste of time," Yarush said.

"Papa say take new wife. I say no. Wife mine. Pyotr and Pasha . . ." He crossed his wrists and clapped them together. "You know?"

"My woman ran off. Took my girls. Two of them. I said good riddance. If you run after a woman, everyone can see you're not worth nothing." Until now he'd forgotten the look of the empty room. The clothes hooks without clothes and the mirror without any faces and the dolly's hat left beside the bed. A hat he made out of straw. Suddenly he was hungry. He pulled a salami out of his pocket and took a big bite, chewing fast and swallowing a hunk that nearly choked him. "You're better off alone. A man doesn't need to be dragged down by a pack of whining women. You have what you get for yourself."

The boy shook his head. His dark eyes flicked from Yarush to the horse. "You go Warsaw?"

"Plotsk," Yarush said. He passed his bottle to the boy. Pyotr drank through his fist, curled around the top of the bottle. Grinning, he mouthed "Warsaw."

"You don't give up. You're all right," Yarush said as he cuffed the boy, though not with all his strength. Flicking his knife open, Yarush picked a piece of salami out of his teeth, then pointed the knife at Pyotr. "You come to Plotsk with me and you can keep half what you make from the bear. Say no and," he tossed the knife and caught it in his left hand, "you come to Plotsk and you don't get nothing."

"You say Plotsk? You want bear? You have bear." Pyotr hooked the bear's chain onto the back of the cart. Then he climbed in, his buttonless jacket flung over his shoulder, the *gudulka* under his arm. Satisfied, Yarush followed, sitting beside the boy.

The old horse stirred restlessly, the smell of bear vaguely downwind. But as Yarush began to turn the cart around, and the full strength of bear odor hit the nag, she reared on her hind legs like charging cavalry. Screaming, she tore off, not in the direction of Plotsk, nor Warsaw, but up the familiar Północna road toward Blaszka.

"You'll pay," Yarush said, "I'll sell you for a ship's boy for this." The cart rocked, axles screeching, wheels scraping the rutted road. Clods of dirt flew up in their faces, farmers' fields rushed by in a blur of gold, a low branch broke off against the cart, sticking up from the side like a giant *shmeckel*. A wheel flew off and still they raced, three-legged, careening from side to side, the wind pummeling them. The boy bounced and fell, rising into the air and dropping onto the seat with a loud smash, his face turning green again. Like souls in hell, the horse and the bear and the green-faced boy hooked together. Yarush began to laugh. They crashed through a flock of geese, honking and parting with a great flutter of wings and falling feathers, the goose girl in her red petticoat swearing at them. One gosling, shaggy with shedding down, neck stretched long, lay still on the road behind them, and the girl hoisted it onto her shoulder. Peasants in the field raised their scythes. The cart tilted, threatened to fall. And still they raced, the rank smell of bear chasing the horse, her eyes bulging, flecks of blood around her nostrils. In front of them a cow and her calf blocked the road. The horse ran mindlessly toward her, ribs and hips almost piercing her hide. "Done for," Yarush shouted. "The horse is finished! Kaput." Tears of laughter ran down his face, a rivulet gathering in the scar below his ear.

Cursing, Pyotr leaned back and unhooked the bear. The cow stood immobile between the onrushing cart and her calf, excavating hot dung. Pyotr stood, bracing his feet against the front of the cart as he grabbed the reins and leaned back, pulling on the horse. She veered off the road, turning out of the wind, the bear smell at last leaving her. She stopped. Her mouth was white with foam. Her legs trembled. Pyotr fell off the cart, the wound in his forehead reopening as he fainted among the crushed stalks of barley. The bear raised his head and howled as he headed for the trees outside of Blaszka.

CARRYING the boy over his shoulder, Yarush stomped into the study-house. The load was heavy and he was getting hungry again. From the village square came cries of, "Buy, buy fresh red apples, apples freshly picked, as if painted, apples like raspberries, so juicy that they're worth a kiss." His stomach grumbled. "You there," Yarush said. But just as the Rabbi looked up, Yarush noticed the portrait of the *Alter Rov*. He stopped, fixed by the gaze of the Old Rabbi with his prominent nose, the long beard hanging over a good-size belly, yes, just as he remembered, the broad fur hat, the plain walking stick. A holy man, not like the new Rabbi, a skinny person with his mop of red hair speckled gray, his beard curling in all directions like the fronds of ferns around a mountain spring. Out of respect for the *Alter Rov*, Yarush just asked, "Where should I put him?" and spit into the corner.

"You?" the Rabbi said, "What do you want?"

"The boy is hurt," Yarush said. "Where do you want him?"

The Rabbi stood up, waving his hands at Yarush as if to push him away. That was Blaszka. Take your money and your goods on market day and throw you out like you're nobody's son. Pyotr groaned. The cut on his temple was dripping slow fat drops of blood down Yarush's back. He started to lower the boy onto the rabbi's chair.

"Not here," the Rabbi said sharply. "Come with me."

Yarush followed him into the house next to the synagogue, where the rabbi pointed to the couch in the front room. The boy groaned as Yarush dropped him, not ungently, onto the couch. "Take off his wet clothes and cover him with my nightshirt," the rabbi was saying to his housekeeper, "and wrap him in my feather bed. I'll see what Misha can give me for the cut." Before Yarush could finish casing the room for valuables, he was being ushered out the door.

"And for my trouble?" Yarush asked.

But the Rabbi ignored him, hurrying across the square to the house on stilts. The house, yes. With the woman. The one that had spit at him. The one he thought would be different when he lay with her, but wasn't. Yet the image that came to his mind wasn't the fight in the village square but his fantasy in the tavern—a table heaped with food for *Shabbas*. A woman calling him to come in. What would Misha's table look like tonight? It was Friday, *Shabbas* was coming. Would she light the candles? Would she spread a white cloth on the table? In the village square he heard she was as big as two women now. It wasn't anything to do with him. Of course not. But why shouldn't he have a look at her? Looking didn't cost nothing, and she'd been promised him once.

Ignoring the Rabbi's mutterings and feeble wavings, Yarush climbed the steps behind him. The Rabbi knocked on the door, then opened it a crack, just wide enough for his narrow frame to slip through. Yarush peered over his shoulder. On the bed beside the wall lay Misha. Bigger than anything he had ever seen. As big as a host of women. Could he have had anything to do with that? He wanted to touch it, that big belly with maybe something of his inside it. He wanted to see how her breasts swelled, the nipples riding on the top of the mound, the way his wife's did, once. He imagined again the white cloth covering the table, the two braided loaves of Sabbath bread, the cup of sweet red wine, the white candles flickering. But the picture wavered, broke apart, and instead he saw Misha as she had lain beneath him, her face white as a silver coin, a round red spot on each cheek. What did she see, then, as she looked up at him? He'd never asked such a question. He'd never thought to ask it. The question stretched, it filled his mind, and stretched some more as he remembered her hands pushing at him uselessly, her eyes shutting tight, head to one side, his hand over her mouth. Look, he told himself, she's had it plenty before. She'd been promised him, right? And any question he had about himself snapped into a small, hard knot, like an indigestible stone that had to be expelled.

The Rabbi slammed the door behind him, shutting him away.

Yarush flushed, the scar under his ear standing out whitely. "It's not mine," he said aloud. "These witch women screw a dozen and don't know the difference." He shrugged and left, thinking of the silver coins in his pouch, and how he'd buy drinks for everyone and they'd call out, To Yarush, to Yarush.

ON THE Sabbath between Rosh Hashanah and Yom Kippur, called the Sabbath of Repentance, Russian soldiers found Pyotr's bear. They broke his arms and crushed his chest, as was the practice with dancing bears, to force them upright and to prevent them from squeezing their captors in a fatal hug. They found great amusement in the dancing bear.

OVER THE next few days, while the Jews of Blaszka were begging one another's forgiveness in preparation for the Day of Atonement, Yarush ate the equivalent of two cows and a mill of flour. He was drinking in Andrei's tavern when a young traveler in a ragged coat with a rose pinned to the collar pulled up a chair, a fresh bottle and a large, round almond torte in hand. Yarush was sitting at his customary table in the back, below the sword hanging on the wall and next to the shrine of Our Lady of the Barley, red candles burning in front of her. The shrine reminded him of his mother.

"You gave me a ride, remember?" the Traveler said.

"So?" Yarush asked. The Traveler cut a good wedge of torte and slid it onto his plate.

"So I'm returning a favor. A torte like this they make only in one place. Can't get that flavor anywhere else. Just Blaszka. They don't stint on the almonds. Not the raisins, either. Can't get a torte like this in Plotsk or even Warsaw."

Biting into the torte, Yarush's mouth filled with a thick and plummy paste.

"I heard that you saved a boy from drowning. Brought him to Blaszka."

"I don't do something for nothing. He paid," Yarush said.

"Of course. But tell me, what's a Gypsy boy doing around here?"

"Looking for his wife. Waste of time. He should have stayed home with his uncle's horses."

"You're right. Horses are worth a lot of money. Russian peasants will poke out a man's eyes and hang him for stealing a horse, even an old nag like yours, if you'll pardon me. I suppose the boy just wants an adventure."

"Nah," Yarush said. "He wants the girl. Stupid. But that's what he wants."

"Well, never mind. He'll forget about her. A man can always find a woman, right?"

"Yeah," Yarush said, but he couldn't shake off the memory of the boy's face as he said, I go look girl, I find her.

"Anyway if he found her, what good would it be?" the Traveler asked.

Maybe she was waiting for Pyotr. In a little house, sitting at a table covered with a white cloth, a bottle of wine on the table, an empty glass. When he came in, he would take off his boots and he wouldn't have to watch his back. Maybe she'd ask him to play a tune for her. And he would. He'd play anything she wanted.

"Well, it's none of your business anyway," the Traveler continued. "Have another piece of almond torte. In Blaszka they make it with enough butter so you know you've eaten something. Sits good in the stomach, so eat up. I have another one. Tonight is the eve of Yom Kippur. A fast day. Eat hearty."

"A fast day? Do I care?" Yarush said.

"Right now," the Traveler leaned forward confidentially, "the great book is open and the Holy One, Blessed Be, is writing your fortune for the next year. It could be good, it could be bad. Who knows?"

Yarush stopped in midchew. "Right now?"

"Oh, yes. But intercession is possible."

"For me?"

"Who else? Maybe you know someone up there who could plead for you? Someone from here?" The Traveler looked around the tavern.

Yarush followed his gaze with consternation. "Not here," he said.

"Somewhere else maybe. Someone who might hear you if you prayed nearby?"

"Yes, yes, I know someone," Yarush said. "The Old Rabbi. From Blaszka. You think he would talk to the saints for me if I prayed to him? Not here, of course. But maybe in the synagogue in Blaszka?"

"Could be," the Traveler said. "It's not too late. The sun is just starting to go down. You could make it if you left now. Here, take the other torte for the road."

KOL NIDREI

Yarush stands against the back wall of the synagogue. He isn't robed in white, like the other men. He doesn't own a *kittel* or even a prayer shawl. He is shrouded in his fur coat, and beneath he wears his plain, peasant clothes layered with lice. Over the heads of the men rising to their feet, he sees the Rabbi in front of the reading platform. His voice is stronger than Yarush would expect from such a skinny man.

"*By the authority of the heavenly court and by the authority of this earthly court,*" the Rabbi calls. "*With divine consent and with the consent of this congregation, we hereby declare it possible to pray with those who have transgressed.*"

These are the traditional words spoken at this very moment in a thousand places. Yarush doesn't understand them. But he knows they are important. Soon the Old Rabbi will speak on his behalf. But what is this? A noise from above and the men are clearing out like thieves from a house where someone's blown the whistle. "What's going on?" Yarush asks, but no one hears. They're looking out the door, not at the strangers leaning against the back wall. Yarush is weak with hunger, stiflingly hot under his fur coat.

No one notices Yarush leave the synagogue. Outside, he sits on a bench near the guest house, where wandering beggars can sleep without interference on the pallets of straw. Now the beggars stand with the crowd of men near the doorway. On this side of the synagogue there is no one except for Yarush and the Gypsy boy, Pyotr, who is also alone, sitting on the bench, looking at the moon. It is ten days old, more than a half moon, not quite full. The voices of the men and women of Blaszka are muted. There is a cool breeze. Yarush could fall asleep sitting here.

"You look better," Yarush says. The boy's cut has healed. His hands are restless in his lap. "Play something," Yarush says. The boy picks up the *gudulka* and plays a mournful song. Yarush plucks at his sleeve.

"Something cheerful," he says. And the boy obliges with a wedding dance. There are tears on the boy's cheeks.

"Take the horse and cart," Yarush says. The boy looks at him wonderingly. "Take it," Yarush growls, "to Warsaw. Even to Moscow. What do I want it for? Go on."

Quickly, before Yarush can call him back, the boy goes to the cart and leaps into the seat. As he drives out of Blaszka, he finds some bread and cheese and kielbasa in the cart. He is hungry enough to eat, even though the food might be impure.

Yarush walks alone along the path through the woods toward the river. What is another hungry day to him?

8

A GIFT OF FIRE

In the coming year, after Pyotr leaves Blaszka with Yarush's cart, after Kol Nidrei, after Yom Kippur, after the fields are bare, after the snow falls and the houses of Blaszka are alight with Hanukkah candles, Berekh the Rabbi will receive a letter from Paris. His oldest friend, Moyshe-Mendel, known more widely as the journalist Maurice LaFontaine, is sick. He will ask Berekh to go to Warsaw to dispose of some important papers. "If anything should happen to me," the letter will say, "I don't want my wife's future to be in any way inconvenienced. I know that I can trust you, Berekh, for the sake of our friendship, to do what is right."

Berekh will leave for Warsaw immediately. He will retrieve the papers from the safekeeping of a lawyer on Nalewki Street whose office is stuffed with antique furniture from the time of Napoleon. On Christmas Eve 1894, sitting in a small, windowless room off the lawyer's office, Berekh will sort the papers into three piles. One pile he will destroy. One pile he will forward through a safe courier to Paris. And the third Berekh will take with him, to read while sitting in a cafe at the back of a bookstore on Nalewki Street. He will have every right to do so, since these are letters that he himself wrote to Moyshe-Mendel.

The proprietor will ask Berekh what he is gazing at with such intense interest. Berekh will reply, "Ghosts."

In the corner of the cafe, a large woman with moon pale hair under a cap strung with golden ribbons nods. He will read, and he will remember.

Lag b'Omer, Monday May 20, 1878

My dear Moyshe-Mendel,

I am sorry to send you the news that my brother Pinye is dead. Drafted last year—killed in action. As they say. But I hear that more die from hunger, sickness, and "disciplinary" punishments than from fighting in the Russo-Turkish War.

I would only like to know if this was the plan of God above. That the good brother who would have followed our father as a cantor in Zhitomir is dead, while the unworthy brother who left the Rabbinical Seminary to wander aimlessly lives. As the heretic Elisha Ben Abouya used to say in days of old: God does not follow His own laws of justice and therefore is not worthy of worship. I do not say so. I merely quote. I say that God is old and therefore nods off while His creatures tear each other to pieces.

If I had had any courage at all, I would have gone to the draft in Pinye's place. My father mourns. As for me, I have returned from Moscow where I sang with the Gypsies and drank with the guliaka, the young Russian gentry that frequent Gypsy cafes. They did not mind drinking with a Jew, as long as I shared my bottle freely. And afterward, when my pockets were empty and theirs, too, we went out into the streets and sang. If our arms were not around each others' shoulders we certainly would have fallen. The girls stood in the doorways, laughing while we blew them kisses until their mothers pulled them inside.

But this is suitable activity for a boy of eighteen not an old man of twenty-four such as I. So when I heard the sad news of Pinye's death, I left my roguish behavior behind and returned to my familial duties. Since I could not comfort my father, I determined to make my amends by attending to the family of my cousin Yekhiel, who was so good to me when I was young.

You remember Yekhiel, the baker in Blaszka whose wife died

*when their daughter, Faygela, was only two years old? It was he
who convinced my father to release me from the prison of the
yeshiva in Zhitomir and send me to the Rabbinical Seminary with
you. I can still recall the odor of our sweat in that yeshiva class full
of boys arguing the fine points of archaic law, while you and I and
some others hid our books behind the sacred texts. What else could
anyone expect in Zhitomir, that den of Jewish enlightenment?*

*In the seminary, our Jewish teachers taught us to seek knowledge
of every kind and I became an educated person. Hence out of loyalty
to Yekhiel's memory, I am now in the village of Blaszka, where my
cousin resided until his death three years ago. His daughter Faygela
still sees him everywhere. There is little I can do for her in this backwoods but let her know that she has a friend in me.*

*The ways of fate are mysterious, my friend. Even here, in a place
where the flatness and dearth of life surpass that of the Dead Sea,
there is an object of interest, a female object. Cupid's arrow struck
in a small house on stilts above the Północna, wherein resides the
lady with eyes as dark as our River Midnight.*

*The lady in question is Misha Fliderblum, twenty years old and
unmarried, I may add. Thank Heaven above, she has no yikhus,
no family stature, her heritage being one of carpenters and mid-
wives—not a pale and tired scholar amongst them. Her great-
grandmother, in fact, was the last person in Poland to be officially
tried for witchcraft, though I hear that in the Russian countryside
the peasants still conduct trial by water. A woman accused of witchcraft is thrown into a pond, a bag of rocks tied to her waist. If she
drowns, she is innocent and is given a Christian burial. If she does
not drown, she is guilty and is burned at the stake. Fortunately, we
are somewhat more civilized, here, and Misha, who is the village
midwife, is in no such danger.*

*This Misha is no wifely girl with modest manners, but how she
laughs. There is more life in her than in the whole of Russian
Poland, and I found it here in the least distinguished plot of land
imaginable. The village requires a "crown rabbi," and I have
offered myself for the position. I will record births, marriages, and
deaths, and should the Tsar's minister have any reason to communi-
cate with the people of Blaszka or, if the villagers wish to convey a*

message (as foolhardy as this would be) to the Tsar's minister, it will
be my duty to act as intermediary. The government may believe that
we "crown rabbis," graduates of a Russian school, will lead the Jews
of the Empire to assimilation, but they are much mistaken. The
people hereabouts trust only the Old Rabbi, who speaks Hebrew and
Yiddish, but no Russian, and whose thinking is unpolluted by secular learning. I am entrusted with no religious functions whatsoever,
all such matters remaining in the hands of the Old Rabbi. I am to
be content with my gold-nibbed pen and the ledger book of village
records.

How naive we were to think that we would become teachers of
the people when we left the seminary. There is some interest among
the villagers who participated in the Polish insurrection of '63, but
there is little material in Yiddish. Meyer the butcher, who was a
friend to my cousin Yekhiel, can read a little Polish and I am
endeavoring to instruct him. Like the other men, his Hebrew is ade-
quate for prayers but not for the newspaper or other modern texts.
Most people are preoccupied with the struggle to earn a living and
have no use for new ways.

I attended my first village wedding today. Hanna-Leah, daughter
of Meyer the butcher, was married to Hershel, the butcher's apprentice and soon-to-be partner. I had the honor of amusing the bride
by performing the Angel of Death dance with our watercarrier,
Hayim. He in turn invited Misha to join him in the kosher dance.
It was not quite the custom, as she is not the bride. But the more
the old women scowled, the higher she stepped and the harder she
stamped, pulling her dress above her calves. Her hair flew behind
her like ravens and I wished that I had thought to ask her to dance.
She teased Hayim mercilessly and the poor man blushed with
embarrassment. I would not have blushed.

Tuesday, July 9, 1878

Dear friend,
I attended another village wedding, today: Misha the midwife
and Hayim the watercarrier. It was all arranged by the Old Rabbi,
himself, and I am told there could be no better shadkhen except for
the Holy One above. The village luminaries acted in place of the

bride and groom's parents, who are deceased, and all was conducted according to custom.

You may wonder why I didn't speak for Misha. Since it has just been a year since her mother died, and the two were very close, I thought that she would be missing her mother too much to think about a suitor. And even if it were not for that, I considered that I should first establish myself in Blaszka. What could she know of me, a stranger in the village who had visited on occasion and settled here only three months since? Well, my friend, I was too slow. Before I made a move, I heard that a match had been arranged, the plate broken, the betrothal fixed. I would not say a word to interfere with another's happiness, so I must forget the foolishness to which I alluded in my previous letter. Clearly it was not meant to be.

I myself have been presented with several candidates by the local matchmaker, all of them good and spiritless girls, very suitable. I protested that I was not worthy, having neither money nor prestige in my situation as the "crown rabbi." The shadkhen *commended my honesty and returned with a list of women who are still good, he assured me, but also somewhat ugly, poor, and lacking family* yikhus. *Hence they have been left sitting, as they say here. I told him I will give proper consideration to the matter, which, being no light thing, requires serious deliberation. I will think about it at great length. Very great length.*

Meanwhile there are tensions in the countryside, and there is rumor of revolt. The peasants are breaking under the double load of taxes and redemption payments. You remember how it was before the peasants were emancipated in '63. They were serfs—let us be honest, practically slaves—property of their masters, with no human rights at all. But things are not so much better now. It's true that the peasants are free and own the miserable bits of land they used to work for their masters. But they are required to pay the former landowners compensation. Many cannot meet the high payments and their taxes, too. This is not chance, but strategy. The finance minister aims to force the peasants into exporting their grain, thus improving the balance of trade, with the gold from foreign buyers stabilizing the paper ruble, which drops in value daily. The peasants, having been liberated from serfdom, go hungry, and every year more of them abandon the land and pour into the cities, where they are even hungrier. The wars cost much, the debt must be paid somehow, and the hungry peasants look for someone to blame for their misery.

Thank you for sending me the article concerning Heinrich von Treitschke and his band of crackpots. Who would think that the worthy professor would ally himself with such backward types? He cannot really think that the Jews are the misfortune of western civilization. It is laughable. A cunning race of snakes gripping the throat of the honest, hard-working, and natural German? This Heinrich should only be our guest in Blaszka, where he could meet, perhaps, the cunning watercarrier Hayim who stammers and stumbles over his yoke, or the still more cunning baker, Shmuel, who fills his baby's mouth with plump raisins.

What would I do without you, Moyshe-Mendel, to send me all the news of the world?

Tuesday, August 5, 1879

Greetings Moyshe-Mendel,

I write to you from my room above the bakery. It was kind of my cousin Faygela and her husband Shmuel to allow me to use this room, but I am quite ready to move out. It may be difficult for you to imagine, though I assure you it is true, that the smell of fresh bread can become a noxious scent as it ascends day after day into the stifling heat of an attic room. There are blotches in the ledger book where the sweat poured from my hands as I entered births and deaths and even a divorce with my gold-nibbed pen.

You know how seldom divorce occurs among these people, though it's easy enough to obtain a Get. *But after less than a year of marriage, Misha Fliderblum and Hayim Bernstein are divorced according to the Law of Moses. No one knows why, though many have tried to guess. I did not wait long, this time, but sent the matchmaker to Misha to plead my case. I eagerly await her answer, but I must tell you, my friend, this Misha is no ordinary woman, and I am quite sure that my little house and my meager income as "crown rabbi" will neither interest nor deter her. It will only be I myself that she will judge as worthy. Or not. And so my friend, I am quite nervous. You would not think that this is the same man who rode by sleigh from Moscow to St. Petersburg, the sole male escorting a choir composed of healthy, young women.*

Through my little window I see the matchmaker coming toward the bakery. He is frowning. It does not look good.

The matchmaker has left. It seems that Misha did not receive him kindly. Moyshe-Mendel, I could ask no one else but you. Tell me. Be forthright. Am I so terrible that a woman should throw a jar at the head of the matchmaker representing me?

Wednesday, April 13, 1881

Dear friend,

Only a brief note this time. I hope that you will have a better Passover than we. The good Tsar Alexander II was assassinated exactly one month ago, and now the Jews are blamed. It seems that among the terrorist group responsible, there was a desperate young woman, Jessie Helfmann, a Jewish seamstress. From this small fact, anti-Jewish circles have woven the extravagant claim that the assassination was a Jewish plot. We have heard that there are to be organized riots against the Jews, authorized by the new Tsar Alexander III. Pogroms. And lives are not to be spared.

Friday, December 23, 1881

To my mentor Moyshe-Mendel, greetings

The pogroms continue, the peasants, who require a scapegoat for their misery, eagerly following the lead of the Cossacks.

We have been safe, so far, in Poland, but there are rumors that there will be trouble in Warsaw. I intend to follow your advice and will not stand idly by while fellow Jews are attacked. A group of us will be spending the Sabbath in Warsaw, where we go to defend the Jews: myself, Meyer the butcher, his son-in-law Hershel, and the Puks, a family of carters, father and three sons. We do not go unarmed, but have amongst us an ax, several cleavers, and an ancient sword. Since God in Heaven does not come down to defend His people, we must march to the call of our ancestors, and not cower like sheep in a storm.

Addendum: December 28

It is over. What do the Gypsies say? "One madman makes many madmen, and many madmen makes madness." The pogrom began three days ago, on the last day of Hanukkah, and we imagined ourselves to be as the Maccabees fighting the Romans. It was Sunday, Christmas Day, the narrow streets of the Jewish quarter crowded with good Christians—pogromchiks smashing shop windows. Goods scattered. Doors of homes broken. Women's cries as they were dragged out and set upon while the church bells rang. Houses set on fire. Snow falling among the feathers of torn pillows stained pink with blood.

Tell me, Moyshe-Mendel, why do they tear up the pillows, a poor girl's only dowry?

I was pushed against the wall of a butcher shop by the crowd of peasants trying to gain entrance, the rusty point of my sword sticking in the wooden sign that said "Kosher Meats." I am ashamed to tell you how frightened I was by this mob armed only with fists and kitchen weapons. They were not human anymore, but something else. Something without a mind. Something that grew large on the smell of blood. And I was a coward before it, slammed against the wall, my arm over my eyes—to protect myself from the broken bottle coming toward my face or because I could not bear to see? I do not know, my friend.

Hershel and Meyer wielded their cleavers fearlessly and, with the Puks holding iron bars, they kept the peasants from overrunning the store, inside which five Jewish families had barricaded themselves. This was before the Cossack leaped off his horse and pointed his rifle at Meyer, who sensibly dropped his cleaver. Then Hershel grabbed the ax from the elder Puk. With one hand he gripped his knife, with the other he flung the ax. The Cossack was most amused. We disarmed Hershel, despite his protests, when the Cossack aimed his rifle at Hershel's lower parts. Then, after forcing Hershel to hand him the ax, he swung it to each side of my head, grazing my ears. Impressed by the Cossack's skill, one of the peasants wanted to see if he could also mark my ears without cutting them off, but Meyer rushed at him, sticking him with a knife he had hidden in his boots. The peasant screamed, though the wound was more surpris-

ing than damaging, the knife partly deflected by his sheepskin. We
turned to run, but a shot from the Cossack's rifle stopped all of us
when Puk's middle son fell.

Then two peasants in big fur coats took Meyer, the snow falling
on them while they tied him up. "Sugar tax," said one, pouring a
bag of sugar, looted from the broken window behind us, over
Meyer's head, laughing as he sneezed and choked. "Kerosene tax,"
said the other man, pouring kerosene over the sugar. "Match tax,"
they shouted together and, while I started forward, the Cossack's
bayonet stopping me in half a step, they set fire to him. I blinked,
and still my vision seemed to waver as the flames exploded.

Avram Puk is sitting shivah for his son, but the younger brother
will not leave Perlmutter's tavern. He drinks and eats, and when I
pleaded with him to sit with his father, he said, "You are too thin,
Berekh Eisenbaum, you will flicker and out you will go like a
match. But I won't stop eating until I can make a huge fire that
will burn for hours, a fire big enough for the Tsar to see in
Moscow."

I have discovered a second truth. While God in Heaven sleeps,
Berekh Eisenbaum on earth is useless. I could do nothing for my
brother Pinye nor for my fellow Jews in Warsaw nor for brave
Meyer who, in defending me, lost his own life. Better to have offered
myself as a sacrifice.

I am on my way to my grandfather's hut in the Tatras. Even on
the mountain among his goats, I will not forget the smell of the fur
coats as they warmed in the fire from Meyer's body, or the smell of
sugar on his skin burning as it blackened and curled away from his
bones.

I could not bear to speak with anyone in Blaszka before I left.
Misha, meeting me on the path through the woods, asked me to
take a cup of hot tea to warm myself in her house. But she must not
have heard what had happened. If she did not see fit to accept my
suit earlier, surely she would not want me in her house now. I
declined her invitation and made ready to leave the village.

Thursday, July 27, 1882

Dear friend,

Tishah-b'Av has come and gone, Moyshe-Mendel. And after my

grandfather prayed for the destruction of the Holy Temple, he said to me only, "Go down. You belong among people." Perhaps he is right. I am a burden to him here. An extra mouth to feed with no skill to offer him. The goats hide from me and I cannot even light his fire. The sight of a match causes me to shake. And from time to time I have the delusion that I am in Warsaw once again. I hear the screams. I smell the fire.

You would not know me, now, my friend. I scarcely know myself. I am not the reckless young man I once was, nor can I pretend to be the romantic who went to Warsaw, dreaming that I could make the least difference in the world. But at twenty-eight years of age I can at least support myself in Blaszka and fulfill the mitzvah of giving charity, even if I can do nothing else. You may wonder that I speak of mitzvah, I who quote the heretic Elisha Ben Abouya, I who hear God snoring. But while I walked in the clear mountain air, I determined that a man needs to follow something if he is not to go mad in this unjust and chaotic world. I am a Jew. I will follow Torah.

Friday, March 30, 1883

Dear Moyshe-Mendel,

Congratulate me, old friend. At the ripe old age of twenty-nine I am betrothed. The girl is of impeccable, if not great, lineage. All the knowledgeable denizens of our village assured me that the match was not only suitable, but perfect. Everyone in the village will attend our wedding, from Hershel the butcher to Misha the midwife.

When I came down from the mountains, I found that the Old Rabbi had died: the real rabbi, that is, the one who determined points of religious law as well as settling local disputes for Jews and peasants alike, as is often the custom in these backwoods places. He judged everything: a boundary dispute between peasants; an argument between husband and wife; whether the stain on the woman's rag means she is still unclean. Everyone went to him with their shaalehs, their questions. If one is lost in the woods and cannot see the sun, when is it time to pray? Is so-and-so obliged to divorce his wife if she cannot give him children? Does the money pouch belong to Haykel who found it or Getzel who owns the land where it was found? You remember the type, a beard like Moses, making no concessions to the modern world.

*The village is too small and poor to offer much of a livelihood,
not that they pay the rabbi, of course. Oh no, that would be to make
an ax out of the Torah, as they say. But the Old Rabbi's wife had a
monopoly on yeast, and that's how they lived. Therefore my stipend
in the post of "crown rabbi" made me a prime candidate, despite the
disadvantage of my secular education. Since the pogroms, interest in
the outside world has been eclipsed by fear and suspicion, but the
fact that I first went to yeshiva has lessened the sin of reading German, Polish, and Russian. In the end, there was no one else. So they
made me the Rabbi of Blaszka, branded me, so to speak, like a stray
sheep, and, having magically transformed me into the local religious
authority, they informed me that I could do nothing else than
marry. After a year of resistance, I surrendered. The deed will be
done on Lag b'Omer and you must attend the wedding, my friend.*

*My betrothed is a pale-lipped, scurrying inoffensive little mouse
of sixteen, whose ears turn red at the tips when she is nervous. I will
do my best not to make her nervous.*

Sunday, June 10, 1883

Greetings, Moyshe-Mendel,

*I cannot tell you how glad I was that you were able to attend the
wedding. My young wife Hava is still rather shy. Except for the cup
of watery tea that suddenly appears and disappears at my elbow, I
hardly know she's in the house. She speaks only to ask me if everything is to my taste, and even then looks quickly away before I catch
her eye. In turn I ask her if all is to her liking, and she replies, her
ears turning red, that all that is lacking is a child, and she hopes
that the Holy One, in His wisdom, will see fit to grant us that joy
soon.*

*We are fortunate to retain the assistance of my predecessor's ser-
vant, Maria, who attends my young bride with kindness and myself
with a touch of scorn. She went to work for the Old Rabbi when
she was fourteen and still reveres him as a saint, as do many in these
parts. For myself, I do not have such fond memories of him. After
my cousin Yekhiel's death, I appealed to the Old Rabbi on Faygela's
behalf. She wanted to go to school, as her father had promised. The
Old Rabbi replied that while secular studies were no danger to a*

female child, if the pious grandmother objected to my sending
Faygela to school in Warsaw, then she should find her contentment
in obedience.

Thank you for sending me Émile Zola's new work. I will share it
with my cousin Faygela, who cherishes every word of print, bur-
dened as she is with three (presently to be four) children, though she
is only twenty-two years old.

Wednesday, October 7, 1891

My dear Moyshe-Mendel,

Please forward my most heartfelt congratulations to your new
bride. Since we are only a few days from Yom Kippur I would like
to ask you if I have done anything to offend you in the past year. I
hope that you will forgive me.

It is good of you to make your house in Warsaw available to the
refugees. Since the Jews were expelled from Moscow, there is hardly
the corner of a room available anywhere. Even in Blaszka, the guest
house regularly has one or two families on their way to Warsaw. I,
myself, have had a peasant family staying with me over the last few
days. They, too, left their home in Russia and are on their way to
Warsaw, having lost everything in the famine, poor souls, and are
nothing but skin and bone. The little one's face is gray and she sits
completely still, holding onto the silver crucifix that hangs on a
leather string around her neck.

I hesitate to tell you my sad news and cast any shadow on your
joy. But Hava, my wife, passed away recently. She died happy in the
knowledge that she had finally been blessed with the son she so
badly wanted. Misha, the midwife, wrapped the baby and held him
to Hava as her eyes closed.

Tell me, Moyshe-Mendel, did I need to have a son? I told her a
hundred times that we have a beautiful daughter. With each miscarriage I begged her to stop. But she wanted a boy, a son to say
kaddish for us when we die. Why did I give in? I am the one reciting the mourner's prayer, and who knows if the baby will even live?

Until Hava was gone, I didn't know how much life came from
the corner where she sat all day knitting and consulting with
Maria. I know nothing, now, of what is going on in the village,

*and the house is so quiet that I am startled by the mice. Yesterday
Maria brought some peasants to me for arbitration in a boundary
dispute. Three brothers, three small farms. I could have kissed them
for disturbing the royal silence of my long days.*

*Please excuse the brevity of my communication. I find myself
overly tired these days. May you and your bride be inscribed in the
Book of Life. Do not forget your old friend, Berekh.*

IN THE Golem Cafe, Berekh puts down the pile of letters. It has been
over three years since his wife died. He is forty years old. Neither of
the children remembers their mother, though they both look like her.
Rayzel can read already and Adam is beginning to learn his letters.
Berekh refuses to separate them and will not send Adam to the heder
where a crowd of boys mechanically chant their lessons in an airless
room.

"More tea?" The proprietor of the Golem Cafe hovers at Berekh's
elbow. Berekh nods without looking up, lost in memory. "And
lemon?" the Director asks.

"Yes," Berekh answers, thinking of the simple headstone, "Hava
Eisenbaum, 1867–1891."

"And sugar?"

Berekh nods, waving his hand to dismiss the Director.

"One or two lumps?"

"One," he answers abruptly, irritated at the distraction.

"Ah," the Director says, "you're sure, one, not two."

Now Berekh looks up. The Director's eyes gleam, a red flicker in
each pupil like a pair of lit matches. "I told you one," Berekh says. "If
it's so important, then give me two."

"Certainly not. If monsieur desires one, then he should have only
one. With the sugar tax as high as it is, I would not like to abuse monsieur's taste for sweetness. But perhaps monsieur would like a cigarette?" The Director proffers a silver case.

"No, thank you," Berekh says wryly, "the tax on matches is rather
high, as well."

"Very good, monsieur," the Director laughs half-heartedly. "Perhaps you require more light for your reading? I can bring over the
lamp. We are not short of kerosene." At Berekh's definitive no, the

Director gracefully deposits a slice of lemon and a lump of rock sugar beside his glass, and slides away.

Berekh puts the sugar in his mouth, sipping the tea as he gazes at the letter, but his concentration is broken, his mind drifting aimlessly while his tongue gouges a tiny hole in the sugar, the crystals melting into the sides of his mouth. Instead of the cemetery in Blaszka, his mind fixes on the sugar, the contrast between the hard intensity of its sweetness and the pulpy slice of sour lemon in the hot tea. It reminds him of his first cup of tea in Misha's house.

AFTER THE *shloshim,* the first month of mourning, he came to thank Misha for taking such good care of his wife, not only during her last pregnancy, but in all the others as well. Both doors were open, front and back, so that the wind blew through with its spicy autumn smell, a leaf scurling and skittering along the well-worn pine floor. Misha offered him tea, motioning to the kettle bubbling on the *pripichek.* "The water just boiled," she said.

"Not today," he answered, "but later, if you don't mind, I would like to visit you."

When summer came, he did. His first cup of tea with Misha, July '92. So bitter it drew the two sides of his mouth together and a lump of sugar so big he could only suck on it for what seemed like hours, rivulets of the bitter tea slowly eroding channels in it. The doors were open, again, and the sweet smell of hay mixed with the wine and rose scent of Misha's decoctions.

She moved with her large grace from the stove to the table, her presence like the fragrance of locust flowers, so thick and musky it is more of a taste than a scent. While Berekh drank his tea, Misha strung garlic, nimbly braiding the silvery leaves, looping the garlic onto a nail in the beam beside the fall of bronze onions. A chest, sanded and half carved with intricate spiral ferns, stood against the wall under the garlic. She turned to the stove, where a bowl of rose petals was soaking in raisin wine. On the blue tiles beside the bowl were rows of leaves, roots, and bark, their function denoted by small pieces of brown wrapping paper marked with cryptic signs. Misha bundled each row, except for one, into paper and string. Berekh noticed that this was the only one marked with recognizable Hebrew letters: a "nun" and a "gimmel." With his mouth still full of sugar, he could only lift his eyebrows questioningly. "*Nisht gut,*" Misha said, no good. "Someone showed me how to write it." She swept the row of leaves into her large hands and threw it under the grate of the *pripichek,* where the quick fire had set the kettle to boil again. "The rose petals in wine are better for cramps," Misha said, motioning to the bowl. Now she knelt in front of the chest, her broad back concealing it from Berekh.

"Who did the carving?" he asked.

"My father, before he died. The trunk belonged to my mother's grandmother. He was refinishing it."

"What do you keep in it?"

"Things."

"What kind of things."

"Oh, my father wanted it to be my bridal chest."

"Is it?"

Misha laughed, her whole body shaking at the joke.

"It could be," Berekh insisted. "It still could be. You might consider a person, one whose children are small and good-tempered, not much of a burden, at all."

"No. I was married. Once is enough."

"Don't misunderstand me," Berekh said. "I mean only in the proper way, with a *shadkhen,* when the time is right."

"Sometimes my bed gets cold," Misha said, looking at Berekh, her dark eyes, with their hint of gold around the iris, narrowing mischievously. "And what good is a matchmaker then? No, I have no interest in a wedding canopy, none at all. But I might consider a person on a cold night. If the person came himself."

"This person, in theory, such a person would be finished with his year of reciting the mourner's kaddish, wouldn't he?"

"Maybe a year, but it could be ten months or three years, too. He would know when enough time had passed." Misha sat on the stool beside Berekh, her shoulder touching his. Not looking at him, she said, "I miss Hava."

"I didn't know that you and Hava were friends."

"She was a good friend to me. If Faygela wasn't able to read me the news, Hava would always come with the Jewish paper, not that Polish *Israelite* that Faygela reads, but the real one, *Dos Yidishes Folksblat.* A shame it went out of business last year. Hava missed it."

"My Hava?"

"Of course, yours."

"You don't mean my Hava. She never read anything."

"I mean your Hava and no one else's. Whenever Faygela was lying in with her babies, Hava took her place and read to me, so I shouldn't miss anything interesting. Once I mentioned that it would be nice to read it myself. She said that Faygela could teach me how, I only had to ask, and she would help, too. I didn't want to. I was too busy. It would take too long. But your Hava said there was no rush, we had plenty of time." Misha shook her head. "I didn't do right by her. The bleeding came too fast. I wasn't ready."

"And me?" Berekh asked. "I didn't even know her."

"After my mother died I thought of everything I didn't ask her. I thought there was still so much time. Then it was too late."

"It's good to sit here," Berekh said. "Just for a cup of tea. Even if there isn't so much time, who has to be in a rush?"

AFTER THE year of mourning, Berekh still found himself waking up sweating and nauseated. He only had occasional dreams of Hava, then, but he had begun to dream of poor Meyer again, the pogrom, the fire. He would wake up in the middle of the night and, hobbling to the samovar, he would pour himself a cup of tea, wincing at the cold, bitter taste, as bitter as Misha's tea. Really, he should put the kettle on to boil for a fresh pot, but he couldn't bear to kindle a fire. His hand shook even putting a match to a candle. So instead he waited for dawn, sitting at the table with his stale tea.

The front room was dense with reminders of Hava, the dark cabinet filled with her trinkets, the sideboard with her dowry, a silver tea set and a dozen silver spoons, on every surface her knitted green doilies, and on the eastern wall the wobbly landscape of the Holy Land, which she had embroidered before they were married, with its doglike camel and its faltering tents. Berekh preferred a plain, functional room, but he wouldn't think to remove these things any more than the charcoal portrait of the Old Rabbi in the studyhouse, drawn by Hayim. A person has the right to be remembered, Berekh said, and one should not begrudge their memory for the sake of his own comfort.

Some nights Rayzel would awaken, stumbling into the room with half-sobs and murmurs of bad dreams, of the darkness, of ghosts and monsters. The child would clamber onto his knees, Berekh stroking the silky head until she fell asleep, held close in his arms. Sometimes Adam would cry, and Berekh would take him from his cradle and rock the baby in his arms while he drank his cold tea.

His friendship with Misha continued to grow slowly, though she would not allow him to approach her in the ways demanded by custom and propriety. "But why can't I even come for a cup of tea without creeping through the woods?" he would ask.

"People will talk."

"So let them. I'm ready to make things right with you. Any time."

"When will you understand? I was married once already. That was enough."

"All right. So it didn't work out. It happens. A man divorces a woman. It doesn't mean her life has to end."

"Dear God, save me from wise men," Misha finally said one day, shaking her hands at heaven in exasperation. "If people know, then they'll badger me day and night. 'It isn't right, you're a woman alone. He's a good man.' And you'll agree with them. 'Am I so terrible?' you'll say. Yes, and you'll look at me with a sad face, and your voice will weep, and one day, even though I know better, one day when I'm not feeling so well, maybe I have a chill, or it's my time of month, I'll agree. And then, oy vey, it's not to be thought of."

Berekh laughed. "All right," he said. "I won't complain. I'll be as quiet as a thief from Plotsk. But you know someone will suspect. In a small place like this, people will talk anyway."

"Ah, but they won't know for sure!" Misha said triumphantly. "In the women's gallery they've matched me up with almost every man in the village, even with old Pinkus the *shokhet*. So how can they tell when the truth catches up with their imagination?"

"What truth?" Berekh asked. "That we talk together, drinking your bitter tea? Or that I sit while you make up your mysterious infusions and powders? Or," his voice softened, "that I never tire of watching you? Every day, something different. The light, the smell of the river, the table covered with herbs, your hands moving. It's like a holy text, like a deep commentary; I find something new in it all the time, I never know it all."

He brought books to her house, but she made him take them away. "Do you think I need to be a yeshiva boy?" she asked. "Are there no children for you to teach?"

"Hava read to you. Now I want to," he said. "There's so much I can tell you."

"If I want to know something, I'll ask a woman. You men don't know anything. Except maybe Hayim. And not just because I was married to him. Let me tell you, he would have plenty to say, if someone has the patience to listen. He watches everything, but as soon as a person looks at him, he hides."

"What is there to see, shlepping water?"

"You would be surprised. Hayim has a deep head. Not like me. Not like you, either."

Berekh was not flattered by the comparison. "Hayim? I don't believe it. What did Hayim tell you? One thing. Anything at all."

She only laughed, saying, "If you want to know something, then sit in the women's gallery on *Shabbas,* you'll hear everything."

Berekh would retort, "You think the men don't talk in the bathhouse?"

"Oh, yes, they talk, but do they know anything?"

Berekh was insatiably curious about the secrets that Misha knew about the villagers. He poked here and there with questions, like a Talmudic master testing a student, but Misha refused to be either student or teacher. She would say nothing more than what Berekh himself could observe if, she said, he cared to notice. "There is always something more to find out about a person. Just look, under each layer is another," she told him.

"Then what about me? What do you see?"

"Isn't it obvious?" she asked.

"What, what?" He smiled broadly, as she ran her fingers through his beard.

"The Rabbi . . ."

"Yes, tell me, what?"

"The Rabbi," she said, "is playing at love with the midwife! Can you imagine such a thing?"

"But I'm not. I haven't," he said. And then, "*Ah,*" as Misha began to undress.

It was June '93, more than a year and a half since his wife had died, and he lay with Misha for the first time. As he undressed, excited by the secrecy, shamed by it, he wondered if he would please her. When he used to make love to Hava, his body covered hers and he worried that he would be too heavy. And here was Misha half sitting on the bed, her breasts large and round and darkly nippled, her dimpled thighs large enough for both his hands to caress and not find any end to the soft heat. His touch was tentative, he was clumsy, and yet she smiled, her gold tooth gleaming as she opened her solid arms to take him in.

The first time became many times. As the days dipped down toward the short Friday in December, Misha's body became familiar to Berekh, his gratitude became joy. And now another year has passed. He is in a cafe in Warsaw, it is Monday—in a few days the short Friday will have come around again.

BEREKH AWAKES from his reverie as the door to the cafe swings open, bringing with it a blast of cold wind. A young man in a ragged jacket shakes the snow from his sleeves and collar, where a silk rose rests incongruously in a snowy lump. He is carrying a worn traveling bag with rope handles, which he deposits beneath the table beside Berekh's. Removing his hat, he runs his hands through his hair until it stands on end like rooster feathers.

The noise in the cafe is as familiar as the village square on market day. The tables are occupied with men and women arguing loudly and earnestly, as if their living depends on it. Instead of the price of a hen or a corset, it's an idea they bargain over, but the sing-song of voices, the slap of the table, the jab of a pointing finger could be Hanna-Leah's or Alta-Fruma's or Getzel the picklemaker's: "Are you mad? Don't you see what's in front of your eyes? What are you talking, Adam *Harishon* wouldn't buy what you're selling." Some are well-dressed, some in rags from the community barrel. They read, they argue, they write, they stand and look over one another's shoulder. They speak quickly, as if to keep up with their short lives while the world rushes into the next century transfigured, mutated, altered beyond recognition, and everyone is trying to guess how. The light is dim, filtered by the damask curtains, reddened by the colored shade of kerosene lamps casting a blush on the cherubs that seem, already, old-fashioned and awkward.

Berekh rubs his stiff neck, tilting back his head as he squeezes the knotted muscle. The proprietor of the Golem Cafe is coming toward Berekh's table. "Something else, monsieur?" he asks. Berekh shakes his head. "Everyone is talking about the French officer Dreyfus," the Director continues. "His arrest is a travesty of justice. It is certain that the document used against him was forged."

"A terrible case," Berekh concurs. "The authorities are insulted that a Jew can be an officer in the French army. But worse are those that stood by and allowed his persecution. Such cowardice. Turning a blind eye to the injury of an innocent person is the worst form of betrayal."

"Indeed. But let me not distract you from your reading."

As the Director retreats, Berekh notices that he has left the newspaper, folded to show a courtroom drawing of Dreyfus. Under the table Berekh's knee jiggles in agitation.

Friday, December 29, 1893

Greetings, Moyshe-Mendel,

It being the short Friday in December, the village is in a flurry to finish its business by sunset. Just an hour past I was visited by one of our esteemed women, Malkah Isaacs by name. She came with a shaaleh, a question of religious significance, the kind that is of the greatest import in our town.

"Please, Rabbi," she said, "have a look and tell me if the hen is kosher. I don't even know whose she is. She wandered into my yard and fell over half dead. Just like that. I asked everyone if they're missing a hen, but no one is. So it's ours, isn't it?"

I nodded in encouragement.

She continued. "But my husband says that if it fell over like that then there must be something wrong with it, even though Reb Pinkus took a good look at her intestines and said she was kosher. He should know, he's the shokhet, after all. So fast with the knife. But still, I have to listen to my husband, don't I? So I cut her into pieces and we all looked at her, my husband, his mother, even though she only has one good eye, and all the children, no evil eye should touch them, they have sharp young eyes. And sure enough, Yankel found this in her throat." The woman handed me a button. It was a tin button, the kind that might be on a pair of boy's short pants. "And here," she said, "I brought the hen so you can look at her." She held out a basket, lifting the cover to reveal an eviscerated hen, with its innards neatly laid around it.

I motioned to a chair, and Malkah sat while I deliberated. I could see that she was highly anxious, sitting on the edge of her chair. It was only natural. Her family has not tasted meat for weeks, and at this very moment the children would be congratulating one another on their unexpected fortune, tasting the anticipated Sabbath soup as if it were already before them. But I have discovered that an immediate and favorable response to a shaaleh *arouses suspicion. Someone in the family, a husband, a mother-in-law, will demand a second opinion from the rabbi of the old synagogue in Plotsk, which might not be so favorable. Compared to Malkah, with her twelve children and her husband who always ails but never dies, Gittel the raisin-wine maker is rich. I heard that the family would starve if it weren't for the pot of cabbage and potato soup that Hanna-Leah brings them every other day.*

So I hummed, I stroked my beard, I opened a volume of the Talmud, looked over a book of commentary, and laid on top of it a book of responsa to shaalehs *from the Gaon of Vilna. Finally, I poked the hen several times, and pronounced her kosher. Malkah went home fully satisfied, and at this very moment I am sure is cooking a delicious soup.*

The inkblot you see is my daughter Rayzel's contribution to our correspondence. She is sitting on my lap, braiding my beard, while Adam is in his favorite place under the table, investigating my shoes. At least he has outgrown the habit of biting my toe where it sticks out of the hole. They both take after Hava, being fair, and Maria looks after them like one of her own, whom they rather resemble.

Hard times occasionally produce interesting flowers, my friend. Even here in the shtetl we have heard of how the tailors in Plotsk have a workers' circle where they study such pamphlets as they can obtain in Yiddish, small renderings of the great thinkers' works. And while here such activities are dismissed as foolishness by some, others respect learning in any form. Certainly the young people hunger for knowledge as we once did in the yeshiva.

As I gaze out the window, I am privy to one of the typical spectacles of our village. An enormous man, wearing a fur coat so encrusted and odoriferous it has a soul of its own, is galloping around the village square in evertightening circles that will surely end in the old nag, which he is whipping frantically, biting him in the behind. This will, of course, cause him great aggravation, which he will be sure to vent on some lesser creature. Yet where will he find such a one? What man is so wretched as to be less than this man, whom we know as Yarush, thief and sometime peddler from Plotsk?

The sun is getting low, my friend, and there seems to be some sort of disturbance outside which I should investigate. Tomorrow, I will let you know the cause.

Addendum:

The Sabbath is over and now I must finish this letter by candlelight.

I left my study, yesterday, to observe the commotion in the village square. There I saw a crowd surrounding this Yarush and our own midwife, Misha.

"I'll show you who's the master here," Yarush said.

Misha answered, "Master? Of me? The Pope will marry our blind Hindela first." And she laughed at the very idea.

Then this Yarush threatened her and the crowd became excited. They looked from Yarush to Misha. Such excitement. Such drama. Better than you could see in Plotsk. Misha's black hair was a storm cloud, her skirts a whirlwind. Yarush was slow and dangerous as a hungry bear.

But I must tell you that I was not entertained. This Yarush would not hesitate, I am sure, to stick a knife in anyone. I was riveted by the violence of his expression. He could have turned on anyone in the square who caught his attention, and with his large hands tear a person limb from limb as easily as pulling the thigh off a boiled hen. I imagined how his hands would feel on my throat, pushing me against the wall of the synagogue, everything blocked from view except that fur coat of his, as old and dirty as the coats of the peasants during the pogrom in Warsaw. But while I was thinking thus, standing like a stick of wood, Hershel the butcher was calling the peddler to join him in a drink. Soon Hershel was leading Yarush toward the tavern. Our Hershel is a man of sense.

Misha stared at me as if she wanted me to follow them. And what good would that do? Hershel took care of everything. There was nothing more for me to do, was there? It is true that Misha is, shall we say, a particular friend of mine, but this is a confidence between myself and you, my oldest friend, from whom I have no secrets. She refuses to entertain any thought of a wedding canopy and requires that our friendship remain clandestine. Well and good. So then she should not expect me now to break the terms of our agreement.

But the most curious thing occurred last night. I was reading the news from Paris by candlelight. The animal scent of tallow melted onto the paper as I studied every word, even the small article on page seven about some army officer named Dreyfus.

But something distracted me. Perhaps it was a flicker of the candle or a sound that didn't fit the noise of the house creaking in the wind. I glanced out the window only to see a shadow separate from the doorway of the tavern and lurch across the square toward the midwife's house. I thought at first it was only the result of a strong wind, a flurry of snow, the strange shapes of night. But I will tell you something I would tell no one else. I also heard sounds that one should not hear at night from the village square. Something like the hammering of a rock on a wooden latch. A door splintering. The clatter of pots thrown aside. I thought I heard a woman's scream ripping across the square and calling someone's name, dreadfully calling, "Merciful God."

I must have been having some sort of attack again. A delusion. I took myself to bed to put an end to it, first blowing out the candle for fear that it would start a fire.

I am sure that it was all just the wind. Do you think that it was? For if it was not the wind that I heard, I don't know what I will do. This time I cannot run off to my grandfather's hut in the mountains. How ironic that I, who am terrified of any fire larger than the little flame of a candle, was named after Berekh Joselewicz, who commanded the Jewish legion in defense of Warsaw in 1794.

Tuesday, March 20, 1894

My dear Moyshe-Mendel,

Tonight is Purim and the swallows have returned from their winter sojourn in Egypt. However, spring has not quite arrived, as I came home from synagogue just in time to avoid the ice storm that is now pelting the roof.

My servant Maria claims that something is amiss with Misha. This evening she said to me, "The midwife sent Boryna's Agata away when she came to her with female troubles and I'm telling you, Rabbi, she's not hanging any rags on the line." Maria often speaks in this obtuse manner, usually punctuated by incomprehensible Polish proverbs. "When the grass grows doesn't the horse starve," she'll say and nod wisely. I do not understand her more often than not, but the children love her, and in truth I am in some confusion regarding Misha's recent behavior toward me.

My friendship with her is in disarray and I cannot help but wonder if it has anything to do with my strange vision on the night of the short Friday. One day I think that what I heard was just the result of an overfevered imagination linked to memory of the pogrom in Warsaw. The next day I am sure that something occurred, what exactly I do not know, but certainly of no benefit to Misha. But the truth is that I was at least remiss in not interfering on her behalf when Yarush accosted her in the village square.

Ever since then she has either avoided me or, to be quite frank, thrown me out on my ear. "Do you think a woman is a donkey you can ride anytime you like?" she asked me.

I protested to no avail. The next time I knocked on her door she said that a man is worse than a hyena that eats dead flesh. I will spare you what she said the third time.

And so I find that I am lonely once more and I must conclude that it is my own unworthiness that has caused it. For if I am paralysed by fear when others have need of my help then certainly I am not entitled to any human succor myself. As my esteemed cousin, Yekhiel, used to say, "Whatever a man fears, there is his destiny."

I must end this letter as I am expecting the arrival of a young boy, Izzie Blau, who is receiving instruction from me in Talmud studies. I can easily listen to him chant, but if he asks me any questions, I must remember not to quote the heretic Elisha Ben Abouya and thus corrupt the poor child's innocent faith.

Thursday, May 17, 1894

Dear Moyshe-Mendel,

A brief note, my friend. I hope you fare well. We in Blaszka are drowning in rain. Some say that it is time to build an ark. But the season of rains aside, I am quite disturbed in my mind. The whole village is talking about Misha. Our midwife is pregnant. Yes, in the synagogue on Saturday it was clear that she was showing. Not that I, myself, would have seen a thing, as blind to such matters as I am. But the women in their balcony have better vision than I, as Misha has always claimed, and even I have heard the talk now. They say that the father is Yarush, the peddler with whom Misha argued on the short Friday in December. It now emerges that Hershel was trying to make a match, but did not succeed. Or did he? people ask.

Of course it cannot be. Misha would not accept that, that . . . I do not believe it. But what if it was Yarush who crossed the village square that night? And was she willing? And if not, and I did nothing. . . . Isn't it written in the Talmud that if a man stands by while a crime is committed, it is as if he has done it himself? My friend, my friend, I can never forgive myself. Not if I live to be one hundred and twenty. If she would only speak to me I would beg her to allow me to give the child a name, whether it is mine or not.

Wednesday, May 23, 1894

Greetings from Blaszka to Paris,

How quickly time passes. Suddenly, it seems, the days grow long again. And now young Izzie Blau, my pupil, has left me with a quandary.

We were studying the portion of the week when Izzie's sister knocked at the window. I did not hear the conversation, except for the concluding comment, when Emma shouted, "God is a cabbage," and slammed down the window.

The brother and sister are strangely similar although she is quick

and excitable, while he moves dreamily, like a person under water.
Yet they have the same blue eyes that, when deep in wonderment,
are swallowed by the pupils until they are black, barely fringed with
an aureole of blue, like the sky as it passes from day into night. I
have learned that when the boy's eyes take on this color, questions
will follow. Difficult questions. The uncomfortable sort that teachers
dread. The kind that my cousin Yekhiel quite loved.

So my friend, as I watched Izzie's eyes darken after his sister
slammed the window shut, I steeled myself for an arduous conversation.

"What is God?" he asked.

I was greatly relieved. There are many lengthy answers to this
question, none of which require any deep thinking on my part. To
begin, I suggested we turn to Maimonedes's thirteen principles. I had
hardly commenced with "God is without form," however, when the
boy interrupted me vigorosly. It seems that his question was something more along the lines of "What use is God if good people like
his parents, caught in a fire, are not rescued, but die in great pain?"

I was somewhat startled, but his sincerity is undeniable. He
reminds me of my cousin Yekhiel, and it breaks my heart.

After many false starts, I finally confessed that I had no answer.
However, I said to him, I could tell him a story. It was a story
that my grandfather had told me when I was his age, herding his
goats in the summer. My mother's family are Hasidim, I said, and
followers of the Belzer Rebbe. The story, passed on directly from
father to son, I assured Izzie, was about the Ba'al Shem Tov, of
saintly name.

He was wandering in the forest when he saw an old woman
gathering wood. She was so hunchbacked she could barely walk,
and yet she pulled a little boy in a small cart. The little boy had no
legs. He was sucking on an old dirty rag, his eyes big in his hungry
little face, and he made not a single sound. Finally the Ba'al Shem
Tov cried out in anguish, "Eternal One, You see the afflictions of
Your children, whom You created with your own hands, why do You
not do something for them, I beg of You?" He waited and waited for
an answer while the trees shook and the wind howled, until at last
a voice came from the heavens. The voice said, "My child, I have. I
created you."

I was embarrassed to offer Izzie nothing more than this small story, but the boy seemed satisfied. He sat and thought, his chin resting on his hand, then he straightened up and asked me what, then, I was going to do about Ruthie.

Ruthie is my cousin Yekhiel's granddaughter, Faygela's oldest. She was arrested yesterday for carrying incendiary propaganda, though the idea of this quiet girl being a revolutionary is preposterous. There is no doubt, as my servant Maria claims, that Emma was behind it.

I am at a loss, however, as to what can be done. The Tsar's wheels of justice are entirely dependable to grind up the innocent unless lubricated with sufficient gold imperials, and where are we to get such in this poor village?

The Russian in charge of this gubernia was transferred not long ago from St. Petersburg, and he is not happy to be sent (for some misdemeanor, surely) to the back end of the empire. His administration reflects his unhappiness, and he orders the public whipping of Poles for even putting up a sign in their tongue. Selling a Polish book is sufficient grounds for exile to Siberia, not to mention his predilection for hanging Jews, and I heard that he has tripled the level of bribes to which we are accustomed.

The community council is in the process of collecting money, but you can be sure that the total will do no more than perhaps allow the girl's mother, my cousin Faygela, to visit her in prison and bring her some comforts. Ruthie's release would require an additional bribe of a rather larger sum.

I cannot see what else is to be done, unless I seek the advice of my former friend, Misha the midwife. She knows the secrets of more people than I can name. Then perhaps a second bribe might be reduced by the whispered promise of revelation. Selfishly, I am embarrassed to ask a favor of Misha, who has had nothing but contempt for me these last few months. But I must do something, at least to warrant the boy's trust.

Addendum:

I have returned from Misha's house. The village square was quiet, it not being market day, and the woods beyond Misha's house were

shrouded in that green mist that appears in spring. I knocked at
her front door, politely, like a stranger, which I have become. When
I entered, she was emptying the contents of her chamber pot out
the back door. She greeted me in the customary way, though it was
evident that she was not pleased to see me. Yet I proceeded to ask
for her advice nonetheless. I anticipated that she would not take
kindly to my request, but I never thought that she would be angry
with me for neglecting her—not after she had thrown me out
three times!

"So I was a little excited. Why shouldn't I be? You think an angel
put this here?" she said.

I swore to her that I was unaware of her condition until a week
past and that I was prepared to make it right with her. She
absolutely refused my offer of marriage with some harshness and I
cannot blame her—what have I done to warrant her confidence? So
I offered to make her a cup of tea. You will laugh at me, my friend.
But I was going mad wondering what I could do for her and all
that entered my mind was this little thing.

Of course, before tea can be made a kettle must be boiled and
before the kettle can boil a fire must be lit. With some horror, I eyed
the innocent pripichek, the square of bricks with the cooking grate
resting on it. Ah. Yes. A slight problem. Sweat began to trickle from
my temples, stinging my eyes. My hands were cold as a ghost's as I
took the box of matches from the mantelpiece. It is only a little
match, I assured myself, it is only a little fire. But I was gasping for
breath as I braced myself against the stove to strike the match. The
match was lit, my fingers so damp that it slid from my hand, the
little flame winking out as it struck the tile. Again I struck a match,
wincing at the eruption of flame, holding my breath as I flung it
into the kindling. Success. The fire was lit, the crackling of flame
loud as a gunshot. I jumped back, stumbling against the table, but
gathered myself to put the kettle on the grate and the tea into the
pot. When I set the cup and saucer before Misha, it rattled in my
shaking hand, tea sloshing over the side. Yet she seemed content with
my clumsiness.

"Maybe there's still something to you, Berekh Eisenbaum," she
said.

And after I managed to swallow some tea myself, Misha told me that she did indeed know something that might be of particular interest to the Governor of Plotsk. How gratified I was that at last Misha would impart to me one of her secrets. But not yet, it seems. She said that I must first fulfill a task, in which she has instructed me, before I would be allowed to hear the story. Nevertheless, my satisfaction did not wane. I was sitting at her table again. And for that privilege I would remake the world.

I only hope, my friend, that everyone will not now begin to ask me to light fires morning, noon, and night.

Thursday, June 21, 1894

My dear Moyshe-Mendel,

As Misha ordered, I have gone, for the second time, to the palace of the Governor of the gubernia of Plotsk. While it is rather less imposing than any of the villas in the Lazienki Gardens, it is surrounded by a sufficiently large retinue of soldiers. In truth, I must confess that I felt completely inadequate to the task I had undertaken, which was simple enough. In my capacity as the local (albeit humble) representative of His wise, majestic, glorious Self, the Little Father, our Tsar Alexander III, was it not my duty to enquire into the circumstances of the conspiracy revealed by the arrest of one Ruthie Shnir?

Although I attempted to gain an audience two weeks ago, wearing my best, but nonetheless rather worn, silk caftan and my fur hat, I was not allowed past the front gate, much to the relief of my knocking knees. The soldiers laughed at me, but beyond tweaking my admittedly unruly beard, they left me in peace to go on my way.

After that I retrieved from its bed of mothballs my old clothing. Attired in the garments of my youth, despite their reek, I felt young again. I recalled the brilliance of a world in black and white, the shush-shush sound of the sleigh flying across the snow, a universe of stars. The pleasure of memory, however, was soon dampened by the possibility that, in my Russian costume, I might actually gain an audience with his honor Alexi Tretyakov, though I would not, as you suggested, shave off my beard for the occasion.

The audience was granted, I think, because Monsieur Tretyakov was in need of some amusement, which, with my wrists and ankles and long neck poking out of all ends of a suit durably patched by Maria, I most graciously provided. Our esteemed Governor is a short, stout man with an enormous waxed moustache, which he stroked lovingly throughout our interview. Due to his good humor, he addressed me as Monsieur Giraffe, rather than Dogmeat Jew (as is his wont), and offered me a glass of vodka, which I accepted. He had little interest in reviewing the case of my young cousin, twice removed. No, his singleminded consumption of large and greasy quantities of pig washed down with vodka, while occasionally wiping the tips of his fingers on a lace napkin, was only equaled by the lengthy list of his grievances against his superiors. Finally when he could swallow nothing more, he began to sing and weep simultaneously. "You don't know the songs of St. Petersburg," he said, "where the Gypsies sing like angels in their cafes."

I replied that I did, certainly, since the songs of St. Petersburg were much like those of Moscow. Now, I amused him heartily since I began to sing like one of the young Russian gentry, the guliaka *who were frequenters of Gypsy cafes in the days of the old Tsar Alexander. Then I tossed back a glass of vodka just like a* guliaka, *which our Governor Alexi had himself been in his day.*

In his increasingly benevolent state, it seemed appropriate to enquire as to how many gold imperials it required to ease the travail of a hapless fellow Russian, such as himself. He replied with little prompting. It was a staggering sum, my friend.

Misha had instructed me to then add, after a polite pause, "And if it is sent with the good wishes of your friend from Minsk?"

At this he sat up sharply and said, "If, indeed, I were assured that this was a favor for my friend. . . . Yes, if I were to receive a letter that proved this case to be of any interest to my friend in Minsk . . . well, in such an instance, of course the price would change." He then named a figure which, though rather less, was still almost inconceivable for our village. I had, however, completed my assignment, and took my leave with many obeisances and flatulent salutations.

I returned from this second venture yesterday and today, I hear that such a letter has been prepared. The contents are unknown to me, but I understand that the letter and the price required were made ready by the women of Blaszka. How is entirely a mystery to me. In these long days when the sun hovers in the sky so that night has no meaning, everything is possible. Ruthie's father, Shmuel, is now on his way to Plotsk to retrieve his daughter and I am on my way to retrieve Misha from her house. I have a bottle of wine, real wine, not our Gittel's raisin wine, and I will hold Misha's arm while we walk along the river. If people see us, what does it matter? Let them talk. What other pleasures do they have in this small village?

Ruthie will soon be in her mother's embrace. Then I must begin to see to her comrades in arms. Their woodland meetings are too perilous a game.

Tuesday July 24, 1894

My dear Moyshe-Mendel,

Honored patron of the B. Eisenbaum Young Adult Learning Society, how can I express my gratitude for the box of books you sent us? My students dive into all reading matter as if it were a secret river of precious gems. At night they study tirelessly though they work all day, and I am kept on my toes to supply their endless appetite. It seems as though every day Izzie brings another young person to me. From the first timid student, there are now a dozen. I have five girls and seven boys in my class, though Emma Blau refuses to join them as yet. Stubborn as a goat, her great-aunt Alta-Fruma says. This study keeps them away from their conspiracies in the woods—at least while they are with me. When they are gone, I am restless. I wander through the woods myself, like the Ba'al Shem Tov, *of saintly name.*

Izzie is not interested in the secular studies that the older children pursue. In exchange for introducing them to me, I am preparing him for the yeshiva. He is as serious as an old man, but from time to time when he eats with me, for our dessert, as childishly as one could wish, he demands one of my grandfather's stories.

Yesterday I overheard him in shul telling another boy one of these tales. A disciple of the Ba'al Shem Tov *asked him when the Messiah would come. His teacher answered with this story. He was walking* across the fields, when he saw from the stones, the stacks of hay, the grass, and the trees, from the cows and the goats and the mice, sparks emerge. The sparks clung to him, purifying his spirit. In this way he saw the Holy Fire. And when he saw clearly, the sparks rose up to the heavens and fell down, like rain, in the form of letters. The Ba'al Shem Tov said "Each of us holds a handful of the letters. And if, together, we assemble them correctly, the whole world will be alight with the Holy Fire, and it will not be consumed." Then his disciple asked him, "How can we know the correct order of the letters?" The Ba'al Shem Tov answered, "With eyes of wonder, and a heart of mercy."

My friend, it was the child, and not I, who added the last two lines of the story.

Misha grows uncomfortably large, but in the summer nights I take her to the silver rocks in the river where the water runs deep. There we may wade up to our waists, and I wash her as gently as I can. I kiss every place that I touch and so I should—for she carries the burden of the child while I am honored to be her servant.

Monday, September 3, 1894

Dear Moyshe-Mendel,

We come to the time of repentance, Moyshe-Mendel, my friend. The ram's horn is blown every morning to awaken us. The village has survived the typhus. Only one child was sick—Emma is well again, thank God. Misha is eight months along.

I brought my children to her house. They looked into all her jars and pots, sniffed herbs and nibbled on the ends of roots, sat in turn on the half-carved trunk, and put their small inquisitive hands on her belly, squealing at the push of an elbow or a heel under their fingers. If only Misha would consent to marry me then they would have a mother once again.

You have asked if people are talking. Of course they talk. And my servant Maria reports every word.

That the Rabbi should be practically betrothed to the midwife, a person of no yikhus, who goes into the houses of peasants, some even say that she casts the evil eye? Evil, shmevil, is the Rabbi such a catch? His father's a cantor in Zhitomir, all right, but what is his

326 • LILIAN NATTEL

mother's family? Hasidim. Goatherds. And you know, he's a little
strange himself, he reads German and Russian, not just when he
has to, but for pleasure. But what about this child of Misha's, who
knows whose it is? If nobody knows, maybe it's even the Rabbi's. It
can happen. Look, this isn't Warsaw. He's all right for our little village. He teaches my Devorah and your Isaak-Naphtali so they're
not hanging around in the woods getting arrested. Let the Rabbi
and the midwife make a match, so long as we're invited to the
feast.

However, there will not be any wedding canopy. She still refuses
me. You know what we read from the prayer book on Rosh
Hashanha: "You open the Book of Remembrance, and the
record speaks for itself, for each of us has signed it with deeds."

Friday, October 5, 1894

To my faithful friend, Moyshe-Mendel,
    May you be inscribed in the Book of Life. If I have offended you
in any way, or done anything to cause you any harm, or even any
discomfort in the last year, please forgive me.
    As always we have a number of guests in Blaszka for the Days of
Awe. One, however, arrived today in an unusual way. A Gypsy boy
by the name of Pyotr Mirga was rescued from drowning by, of all
people, Yarush the thief and peddler. I could scarcely contain myself
when this Yarush came into the studyhouse, still in his filthy fur
coat, a bleeding boy slung over his shoulder. This was the man who
accosted Misha in the village square, who may indeed have . . . I
cannot write more regarding that. Particularly since my anger
quickly gave way to shame at my own inaction for which I cannot
forgive myself, though I attend Misha every day. Nor am I alone in
this. For everyone in the village brings something to Misha. The
children work in her garden, the women clean her house and comb
her hair, the men repair what is broken. Our villagers are one in
their attentions to Misha. They bring their gifts freely, without
argument, without recrimination. Can it be that the Messiah is
indeed on his way, as some people claim? No, my friend, I cannot
believe that the messianic age is at hand. But perhaps there are
islands of time when we have a taste.

My unexpected guest is comfortable on a couch in the front room, having drunk the restorative tea I obtained from Misha, his head anointed with a medicinal salve. While I write to you, I hear that he has already picked up his instrument and is plucking the strings in a sad tune that suits these days of judgment. Izzie, who came to study with me before the Sabbath, is instead listening to Pyotr's music, his arms clasped around his knees, staring at things we cannot see as if he is listening to the song of heaven. And perhaps he is. Now, Izzie insists that Pyotr must accompany him to Kol Nidrei and sit with him in repayment for this music. For no one will understand the ancient melody as well as Pyotr, he says.

IN THE Golem Cafe, Berekh returns the letters to their folder. It is getting dark and difficult to read, and in any case he has finished all the letters. He has discharged his duty to his friend Moyshe-Mendel. It is time to return home. It is the 26th day of the Hebrew month of Kislev, 5655, or December 24th, 1894, according to the Christian calendar. Monday. Tonight Berekh will light candles for the third day of Hanukkah. It is both the dark of the moon and the dark of the sun, three months since the Day of Judgment. And how was he judged?

THE SAGES call Yom Kippur the long day. There is no night, time hangs on a thread spun by the haunted melody of Kol Nidrei. It is said that there are some whose singing makes the demons weep and the souls of hell fly up to heaven. But as the sun lowers on the eve of Yom Kippur, the Rabbi's throat is dry. Though he opens his mouth to begin Kol Nidrei, nothing emerges but silence. His throat is closed. Why? he wonders, attempting again to sing, without success. It can only be because he has not atoned for the sin of his cowardice. Pinye. Meyer. Now Misha. She most of all. At this very moment she suffers alone and if she lives through the labor, still he cannot undo one moment of her pain. Across the square she lies alone. How many are alone? Women and men, each naked before God. His eyes blur. The walls of the synagogue melt like tallow, and he sees in the distance sparks flying toward Blaszka. Is it the Holy Fire or the Angel of Death?

"Where?" asks Pyotr Mirga, sitting beside Izzie.

Hershel thinks he means the Rabbi. "Right there," he says.

The Rabbi thinks he means the fire. "Coming," he whispers.

But Izzie is sure that he must mean the Eternal One, Blessed Be, the Holy Flame out of which leap the sparks of life. "Here," he says, touching Pyotr's hands, not knowing what makes him say this, "here," holding out his own hands, and "there," pointing to the women's gallery where his sister, Emma, stands beside Alta-Fruma.

"Can I find my wife somewhere," asks Pyotr, "after so long?"

"Here," says the Rabbi, holding up his hands. "Dear God, I am Yours."

"Do you hear?" asks Hanna-Leah in the women's gallery as the moon slides across the village square. "How long must she suffer without anyone to give her a drink of water even?"

The men point. They whisper, "Misha, it's her time."

Ignoring their calls, Berekh pushes his way between them, even though it is too late to erase his betrayal nine months past, when a gust of snow blew across the village square.

The sea of women parts. Berekh enters Misha's house.

IN THE coming year, the proprietor of the Golem Cafe will retrieve the Paris edition of *Fleurs de Lis* from Berekh's table. Tucking the newspaper under his arm, he will say to Berekh, "Just think of that poor fellow Dreyfus in his confinement on a barren isle. While all those who allowed this tragedy—"

"Yes," Berekh interrupts him excitedly, "how can a person call himself a man when he hides behind his own inaction? Such a man can never escape his guilt. Never. No matter how hard he tries."

"And yet," says the Director, "he is not the criminal."

"No, he is worse. The criminal is pitiable. He is ignorant, or mad. But the man who stands by has no excuse." Berekh pounds the table. "None. None at all."

The young Traveler at the next table turns in his chair, crossing one leg over the other, calmly clasping his hands over his knee. "Every man can atone," he says quietly.

"How can he? The past cannot be changed. Such a man, though he atones all his life, cannot erase one minute of pain and suffering."

"How true," the Director admits. "How wise, how perspicacious are the monsieur's words. A deed once enacted cannot be recalled."

The Traveler sees Berekh tense, his shoulders drawn inward, a muscle in his cheek twitch. "God in Heaven," the Traveler snaps, "a person atones all of his life, and you're telling me it's useless?"

"Yes," Berekh says. He rubs his forehead as if it aches.

"Even if such a man devotes his life to attention and action?"

"He can't erase the past," Berekh insists.

"Right," the Traveler agrees. Berekh nods with grim satisfaction. "But," the Traveler continues, "such a man hears the call of the ram's horn not only on the Day of Atonement, but every day. Awake, always ready to make amends by acting on behalf of others. Always alert lest he fall asleep again."

"Perhaps," Berekh agrees tentatively.

"How fortunate," the Traveler says, "are the friends of such a man. How lucky are those who know him. They'll always have someone to turn to in time of need, a man who won't look down on them for their sins, knowing his own."

The Director claps his hand on the young Traveler's shoulder. The Director smiles, the Traveler smiles back. Berekh thinks that they look like brothers. And if he were telling his students a story, he would say, For an instant I saw *Netzakh* and *Hod*. The light brightened around them and I saw the twin aspects of the Holy, one crashing through all barriers to the outflow of God's benevolence, the other holding back lest it be dissipated uselessly. The light was like a fire that does not burn.

"But you, monsieur, have a train to catch, I believe," the Director says, and the light is ordinary again.

"Yes, I'm expected in Blaszka, this evening. My children are waiting for me. But take this." Berekh turns to the Director. "To make up for the sugar tax." He hands him a box of matches. "I have another."

"Au revoir, Rabbi," the Director calls after him.

In a few days, Berekh will light a memorial candle for Meyer, who died on the third day of the Hebrew month of *Tevet*, which this year will begin on the eve of the 29th of December, exactly one year since the day that Misha conceived.

In fifty years, one of Berekh's grandchildren will survive the war, though just a boy at the time. He will eventually settle in the new world. One weekend in the early 1960's he will stand with his friends in front of the tents at a Jewish Boys' Camp, brandishing baseball bats at the neo-Nazis who have threatened to attack it.

In a hundred years, this grandson of Berekh's will say to his own children and grandchildren that he survived the war because he didn't fight. Time after time, he let chance take him from a situation that seemed better to one that seemed worse, only in the end to save him from death. He was lucky.

Or perhaps, the Traveler might have said, restraint is as much a sign of the Holy as is courage.

PART THREE

MISHA

9

THE SECRET RIVER

In the village square, a crowd of women jostled like geese around Misha's stall. From the array of jars on her table, she picked a mixture of fennel seed, nettles, raspberry leaf, motherwort, and wild oats. "Listen," she said, tying up the herbs in the handkerchief of a woman with red eyes and a scar along her chin. "Boil a spoonful of this in a small pot and drink it morning and night. Between us, it would work better if you . . ." Misha whispered the rest in her ear.

A tired tear trickled along the woman's broad nose as she nodded, slipping a few *groschen* into Misha's hand. Again, Misha whispered into her ear. She smiled crookedly and Misha laughed, her gold tooth gleaming, holding onto the woman's arm with her large hand, laughing and winking until the red-eyed woman laughed creakily. They looked so foolish, rocking from side to side, huge Misha and Agata the stick, laughing at nothing, "at cheese," the women said, that soon they too were laughing and pointing until their sides hurt, arms lifting and falling like beating wings. "Give him to me," Misha said to Agata, pointing to the baby riding in her shawl. "You go to Rivka's table. She has new fabrics from Warsaw. Like no one else's. Just go and look," Misha said, humming as she took the colicky baby and Agata headed across the square.

INSIDE THE bakery, Faygela, surrounded by her daughters, was saying, "But in walked Misha, like a queen. She threw out the doctor, turned the baby around inside me with her own hands."

INSIDE THE butcher's shop, Hanna-Leah was saying, "Did you hear that someone saw a pair of man's pants sticking out from under Misha's bed?"

Who do you think they belonged to? the women asked.

"Anyone she wants." Hanna-Leah's eyes narrowed. "She wouldn't hesitate."

BREAKING the ice in the well with his ax, Hayim thought, A woman you can look at, but never see.

In the tavern, Hershel said, "A wild wolf."

In her cottage, Alta-Fruma said, "Who knows things."

With defiance Emma answered, "From the dark ages."

Looking out of his study window, Berekh thought, Who's more alive than the earth itself.

Driving toward Blaszka, Yarush spit over the side of his cart. "Women? There's not a good one among them."

AT MIDAFTERNOON, Misha was thinking that it was time to dismantle her stall and go home to prepare for the Sabbath. But look, Hanna-Leah was coming across the square from the butcher shop. It had been a month since she'd last gotten a remedy from Misha and apparently it was time for another.

"You have something different?" Hanna-Leah asked.

"What I gave you before didn't help?" Misha could see that it hadn't. Was this a happy woman, tapping her foot, looking over her shoulder to see if anyone was listening?

"Just give it to me. I don't have time to stand here all day."

Once Hanna-Leah had been the most beautiful of the *vilda hayas*. Now her golden eyebrows were drawn together, a deep line between them, her mouth pulled down into a tight crescent. "Put it in the soup," Misha said gently, reaching toward Hanna-Leah's shoulder, but Hanna-Leah pulled away, grabbing the package and slapping a few kopecks onto the table.

AFTER MISHA took down her stall, she stopped to check the stores in her cellar on her way home. Because her house was on stilts, the cellar was dug into the earth beyond the floodline of the river, on the edge of the woods. Bending low to enter the half door, Misha climbed down the steps with the agility of someone who was coming home.

The deep, dark cellar was filled with everything good. The straw insulation, with its faint hay smell, the hanging bunches of dried leaves and roots, the baskets of flowers and bark, the shelves of bottles and jars. Here she used to stand beside her mother, storing what they had gathered in the woods. "So Misha," Blema would say, "do you remember what I told you about tansy?" Or it might be belladonna or ergot or something more ordinary like raspberry leaves. Misha would answer—where it grew, the shape of the leaves, color of flowers, how to prepare it, when to use it, any dangers. If she made a mistake, her mother would make a clicking sound in the back of her throat, and Misha would ask, "What is it, Mama?" Blema wouldn't tell her. She would only say, "Watch more carefully, Misha. I won't always be here." But in the dark cellar, with its fragrance of spring even in the middle of winter, Misha could still feel her mother near.

As Blema did when she was alive, Misha conducted an inspection every week. Were the raspberry leaves still white and green? Was the clover a good purple-pink? In the winter, when all she had was the light from the kerosene lamp, she relied more on the smell and the taste of the herbs. "Look at this," she now murmured. The willow bark was crumbly and musty-smelling. A shame, especially in the winter, when there were so many fevers. And half of the plantain leaves were soft and sweet-tasting because Ruthie had picked them still wet with dew. "What can I do, Mama? She has to learn," Misha said, speaking to her mother casually, as she often did.

"At least I have plenty of comfrey if I need something for a cough. But look at this getting spoiled." Misha picked up a jar of plantain oil, clumps of mold along the glass rim. "Never mind, I'll make an ointment out of it. I need more anyway, and right before *Shabbas* is the best time to make it." Misha continued along the rows of shelves, inspecting the glass jars of infusions and decoctions, the brown bottles of tinctures and syrups, the tins of ointments.

There were times when Misha thought her mother could hear her, and other times when she thought she was talking to herself. What does it matter, she often said to Berekh, a person has to talk, even to air. "Mama, I know what you'd think," Misha said as she climbed out of the cellar, swinging her basket. "But look, I'm not a child anymore. I can't be alone all of the time. So get married again, you'd say. Be like everyone else." Misha sighed.

Her mother used to say, Don't be like Manya. You know what happened to your great-grandmother. She got pregnant not once, but twice. Two beautiful girls. But a father for the children? None. And when she was accused of all kinds of nonsense, she was taken away from them. Her hair turned white and she died. All because she wasn't like anyone else.

Once in the house, Misha placed the jar of moldy oil on the stove beside the pot with her soaking laundry. Then she turned to the clutter on her table. Pushing away half a loaf of dried bread, a cracked jar, a shiny stone, three pots of flower bulbs, and a fishnet, she tore *The Israelite,* which Faygela had left on the table last week, into narrow strips. Half the strips she set aside for the outhouse, and the other half she divided between the stove and the cracks around the window.

"How could I be like anyone else, Mama? I have to hold the secrets of the whole village. And let me tell you, a married woman has plenty. Not like an unmarried woman—she can have only one kind of secret. Where they hear about me, I don't know. But if the Countess of Volhynia is late one month, she comes to me. You'll take care of me, she'll say. I know you won't tell anyone. Well, I don't. But am I fat? Not half big enough to have a place for all their secrets."

At the stove, Misha carefully poured some of the plantain oil into a pan, adding grated beeswax. As she talked she stirred, checking the consistency of the salve, now adding a little oil, now a little beeswax. "Berekh is something different. He doesn't tell me secrets. Instead he wants me to talk. Every day people are pestering him with *shaalehs;* Rabbi, tell me this, Rabbi what about that? It's good for him to listen to someone else for a change. And don't I deserve a little comfort? A little pleasure? Just don't expect me to marry anyone. A woman who marries doesn't own her own soul. She's her husband's. It shouldn't be, but that's how it is." Misha could almost hear her mother making the clicking noise in the back of her throat as she shook her head. "Look, Mama. There were four *vilda hayas*. And what happened to them? Hanna-Leah married and she's unhappy because she has no children. Faygela married and she grinds her teeth because she has too many. Zisa-Sara married, went to America for her children, and there she died with her husband. Look at me. I have my house and I do what I want."

There was the sound of clattering on the steps outside. "Misha, Misha." Faygela, surely with the new issue of *The Israelite*.

"Sit. I'm making ointment," Misha said as Faygela came in. If a married woman didn't have a friend to talk to, you can be sure she would go crazy. But at least with Faygela, there was always something interesting to hear.

Faygela had left and Misha was putting the potato pudding into the oven when Hershel came in, flushed, his breath short, his hat pushed back from his forehead.

"What do you need?" Misha asked.

"I have a little weakness. It's nothing, just a sort of weakness," he said. Of course Misha knew very well what kind of weakness. But she couldn't say, could she? And when Hershel complained of a problem with his leg, she had to watch him walk around the room, all the while wondering what she should do. Well, he was here, wasn't he? He must want something. Maybe a word of advice. Wasn't the midwife supposed to know about these things? So at last she said, "Some men can have a weakness in other parts. Not you of course, but when a man has a weakness in those other parts, the best thing to do is to forget about it. The man should remember that he has strong hands and soft lips. He should remember how it feels to touch his wife. These weaknesses aren't that important."

"I told you it's my leg. Of course you can't see anything wrong with my leg. What was I thinking? I should have my head examined. The *feldsher* would give me a leech or a good cupping and I'd be good as new. But you're a witch, not a doctor." Hershel's fists came up, his face darkened and he yelled as he left, "God protect me from the evil eye!"

"So who asked you to come to me?" Misha called after Hershel.

She slammed the door shut. "You see, Mama, what I have to deal with? Is this a way to start *Shabbas?* Never mind. It doesn't matter. Let me clear off the table and get things ready."

The brass candlesticks were shined and set in the center of her mother's pine table. A broad-lipped maple bowl, etched with leaves, was filled with smooth stones, the river's eggs, that would glint red and green in the Sabbath flames. The fire was banked to last through the night. In the oven a potato pudding was growing a golden crust. Later she would take it to Alta-Fruma, where she would have *Shabbas* dinner and meet Zisa-Sara's children.

As the back door creaked open, Berekh poked his head through the opening like a turtle stretching his neck out of the shell.

Misha lay in her bed, an old blanket pulled up to her chin. "Come closer," she groaned, with a few coughs thrown in for good measure.

Berekh bent over her anxiously. "What is it?" he asked, "What's wrong? Are you cold?" he put a hand on her forehead.

"Oh," she sighed, "don't look. It's too much for you."

"Please, don't say that. Let me help. Show me. Is something hurting?"

"It's my skin," she said sadly. "It itches all over. The blanket is scratching me something terrible."

"Then let me bring you my featherbed. I'll go right away."

"No, no," she said gripping his hand. "Just take away the blanket." As Berekh lifted the edge, she gave it a healthy kick, revealing her nakedness in the soft ebb of daylight.

"I don't see a rash," he said. "Your skin itches all over?"

"Something terrible. And only one thing can help."

"What is it, Misha, tell me."

"Your beard!" And with that she sat up. Throwing her arms in wide welcome, she shook with laughter, the bed frame creaking as Berekh leaped onto the bed like a goat. He flung his clothes to the floor and burrowed into her, his red beard scratching and tickling her from the nape of her neck to her thighs.

When Berekh left, she lay, still naked, one leg bent, her arm over her head. She wasn't regretting the ten years that had passed between the time he first sent the matchmaker and the day that he finally had a cup of tea in her house. That's how it is in life. She wasn't a person who thought too much about the past. She was, however, realizing that she should be lighting candles soon. The shadows were lengthening quickly, merging with darkness. It was early, very early. In fact, she counted on her fingers, it was the short Friday of December. She sat bolt upright, swinging her feet to the cold floor. You're a fool, Misha, she thought. It had only been one week since she had finished bleeding, not two as she had figured. Of course, that was why she had been so eager for Berekh's visit, as reckless as a child at play. She dressed herself, yanking the strings and wooden buttons roughly.

When she went outside to get a breath of fresh air, she saw a commotion in the village square. "What's going on?" she called.

"It's that thief Yarush," Faygela said. "He's all excited because his cart broke and the horse fell over."

An oversize, yellow-bearded man was kicking and punching a horse lying on the snowy mud of the square. Just like a man, Misha thought. What are they good for? Getting a woman pregnant and kicking a defenseless animal. Well, I'll give him a good one for the poor nag.

The village square, empty when Yarush had arrived, was filling up with curious gawkers as Misha made her way between them. Now something's going to happen, people said. "You're right," Misha answered, her red shawl falling back from her head. She was so angry that she'd forgotten her coat, her boots crunching the hard mud.

"Take your hand off the horse," Misha shouted.

The big man turned his head slowly. "You talking to me?" he asked.

"Who do you think I'm talking to? God in Heaven?"

The crowd laughed. "Go back inside, woman," Yarush growled. "Mind your own business."

"If it happens in Blaszka, it's my business," she said, throwing back her head proudly, her long hair lifting in the wind.

"You think you're something, don't you?"

"Leave the poor nag alone," she said as Yarush kicked the horse.

"What do you mean, ordering me around? Can you say what I should do with my own animal?"

"I told you once, and I'm telling you again. Leave the poor nag alone." Did he think he could browbeat her like some starved horse? She'd show him.

"I'll show you who's the master here." He grabbed her shoulder.

"Master? Of me?" She laughed. "The Pope will marry our blind Hindela first."

"I'll give you something to laugh for," he said. His hand was surprisingly heavy. She couldn't shake it off.

"You'll show me some respect." Lifting her skirt, she gave him a good kick in the leg. It should have made him let her go, but it didn't. He hardly moved, standing so close she could see the lice crawling around the edge of his hat as if to get a better grip on his eyebrows. He squeezed her shoulder, the thumb pressed painfully into her collarbone.

The crowd danced with excitement. Children were jumping up and down, the boys climbing onto their friends' shoulders and butting heads in the general enthusiasm. The adults nudged one another. Who do you think? they asked. Yarush, some said. No, Misha. There isn't a man who can better her. What are you talking, she's a woman, isn't she? So? She's not like anyone else. Her great-grandmother was a witch. Don't be an idiot, you believe that old granny's tale? Well, it doesn't pay to get her angry, let me tell you. All right, don't argue, just look what's happening.

Misha pulled back her head, gathered a thick gob of spit in her mouth, and slapped it into the ugly forked beard. "Go to hell," she said.

Yarush lifted his fist.

"Sure, use your fist," she said, only the slightest bit afraid. "You can't get your horse to pull the cart, so you think you'll get a woman instead?"

But he was distracted, turning his head at the sound of a voice calling him. "Friend, friend, join me in a drink," Hershel was saying as he waved a bottle at Yarush.

"Schnapps. *Mph.*"

"Ah. A man of few words. The best," Hershel said.

Yarush let her go, forgotten. She stared at his retreating back. What would have happened if Hershel hadn't taken him off to the tavern? If, if, she chastised herself. If men had to give birth, the whole world would die out.

And Berekh, what was he doing all this time? Standing. Watching. Like a man. What are they good for? To get a woman pregnant and watch her work. She looked at him as if to say, Go to the synagogue and study. Leave the real world to the women.

WHEN *Shabbas* began, Misha was standing in the hallway of Alta-Fruma's house. Blowing on her hands and rubbing the feeling back into her cold fingers, she spied the children, arms around each other, leaning into the warm angle of wall and oven. "Good *Shabbas*," Alta-Fruma greeted Misha with a kiss on each cheek. "Come in, take off the wet coat, get warm."

"And what do I smell? Aahh. Cabbage rolls like no one else's," Misha said as she shucked off her coat. Alta-Fruma laid it over a bench near the stove.

"Come here, children." Alta-Fruma hustled them forward with a push between their shoulder blades. Emma held back. Izzie stumbled forward sleepily.

"So these are Zisa-Sara's children?" Misha said. "The boy looks nothing like her. He takes after the father. But the girl is her exactly."

"Not the eyes. She has my sister Rakhel's eyes, no question. I look at her face and there is Rakhel," said Alta-Fruma.

"All right, the eyes, but everything else is Zisa-Sara, even the tiny mole above her lip." Misha reached out a hand to brush back the curls that had sprung from Emma's braids. The girl jerked aside, lifting her arm as if to block a blow.

"Who are you?" she asked. She was holding her brother by the shoulder to keep him from falling over with tiredness.

"Who? Your mother and I were like this," Misha crossed her fingers. "We grew up together like two flies from the same egg. Closer than sisters. Didn't she tell you about the *vilda hayas?*"

"I don't care about old stories," Emma muttered in English.

"When someone asks you a question, you answer in the *mama-loshen*," her aunt said, "not in a *goyisher* tongue that no one understands."

"I said nobody cares about old stories," Emma answered defiantly in Yiddish.

"You see?" Alta-Fruma asked. "A handful. All right, children. Pull out the bench for Misha."

Unloading her basket, Misha placed the pot of potato kugel on the

342 • LILIAN NATTEL

table, and the tin jug in Fruma's hands. "I made this special for the children," she said. "Put a teaspoon in a hot tea before they go to sleep."

Emma poked her head over her aunt's shoulder to peer into the jug. "What is it?" she asked.

"Five leaf tonic," Misha said. "I don't have very much of it this time of year, but after such a long journey, a person, especially a little girl, needs a tonic."

"What's it do?" Emma asked.

"It protects you from the Evil Eye," Misha answered. "The best mix has seven herbs, but in the winter, five is all right." People came from far for her tonic, and she had put her last pinch of it into the tin jug, thinking that for her best friend's children even the last drop of her own blood wouldn't be too much.

"The evil eye," Emma echoed, now as wobbly as Izzie with fatigue. Wrinkling her nose, she turned to her brother. "We're not having any of it," she said to him in English. "Who knows what's in it? It could even be poisonous. They're living in the dark ages. Old hags." Neither her great-aunt nor Misha understood a word, but the expression on Emma's face they understood quite clearly. Misha bit her lip.

"Emma," Alta-Fruma said, "it's *Shabbas*. We have a guest. Don't make me ashamed. In my house you behave like a Jew, not a *goy*."

Emma reddened, but before she could say anything back to her aunt, Misha jumped in. "What does she know? She's from America. Just a child."

"A child? A mule. As stubborn as her grandmother Rakhel. But never mind. It's *Shabbas*, we won't speak of it now. Sit children. Who's going to say the blessing over the wine and the bread? Izzie?"

All through the meal, though Misha tried to draw her out, Emma wouldn't say a word but just peered sullenly through the strands of hair unraveled from her braids. From time to time, she poked her sleepy brother and hissed at him in English. This wasn't the way Misha thought it would be. She had expected to do something for Zisa-Sara's daughter, to let her know that she could always come to Misha just the same as if she were Emma's aunt. Wasn't Emma's mother, Zisa-Sara, like a sister to Misha? Even when they were small, Zisa-Sara and Misha had promised that they would watch over each other forever.

*　　*　　*

"YOU'LL BE the godmother of my children," Zisa-Sara would say when they were ten or eleven years old, playing wedding. Misha would have no husband or else two, even three, while Zisa-Sara always had one, a scholar, draping her head with an old shawl of her mother's for a veil, practicing how she would walk to the wedding canopy. Misha would tear the shawl from her head and run, and Zisa-Sara would run after her until they were deep in the woods. There Misha would tell Zisa-Sara everything she'd heard from her mother about the getting of babies. A few years later Misha said, "I'm never going to have one. Women bleed to death when they give birth. And there's not one thing they can do about it."

"Sometimes," Zisa-Sara said. "But if you don't have any children, who will love you when you're old?" They were wading in the river, splashing water at each other. It was summer, the raspberries ripe. They were fourteen, the same age as Emma was now.

"Well, you, of course. We'll be two old women together." Misha hunched her back and drew in her lips as if she had no teeth. "Oh Zisa-Sara, remember when we were young and beeeautiful? You had one husband and I had thirteen."

Laughing, Zisa-Sara said, "How could I forget? You had two children with each of them and with every pregnancy you lost your teeth. I, of course, still have my teeth. But that's the price you pay for thirteen husbands."

Straightening her back, Misha leaned toward Zisa-Sara and whispered, "There's a crack in the wall of the bathhouse. We could take a look. See what one looks like."

"Misha, we couldn't."

"Yes, we could." Misha winked. Zisa-Sara pursed her lips and twisted her shoulders back and forth. "Come on," Misha said.

"All right. Just once."

"Of course. Just once."

They snuck behind the bathhouse and Misha looked, but Zisa-Sara thought she heard a noise and ran off into the overgrown lanes. When Misha caught up with her, Zisa-Sara was blushing even though she hadn't seen a thing. As they walked back across the bridge, Zisa-Sara said, "I like Mikhal. Who do you like, Misha?"

"Oh, I don't know."

"I know that look, Misha. You're hiding something. Tell me."

"Well, maybe Hayim. The miller's son."

"The watercarrier? He's so old. He must be twenty-two."

"I like his eyes," Misha said.

"Well, I'm going to marry Mikhal."

And she did. She married him. They went to America. She died. And now look. Her daughter was scowling at Misha with Zisa-Sara's face, one arm around her brother's shoulders to protect him from strangers.

After dinner, Misha left Alta-Fruma's house, walking home in the darkness, her boots like black roots kicking up the snow. The night brought with it a deep cold. Her nostrils pinched, the snow squeaked underfoot, an owl shuddered over her shoulder, heavy with the rabbit in its talons. She was edgy with disappointment and when she got into bed, she tossed and turned, dreaming that Zisa-Sara was calling her. She woke up to the sound of banging on her door, groggy, unsure of herself.

"What is it?" she called. None of the women in Blaszka were near their time. Could it be a miscarriage? An accident among the peasants? She rose from her bed, throwing a shawl around her shoulders.

"Let me in," someone said gruffly. That voice, so familiar. Who was it? That rough slur of a man half full of vodka. Yes, Yarush.

"Go home," she yelled at the closed door.

"I want to come in."

"Sleep it off. It's late, go home."

Then the banging began again, but it wasn't the sound of a fist knocking. She looked around for something to grab, a heavy pot, an iron rod, but she was slower than she should have been.

THE NEXT day in shul, Misha expected the women to ask her what had happened to her. But no one in the women's gallery said anything, not to her cut and bruised face, not to her trembling hands. Since no one asked, she told no one. Not how the latch broke and the door swung open. The flash of light on snow. The man like a shadow blotting out the moon. Nor did she tell them how they struggled. The pots and pans clanging like the end of days. Bottles shattering, spilling a season's work. The water barrel falling on her. The icy water. His hands on her neck. She would have made any sacrifice to remove those hands. Nor did she say how her head still ached, or show them the lump where he cracked her head against the iron bed stand, her throat hoarse from choking. She could still taste the blood from when she bit him. The skin of his neck was under her fingernails as if he had become a part of her, and she would never rid herself of him. She would say nothing of how she remembered her screams with shame. Not how she cried out, "Berekh, merciful God, please, Berekh, come to me," unaware that Yarush was already inside her. Not that she had discovered she was just a woman like any other, and nothing could help her.

And the women, even amongst themselves, said nothing. If they acknowledged that any harm could come to the midwife who laughed at the Angel of Death, wouldn't it bring his presence among them? So Misha told them nothing. And when Berekh visited her, she couldn't bear the nearness of him. "Do you think a woman is a donkey you can ride anytime you like?" she asked him.

"No," he answered. "Let me just have a cup of tea with you. That's all." But she couldn't stand to be in the same room with him. Not him, not any man. Not for months.

At night she told herself to forget what had happened. She said this as she lay in bed, staring at the door, waiting. On her table the piece of amber that she'd found on her doorstep winked in the moonlight like a red tear.

THE DAY OF THE ICE STORM

Nearly spring and Purim was coming. Misha crossed the village square to the bakery, taking her shawl from her head and swinging it around her shoulders. As she walked, she hummed. Though her period was a little late in coming, that happens. It's not so unusual. And if she didn't feel so well all the time? Wasn't it a bad piece of fish, a touch of the grippe? In the cold weather no one feels too well. But spring was on the way. A person could taste it in the wind. The larks were singing. The mud slopped and sucked at her heels. The ice in the river crackled like a fire.

"*Sholom aleikhem,*" Misha called to Hanna-Leah, who was leaving the butcher shop. "Where are you going so early on market day?"

Hanna-Leah stopped. "And why aren't you at your stall? Don't you have any poison to sell today?"

"It's Purim. I have presents to bring the children."

"Sure, why do you have to work? A woman alone has time for everything."

"How true. And a married woman has time for only one thing."

"And what's that?" Hanna-Leah asked.

"Complaining."

"Well, thank God she has someone to complain to instead of talking to the four walls," Hanna-Leah said. And having had the last word she continued on her way toward the woods, where she would soon meet the Traveler, while Misha, invigorated as usual by the exchange of a few good words with Hanna-Leah, went on to the bakery.

"A good day, a good hour, children," Misha said as she entered the bakery. Faygela's bare arms were sunk to the elbows in dough. The older girls were stoking the fire, and Berel waddled underfoot, thumb in mouth, his naked behind sticking out from his undershirt. "*Sholom aleikhem,*" they called.

"Come to me, Dina, so I can have a look at your hand," Misha said, seating herself on the bench, "but first let me check your neck."

"My neck?" the youngest girl asked. "But that's silly. I cut my hand."

"Is it silly? Come over here and let me see." Misha patted her knees, as Dina confidently climbed up. "*Hmm,*" Misha said. "There's something here, right in the corner, and on this side, too." The child twisted her neck, squealing as Misha began to tickle her, giggling and sliding around the huge lap, clinging to Misha's neck.

"Stop, stop," Dina said at last, hiccupping. "No more, Auntie Misha."

Misha rounded her mouth in astonishment. "You have a hiccup? Can this be?" she asked. Dina nodded solemnly. "Then there's only one thing to do. We have to cut off your nose," Misha said. Dina covered her nose with both hands, not quite sure if Misha was serious, but not yet ready to run away. "Well, if your nose is hidden, then I have no choice." Pausing for effect as she pursed her lips and tapped her chin with her finger, Misha added, "*Harrumph.* Then, well then, I just have to give you something for your mouth." She popped a piece of rock sugar into Dina's mouth.

"Me, me," insisted Berel, watching the proceedings with interest and pounding Misha's knees.

"Of course, you," Misha said, putting a piece of sugar in his mouth, too. "Now let me see this hand."

Carefully, Misha unwrapped the bandage. The cut ran jaggedly from Dina's wrist to the center of her palm. "You see," Misha said, as Faygela leaned forward, "it's rough and red, but it isn't hot. No swelling. Very good, Ruthie. You were right to put the onion on it." Faygela's oldest daughter flushed with pleasure. "Now, we'll just put something on it so it won't itch so much. Right, Dina?" Misha took a tin of plantain salve out of her basket. The little girl's pulse beat quickly under her hand as she smeared the cool ointment. "Now you can go and play. But no more trouble from you. Remember."

"Thank you," Faygela said. She wiped her eyes, remembering Dina's hand pouring blood, her sisters screaming while the little girl stood stock still.

"Don't say a word, it's nothing." Misha put the ointment back in her basket. "After all, I pulled out each one of your children. We're not putting even one back." Misha winked at Faygela. "And so you shouldn't think I've forgotten, children, I have *shaalakhmonas* for you. After all, it's Purim." From her basket, Misha pulled out packages of raisins and nuts, each in a bright square of cloth tied with new hair ribbons for the girls. "And is Ruthie coming with me today?"

"I need her here," Faygela said. "We have a lot of baking to do for Purim. It's too bad—she'd rather help you. Wouldn't you, Ruthie? But you know what they say. A girl can't do what she wants, only what she has to."

"It's true. It won't be long until she's a bride. She has to get used to it," Misha said. "They say a wedding canopy erases all of a man's sins. So? Then he has to get busy to make more. *Nu*, bride girl, do you have your eye on a man yet?"

Ruthie sputtered and blushed while Faygela said, "My Ruthie? So modest? She doesn't even look at a boy. Not like her next sister, who prays to be noticed. You," she said to Freydel, "get more wood. Make yourself useful. And the rest of you, too. What are you standing around for?" As they scattered, she turned again to Misha. "I have something for you," she said, sitting on the bench beside Misha, taking a small blue book from her pocket, the corners unraveling, the binding loose. "It's nothing special. An old book of mine. It's a nice story and easy. I think you're ready for it now. We'll look at it, together. After *Shabbas*. And don't forget to take the *hammantashen*."

"Forget? How could I? All year I look forward to them. No one makes a *hammantash* like you. Do you have prune and poppy seed for me?"

"And a new one, too. Almond."

"Maybe I should test one. To make sure that you haven't forgotten how to make them."

"Well, if we're going to have pastry, then we need some tea to go with it. Ruthie, get us some tea," Faygela called.

From the bakery, Misha went to bathe the arthritic fingers of Old Mirrel in warm wax. She passed the dairyhouse and asked after Emma and Izzie's health. She walked down to the peasants' cottages with a remedy for Agata's cramps. On the way back, sure that Berekh would be in the studyhouse, she stopped at his house with Purim treats for the children, who peeked at her from behind the skirts of the house-keeper, Maria. When a woman dies in childbirth, Misha thought, a stranger becomes mother to her children. If they're lucky, she's good to them. If not, there's no one to take them from the fire. "I see a pair of baby birds," Misha said. "Do little birds want *shaalakhmonas*? Or should I take this away."

"No, don't," the little girl, Rayzel, said, leaving Maria and taking a step toward Misha, her hands out for the treats. Her baby brother kept one fist wrapped in Maria's skirt, the other held out for his share.

So Misha gave them the bundles of nuts and raisins and left them. Could she do otherwise? She had no claim to them. She had rejected their father's offer and, anyway, he was nothing to her now.

It was only when she was already at home, preparing a fresh infu-sion of ergot for Shayna-Henya, who was near her time and prone to bleeding, that Misha was struck with her own stupidity.

The nauseous, penetrating smell of ergot rose from the glass jar as she poured boiling water over the buds. The odor reminded her not of the times she used ergot for other women to contract the uterus after labor, but of her own abortion.

OF THE FOUR *vilda hayas*, Faygela got her period first, and Misha next, although she was older. She knew what to expect. The girls talked, and she wasn't too ashamed to ask her mother. "If you're old enough to ask, you're old enough to know," her mother used to say. When she began to bleed, she was already a head taller than her mother. She had monthly cloths prepared, and after she fixed herself up, she went to find her mother in the cellar. It was summer. The cellar door was open, and she climbed down slowly, as befit her new dignity, moving from light into darkness. The smell of hay baking in the sun gave way to the smell of moist earth, and there was a moment of blindness until her eyes adjusted to the cellar dusk. Her mother wore a wide apron, embroidered with red thread, and in the muted light it seemed to float as her mother reached up to hang a basket. Strangely shy, Misha bent to lean her head on her mother's shoulder, and whispered, "Mama, I'm not a child anymore." Her mother didn't slap her face, as was the custom to keep away the Evil Eye. Instead Blema stroked Misha's hair. "May the Holy One be praised, that I lived until today," she said, her arm around her daughter's waist. "Now I have something to give you. Come, Misha," she said, taking her hand. When they came home to the room they'd shared for so long, Misha looked around curiously, wondering what there could possibly be in these four corners that she hadn't looked under and over and behind a hundred times. There was the table, and the bench, and the stove, the braids of garlic and onions and drying mushrooms, the shelves of dishes and cups and jars, the big cooking pot, and the clay bowls, the landscape her grandmother had embroidered with its elephants in blue-tassled cloths, the braided rag rug beside the bed she shared with her mother.

"Misha," her mother said, "you're sixteen years old and a woman now. I'm giving you the key to my grandmother Manya's trunk. Your father was refinishing it for a bridal trunk before he died, and I hope that you'll fill it with good things. Come, here, *shaynela,* and let me show you what's inside. It's not very much, just a few things for you to start with. So when I'm gone you remember what you need to." Her mother moved the brass candlesticks, the wooden bowl, and the red woolen shawl that had covered the trunk so long, Misha had forgotten that it was anything but a shelf or a bench.

Lifting the lid of the trunk, her mother took out a folded cloth. "This was my mother's," she said, "whom you were named for. She made it before I was born."

As she pulled back an edge of the cloth, Misha saw the carefully detailed stitching of leaves, flowers, and roots. "Tansy, hellebore, bryony, belladonna," Misha said with delight. "And this one?" She pointed to a bell-shaped rose-and-purple flower, the inside speckled with red dots.

"Foxglove," her mother said, unfurling the finely spun cloth so that it lay shimmering across the floor between them. "Very strong for the heart. Strong and dangerous, every one of these flowers." Her finger traced the delicate threads. "Your grandmother hung this cloth over my cradle when I was born. I did the same, and it protected you until you could walk. Now, it's time for you to come with me to the women, and I'm sure that you'll be strong enough to see what you have to see. Soon you'll know that when a woman is in labor, the midwife shakes hands with the Angel of Death."

Misha was silent as her mother folded the cloth and returned it to the trunk. She would be glad to go with her mother, she thought, she'd been waiting so long for it. "I'm not afraid, Mama," she said proudly.

Her mother put a cold hand over hers. "You will be," she said.

By the time her mother died three years later, Misha had seen many things. A pregnant woman who got the sugar sickness and wasted away as if she was dying of starvation. A woman who swelled up, nose bleeding, eyes blurred, convulsing. Another whose uterus came out during labor. A woman too tired to push anymore who bled to death. A baby who was strangled by the umbilical cord. Two babies, brothers, who were born live but a year later still couldn't sit up or lift their heads. The mother drowned herself. Misha tried not to think of them. She couldn't or how would she be able to laugh and joke and prepare the right remedies for the women who needed her and their children, too. But she swore that she would never go through it herself.

After her mother died and she was alone in the room they had shared, Misha said, "I don't need anyone else, Mama. My life belongs to me. Isn't that enough?" But she found that it wasn't so easy sitting alone at the table, turning around to say something to her mother and having to remind herself that there was no one there. So when the Old Rabbi himself approached her about marrying Hayim, she thought of his golden eyes and the strength of his hands when she danced with him at Hanna-Leah's wedding and she agreed.

Right after her own wedding, she'd known it was a mistake. There wasn't enough room in the little house for her herbs and jars and boiling pots and Hayim, too. He was always in her way, looking at her with those serious eyes of his, asking her over and over what he could do for her until she wanted to scream with impatience at his stammer, his drawings pinned to every wall so that she couldn't rest her eyes on anything but an image of herself. And just when she wanted to throw his buckets into the river, the gentleness of his touch would soften her and she would find herself forgetting everything except the heat of her body. Until the next day. Then she would walk around muttering to herself, "Idiot. Don't you know what time of month it is? Do you want to get pregnant like every other woman?" She would wait for her period in a panic, checking her underwear, wondering if she'd made a mistake about when it was due. She couldn't sleep. She was too hot. Hayim let her have the bed to herself.

When her period didn't come, she was almost relieved. So now it had happened. She would have a baby. Hayim would be very happy. She watched him stretch, his back stiff from sleeping on the floor. "You shouldn't be sleeping there," she said.

"It's, it's all right. You need room in the bed."

"No. You should sleep here with me."

He smiled. Hayim smiled so seldom and here he was smiling at her, his eyes crinkling, his hands reaching out to clasp hers, the fingers grayish from charcoal dust. "Very good, Misha."

But all day she could do nothing. She thought of everything that could go wrong and how she'd be as helpless as any other woman. Her heart pounded. She could hardly breathe. Finally she said to herself, Look you're not like other women. You know what to do. You can take care of it. And Hayim? He wants children so badly. A son to name after his father. What will he say? He won't know. Women lose their babies all the time. Let him divorce me. It would be better for him. He can marry someone else and have a dozen children.

Of course Hayim was angry. That was good. It would make it easier for her to do what she had to. She took enough tansy and ergot to abort a horse. The pain was worse than she'd expected, the unstoppable blood frightened her. Then Hayim's pity made her cry because he didn't know that she'd done it to herself, so sweet that she almost agreed to forget the divorce. But she refused to go through any of this again. He'd remarry, she assured herself. And she didn't need anyone. She preferred to be alone.

Yet when Berekh came to her after his wife died, more than enough time had passed for her to want to be with someone again. For his red beard curling in all directions and his walk like a restless horse and his clean hands that smelled of nothing but old books, she was ready to give up a piece of her solitude. And now look what had happened.

Misha sat down heavily, realizing that she had missed her period not once, but twice, and that her sickness was not any bad fish. Well, she knew what to do. There was nothing moving inside her, no quickening yet. She was just, let's say, irregular, and she could make herself regular again.

Soon, Misha had set aside some of the ergot for her own use, and the tansy tea was brewing while she sat with her elbows on the table between the jar of honey she used for making syrup and the bottle of vodka she used to preserve strong herbs. Resting her chin on her fists, Misha waited and thought. She had warned Ruthie about ergot. It's dangerous, she told the girl. It's not an herb, but a growth on the rye plant, and don't you touch it. Misha dropped her fists, upsetting a pile of roots. "You raised an idiot, Mama. How could I, of all people, not know that I was pregnant? The remedy is supposed to be taken two weeks after a woman misses her period, even four, but now?" She shook her head. "I waited too long. But what can I do? I'm not putting a wire inside myself. I'm not so desperate to die like that.

"When I was pregnant the first time, I was just a girl, only twenty years old. Having a baby would be more dangerous now—I'm thirty-six already. And a woman in labor is as helpless as a piece of wood in a fire." She poured the tea into her cup. "Even if nothing goes wrong, to have a baby alone in a place like Blaszka wouldn't be easy. Remember what happened to Manya. Well, that was a long time ago. And what if I bleed too much again? I could die for nothing."

She was still undecided when Hayim came in. Silently, he poured the water from his buckets into the barrel in the hallway. The tea was steaming in front of her, the ergot on the stove. She was so far away in thought, she hardly noticed him come to the table.

"Mazel tov, Misha," he said.

She was startled as if he'd materialized out of her reverie. If he knows, she thought, then the whole world must know, and my humiliation will begin. The entire village can watch Misha the midwife brought low, her belly growing willy-nilly before her without any say on her part. And Misha would have drunk the tea down right then, without any further thought, if she hadn't knocked it over in shock first.

"How did you find out? Does everybody in Blaszka know?" she asked.

Shaking his head, he picked up her cup from the floor.

"Who's talking? Tell me. How did you know?" Were they laughing behind her back? It was just too ridiculous, the Rabbi with her. For the moment she'd forgotten completely that there was a second possibility for the father, a large figure shrunk to a pinpoint and then locked away in the closet of her memory.

"Why, I, why," he stammered.

" 'Why not?' Is that an answer?"

"Shouldn't I know? I was, I was . . ."

"My husband? Only for eight months."

"Long enough. I see. In your eyes, I see it."

"My eyes? What's wrong with them? If you know, the whole world will be pointing fingers at me."

Hayim looked at her, his face unreadable. She could get nothing out of him. It was useless.

"It's not. Don't. Don't trouble yourself, Misha. I can't put two words together when I want to." He was wet, dripping on the braided rug, the water mixing with the spilled tea.

Maybe it's *beshert,* she thought. Maybe this was written. It could even be that my mother made me spill the tea. Hayim is a good man. I divorced him and he never remarried. What's a man without children? Maybe this is my payment. But before she could offer him a cup of hot tea and a chance to dry off by the fire, he was gone. It's Purim, she said to herself. Everything is upside down. And she rose to dress herself like a queen for the reading in the synagogue.

SEASON OF RAINS

"Haia-Etel's baby is coming early. That's not so good," Misha said. It was just before Passover. Drizzle hung like a string curtain across the houses of Blaszka as Misha and Ruthie walked arm in arm. Misha's red shawl covered her head and shoulders, falling across her belly in generous folds. Her dress was tied a little looser, but she wasn't showing noticeably yet.

"Don't be so serious, Ruthie. It won't help you, and it won't help Haia-Etel. Smell the good air. Take a deep breath. *Aah.*" Misha prodded Ruthie in the ribs until she inhaled noisily. "That's good. Again. Like the piggie sniffing at Alta-Fruma's turnips." Misha smiled as Ruthie giggled. "A girl in labor getting tired and maybe scared doesn't need to see a sour face," Misha said. "She needs a good laugh. A bright color, red is good." Misha fluttered her shawl at Ruthie's cheek. "Some light, so she doesn't think she's ready for the coffin already. It's good even to make her angry. Anything, so long as she has some spirit. Whisper something immodest in her ear. Make a joke about her husband's 'little thing' and don't be afraid to be crude. Call it a *shmeckel.* It gives her strength. Don't expect Haia-Etel to be like Gittel. She pops them out like a nut from a prune, but Gittel's had five already, all boys."

"I know," Ruthie said. "It's Haia-Etel's first."

"And she's young, too. I want you especially to see Haia-Etel because you're the same age," Misha said. "She just left her mother's house nine months ago. Now she's alone with a husband who is twenty years older than her, in a room behind the shop. Her Mendel means well, but he's too rough."

"At the wedding she looked like she was going to faint," Ruthie said.

"You listen to me, Ruthie. A girl should wait a few years after she starts to bleed before she gets married. Not before she's maybe eighteen. If she's too young, then . . ." Misha shook her head. "Often she loses the baby, or God forbid it isn't normal, or even worse. I knew of a girl who had a baby when she was thirteen. It was terrible."

"Thirteen? Really?"

"My mother attended her, and she told me herself what happened. The baby only had half a head. The top was completely open, and the girl couldn't walk afterward. So you listen to me, Ruthie, and don't get married too soon."

"I don't want to get married."

"Good, you're a little nervous, you should be. That's right in a girl."

"I'm not nervous. I just don't want to get married."

"And what do you think you're going to do?"

"I'll live alone. Like you."

Misha stopped. There was something in the girl's tone. It had gone suddenly quiet and trembly like the voice of a married woman who wanted a different man. "A girl like you to live alone?" Misha said firmly. "It's not to be thought of."

"But you do it."

"I'm not you, Ruthie. I'm used to being on my own. You always have someone to turn to, sisters, uncles, your mother and father"

"You don't know how it is to have a pack of sisters breathing down your neck," Ruthie protested. "It would be a nice change to sleep alone. I wouldn't be black and blue from being kicked in bed. I wouldn't lie awake listening to Leibela wheezing next to me. I could stretch without someone complaining. What a pleasure."

"All right, all right. But don't fool yourself. It's not always easy to live alone."

"What do I need a husband for? Men are hairy and ugly. Not my papa, of course, he's sweet, but then he's my papa."

"Tell me, Ruthie dear," Misha said, remembering the knot hole in the back of the bathhouse. "Aren't you even a little curious?"

"No," Ruthie said so forcefully that Misha was startled.

"When a woman lives alone, people are always ready to think the worst of her. Could you bear that? Remember what happened to Manya."

"Oh, that old story. It was a hundred years ago. And besides, she had a baby and no husband. I won't let a man come near me. What would I want from him? I'll tell you a secret," Ruthie said shyly. "I read in my grandfather's books about English women who traveled all over the world. Even to the islands of Japan. I like to sit on the silver rocks in the river with my eyes closed and dream that I'm on a ship going to Japan."

"And you're not lonely in this dream? Without any family, any home. Nobody knows if you're alive or dead."

"Who says I'm alone? I'll go with someone."

"Maybe one of your sisters?" Misha asked as if the dream were reality.

"Oh, not my sisters. Maybe a friend. There's nothing like a good friend who knows your every thought." Ruthie looked softly into the distance. "A friend who shares your soul," she said.

"You read too many stories," Misha replied. "I suppose this person is tall and mysterious. Maybe he has a wax mustache like a nobleman?"

"I said a friend, Misha. A woman like me."

Misha had met enough girls who weren't so keen on getting married. Why should they be? It was hard to leave sisters and friends, the home they knew and the father who indulged them for a strange house with a husband they maybe never saw before, a mother-in-law to pester the life out of them, the burden of pregnancy, and the danger of giving birth. But there was something different in the way Ruthie spoke. It wasn't just a matter of being afraid. She wasn't even curious. There was something else that made her eyes shine, a dream that contained no husband. Instead there was a friend. A girl. Or a woman. Misha noticed that the hand on her arm had tightened, and she recalled how lately, whenever she came into the bakery, Ruthie's fingers would quiver slightly as their hands touched across the loaf of bread. Now that she thought of it, she remembered how Ruthie colored, and sometimes she even stammered. A girl who was known for her cool head. And what about the last time Misha went to Faygela's house for *Shabbas* dinner? Ruthie helped her take off her boots. Misha was sitting, Ruthie kneeling in front of her, pulling. "Your foot is so cold," she said, "your poor, dear foot, let me rub it." Yes, and when she rose, Ruthie kissed her on the lips, as a daughter might kiss a mother, but the girl was breathing quick, ragged breaths. Then three of her sisters were pulling her to the table, scolding her for forgetting the braided loaves that were pouring black smoke from the oven.

If I was a man, Misha thought, the mother would either be thinking of a matchmaker or would be slapping her daughter for shaming her. But people see what they want to see, and not something different. The girl herself seemed to be unconscious of her feelings. And why should she be? A good girl, a responsible girl, maybe with a few dreams that no one knew. Completely normal. Misha tapped the roof of her mouth with her tongue. It was Esther, she remembered, Faygela's own aunt, who left Blaszka for Warsaw, where she found a new flat on Nalewki Street, and there she lived with her second cousin, also a spinster, to the end of her days. Women left sitting, people said. They felt sorry for them. But Misha heard, well, what she heard she never told anyone. But they were content. She would have to be careful with Ruthie. A young girl is sensitive.

"Doesn't Emma always say that women don't need to get married?" Misha asked.

"Yes, exactly. I told my mother. And she said I shouldn't let Emma influence me with her American ideas."

"Well, child, you know I'm older than you. I have more experience, but," Misha sighed, "I'm no company for a young girl."

"No, that isn't true. I like to help you. I feel useful." Ruthie squeezed Misha's arm, hugging it close.

Oy vey, Misha thought. "Useful, of course useful. A young girl with energy is always useful to a tired woman."

"You don't look tired," Ruthie said.

Misha drooped her shoulders, walking slowly like Old Mirrel, the girls' teacher. "Some days, I'm telling you the truth, I feel older than Moses our Teacher. And when I look at you, what do I see?" She pinched Ruthie's cheek between two toughened knuckles. "I see a sweet little baby, making such a pee, like the Sea of Galilee. I look at you and I remember a squirming, red worm wriggling out from her mother, with wrinkled skin and a mouth full of mucus. You'll see how it is with Haia-Etel."

Ruthie pulled her hand away, fluffing like a ruffled hen. After a moment's silence, she said, "So, tell me. What should I get ready for you at Haia-Etel's."

It was then that Misha felt it. The quivers in her belly, like a burst of minnows, like moths beating their wings at a lamp: it was the quickening. She really was pregnant. She caught her breath. Misha the midwife, nervous? And why shouldn't she be? she thought. Her life was no longer her own. Is a person who gets drafted happy? But what disturbed her was the excitement, that her hands, knowing and capable, intertwined over her belly as if to welcome the mystery. And that it suddenly seemed to her that she might give up anything to keep her child safe.

HAIA-ETEL lay between the coils of rope on one side of her bed, and the stacks of corsets on the other. Sitting in a chair in the corner, below the shuttered window, her mother-in-law was speaking in a hoarse, grating voice, "My patience is at an end, I tell you. When a girl is young, she's useless. How many hours has she been lying there? Mendel's first wife, may she rest in peace, pushed them out in no time, one after another. Such a pity they were all girls. But this one, if she has a boy, he'll be tired of life before he gets out." The room had an oily smell from the barrels of kerosene pushed into the corner with no care for the candle dripping on the nearby table. Ruthie prepared two washtubs on the table, one filled with cold water, the other with hot. The mother-in-law was knitting. "Not for the new baby," she said, "God forbid I should call down the Evil Eye before it gets here. Of course, what can I do if this one," she pointed with the knitting needles, yellow wool hanging from them, "is too clumsy to make her own baby clothes. And lazy? Let me tell you. I stood up from each of my ten children one hour after they came out. But her? I have to get after her every minute. She wants to lie in bed like a queen."

While her mother-in-law was talking, Haia-Etel was holding onto a rope that had been tied to each of the bedposts, pulling and panting with each contraction. She had been in labor for nineteen hours. "I opened the shutters yesterday," Misha said to Ruthie in a low voice, "but you see, the old woman closed them after I left last night. She was afraid the demon Lilith would come to steal the baby. You see the amulet hanging over the bed? It helps like putting leeches on a corpse. Open the shutters and take the mother-in-law into the front room. Try on a corset. Ask her advice. Just keep her away."

After speaking calmly to Haia-Etel and giving her some water to drink, Misha told her that she was going to check the baby's position. She reached between her legs, putting two fingers inside to touch the baby's head. "It's good," she said to Haia-Etel, "the baby's facing down. It won't be too long."

Misha looked at her fate. The haggard face, the smell of sweat, the skin swollen and tense, striated with dark stretch marks, the look of panic alternating with vacancy. It was the look of a horse, not a human being. Misha had attended these things countless times, always with pity, knowing that she herself would never be so helpless. Well, soon enough she'd be the one begging for the labor to end. Misha felt a wave of disgust rise up and threaten to smother the life from her, like the hand of God, like the contraction driving Haia-Etel's fist into her mouth.

Haia-Etel was completely open, but the membrane, unbroken, hung out of her like a balloon. Misha would have to break it. Mechanically, she heated the end of a needle in the candle, waiting until it cooled before she reached carefully into Haia-Etel and broke the membrane. Out shot a gush of warm, colorless half-jelly. As the contractions strengthened, Haia-Etel gasped. Then she leaned over and threw up. "I want to go home to my mother," she moaned. "I'm so tired."

Misha had to get the girl out of her lethargy. Lying there flat on her back wasn't helping. She would need to push hard to move the baby down. "Get out of bed," Misha said harshly. The girl looked at Misha confusedly. "I mean it, Haia-Etel. Right now." As the girl attempted feebly to sit up, Misha put a strong arm behind her back, and swung her legs over the bed. "Kneel on this," she said, throwing a pile of corsets under Haia-Etel's feet, holding tight to the girl's shoulders as she lowered herself, her huge, taut belly unbalancing her. "Now put your hands forward, on the floor."

"What are you telling me? Am I a dog to stand on all fours?" asked Haia-Etel, sitting back on her heels, and looking up at Misha. Angry is good, Misha thought. No more begging, only anger.

"You? No. But your mother-in-law, *ahhooh!*" Misha lifted her head and howled. The girl laughed and gasped. "Now put your head down, chin against your chest. Good girl." Misha rubbed her back firmly, feeling each bone under the yellowish skin, the muscles ridged like ropes. Haia-Etel was pushing in a ferocious, helpless grip of energy. Misha rubbed, Haia-Etel pushed, looking down between her open legs. "I see him," she cried. "I see him."

"Don't breathe so hard or you'll tear yourself," Misha said. "Little breaths, Haia-Etel."

The girl's breathing was uneven, ragged, her eyes open wide as the baby squeezed out of her. It was tiny. It was blue. Misha's throat tightened as if this was her own. But if she were Haia-Etel, she wouldn't know that the small ones often don't live.

Holding the wet, twisted cord, Misha waited until the pulsating stopped before she tied the cord in two places, cutting in between, half a hand's length from the baby. The child was still not breathing. Not even after the second smack.

Quickly, Misha put the baby first in the cold tub, then the hot, then cold and hot, again and again, while Haia-Etel cried, "Where is he? Give him to me! He isn't yours. Misha, I want my baby." Again the water, hot, cold, hot, cold, until there was a mournful wail. "Good," Misha said, "Very good. Cry little one. Cry." She rocked the baby in her arms, massaging the temples with lemon, ignoring Haia-Etel's outstretched arms. Only when it was breathing steadily with tiny, intermittent shuddering sobs, did she give it to Haia-Etel.

"A girl, Haia-Etel," Misha said.

"Not a boy? Then, I'll name her after my grandmother, won't I, *shaynela,*" said Haia-Etel. She kissed the baby's hands.

"It's not finished yet," Misha said. The words were hardly out of her mouth when Haia-Etel's face twisted with the surprise of another contraction, and the placenta came out. Misha dropped it carefully into a pan. "Your mother-in-law will want to bury it so that you'll have a boy next time. Now it's over, Haia-Etel. But don't close your eyes yet. I want you to drink this," Misha said, giving her a decoction of ergot to contract the uterine muscles. "We're not going to have any bleeding from little Haia-Etel. You have too many more years to make yourself some sons."

Afterward, as Ruthie walked back with her, Misha said, "So you're going to play a little, Ruthie, and not spend all your time working with me when you're not in the bakery?"

"But I like helping you and I have so much to learn."

"Yes, of course. But what's the rush? Don't you have anything to do with your friends?"

"Well, I have been helping Emma with something."

"What is it?"

"Oh, just something."

Very good, Misha thought. A something that Ruthie doesn't want to tell me about. That's how it should be for a girl who's talking to her mother's friend. "You know what, Ruthie? I'm invited to Alta-Fruma's house for *Shabbas,* but I'm feeling a little tired. You go in my place. You can take the strengthening tonic for Izzie, and tell Emma that I asked after her. Her mother would have liked me to keep an eye on her, but what does a woman my age have to say to a young girl like her? So you watch out for her in my place. All right?"

Ruthie nodded contentedly.

THREE WEEKS later, on the second Sabbath in May, Faygela was in Warsaw, Ruthie was sitting with her sisters in the synagogue, and Misha was in the back listening to the women's whispers.

Look at Misha, isn't she showing? Yes, I think she is. No, it couldn't be. And why not? You see how calm she is.

"So? That's Misha," Hanna-Leah said. "Her feet stick in the mud like everyone else's, but she laughs at everything, even the Evil One himself. I tell you she won't be so cocky when the baby comes without a name."

Lifting her head even higher, Misha thrust the ends of her shawl to each side of her belly so that nothing should obstruct the women's view of it. When they turned back to stare at her, she met their eyes directly, nodding as if to say, "Good Sabbath."

The women faced forward in a hurry. Misha thinks she knows everything and she can do anything, they said. Well, she'll find out soon enough. A woman alone is nothing. And in her condition, even less. Wait until she can hardly walk and she can't feel her feet anymore. Who's going to do something for her then? Not me. Let my daughters learn a lesson from this. They should see what it means for a woman to be alone. You hear the *zogerin?*

"Give me the strength to turn away from the sinful people that walk

in hidden ways, pulled by their lusts." The *zogerin* was standing, eyes closed, silver prayerbook clasped against her Sabbath pearls as she prayed aloud for the women.

If Faygela was here, Misha thought, she'd have something smart to say to them. Look at Ruthie. Her sisters are pointing fingers at me and she pushes their hands down. She's a good girl. But she looks worried. I'll tell her there's nothing to worry about. No, I should leave her alone. She shouldn't be helping me. Not now. It's all right for me. I don't care what people say. But she's young. Let her keep company with her sisters and Zisa-Sara's girl, Emma. So no one will come to visit me on *Shabbas?* Don't I need a rest?

But for the first time, Misha felt lonely. Even Berekh was avoiding her. Just because she'd thrown him out a few months ago. If he gave up so easily, she couldn't be very important to him, could she? That very morning when Misha had passed him in the synagogue courtyard, she'd glared at him. Just say one word to me, she dared with her eyes, and I'll take your head off your neck like an old scrawny rooster for boiling.

As far as she was concerned, there was no father. It was nothing to think about. The baby was hers and only hers. But in the blackness of night, when she saw herself alone in her house above the river, she felt a terrible dizziness, as if she lived in the house of *Baba Yaga* the witch, with its gaping mouth for a door, and its spinning chicken legs for stilts. It seemed to fly above the village in a wild and solitary spin, while below, Blaszka slept peacefully, each house linked inextricably to its neighbors.

When Misha left the synagogue, she walked with her head high, alone, to her little house above the river.

Two weeks later Ruthie was arrested.

THE LONG DAYS

The day after Ruthie's arrest, Misha sat at her table, grinding a mixture of roots and bark. She didn't like the smell. Why didn't she like the smell? Who knew? These days something she'd always liked could make her sick and something she'd never liked could be exactly what she had a craving for. But why should she complain? "Don't I have enough customers, Mama? Everything's the same. So I'm a little bigger. It's nothing." All right, so she had to pee all the time. The veins in her legs were swollen. Her nipples were so tender she could hardly stand to cover herself. Her nose bled when she said hello. She was itchy between her legs. But thank God, the village never changed. Hanna-Leah came once a month for her potion. Leybush got a black alder wash for his lice. Boryna's Agata came to her for advice about her female troubles. Ettie got her fennel tea for morning sickness. Haykel the blacksmith dropped a burning rod on his foot. Yosele was born with no trouble, and Gittel's sister, Naomi, boasted that she had six sons now.

So why did Misha wake up at night and wish that her mother was with her? Why did she lie in bed with her eyes wide open, worrying that she wouldn't have enough milk? Wondering if she would survive the delivery? If the baby would be born alive? If she carried a monster inside herself?

Everything was normal. Except that she was five months pregnant. Ruthie was sitting in prison and Faygela was coming home from Warsaw today. What was Misha going to say to Faygela—that she had pushed Ruthie to spend more time with Emma? And now she had to pee. Again. Though she'd just been to the outhouse. All right, she'd use the chamber pot this time. She'd just finished and was standing up, lowering her dress when she heard the knock at her door. "Who is it?" she called a little nervously.

"Berekh Eisenbaum," he answered, as if there were a dozen Berekh's in Blaszka.

"So what are you waiting for? An invitation from the Messiah? Come in already," she snapped.

Misha was not pleased about her suddenly rapid breath, the quick flush of her throat, or the tingle in her lower regions, which had no business provoking her when she was fully occupied in producing a baby. Is it his? she thought, let it be his. You're a woman alone, she scolded herself. You remember your pleasure with him? What for? It's finished. There's no reason to think of him. Not any more than in remembering the other one.

To steady herself, Misha picked up her chamber pot and opened the back door to empty it. There was nothing like the sharp smell of pee to bring a person back to earth. What right did he have to come to her house after so long? She would throw him out so fast his head would spin, she reassured herself. But when she saw him, her resolve weakened. "*Sholom aleikhem*, Rabbi," she said huskily. Maybe he would apologize, yes, and plea for her forgiveness.

"I need your advice, Misha," he said. He spoke like a stranger. Politely, inquiringly, impersonally.

Not even, Misha, are you well? she thought. "So you need me? I should be so honored. You don't talk to me for months, but when you need advice, then you remember Misha."

"I wouldn't bother you if I had another choice," he said. "I didn't know what else to do. I've gone over the problem again and again in my mind, but nothing moves. I'm completely stuck."

"Well, Misha is not an enema. If your hole is closed, go to the *feldsher*. Now get out."

The politeness peeled away like birch bark as his face twisted. "I thought you didn't want me to come here anymore."

"You thought. The great Rabbi thinks, of course. Asking? No. Why should he ask? He knows everything."

"But you threw me out," he said. "You told me a man is worse than a hyena that eats dead flesh."

"So I was a little excited. Why shouldn't I be?" she said, agitated. "You think an angel put this here?"

"I didn't know, Misha. I swear it. Not until a week ago. Please believe me." His voice choked. She felt a small glow of satisfaction.

"Maybe. I'll think about it," she said. If he begged her forgiveness, she would forget everything. She waited, but he didn't. He couldn't. And Misha's irritation rose up, as bitter as bile. "Maybe it's not even yours," she said. "Are you surprised?"

He took her hand, stroking it slowly and tenderly. "It doesn't matter. I'll make things right. Don't worry, Misha, please. The child will have a name. We can get married right after *Shavuos*."

This was unexpected. Certainly he had asked her to marry him many times, but now, when everyone knew that she was carrying, and she couldn't even promise that it was his? Misha pretended to busy herself among her herbs. Maybe she should. Why not? Is it so good for a woman to be alone? She was tired. She had even found herself crying on occasion. But to belong to a man? To have no rights apart from his say so? To be his irrevocably unless he was willing to grant her a divorce? And there would be more children. Each one a possibility of killing her. No, she wouldn't do it. She wouldn't give herself over to anyone. "You're a singer with one song," she said harshly. "And the song has one verse. You want some advice? Find an old graybeard and ask him when the Messiah is coming."

She held the door open, but Berekh didn't move. "Would you like a cup of tea?" he asked.

She was very thirsty for a cup of tea. "Maybe," she said, "but it's not so easy to bend down already. I don't want to light the stove."

"Never mind," Berekh said. "I'll do it."

She sat down heavily. It was too much. That he would light a fire for her, this man who flinched when she struck a match to light a candle. She had no more strength.

"Well, well. Maybe the Messiah is on his way already." She smiled slightly. "A cup of tea would be nice." While he fussed around the *pripichek* she polished a stone she had picked up from the river bed. It was three-cornered like Haman's hat, flat, banded red and cream. As the stone smoothed under her hands, she watched Berekh kindle the fire and then make the tea. When he brought it to her, the tea sloshing over the side of the cup in his shaking hands, she said, "Maybe there's still something to you, Berekh Eisenbaum." It was a good cup of tea. "So tell me."

"It's about Ruthie. You know how it is with these things."

She nodded, though she wasn't certain.

"What does the Governor of Plotsk care about one young Jewish girl? She can't send him back to St. Petersburg, and she can't harm his career, either. She's nothing to him. If he receives a bribe, of course, it's a different story. It makes his life more pleasant. But this new Governor is very unhappy about his posting. He was expecting a promotion, and instead he was sent to the far provinces. They say that his price is unreachable. No one in Blaszka has that kind of wealth. We need to persuade him to lower his price. I know, it's a small chance," he took her hand again, "but people come to you. They talk to you. From Blaszka, from Plotsk, even farther. I thought you might have heard something that would be important to the Governor."

"The Governor?" Misha put a piece of sugar in her mouth and sipped the tea. "Yes, I heard something." So there was still something she could do for Ruthie. The sugar melted in the good, strong tea. Her spirits lifted. "You just go to Plotsk and tell the Governor that we'll send him a gift with the good wishes of his friend from Minsk."

"That's all? Nothing more?" He looked at her with the eager curiosity that had so often made her laugh but say nothing. He always wanted her to give away her secrets. She wasn't going to. Why should she, now, when she never had before? She was still angry that she had even considered a wedding canopy, and this was women's business anyway. Hers and Faygela's. Still, the tea was good, and she noticed a red mark on the back of his hand where he'd burned himself. "You just go to the Governor with the message about his friend from Minsk," she said. "Find out his price. You do that for me and I'll tell you the whole story."

"Yes, yes," he said, like a little boy with a handful of chocolates.

"But I'm not going to say anything more about it yet," she said. His face fell. Drawing closer to him, she added, "One day, I'll tell you everything. I promise."

They sat quietly, without speaking, looking at their own reflection in each other's eyes, Misha's eyes of night and Berekh's blue as the day.

As MAY gave way to June and Misha was in her sixth month, Ruthie was still in prison. Berekh had tried to see the Governor, with no luck. Faygela hadn't spoken to Misha since Ruthie's arrest.

Of course, Faygela won't have anything to do with Misha now, people said. You see, a mother should be more careful about who she lets her daughter associate with. Especially these days when there are all kinds of people spouting dangerous nonsense. Someone says you have to be a Russian, someone else a loyal Pole, a third says you should join the workers, a fourth that you should go to the Holy Land, and they're all ready to beat you up for being a plain Jew. From one day to the next, you don't know where you stand. A young girl is vulnerable, she can be caught up in any kind of enthusiasm. This is what comes from Ruthie being friends with a girl like Emma and assisting the midwife. Look there, you can see Misha's morals growing right in front of her.

In the synagogue on *Shabbas,* Faygela didn't say a word to Misha, but brushed past her, leading her four remaining daughters and holding her little son by the hand as if he might disappear.

After the May rains, June was unusually warm and dry. In the second week of June, Misha went down to the river to cool off, tying the hem of her dress above her belly as she waded into the water. The cold rush against her legs was pleasant in the furious sun, the river broad and open, though she couldn't be seen unless someone stood right on the embankment and looked down. She was feeling better these days. She didn't itch, she didn't bleed. Plantain seeds, slippery elm, you just had to know what to do. An hour in the dark, cool cellar with its good smells of leaves and roots, and she was a new person. Inside her, the baby was frolicking like a litter of puppies. She thought about names, but never said them aloud. Instead, she called the baby *Alter,* Old One, to fool the Evil Eye. "Can you smell the locust blossoms, *Alter*?" she asked, taking a deep breath of air. "Listen. That's the train from Warsaw whistling." The baby hit the side of her stomach. "You heard it, I know you did, you little *pisher.*" At the edge of the water, blue dragonflies hovered above the reeds.

Sometimes she could see a foot or a knee push out her skin. It looked to her like a terrible growth. A shame on you, Misha, she said to herself. What kind of mother has these ideas? Patting the baby, she sang, *"You make the girl a bride, And lead her to the sacrifice You bind her eyes, And then her courage dies, da-da-dum."* As she sang the old song, the baby danced, and Misha swayed from side to side, buoyed by the river.

Coming toward her from the direction of the wood was the large figure of a woman. As Misha squinted against the sun, shading her eyes, she saw a wild halo of pale hair. For a moment she thought it was her great-grandmother Manya coming up the water toward her. Is it a sign? Misha wondered. The rains had been unusually heavy, and now the sun was very hot. Strange things were happening in the world. Could it be a message from the other side? Heat swelled from the river's surface. The woods wavered. A raven cawed. The still air parted for a sudden slice of wind, bringing the scent of wild roses. The figure neared. Her vague outline came into focus, and Misha nearly lost her footing. It was not Manya, coming from the other world, but even more strangely, it was Hanna-Leah, swinging her kerchief in her hand, her wet dress clinging to her, her face turned up to the sun, her hair windblown and shining like thick twists of barley. The two women came face to face, the noise of the village square far away.

Hanna-Leah smiled, then frowned, then smiled again, unable to contain herself. "Everybody knows," she began conversationally, as if they were standing in the village square, "that Faygela isn't talking to you."

"Is it your business?" Misha asked, ready to do battle even in the middle of the river.

"It's a shame, the four *vilda hayas,* one is gone from us, the other three don't speak."

This wasn't the Hanna-Leah that she knew, her voice mild, smiling as if she didn't have a care in the world. When did this happen?

"And I don't want any more remedies," Hanna-Leah added. "I just wanted to tell you. If I don't come next month, it's not that I'm aggravated with you." Hanna-Leah hesitated as if there was something more. "I think you should know that Hayim has been cutting wood for you."

"Hayim? Impossible."

"It's true. Of course you might not notice, you have something else to think about," Hanna-Leah said.

Ah, here it comes, Misha thought. Wait until she hears what I have to say to her.

"I just thought you should know," Hanna-Leah said. So that was it. No digs, no sarcasm, nothing that Misha could answer to. Hanna-Leah just turned around and walked down the river away from Misha, the water swishing around her dress bulging and bubbling behind her.

So how could I not know? Misha asked herself as she watched Hanna-Leah go. Where did you think the woodpile came from? She hadn't paid attention, that was all there was to it. The woodpile lowered and filled, and if she had noticed at all, it was a passing thought that one of the peasants from the cottages downriver must have left some wood for her. She'd always known everything that happened in the village. What was wrong with her that she didn't know things that other people knew? she asked herself as she went home.

She was tired. She got tired easily these days. She needed to lie down, but first she had to rub her sore back a little. Kneading her back, she looked around the room at the infusions and tinctures she'd prepared to replace the jars that had broken on the short Friday, at the piece of red amber she'd found on her doorstep, at the bridal trunk that had once belonged to Great-grandmother Manya.

Manya had two girls, the story went, and it was the older one who took care of the younger after Manya died. There was no father in the story. Did Manya know who it was? Did her bed ever shake while she tossed and turned in the night, wondering? Did she throw up over and over until she thought she might throw up her own baby growing in her? She couldn't have, Misha thought. She wouldn't wish, even for a moment, that if the baby was that man's, the stranger, it would wash out of her body. She wouldn't worry that she would see him in the child, and maybe hate it. Not Manya. What did they say about her? She was bigger than any man and thought she was twice as smart. Misha fell into a restless sleep, waking up just as the light was softening to a buttery glow among the trees. Still groggy, she sat at her table, drinking a cup of tea. Opening the book that Faygela had given her, she picked out a few words, then threw it down, knocking a pile of herbs onto the floor. What did she need to read for? Was she a scholar?

Someone's coming, Misha thought. She turned and began to rise from her stool. She'd heard Faygela's quick, light tread on her steps. But when she opened the door no one was there.

So Faygela didn't come to her with *The Israelite* anymore. It was better to be alone and not be bothered.

ON MARKET DAY Misha folded up her stall early, so she didn't hear the women saying, Where's Misha? Did she go home already? I didn't get the syrup for my mother's cough. I'll have to go to her house now. No, don't bother Misha. She has to rest. What if something happens to her? Who's going to bring our babies safely into the world?

IN THE third week of June, Berekh told Misha that he'd seen the Governor, who wanted a letter to prove that Ruthie's case was of interest to the *friend from Minsk*. "I'll ask Faygela to write the letter tomorrow," Misha said. She was sitting at her table, measuring vodka and adding it to a tincture of nightshade. Berekh perched on the stool opposite.

"Faygela? What about me? I'll do it. Just tell me what to say."

"No. Leave the letter to me." It would give her a reason to talk to Faygela. A good reason.

"And the money?" Berekh asked. The price for Ruthie's release had gone down, but it was still more than anyone had.

"That I don't know. We'll have to wait and see."

The next day, in the bakery, Misha stood with her hands gripping the small of her back. "Faygela, you have every reason to be angry, but listen to me. Your cousin Berekh already spoke with the Governor. He's ready to lower the price for Ruthie's release. All you have to do is write a letter, and I promise you that Ruthie will come home."

"That's all is it? After I trusted you to watch out for my girls . . ." So Faygela, who had not looked Misha in the eye or said a word to her since Ruthie's arrest, now had plenty to say. Misha looked out on the village square. The colors were too bright in the strong sun. Even the horse dung shone golden while Peysekh-Hersh, the Hebrew teacher, sang as he swept it away. Misha winced, the baby kicking, heels and elbows jabbing her everywhere, as if the child were a dozen.

"You think I don't know what it is to be afraid for your child?" Misha asked, putting her two large hands over her belly protectively.

"You think you know so much just because you have something in the oven?" Faygela flashed. "Any stupid girl can do that. You bring a few up, then you come and talk to me."

"When did I ever lead you the wrong way?" Misha asked.

"You lead me? A fine story. The watercarrier is suddenly a rabbi."

"Faygela, don't talk nonsense. Just do what I'm telling you. I know what's what."

"What do you know?" Faygela looked now at Misha, her eyes full of anger, her voice scornful. "A grown woman, who knows 'what's what' can let this happen?" She nodded at Misha's stomach. "I told my girls to look up to you. A fine thing. Now my oldest, my first, is sitting in prison. And what I saw there? It's enough to make your skin crawl."

"I promise you, Faygela. Write the letter. Ruthie will come home."

"Promises, promises. Everyone has something to say. You'll forget your foolishness after you're married, Faygela. Your baby won't die, Faygela. But you were different. You never told a lie. I thought you weren't like other women."

"So, you were wrong," Misha said. "I'm just the same."

"And look at you." Faygela's voice cracked with disdain. "The big woman who can fix everything. Like a queen, I told my girls. But now I see she's the servant girl who gets caught with her legs open, and thinks the father will make her a princess. I'm fed up. I don't want to talk anymore."She stood up and turned her back on Misha. Then she sat down and shook her finger. "Just let me tell you . . ."

And tell she did. She stood up. She sat down. She pointed. She shouted. And she looked at Misha, how she looked, as if her eyes were bayonets. I'm going to shake her until her teeth fall out, Misha thought. But at last, the letter was written exactly as she dictated it. "To our esteemed and honored Alexi Tretyakov, Governor of Plotsk, from the community council of Blaszka, a gift in appreciation. May you be healthy and live a long life, and may no trouble come to you from foolish people who might bear a grudge. May Heaven bless your daughter's wedding, and may no person, not even from Minsk, not even a count's son, come to disturb your happiness on this occasion."

"And now what am I supposed to do with this precious letter?" Faygela asked. "No one has enough money to bribe the Governor. Not even the whole village put together. I have two rubles in an old sock. You think that's enough?"

"We'll see," Misha said. "The Governor changed his price once already. Maybe he'll decide a few rubles are better than none."

"Maybe, maybe. It's as good as a promise." But Faygela's voice wasn't quite so harsh, and she was at least looking Misha in the eye.

After she went home, Misha prepared something for Izzie, who was suffering from the hot sun. With the salve in her basket, she climbed down the stairs carefully. The village was quiet, getting ready for market day on Friday, and Misha saw no one as she walked to Alta-Fruma's. Not Hanna-Leah, who was picking strawberries in a clearing in the woods, and not Hershel, who was on his way back from Plotsk after his little talk with Yarush.

In the dairyhouse, Alta-Fruma was checking the milk, Hayim repairing a bench. Misha nodded to Hayim. He nodded back. If the baby had been his, it would have been named Ari after his father. Misha turned away. "I have something for Izzie's rash," she said to Alta-Fruma.

"Good, good. But come out with me. I want to talk to you."

Alta-Fruma took her arm as they walked along the river bank. "You're feeling all right, Misha?"

"Not too bad."

"The strawberries are ripe. I'll send Emma to you with a basket."

"I'm not making any jam, but fresh strawberries would be nice." They walked a little farther in silence, no sound but their boots in the grass, the rippling of the water, the lowing of a cow. "So?" Misha asked.

"It's my fault that Ruthie's in jail," Alta-Fruma said.

"You?" Misha asked in surprise.

"I'll tell you the truth. If I wasn't so stubborn myself, then Emma wouldn't always be running off looking for trouble. And where she goes, Ruthie follows."

"No," Misha said. "You're good to her. Better than a stranger. Sometimes a girl has to go wild. Don't you remember?"

Alta-Fruma paused as if she were indeed remembering something, but now they had come to the edge of the woods. Misha blinked in the sudden gloom as they passed from the sun bouncing off the river to the quiet, greenish shade. "Tell me," Alta-Fruma said. "I heard the Rabbi went to talk to the Governor. Is it true?"

"Yes. He came back from Plotsk yesterday."

"And?"

"The Governor will let Ruthie go if he gets a bribe, but there isn't enough money in all of Blaszka to meet his price. Who has more than a couple of rubles?" Misha asked.

"I have a little something. I want you to take this for me." Alta-Fruma held out a pouch. Misha gave it a squeeze. Coins. She looked inside. It was full of gold imperials.

"What's this?" Misha asked.

"You don't have eyes? It's money. Good money. Not like the paper rubles you can't do anything with except to wipe your behind."

"Of course I see it's money. But where did you get it?"

"Never mind. It's not important. Just take it to Faygela. Only don't tell her I gave it to you. It's nobody's business. I know I can trust you to keep things to yourself, just like I trusted your mother," Alta-Fruma said.

"But it's crazy. Where do you come by such a thing? You must be a witch."

The older woman chuckled. Misha's baby kicked as if it were laughing, too, the black cow mooed, the calf lowing as Alta-Fruma said, "Misha, the plain truth is that the dairy makes a good business."

So who knew? Misha took the pouch with promises of silence and the old woman's blessings to Faygela's house.

SIPPING A glass of water and picking at the honey cake, Misha sat across from Faygela at her grandmother's mahogany table, while Faygela fingered the gold coins. "It's a miracle," she said. "Where did you get it?"

"I told you not to ask me. It's not any of my doing, that's all I can tell you."

The two friends looked at each other awkwardly, Faygela's earlier accusations hanging in the air between them like a curtain of rain. "Maybe before *Shabbas,* I could come and read *The Israelite* to you?"Faygela asked.

"That would be very nice," Misha said. "But you don't need to go to any trouble."

"No, it's nothing. If you still have the book I gave you, maybe we can have a look at it together." They glanced at each other and away, Misha solemn, Faygela grave, Misha as big as two women, Faygela as small as half a one, both with folded hands and thumbs twirling.

"You know, later it won't be so easy for you to run up and down the stairs all the time. You just tell me what you need and I'll send one of my girls to you," Faygela said.

"What I need?" Misha asked. Faygela nodded. "What I need," Misha repeated, "is a man to have the baby for me." Then she laughed, her gold tooth shining in the bright light of the summer solstice, while Faygela threw up her hands, saying, "You're impossible. Thank God in Heaven."

WHILE SHMUEL harnessed his horse to the cart, the gold and the letter safe in his pocket, Misha was back at home, sitting on the steps, looking at the river with the uncomfortable feeling that everything was changing. Hanna-Leah smiling, Hayim cutting her wood, Alta-

Fruma with gold, even the baby inside her. All that Misha thought she knew seemed to be leaking out of her, leaving her uncertain and ordinary in a place that was growing more unpredictable by the minute.

"Walk with me?" Berekh asked, standing on the bottom step, and smiling up at Misha. A sack was slung over his shoulder.

"Isn't it late?"

"Not today," he said, "just look at the sky." Leaning on her arms, she titled back her head. The sky had not a trace of pink. It was a day without end, as if the sun enjoyed herself too much to give way to the moon, and night would never have her turn.

"Everyone will talk," Misha said.

"So let them have a little pleasure."

They strolled along the riverbank where it wound through the dappled woods, Misha's left hand on Berekh's arm, her right hand on her belly. Poplar leaves shimmered white and oak leaves caught the sun between their horns. A woodpecker tapped for grubs in a scabrous beech tree. Misha heard laughter and distant voices, but they met no one."Do you see anything?" she asked Berekh.

"I see you," he answered.

"Something else?"

"What else should I see?"

"Nothing," she answered. He whistled happily, while Misha continued to watch the shadows and lights flicker among the trees. This is what happens when a woman is carrying a baby, she said to herself. It grows inside her without any thought or doing of hers, and she loses her mind. When she's asleep she dreams that her baby is born with four arms. When she's awake she sees ghosts. Gazing with interest, Misha noted how the shadows seemed to take the form of women. And why not, she thought. Wouldn't her mother be looking out for her now? Wouldn't all the mothers in heaven walk in the woods of Blaszka to watch their own in the unearthly light of the summer solstice? *Allevai,* she thought. Let it be so.

Berekh whistled as if he saw and heard nothing, picking up a lithe branch and swishing it in the air like a boy thrilled with the pleasure of sound. "You're sure you don't see anything?" she asked.

He peered to the left, he peered to the right. "No wolves. No bears." He squeezed her hand. "Maybe a girl and a boy holding hands down there, where the river bends to the left. But you must be getting tired, Misha. Sit here with me." From his sack, he brought out a blanket, spreading it over the pine needles, and a pillow for Misha, which he propped against the smooth trunk of a beech tree. After he helped her down, he took a bottle and a glass out of his pockets. "Wine for you, to give you strength," he said. They drank companionably. The wine was thick and sweet and dark as the purple shadows under the trees.

"Now, I'll tell you," Misha said.

"What?"

"You forgot already? About the Governor's friend in Minsk."

"Really? You don't have to," he said, not meaning it.

"Do you want to hear or not?"

"Yes, yes," he nodded vigorously, his hat flopping up and down on his incorrigible red mop.

"I'll tell you what it is," she said, smiling at his excitement. "I don't know our Governor Tretyakov at all."

"No? Then what . . ."

"But I know his daughter very well."

"Ah," he said enthusiastically.

"Yes. She came to me when she was in trouble. Her father heard, how I don't know. I never know. But he did, and it was better to send her to me than to someone in Plotsk who might say something to the wrong person. The father came here from Minsk, you know?"

Berekh shook his head.

"Well, there was someone who liked his daughter very much. She's a beauty, this Katherina, and the second son of the Count of something or other took a fancy to her. He had business in Minsk and there he met her."

"And this is the Governor's friend from Minsk?"

"Yes. And he's a friend like the Tsar is your brother. He caused all of Alexi Tretyakov's problems."

"Why, if the Count's son was so taken with his daughter?"

"Yes, he liked her, and she liked him. Too much. He wore a captain's uniform. He had a sword with rubies on the handle. This is what she told me. She couldn't forget the way the rubies shone in the light from the chandelier."

"Then why didn't they get married?" Berekh asked.

"Oh, listen to the worldly man talking. The Count's son, even the second son, marry the daughter of a minor official? It would be like the rabbi marrying the midwife."

"So is that so terrible? I think it's a very good match." He stroked her thigh.

She slapped his hand lightly. "Do you want to hear the story or not?" He nodded. "In the meantime," she said, "Tretyakov was talking marriage to someone else. And not just anybody. The Deputy Minister of Railroads met Katherina when her father was in St. Petersburg, and he couldn't live without her. Who knows why? He was possessed. She flirted with him and forgot him. He was old, maybe even forty, she said to me. What was he compared to a count's son, even a second son? She was sitting right at my table, shivering under her cloak, even though it was lined with a good fur. Silver. A few wolves died for that cloak. She came here in the middle of the night with only her old nurse and one servant to drive them.

"What happened to her you can guess. The Count's son had his way, and she enjoyed herself until she discovered that she was pregnant, and he was gone. She wrote to him. He didn't answer. She was beside herself. Frantic. She confessed to her father in tears. The usual story. By then they were in Plotsk already. Someone, who knows, maybe it was the Count himself, put in a bad word for the girl's father. Instead of going up, he went down. We have a new governor. He blames the daughter. His only hope was to marry her off to the Deputy Minister. A girl can be a virgin twenty times if she wants to, but if she's out to here, it gives the whole story away. So he sent her to me, and I got rid of what wasn't wanted. Are you shocked?"

"Maybe one day I'll tell you a story that might surprise you," Berekh said. "I'm not so easily shocked. Go on."

Misha raised her eyebrows, but continued. "Now she's engaged to the Deputy Minister and the wedding is planned for the summer. She told me that her father is spending a fortune. Afterward, if everything goes well, then her new husband will find something better for her father. But if the whole story should get out, and people are laughing up their sleeves at the Deputy Minister, it won't go too well with our Governor."

"Ah," Berekh said, "Now I know." He leaned back, his hands folded over his belly as if he'd eaten an enormous meal, smacking his lips until Misha laughed at the immensity of his satisfaction. Leaning forward to thank him for the wine, she kissed him on the cheek, but he turned so that his mouth was on hers, tasting of wine, his tongue lightly tracing the outline of her lips. She pulled away. "It's impossible," she said.

"Is it?" Berekh asked, kissing her neck. As the moon found her way into the purpling sky, they embraced, and Misha's belly found itself no encumbrance at all for the inventiveness of a rabbi.

NIGHTS OF THE SECRET RIVER

The barley was high, the potatoes flowering white, and small green apples were thick in the summer trees. Hershel had given the money he got from Yarush to the Rabbi, who had given it to Faygela, who brought Misha what a woman needs and rarely gets when she's going to have a baby—eggs, milk, soft rolls, a hen now and then for roasting, and lotion for her swollen feet.

Evening brought the men from their workbenches and stalls and carts to the synagogue courtyard, where they waited for Getzel the Beauty, whose limp made him slow to walk. Did you hear the latest? Our beloved midwife has a new assistant, they said. Who? The Rabbi. No, you're joking. What's the matter with you, are you half-blind and completely deaf? Everyone knows. So he walks with her. Is that a sin? Well, I say that he must be the father of her baby. There's no other reason for him to have business with her. What are you talking? Anyone can see that the father is Hayim. He's been cutting wood for her since the ice storm. Well, what about Pinye, you know, the young carpenter from Plotsk, he fixed her door. Pinye? One of the boys who are studying with the Rabbi. So, what about you? Me? Fingers pointed. Yes, you, who else fixed her roof on market day? You think no one saw you sitting like a rooster on the hen house? Of course I fixed the roof. It's only right. She fixed my foot. And you, didn't you bring her a salami, and not a small one, either, but one as long as my arm? All right, all right. Look, here's Getzel. Let's go in and pray already. While you're talking, God is falling asleep.

*   *   *

MISHA half sat in bed, her nightgown pulled up so she could watch her baby swivel from one side of her belly to the other in the twilight. Through the open window, she heard the man calling, "Getzel, move your feet, or we'll be saying morning prayers soon." Before they left the synagogue, she was asleep, voices fading into the night, the river gently slapping the banks below her house.

Misha opened her eyes. It was dark. The moon had set. The contraction came again. It's just your womb practicing, she told herself. It's normal. She was a woman of years, a woman of experience, not some girl who needed her mother. But she was afraid. Staring into the darkness, she could only think of everything that might go wrong. "This is no good, Misha," she whispered. "You have to take your mind off yourself. So what am I going to do in the middle of the night? Well, first you can light a candle." The shadows that sprang from the small light were not reassuring. "All right. So find something to make yourself busy with." Taking the candle, she walked across the room, glancing at the table, the stove, the shelves of jars, the trunk in the corner. Her bridal trunk. Her mother had given her the key when she got her first period. Touching the half that was carved and the half that was as smooth as water, she lifted the lid. Inside the trunk lay her memories, wrapped in silk.

SHE WAS sixteen, kneeling in front of the trunk while Blema took out the embroidered cloth made by her mother, whom Misha was named after.

"Is there anything else in the trunk?" Misha asked.

"There's this," Blema answered, lifting out a hair wreath, plaited like the braids of a round Sabbath bread, fair and dark and russet-colored, and in the center a lock of moon white hair. "All the women in the family, when their hair is cut after the wedding, braid a lock of their hair into this, so their daughters won't forget them."

"And this one?" Misha asked, touching the lock in the center.

"Manya's. Her poor mother cut off a piece of her hair before she went into the ground."

Misha saw with great interest how the white hair in the center set off the other braids, like the moon rising above a newly ploughed field, the browns and blacks of the earth rich in its glow. How soft the white hair looked, but just as she reached out a finger to touch it, her mother returned the wreath to the trunk.

"Is there anything of yours, Mama?"

"Of course," she said lightly, picking up a silk-wrapped bundle, "my dowry."

"That was your dowry?" Misha asked in astonishment as she looked at what her mother held.

"Well, the silver candlesticks I brought with me were ugly. My papa was proud. The candlesticks were heavy. Everything he owned was in them. But so ugly. I begged your father to sell them. I wanted him to make something for me. Something beautiful." Tenderly, she put the wooden carving with its large round base into Misha's hands. "Feel how smooth." Misha ran her fingers across the carving. A winged figure was blowing the ram's horn, its head tilted back, the shofar pointing upward, and out of the horn tiny leaves and flowers curled upward and around the rim, climbing the point of a wing. "You see?" Her mother put a key into the back of the base and turned. Music cascaded from the horn. Misha recognized the song. "*Ani maamin,*" she sang softly as she stood up, "*I believe in the coming of the Messiah, even though he may tarry, I believe.*"

"Wait, daughter," her mother said. "There's one more thing." She took out a silver box with ivory inlay. "This belonged to her, Manya's mother. I was named for her, my Great-grandmother Blema. She was a pious woman. When she was the *zogerin,* she copied out prayers for women and kept them in this box." She lifted the lid and inside was a parchment-thin pamphlet. "We only have one left, the prayer for the New Moon, *Rosh Hodesh.* Now that you're a woman, you can't run around the same anymore. On *Rosh Hodesh,* you'll pray with the women. I know you won't bring shame to your mother the way Manya did to hers," and Misha, who was kneeling beside her mother, bent low so that Blema could kiss and bless her head. Her mother died three years later, and the bridal trunk remained empty except for her mother's gifts under their layer of darkness.

THE CANDLE cast Misha's pregnant shadow across the room as she wound up the music box. Taking out her grandmother's fine cloth, she draped it over her head and across her shoulders, its threads gleaming with a silvery sheen over its many colors. As the notes tumbled from the ram's horn, she whispered the prayer for the New Moon.

"*In Paradise dwell our Mothers. There is Batia, the Pharaoh's daughter, and our dear Yokheved, the mother of Moses our teacher. They sing the Song of the Sea with great joy and many holy angels with them, Miriam the prophetess beating her timbrel, Deborah the prophetess and a hundred thousand women who praise the Name and sing. In the time-to-come, the Holy Presence, the* Shekhina, *will return from Her exile in the world and we will stand on the holy mountain and see with our own eyes as the Lord returns to Zion and She, the* Shekhina, *will become great.*

"*Holy One, spread Your wings over us. Do not turn away. I entreat You like a motherless child . . .*"

MISHA covered her face with her hands and her tears fell between her fingers. "Dear God, don't punish this child for my sins," she prayed.

DAWN ROSE in a musky haze. Misha lay on her bed, asleep, her grandmother's cloth spread over her belly. On the riverbank below her house, the women stood knee-deep in the water, washing clothes on the flat rocks. Linens bunched and unfurled between their knuckles as curls of mist rose over the bridge. Did you hear the latest? Our dear midwife has a new assistant. Emma. Yes, it's true. It turns out that working in the bakery wasn't enough of a punishment for her. No? What do you think? Faygela's girls hang onto her every word, and believe me she has plenty. I heard Dina, the smallest, telling my Devorela the story of Little Red Riding Hood. She goes on strike, and the big, bad boss has no choice, he has to give her grandmother her pay. You think it's a good idea to send a young girl to the midwife? For Emma, yes. Who else is a better example to her of what happens when a person follows her own way? Maybe you're right, but I don't know if it's such a punishment. Ruthie helps, too, and I hear that the girls chatter from morning till night. They spend half their time in the woods and I'm telling you it's not going to lead to anything good. In my day a girl their age was married with babies and she didn't dare say a word or her mother-in-law would give her a *zetz* that would send her flying. In your day, what are you talking? Your mother-in-law went deaf just to save herself from listening to you.

*　　*　　*

ON THE road to Blaszka the raspberries ripened. Yarush moved a fallen tree with Hayim's help. Hayim and Alta-Fruma ate raspberries with cream in the dairyhouse. On the riverbank, goslings shed their down and began to fly. Heavy clusters of blueberries darkened from green to purplish blue. The children of Blaszka filled buckets of blueberries, cramming handfuls into their mouths, sticking tongues out to see whose was the purplest.

There was a clatter on Misha's stairs, the door flying open as Ruthie burst into the room. In one hand she held a bucket of blueberries. The other hand pulled a reluctant Emma. Misha could see that Emma had been crying. Her face was blotchy, her eyes swollen, and there was a tight catch to her voice as she said to Ruthie, "Let me go."

"She hit her head," Ruthie announced.

"Oh, make it sound like I did it all by myself, when it was the oppressor that threw me to the ground."

"She means Hershel," Ruthie said. "He pushed Emma away when she tried to stop him."

"Stop what?" Misha asked.

"He had no business breaking up the printing press," Emma shouted. "It doesn't belong to him."

"Yes, of course," Misha said soothingly. "Come over here and let me look at you."

"We fixed it up. It's ours. Nobody else has any right to it." Emma began to cry again. It was her crying that worried Misha more than the cut on the side of her head.

"This doesn't look too bad," Misha said.

"Nothing looks bad when the head of the community council does it," Emma cried. "It's the same everywhere."

Misha stirred a powder of valerian root into a glass of water. "Drink this down, Emma. You'll feel better."

"What is it?"

"It's good for you. Believe me."

"It's probably poison," the girl muttered, but she swallowed it anyway.

"You should go to bed and have a rest," Misha said.

"I'm not going home. I'm going to picket the community council." Rubbing her forehead, Emma sniffled.

"What's the matter?" Misha asked.

"It hurts," Emma answered in a small voice.

"Take her home, Ruthie, and I don't want to hear a word from you, Emma. You have to have a sleep and that's it."

With a worried frown, Misha watched them leave. It wasn't like Emma to be so obedient.

WHEN EMMA woke up from her sleep, she complained that she was cold. Within a few days everyone knew that the doctor from Plotsk had come and gone, and there was nothing he could do. Izzie was sent to stay with Hanna-Leah. On Saturday evening, August 11th, the synagogue was draped in black for Tishah-b'Av.

THE CHILD'S face was mottled red, her lips cracked, her fingers plucking at the blanket while she shivered helplessly. "Emma," Misha said, "can you hear me?" But the girl only continued her incomprehensible murmuring.

"She's been like that for hours," Alta-Fruma said.

"Has she drunk anything?" Misha asked.

"Nothing. You see the oranges the children brought for her? I can't squeeze even a drop into her."

Misha uncovered her basket, considering the jars and powders. Alta-Fruma looked at her hopefully. "There's nothing new in here," Misha said. "Everything for a fever, for chills, for confusion, I sent with Ruthie." At the sight of Alta-Fruma's stricken expression, she added, "But I'm not going. Let me show you what else I brought. See how restless she is. It's stealing her strength. We have to calm her." Misha's voice lowered shyly as she took a silk-wrapped bundle from the basket. "My father made this. You remember him?"

Alta-Fruma nodded, intent on the musical angel Misha was now winding up. "If you just looked at him, you felt that *Shabbas* was here, he was so calm," Alta-Fruma said. "But I never saw anything like this."

"He made it during the cholera epidemic. In Plotsk they said it was their rabbi who stopped the epidemic. In Blaszka they said it was the wedding of the orphans in the cemetery. But my mother said it was my father's music box. I had it all these years in my bridal trunk. Now, I'll put it here, right near Emma. Listen."

The two women stood side by side, Alta-Fruma, gray-haired and green-eyed, her hands twisting, and Misha in her red shawl, the knotted ends rising and falling with the breath of her pregnancy. *"Ani maamin,"* the notes called, "I believe," turning Emma's head toward the music, her hands lulled into stillness. Her eyes fluttered open and closed. But how her cheeks still burned.

"The fever has to break soon," Misha said. "If you just touch her you feel how fast her heart is going. If the fever doesn't break . . ."

Alta-Fruma groaned. "What can I do?" she asked. "There must be something. I can't just sit and watch her go from me. Please, Misha, tell me. Anything."

"You're upset and tired. Here, all you can do is watch. But your sister was a *zogerin*. It must mean something. Go to the shul and pray. Maybe the Holy One above is listening and waiting for you."

Alta-Fruma kissed Emma on the forehead. "Watch over her," she said, covering her head with a shawl. As Alta-Fruma left, the door swung wide in a gust of wind.

"Never mind," Misha said, "I'll latch it shut. Go on."

The wind smelled of dust and dryness. There were no stars in the sky hanging low like the belly of a pregnant horse, a black horse with angry nostrils and hooves like rusty iron. Misha closed the door firmly, dropping the wooden bar into the latch. Turning around, she didn't blink at the figure seated on the stool beside Emma's bed.

"Good evening, madam," he said, tipping his hat.

She didn't answer, but rewound the music box before she set about forcing Emma's jaw apart so that she could put a tincture of willow under her tongue. Then she took two jars, poured a liquid from one into a bowl and from the other added a powder, using a wooden spoon to stir it.

"*Tsk, tsk.* Won't you even wish me a good evening?"

"When a woman is pregnant, she sees many interesting things. Does that mean she wants to talk to them?" Misha said without looking up. Bending over Emma, she hummed, "*Ani maamin.*"

"In that case, I'll take my charge and be off." The figure snapped his gloved fingers, and the music stopped midnote. Misha straightened quickly, facing him as he stretched out impossibly long arms. Were those hands reaching toward her? Inside the white gloves anything could be hidden. She could still be at home, dreaming, she thought. But it wouldn't do to treat this, this person lightly, even in a dream.

"You don't look to me like someone from the Holy One," she said. "Maybe you're from the other side. Then you can't be here for Emma. She's a good girl."

"Don't be so provincial. There is only one side. And I have my requisition papers right here." The figure took from its pocket a scroll with seals that flickered like blue flames. Misha was frightened then. Not because of the seals. Anyone could imagine a fiery scroll. But it, the figure sitting with its knees crossed, used words and terms she didn't know, that she couldn't have made up. So I'm not asleep, she thought. And maybe this one's not here for Emma. It's come for me, or for my baby. Yes, that's it. She felt a sharp pain in her midsection, a pull as if wires were dragging out her insides. This is the punishment for my sins, she thought. It isn't right, she wanted to shout. I don't deserve this. But she had no breath for even a whisper. The figure was pointing a gloved finger at her. It's a dream, she said to herself, closing her eyes. Nothing but a dream. Calm down. Don't scare the baby out of you. What would your mother say? But she could only remember the wreath of braids. After she died, would someone cut off a lock of her black hair to intertwine with Manya's? It seemed important, but she couldn't think why.

The figure bent its finger and the pain intensified, driving through her back like a spike. She fell to her knees. Her heart raced. "*Sh'ma Israel, Adonai Elohainu, Adonai Ekhad,*" she prayed, lowering her head to her clasped hands. I'm finished, she thought and, once she made up her mind to it, she could calmly watch herself humbled with pain and fear. Her mother would be waiting for her. And with her would be her mother, and her mother before her, all the women whose lives were braided in the wreath in her bridal trunk. And surely her mother would forgive her.

But she couldn't let go yet. There was one more thing to do. The gloved angel could have her, but first she would have to do something for Zisa-Sara's child. "Dear God," she said aloud, forcing the words between groans. "Before You take me, please let me help this girl. I only ask for a little time with her, until her fever breaks."

The figure clapped its gloved hands. There was a dry rattling sound. "I applaud your selflessness," it said, "but that's hardly necessary. I'll tell you a secret. I was only having a little fun because you, let's just say, you irritate me. Don't misunderstand, I truly admire you. One always appreciates stimulating opponents. Isn't that so?"

Misha nodded weakly.

"Well, I'm not here for you, but for the girl."

Now that the pain was gone, and she was sitting up straight, she felt a little better. "You expect me to trust you?" she asked, the spark of the old Misha reviving.

"I'm offended," it said, putting a gloved hand over its waistcoat, where a heart would be if such a being had one. "You've met me often enough to know me by now. Surely we're old comrades. Is it so different meeting, as they say, face to face?"

"If," she said, "you are who you say you are. But I'm not going to give Zisa-Sara's child to just any person who comes in when my back is turned."

"My card," it said, presenting a card with a black border.

"I don't read," Misha said curtly.

It took a gold watch from its waistcoat pocket, and flipped the lip up. "I'm getting rather late," it said. "It's been quite amusing having this conversation, but I must leave and you're in the way." Misha didn't move. "If you prefer I can take you," it said threateningly. "My requisition states one female."

"And you always follow your orders?" Misha asked.

"Oh, quite precisely. Without fail."

"Then take me." Misha ignored a tremor of fear. People said that the soul pleaded not to be sent down into a human body. Life was too hard. But once joined to a person, the soul clung to life because it was so painful to be torn from the body and flung back to where it came from. This is the reason that no one is condemned to hell for longer than twelve months. The death agony is cruel enough to make up for almost any sin.

The figure tilted its head to one side, putting one gloved finger to its, what one might call, mouth. There was a stony sound as it tapped its chin. "Well, well. I heard that Misha of Blaszka was brave, but now I see she is foolhardy, too. But who am I? Only a servant. Only a soldier. Just following orders. Take my hand."

Misha reached out to the gloved thing and felt a profound tearing, an unbearable stripping of skin and bone and muscle, of color and texture and shape, sucked upward in a whirlwind to a blaze of light. For a moment, she thought she saw a replica of Blaszka in the light, a shimmering village square, a synagogue of shifting iridescence, a bridge of fragrant dew across water so clear she could see smooth stones of every color and fish like stars that flickered among the whistling reeds. Coming toward her streamed a river of light made of a hundred familiar faces, their arms outstretched in welcome. And wasn't that Zisa-Sara? She felt a movement inside herself, though she had no inside, of something that meant to leap into the arms of light, and whether it was herself or her baby, she didn't know, only that she didn't want to be left behind, alone.

"You idiot, the orders were for one female," a voice said. Who was it? Misha wondered, turning. Away from the light, everything was a confusion of undarkness.

"So what's your problem? Here you have one female."

"Not one. She's pregnant."

"And that counts?"

"Do you want to take a chance with the Boss? You know what's written. If you add even one dot to the Boss's orders, it goes on your record in red. When your ledger is reviewed . . . let's just say that I'm not going to the Boss with this."

"Well, then, I'll just put her back and take the other one."

"Oh, no you don't. You know the rules. Only one death agony per requisition. Back she goes, and you just go to the Boss and take what's coming to you."

The first voice, the dry raspy one that she remembered from the sickroom, seemed to turn to her. "It looks as though I have to take you back, Misha, but I'll enjoy the memory of our time together until we meet again. Don't forget that we have an engagement, and I'm looking forward to it."

As the dizziness increased, Misha thought that the gloved angel must not realize that it couldn't frighten her that way twice. She had seen the real Blaszka, even if just for a moment. It was enough. Nothing would be exactly the same again. She would always see the light inside the stones of the village.

Opening her eyes, Misha found herself sitting on Emma's bed, supporting herself with one hand on the table where the music box still played. It was a dream, she thought, but in her other hand was the wooden spoon she'd used to stir the tonic for Emma, and there was a scorch mark on the spoon.

"Auntie?" came a voice. "I'm thirsty." It was Emma, the flush fading, her forehead covered in a cool sweat.

Alta-Fruma, coming through the door, cried out, "Emma, dear Emma, I'm here." She rushed to the bedside as Misha put a glass of water to Emma's lips.

"Look, the fever has gone," Misha said. Emma drank a little water, then lay back, her eyes closed, her hands still. "She's asleep."

Alta-Fruma sat down and cried.

"How can I thank you, Misha? How can I repay you?"

"I did nothing. It was you. You prayed, and she came back to be with you. Look, all I did was make up a tonic for her."

But Alta-Fruma shook her head. Brushing Emma's hair back from her forehead, she said, "I have a long memory, Misha. I won't forget what you did for me."

IN THE days afterward, Misha was very tired. It could have been because she was getting close to her time. Though she wasn't able to go out, everything she needed found its way to her house. Faygela came, and Ruthie, and Alta-Fruma, and Berekh.

On a hot, sticky day, he bathed her with cool water and almond soap, his hands so careful and light that even her edgy nipples approved as he lifted her shift and caressed them ever so slightly. Dipping the cloth in the pan of water, he wiped under her breasts and over her belly, a strange smile on his face that widened into amazed delight.

"What is it?" Misha asked.

"I felt it. The baby."

"So, didn't you feel it before?"

"This was different. It tried to grab my fingers. It knows me."

"Don't be silly. How could that be?"

"No, no. The baby knows that it's mine," he said, "I'm sure of it."

Misha pushed him away. "The baby is mine, and no one else's." She crossed her arms.

388 • LILIAN NATTEL

"Misha," he said with a mother's tenderness, his long arms reaching around her waistless abdomen. "Are you sure? Are you really sure?"

"Well," she said, softening. "It's possible. It could be a little bit yours."

"A little bit is good enough." Lifting her hair, he kissed the nape of her neck, then rubbed her shoulders, singing the old song, "*Last night I went to a wedding, I saw many women there But none with your black eyes, and none with your raven hair, da-da-dum.*"

As he massaged her back, Misha relaxed, leaning against him, surprised by his sturdiness. After a while she turned to face him, sinking her fingers into his wild beard, with its flecks of moonlight, as she kissed him.

THE DAYS OF AWE

After the ram's horn called in the New Year, Misha could no longer leave her house. She felt the baby's head like an overturned bowl between her legs, and it was a good idea, she found, not to sit down too quickly. From time to time she felt a peculiar spark in the birth canal, like a tiny strike of lightning. There was not an inch of room left inside her, and all afternoon she slept, half-sitting on her bed, with three feather pillows behind her back, and two under her knees. Alta-Fruma had brought the pillows, saying that with two children in the house, she had no room to spare for old things.

Tzipporah came and prayed over Misha.

Emma weeded her garden.

Ruthie brewed pots of raspberry leaf tea to tone her womb.

Hershel brought her his mother's amulet to hang over her bed.

Haykel the blacksmith brought her a horseshoe to put under her bed.

The farmer Boryna brought her a cache of fish.

Ambrose the beekeeper brought her honey.

Nathan the tinsmith pounded out her dented pots.

Pinye, the young carpenter, red-faced, brought her a new birthing stool.

Rivka the cloth seller washed her floor.

Haia-Etel brushed her hair and braided it.

Getzel climbed her stairs with a great effort so that he personally could bring her a jar of strong pickles. "Everyone knows," he said, "that a pregnant woman likes nothing better than a good pickle. Maybe with some sour milk?" he asked. "You like I should bring you some kefir?"

The Gypsy boy came to thank her for the medicine that healed the cut on his head. Afterward he sat on her stairs and played his *gudulka,* Avigdor the fiddler joining him. Berekh sang with them, though most of the time he wouldn't stir from Misha's room, stroking her hand and rubbing her sore back.

Faygela read to her from *The Israelite.* "The last few days are the hardest," she said. "When you can hardly breathe already, and you can't wait for it to be over, you should try to think about something else." Then Hanna-Leah added, "Yes, and let me tell you what's going on in the village. Shayna-Henya is playing at love with one of the klezmer. You know Avigdor, the fiddler? Well he's fiddling something else now. I'll tell you all about it . . ."

And Misha thought that although she had never been so uncomfortable in her whole life, it wasn't so bad to have a table loaded with food that she didn't have to prepare, a crowd of women entertaining her, the men fiddling outside, the children pulling up the rows of cabbage and peppers and turnips and carrots in her garden, which had grown larger than sin. It wasn't so bad at all.

But at last, when Misha couldn't stand the shortness of breath and the weight of her belly and the pressure between her legs another day, she took charge of her fate. Dosing herself every two hours with castor oil and vodka, she didn't think at all of what day it was. When her waters broke, she nearly cried with relief, but ten hours later she wanted to cry with tiredness. It was Kol Nidrei, the most important night of the year, and everyone had to go to the synagogue. When they left, she was alone with the pains that went on forever, gathering her body up and dropping it aside with no thought for the person inside.

KOL NIDREI

She is alone. The village is silent. Everyone is in the synagogue. It seems as though she has been alone since Adam *Harishon,* staring at the tiled stove, her table, the wreath of garlic, the string of onions. She shivers. The hot water bottle that Faygela lay at her feet is cold now. The pains are bad, the baby pressing on her back. The head is in the right place, but it must be facing up. A midwife would tell her what side the baby is lying on. Then she would lift Misha's leg and the baby might turn and come down. At least I should sit up, Misha thinks. But the bad pains have made her more tired than she could have imagined. There's no midwife to help and who's here to scold her? Everyone is in shul, being washed clean of everything bad, while she's being squeezed and twisted like a rag with just the four walls to keep her company. The baby won't come out, she's convinced of it. She's going to die with it still inside her.

The walls pulsate with her staring. Points of memory shine in front of her. Her mother, Berekh, Zisa-Sara, Yarush from Plotsk. . . . She puts her fist in her mouth as a contraction sweeps over her.

When her eyes focus again, she sees that she's not alone. Someone is standing in front of her. A big woman, as big as she, with long pale hair, and a blue cap with gold ribbons dangling.

"Who are you?" Misha asks. She wonders that she has time for this conversation, as if an eternity stretches between contractions.

"Don't you recognize me?" the woman asks.

"No. I never saw you before."

"You did. You saw me in the river, and again in the woods."

"You are . . ."

"Who else? Your great-grandmother, Manya." The woman laughs. "Yes, finally I had a minute to visit you. Your mother sent me. She couldn't come herself or she would."

"My mother?" Misha asks, sitting up. "What did she say?"

"She said to tell you, 'Misha, don't wait. Fill up the bridal trunk. You have children coming to this world, and they will need to remember you.' "

"Remembering makes trouble."

"Since when does trouble bother you?" Manya asks, her hands on her hips.

"Anyway, what does it matter? Why does anyone need to remember me?"

Manya grins, splitting her round face as she nods, her gold ribbons fluttering. "*Ahh.* It's good you should ask."

Misha sees without surprise the walls of her house falling away.

Should such a thing surprise her when she's talking with her great-grandmother, her *Alta-bubbie,* who doesn't look a day older than Misha herself? And now her bed is riding the sea. It must be the sea, it's so wide and cold and it smells of the huge blue fish she sees spraying water out of the top of its head like a fountain. It jumps into the air and dives under, smacking the water with its tail and splashing her. Is that what you do to a woman about to give birth? Misha scolds. But she isn't quite sure that she's still in labor. The contractions seem to have stopped. Above her Manya floats, her dress billowing as she tows the bed with a rope of silver. Where are you taking me? Misha asks, but Manya doesn't answer.

Here the sea narrows, like soup poured into the bowl of the red cliffs on either side. The bed is swimming up a river, past stone pylons where black birds congregate like the parliament of Old Poland. The bed floats under the criss-cross metal beams of the bridge, between herons walking in the shallows with their skinny long legs like Berekh's. As Manya nears a little house on the right bank, the bed slows. Look, Manya says, and Misha looks, seeing as clearly as if she were standing right inside the house, where a woman, nearly as small as Faygela, is dressing herself in white. Of course, it's Kol Nidrei. Who is she? Misha asks. Look, Manya answers. So she looks. Why not? Shouldn't a person enjoy her dreams? The woman's hair is dark as night with flecks of red like faint firelight, and her eyes are blue, as round and blue as Berekh's eyes. The woman lifts her eyes as if she sees Misha and Misha waves. The woman waves back. Then she turns to a box on her table, a box with a window. On the window there are letters, unreadable letters, in neat rows of black. The woman touches the box and the window goes dark. Have a good fast, Misha calls, and the woman smiles.

Kneeling beside Misha on the bed rocking in the light waves of the river, Manya puts her hands on Misha's belly. Warmth spreads through Misha as her *Alta-bubbie* nods at the house on the riverbank. Before you leave, give your great-granddaughter your blessing, Manya says. The gold ribbons on her cap shine in Misha's eyes. She blinks, and then there is only the rosy blaze of the setting sun through the window of Misha's house, where her bed has settled back into its accustomed place.

Misha gasps. The contractions have begun again. She has the urge to push. The baby turned, she thinks. It's really coming. No, no. Wait. It isn't time yet. How often has she said to a woman, wait until you can't wait anymore? It's not so easy. Dear God, let the baby be all right. Never mind about me. Just let it be whole and alive. She half-sits, listening, hoping to catch the sound of Kol Nidrei though it's impossible. She thinks that if she can just hear Kol Nidrei then the baby will be all right. But how can anyone hear the small sound of a human voice from one end of the village square to the other? There's only the wind.

IN THE synagogue the women and men look at one another, whispering, Did you hear? That moaning. There it is again. It must be Misha. It's her time, and she's alone.

They all hear it. They all know what it is. Even though what they really hear is just the wind pushing its way into the walls of the old synagogue. But on the eve of Yom Kippur, when the Gates of Eternity swing open, even the wind can speak to an open heart.

The Court of Heaven looks down on earth to this small dot, this ordinary village, where the women and men in their white garments pour from the synagogue, a stream of light under the dimming sky. On Yom Kippur there is no night.

THE DOOR to Misha's house opens. Who is it? she wonders, frightened, remembering. She expects someone large, someone who has no good in mind, or someone, perhaps, who wears a white glove. But look, it's Faygela, taking in everything with her dark eyes, pursing her lips and tying up the hem of her skirt into her waistband as if she means business. "So you're here," Misha says, faint with relief. She leans back on her pillow, closing her eyes thankfully.

"Lying on your back? This is how you're going to have a baby?" her friend asks. Startled, Misha sits up. Ruthie has come in, smiling timidly at Misha and clinging to the doorpost as if she never saw a woman giving birth before. Behind Ruthie she sees Hanna-Leah and behind her all of the women, arm in arm, in their white finery, laughing and talking excitedly, walking up and down the stairs like the angels on the ladder to heaven in Jacob's dream. Why, her house has become a wedding party. "The guest of honor isn't in any hurry," Misha mutters.

"Well, you know what they say," Hanna-Leah says as she comes toward the bed. "When the band starts to play, the bride goes to pee. So we'll just have to wait for her."

"But Kol Nidrei?" Misha asks.

"The Holy One above can wait a minute, I think. Our lives may be short, but the Blessed One is eternal."

"Well, I don't have time to stand around," Faygela says. "Young Pinye worked very hard to make this good birthing chair for you, Misha, and you're going to use it. You think you're the Queen of Sheba? God save me from women in labor. Get up, already."

"All right, don't nag," Misha says as Hanna-Leah helps her to her feet. Leaning on the two women, Misha moves from the bed to the birthing chair.

Faygela nods. "Now, isn't this better?"

"For you, it's fine. For me nothing is better," Misha says between gritted teeth. Then she says nothing, losing her breath for a moment as the contraction breaks her in half. She is sitting with her legs apart, bearing down, squeezing Faygela's hand until the smaller woman pales.

Outside the women are singing. What are they singing? Do I care? Misha asks herself. Let them sing me into my grave. Hanna-Leah has a pot of water on the *pripichek*. What does she want with water now? Is it a time to have tea? The front door creaks open, a nail-scratching noise that makes her want to scream. Half-blind with a mixture of sweat and tears, Misha doesn't quite see the figure coming through her door now. "*Nu*, someone else. Is my house suddenly the train to Warsaw? At least let me charge a ticket," Misha says, rubbing her eyes.

Berekh sidles through the door, shy, embarrassed. This is not a place for men. "I'm here, Misha," he announces.

"We're not making chicken soup," Hanna-Leah scolds. "Go back to your holy books. Go to the synagogue and pray with the men. You don't belong here." She dips a cloth in the pot of hot water, wrings it, shaking it, spattering the Rabbi's prayer shawl before she takes it to Misha, wiping away the blood and mucus between her legs.

"It's coming, I see the head. Look," says Hanna-Leah.

"Very good. Take Misha's hand, mine is already crushed and you, Ruthie, don't stand in the doorway staring. Let's see if you learned something about bringing babies into the world." Faygela rubs the feeling back into her hand while her daughter comes to Misha tentatively. Berekh hangs back, whistling at the onions hanging from the ceiling as he tugs at his beard, pretending not to notice the strange grunts and half-screams coming from Misha as she pushes.

Ruthie crouches, peering apologetically between Misha's legs. "The head's not coming out. It's going back and forward, back and forward. You have to push harder, Misha."

A big woman like you, Misha thinks, surely you have a little more strength. She pushes as hard as anyone can who is tired out from a hard labor, but Ruthie is telling her that it's not enough. She tries again, but it's still no good. The women's faces are swimming in and out of her vision like flat moons. They are so far away and she's cold. "It's no use," Misha says. "Let me go." Her voice is weak. A pool of blood has formed at the foot of the birthing stool. Her head is rolling back, her eyes closing as if she's going to sleep. The women look at one another. It's from this tiredness that a woman can die.

Hanna-Leah shakes Misha's shoulder. "You look at me, Misha. Do you think I'm letting you go somewhere? No. You're staying right here with me." She squeezes Misha's hand, but there is no returning pressure.

"Ruthie," Faygela warns, "something has to be done."

Ruthie gets to her feet. She stands, her fingers plucking at her lips. She is wearing white, as they all are, and for a moment she's frightened that death might find the color of the shroud too inviting. Taking up Misha's red shawl, she throws it over her dress, thinking that even if she doesn't believe in it, red is supposed to keep away the Evil Eye. Then she goes to Berekh, who stands beside the bridal trunk in the corner, twisting the fringes on his prayer shawl. Blushing, Ruthie whispers something to him.

With a startled look, Berekh listens to Ruthie's instructions. His face turns as red as his beard, but he nods. Quickly walking to Misha's side, his tall frame bends over her as he takes her hand. With his lips close to her ear, he says in a voice so quiet only she can hear, "So, this is what comes from having a little fun with a *shmeckel?*"

"Fun?" she murmurs. "You think yours is so great? I've heard of plenty better. Plenty."

"Well, bigger, sure," he says, still whispering. "But tell me. Did you ever see one prettier? Let the women be the judge. How about Hanna-Leah? She would be fair." Berekh moves as if to take off his trousers.

Misha laughs, her gold tooth gleaming. "You're a fool, Berekh," she gasps.

"What else?" he shouts as she squeezes his hand with all her strength. "Wisdom and wisecrack, the same root."

The stool rocks, blood breaks, and the baby slips into Ruthie's arms.

A girl, squalling mightily, hair as red as fire. Another push. A boy, hair as dark as earth, holding onto her heel.

"One isn't good enough for the midwife of Blaszka, of course not," Hanna-Leah says, smiling as Misha demands her babies, both of them, though she can hardly keep her eyes open.

Standing beside Misha, Berekh says the blessing for new things.

WITH THE door to Misha's house open to the last glimmer of light in the sky, Berekh faces the congregation. They stand on the stairs and around Misha's garden and along the embankment of the river, flowing into the night, the women in their white dresses and shawls, the men in their *kittels,* worn under the wedding canopy, and worn to the grave.

"It's time," Berekh says loudly from the top of the stairs. "There's just a minute of daylight left. Listen to me." They look up to see him in his blood-spattered *kittel,* framed in Misha's doorway, his beard a glinting fire in the falling mane of night. The wind dies down. The sun hovers in the sky, waiting for them. The women stand with the men close by. There is no *mekhitzah,* no wall between them here. Their rabbi stands in the doorway of the little house on stilts above the river. And as Berekh's voice lifts in the ancient melody, the river is the silver crown and the sky the velvet robe of the Torah. The night is the Holy Ark. And they are the Host of Heaven. The souls in hell are rising to the place of hope, right here in Blaszka, while the willow trees weep for joy as Berekh sings Kol Nidrei: *"All vows, oaths and promises which we make to God from this Yom Kippur to the Yom Kippur coming and are not able to fulfill—may all such vows between ourselves and God be annulled. May they be void and of no effect. May we be absolved from them. May these vows not be considered vows, these oaths not be considered oaths, and these promises not be considered promises."*

Inside the house, Misha rests, her babies asleep in the cradle, her grandmother's embroidered cloth hanging above them protectively, while the women stand with their arms linked, listening to the song of peaceful breathing.

In a hundred years, five thousand miles from Blaszka, Misha's great-granddaughter will stand in the synagogue among the men and the women, listening to Kol Nidrei, her prayer shawl draped over the child in her arms, its father standing next to her, his shoulder touching hers. And she will know that her great-grandmother at that very moment, in the house above the River Północna, is listening to her lover sing the prayer that opens the door beyond time, her babies resting after their long swim.

YOM KIPPUR

In the women's gallery, Faygela holds Ruthie's hand. Hanna-Leah sits on her left side, Emma and Alta-Fruma behind them. Beside Hanna-Leah, Misha holds her babies close. Around her are the women of Blaszka, leaning shoulder to shoulder in these last moments of their fast. Malka. Gittel. Little Haia-Etel. Naomi. Old Mirrel. Shayna-Henya. Shayna-Perl. Ettie. Rivka. Tzipporah. Old Liba, though she can't see and she doesn't hear. Together they pray:

"Gotteniu, the precious day of Yom Kippur is almost gone. The sun that was too bright for our eyes is falling, its light dimming. Yet I have a few sweet moments to plead for Your pity. Remember that we are Your children, and You our Father, our King. Have mercy on us. I have no more strength. My tears are tears of hunger and weariness. I cry out to You. Every part of my being begs You. Open Your holy eyes and look at Your children, see the river of tears flowing from our eyes. Our father, our King, seal us in the Book of Life for a good life, all of us who are Your children . . . "

Down below, the men stand as Hershel lifts the ram's horn, Hayim between the dungsweeper and the picklemaker at the back and Berekh at the front, facing the scribe and the blacksmith and the ritual slaughterer and the wheelwright and the carpenter, whose sons and grandsons will leave Blaszka for Warsaw, Jerusalem, Paris, London, New York, Montreal, Shanghai, the fathers kissing their sons on both cheeks, wishing that they would stay and some will, indeed, stay and wish that they had gone.

IN THE coming year, Misha's son will be called Ari the Lion, after Hayim's father, and the girl will be called Blema, after Misha's mother. Blema means bloom, and when she grows up, she will marry and bear a son called Zev the Wolf, after Berekh's father.

In 1940, Misha's son Ari, a partisan, will bring food to a woman from Plotsk and her ten-year-old daughter, hiding in the Północna woods, sheltered by the hut that once held the printing press.

After the liberation this girl, then sixteen, and Misha's grandson, Zev, will find each other and fall in love. Aidel-Mariam will teach Zev to dance and not to swear and they will emigrate to the new world, via London, where Emma Blau will assist them with their papers.

In the new world, they will give their middle child a flower name to remind her of Zev's mother, Blema, the daughter of Misha, and this child will grow up to dance as her mother danced, as her father's mother danced, as her great-grandmother might have danced in the woods beside the Północna River.

One summer evening, this great-granddaughter will look out on a river on the other side of the world from Blaszka, where yet the flat landscape and the smell of the lindens in bloom are a little like that old world. Before it sets, the sun bursts through her window, dazzling her eyes. So how can she be sure of the shape that she sees on the water, a wave of the hand as if her great-grandmother were greeting her? Yet she lifts her own hand in greeting, and while the sky darkens she thinks of Misha, who comes to her in dreams to tell her about the real Blaszka, the one that shines through the stones. Then the great-granddaughter picks up her pen to write it all as she promised she would:

In her bridal trunk Misha put . . .

IN HER bridal trunk Misha put a scorched wooden spoon, a sliver of almond soap, a blue book with a worn cover, and a piece of red amber with a fossilized feather in it. From time to time, she adds something to the trunk, lifting the lid to show what's inside to her family and her friends and to strangers when they are guests in her house.

But for now in the year 5655, the men stand below and the women above in the balcony of the synagogue. They have recited the public confessional, admitting to lies and slander and robbery and violence and stubbornness and immorality and tyranny, willingly and unwillingly, with disrespect and mockery, in gossip, in business, in swearing up and down that something was true when it wasn't. And for all this they are forgiven.

The village of Blaszka has reached the final moment of Yom Kippur. The Rabbi calls *tekiah gedolah,* the great blast, the long call that closes the Gates of Eternity. Hershel raises the shofar. As he sounds the call, the ram's horn curls in its spiral toward heaven. Awake, awake, the gates are closing, and we are left again in the world of time, alone with one another.

In the village of Blaszka, as in every other place, even in fairy tales, there was an oldest son and a youngest son, a rich sister and a poor sister, the clever, the wise, the wicked and naive, a constellation of people, seemingly motionless, a river of stars in the midnight sky. But go closer and the stars are exploding suns that come into being and die, and in between give life to all manner of things. Look and you'll see the planets with their seas rising and falling under the pull of the circling moons. Even closer, you'll see the trees of the forest and mushrooms sprouting in the dark places. Watch how the mushroom pickers, when they find one that's wormy, cut it into pieces which they scatter on the ground to spread the spores, so new mushrooms will grow.

Mushrooms are the fruit of the fungus. Below ground are cell-wide threads that take sugars from the roots of trees, giving in exchange water and minerals. Because the roots are hard and thick, they would have trouble getting what they need without these threads, this network of life blood running through the ground connecting all the trees, making of the woods a single living thing. So make yourself a bowl of mushroom soup, and as you lift the spoon to your lips, remember that this, too, is the river midnight, and as you drink, know that Hanna-Leah made this exact same soup for Hershel, once upon a time.

AUTHOR'S NOTE

BLASZKA IS A fictional village, mythical as shtetls must be, since they're gone now. My parents and my grandparents on both sides came from cities in Poland. The generation beyond that, my great-grandparents, most likely came from a shtetl somewhere—but who they were and what that shtetl might have been is a mystery. As I was writing the first draft of the novel in a cottage on Prince Edward Island, it seemed natural to link these two myths, the shtetl and my lost family history, by tracing my lineage through Misha. And why not? After all, couldn't she have been my great-grandmother as much as anyone?

Yet, once there were shtetls. Their people had existence. And out of respect for them, I wanted the novel to be as historically accurate as possible. So let me say that while Blaszka is fictional, as is the Północna River, all of the details of people's lives, their songs and prayers, the geography of the cities and the landscapes described are factual, with the exception of Whorehouse Row, which is an imagined street in the city of Plotsk (though the whorehouses themselves are based on fact). Any dates given in connection with historical persons or events, including the cholera epidemic of 1867, are also factual. All of the characters in the village of Blaszka are fictional.

Doing the research for this novel began as a challenge, frustrating because unearthing specifies of daily living was difficult, but it ended as a privilege: I stepped into another world and was honored to do so. For historical events, I used contemporary sources as well as looking for the most up-to-date historical research. To get the details and flavor of daily life, I used contemporary sources first of all, secondly sources prior to 1905 (when certain restrictions, such as censorship, were relieved), thirdly sources prior to the First World War. Between the wars, when Poland was independent, life changed in many ways for the Jews: access to secular education increased tremendously, but the economic situation and local anti-Semitism worsened, so material from that period doesn't accurately reflect life for Jews as it was earlier. I used very little material written after the war; the Holocaust overwhelms memory at that point, the shtetl is cast in a nostalgic glow, the surrounding culture remembered in the bitterness of loss.

For those of you whose curiosity has been piqued, I've put together a selection of interesting sources. A number of these books are out of print, but are available in libraries. All of the sources below are written in, or translated into, English. They are organized by category, arranged alphabetically by title.

Researching and writing this novel has been a journey of discovery sweeter and more demanding than I could have imagined. May your journeys bring you much *nakhes,* that untranslatable joy of a full heart.

RECOMMENDED READING

History of Jews In Poland

A good place to start for short, informative articles is *The Encyclopedia Judaica.*

For more in-depth reading, The Institute of Polish-Jewish Studies in Oxford, England, has published a number of very good books through Basil Blackwell Ltd., Oxford. I would especially recommend:

The Jews in Poland, edited by Chimen Abramsky, Maciej Jachimczyk, and Antony Polonsky. The Institute of Polish-Jewish Studies, Basil Blackwell Ltd., Oxford, England, 1986.

The Jews of Warsaw, edited by Władysław T. Bartoszewski and Antony Polonsky, The Institute of Polish-Jewish Studies, Basil Blackwell Ltd., Oxford, England, 1991.

Polin, a Journal of Polish-Jewish Studies, The Institute of Polish-Jewish Studies, Basil Blackwell Ltd., Oxford, England.

I would also recommend:

History of the Jews in Russia and Poland: From the Earliest Times Until the Present Day by M. Dubnow. The Jewish Publication Society of America, Philadelphia, 1916–1920. This is a classic, multivolume history.

Images Before My Eyes: A Photographic History of Jewish Life in Poland 1864–1939 by Lucjan Dobroszycki and Barbara Kirshenblatt-Gimblett. Schocken Books, published in cooperation with the YIVO Institute for Jewish Research, New York, 1977. The best pictorial history I've seen.

The Jews in Polish Culture by Aleksander Hertz, translated by Richard Lourie, with a forward by Czeslaw Milosz. Northwestern University Press, Evanston, Illinois, 1988.

Poles and Jews: A Failed Brotherhood by Magdalena Opalski and Israel Bartal. University Press of New England, Hanover, NH, 1992.

The Polish Jews by Beatrice C. Baskerville. Chapman & Hall, London, 1906. A fascinating (if somewhat anti-Semitic) contemporary account. Ms. Baskerville was an Englishwoman who traveled to Poland and subsequently wrote a book about her experience.

History of Poland

God's Playground by Norman Davies. Columbia University Press, New York, 1982. An excellent general history.

History of the Shtetl

Non-Fiction

From a Ruined Garden: The Memorial Books of Polish Jewry, translated and edited by Jack Kugelmass and Jonathan Boyarin, with geographical index and bibliography by Zachary M. Baker. Schocken Books, New York, 1983. This is a compilation of brief memoirs, categorized by subject, taken from the memorial books put together after the war. Wherever possible, survivors were contacted for stories of life before the war, their stories gathered into books, one for each city or shtetl. I have the memorial book for Plotsk (my mother's hometown, in Polish spelled "Płock"), written in Yiddish and Hebrew with some English translation, and it's an invaluable source of information.

Konin: A Quest by Theo Richmond. Pantheon Books, New York, 1995.

Life Is with People: The Culture of the Shtetl by Mark Zborowski and Elizabeth Herzog, foreword by Margaret Mead. Shocken Books, New York, 1962, reissued 1974. I mention this book because it is everpresent. I even found a copy in a used bookstore in Wolfville, Nova Scotia. An anthropological study of the shtetl, using oral histories to create a study of daily life, it was an original approach in its day. Unfortunately, one person's individual experience doesn't necessarily reflect the way of life for a whole town, or in another place. I found that, in addition to being somewhat sentimental, a number of the descriptions in this book were not corroborated by other sources. One difficulty with historical research is that material, though well-intended, can sometimes be misleading through lack of attention to detail or relying too heavily on other sources that are in themselves inaccurate.

The Shtetl Book compiled by Diane K. Roshkies and David G. Roskies. Ktav Publishing House, New York, 1975. This book is geared for use with students in schools, and is somewhat simply written, but provides interesting and reliable information.

Shtetl: The Life and Death of a Small Town and the World of Polish Jews by Eva Hoffman. Houghton Mifflin, New York, 1997.

Yesterday: Memoir of a Russian Jewish Family by Miriam Shomer Zunser. Harper and Row, New York, 1978. The author is the daughter of the Yiddish author Shomer. Her memoirs begin with the marriage of her grandparents at the ages of thirteen in the 1830s and continue up until the twentieth century. A fascinating picture of shtetl life.

Fiction

I'm very interested in Yiddish literature. There are many good anthologies in translation, so I'll just recommend a few of my favorites, here:

Found Treasures: Stories by Yiddish Women Writers, edited by Frieda Forman, Ethel Raicus, Sarah Silberstein Swartz, and Margie Wolfe. Second Story Press, Toronto, 1994. The introduction by Irena Klepfisz is a fascinating, brief history of Yiddish language and literature, its changing social meaning and impact on the lives of women and men.

I. L. Peretz, Selected Stories, edited by Irving Howe and Eliezer Greenberg. Schocken Books, New York, 1975.

A Shtetl and Other Yiddish Novellas, edited By Ruth R. Wisse. Behrman House, New York, 1986. Includes an excellent introduction by Ms. Wisse.

The Great Jewish Plays, translated and edited by Joseph C. Landis. Horizon Press, New York, 1972.

History of the Rom (Gypsies)

As a Jew, I think it's important to remember another group that has been persecuted and repeatedly evicted from its home, and still is. I would recommend the following:

The Gypsies by Charles G. Leland. Houghton, Mifflin, Boston, 1882. You may be able to find this book at a university library. It's a fascinating contemporary account by an English traveler to eastern Europe. Leland had also spent time with the Rom in England and spoke their language.

A History of the Gypsies of Eastern Europe and Russia by David M. Crowe. St. Martin's Press, New York, 1994.

The Pariah Syndrome by Ian Hancock. Karoma Publishers, Inc., Ann Arbor, Mich., 1987. This book, written by one of the Rom, movingly describes the history of persecution endured by the Gypsies.

History of the Russian Economy

The Tsarist Economy, 1850–1917 by Peter Gatrell. St. Martin's Press, New York, 1986.

Russian Imperialism: The Interaction of Domestic and Foreign Policy, 1860–1914 by Dietrich Geyer, translated from German by Bruce Little. Yale University Press, New Haven, 1987.

Life In New York At the Turn of the Century

Love, Anarchy, and Emma Goldman by Candace Falk. Holt, Rinehart and Winston, New York, 1984.

Out of the Sweatshop: The Struggle for Industrial Democracy, edited by Leon Stein. Quadrangle/New York Times Book Co., New York, 1977. A compilation of brief first-person accounts and contemporary documents. Gives a real flavor of life as it was then.

The World of Our Fathers by Irving Howe. Bantam, New York, 1976. Still a classic.

The Milieu of Crime

The Courage of His Convictions by Tony Parker and Robert Allerton. Hutchinson, London, 1962. This is a book of conversations between a journalist and a repeat armed robber. Intelligent, morally aware, and brutally callous by turns, Allerton's story is intriguing, both revealing much and leaving many unanswered questions.

Crime Among Jews: A Comparative Study of Criminality Among Minorities and Dominant Groups by Zvi Hermon. Center for the Study of Crime, Delinquincy, and Corrections, Southern Illinois University, Carbondale, Ill., 1991.

Criminal Russia by Valerie Chaldize. Random House, New York, 1977.

Sexuality

Jewish Explorations of Sexuality, edited by Jonathan Magonet. Berghahn Books, Providence and Oxford, England, 1995.

Love, Sex, and Aging: A Consumers Union Report by Edward M. Breecher, and the Editors of Consumer Report Books, Consumers Union, Little Brown & Co., Boston, 1984.

Socialism and Anarchism

Class Struggle in the Pale: The Formative Years of the Jewish Workers' Movement in Tsarist Russia by Ezra Mendelsohn. Cambridge University Press, Cambridge, England, 1970.

Some Aspects of Polish Culture

The Peasants by Władysław Stanislaw Reymont, translated by Michael H. Dziewicki. A. A. Knopf, New York, 1924–25. Written in the early years of the century while Reymont was in Paris, this novel later won the Nobel Prize.

Polish Art and Architecture, 1890–1980 by Andrezej K. Olszewski. Interpress Publishers, Warsaw, 1989.

Stanisław Wyspianski by Tymon Terlecki. Twayne Publishers, Boston, 1983.

The Wedding by Stanisław Wyspianski (1901), translated by Gerard T. Kapolka. Ardis, Ann Arbor, Mich., 1990.

Warszawa Zapomniana (1898–1915) by Krystyna Lejko. Wydawnictwo Naukowe Pwn, Warsaw, 1994. This little book of postcard photographs of Warsaw at the turn of the century gives a lovely visual sense of the city at that time.

Spiritual Life of Jewish Women

A Book of Jewish Women's Prayers: Translations from the Yiddish, selected and with commentary by Norman Tarnor. Jason Aronson Inc., Northvale, N.J., London, 1995.

Four Centuries of Jewish Women's Spirituality: A Sourcebook, edited and with introductions by Ellen M. Umansky and Dianne Ashton. Beacon Press, Boston, 1992.

The Weekly Midrash, Tz'enah Ur'enah, translated from the Yiddish by Miriam Stark Zakon, introduction by Meir Holder. Mesorah Publications, Ltd. New York, 1995.

Yiddish Folk Songs

Voices of a People by Ruth Rubin. McGraw-Hill, New York, 1973. Any collection of folk songs by Ruth Rubin is fascinating.

GLOSSARY

All words and expressions are in Yiddish unless otherwise indicated. Words that are Hebrew in origin but pronounced with a Yiddish accent and incorporated into Yiddish are not indicated separately.

Adam Harishon Adam the first

Aguna A woman whose husband has deserted her, whether intentionally or not; she cannot remarry because there is no mechanism in Jewish religious law to declare a man that is missing dead or to force a man to grant his spouse a divorce other than through social coercion.

Allevai If only

Alta-Bubbie Great-grandmother

Alter (m) or **Alta** (f) Old one, often added to a baby's name to confuse the evil eye, hence "Alta-Fruma."

Ani mammin Hebrew, "I believe," the first two words of an old prayer, "I believe in the coming of the Messiah although he may tarry."

Ba'al Shem Tov Founder of Hasidism

Baalebatim Middle-class, often business people who had money but were not considered "shayner" because they dealt directly with peasants.

Baba Yaga Witch-figure in Russian folk legend

Babka Pound cake

Badhan Wedding jester, entertains guests and bride and groom at a Jewish wedding.

Bakenta Bilder *Familiar Pictures,* title of book written in Yiddish by I. L. Peretz

Barukh hashem Blessed be the Name

Bedecken Covering, the ceremony of covering the bride with her veil.

Beshert Intended

Boim Tree

Broygez tanz Literally "angry dance," one of the dances that involve miming characters and situations, performed to entertain bride and groom; the object of the wedding feast was to entertain the new couple.

Bubbie Grandmother

Cack Defecate

Daven Pray

Dayeinu Hebrew, literally "Enough for us," refers to a Passover song.

Der kleiner Literally "the little" [one or thing], perhaps abbreviated from "der kleiner mann," the little man. Polite euphemism for penis.

Dodi li v'ani lo Hebrew, "I am my beloved and he is mine," a quote from the *Song of Songs* in the Bible.

Dreck Feces

Dybbuk The soul of a dead person that has moved into the body of a living person.

Ein Sof Hebrew, literally "without end," a term for God

Feldsher Barber-surgeon, someone who attempted to heal the sick by the use of leeches, enemas, and cupping, that is applying heated glass cups to the skin, creating a suction effect in which the skin swelled, sometimes cutting the skin first to bleed the patient just as in medieval times.

Gadje Romany for non-Gypsy

Gan Aeden The Garden of Eden

Get A religious divorce

Golem In Jewish legend an artificially created person brought to life by supernatural means.

Gott in himmel God in heaven

Gotteniu A term of endearment for God.

Goy/goyisher Gentile

Groschen Penny

Gubernia Governing district under Russian rule

Gudulka Romany string instrument

Gut Yom Tov Good holiday

Haggadah Hebrew, literally "the telling," refers to the book of songs and stories recited at the Passover seder.

Hallah(s) White egg-bread, usually braided and eaten on the Sabbath

Haman In the story of Purim, Haman is the Persian king's advisor who persuaded the king to decree the death of the Jews.

Hammantash/hammentashen Three-cornered pastry filled with prune, poppy seed, or almond paste, eaten on Purim. It is supposed to represent the villain Human's three-cornered hat, some say his ear, others his purse or pocket.

Hanukkah The eight-day winter solstice festival that commemorates the victory of the few over the powerful and the miracle of lights.

Ha-ra Hebrew, "the wicked one" in the story of the four sons told at the Passover seder, illustrating four responses to the telling of the story. The wise son wants to know all of the commandments pertaining to the observance of the festival. The simple son just wants to know the story. The wicked son denounces the story as irrelevant to him. And the son that doesn't know how to ask any questions must be initiated by the storyteller.

Haroses A sweet mixture of crushed nuts, apple, honey, and wine representing the bricks made by the Hebrews when they were slaves in Egypt and eaten with matzo at the Passover meal.

Hasidic, Hasidism A sect of Jewish mystics founded in Poland about 1750, characterized by religious zeal, and emphasizing joyful worship.

Hazen Cantor

Hazzer Pig

Heder Primary Hebrew school for boys, usually from age three to ten.

Hod See *Netzakh*

Hutzpah Nerve

Kaddish An ancient prayer most commonly recited as the mourner's kaddish in memory of the death of someone close.

Kasha Boiled or baked buckwheat

Kassa Union

Kefir Soured milk, similar to buttermilk.

Khapper Kidnapper, specifically a person who earned money by kidnapping Jewish children for induction into the Russian army.

Kiddush Blessing recited over wine at Sabbath and religious festivals.

Kielbasa Polish salami.

Kind/kinder/kinderlekh Child/children/little children

Kishka Intestines

Kittel White robe, worn by men at Yom Kippur, the Passover meal, and when buried.

Klezmer Musician

Kol Nidrei Aramaic, literally "All Vows," refers to the prayer that is recited at the beginning of Yom Kippur. Its origins are uncertain. Rabbinic authorities were at one time opposed to it, but popular acclaim made Kol Nidrei such a beloved ritual that rabbinic authority accepted it by about the year 1,000 C.E. There are two versions. The Hebrew version refers to vows made in the past year; the Aramaic, used by Jews from Eastern Europe, refers to vows of the coming year. A vow to God was no light thing. Such a vow unfulfilled meant that God's name had been used in vain, uselessly, and that was considered a great sin. Both versions of Kol Nidrei arose from the anxiety of being unable to fulfill a promise made to God under stress, as people often do.

Kopeck Smallest demonation of Russian currency, a penny.

Kosher Permitted according to Jewish dietary law; also used colloquially to mean something allowed.

Kugel Baked pudding, usually made with potatoes or noodles.

Kupka Cap worn by married women at the end of the 18th century.

Kuvod Honor, respect

Lag b'omer A minor festival about halfway between Passover and Shavuos; the only day during this season on which a Jewish wedding can be performed.

Loshen-hora Literally, "evil tongue," meaning malicious gossip.

Ma Nishtanah Hebrew, literally "How is this different?" refers to the four questions recited by the youngest child during the Passover seder to initiate the telling of the story of the exodus from Egypt.

Maggid Preacher

Mahrime Polluted, impure in Romany. Among the Rom (Gypsies), certain foods are considered appropriate for eating while others are *mahrime*. Similarly certain uses of utensils can render them *mahrime*. Using a stranger's knife is inappropriate because one does not know how the stranger used it; similarly drinking directly from a stranger's bottle.

Mamala "Little mother," a term of endearment

Mama-loshen The mother tongue, Yiddish

Matzah/matzos Unleavened bread eaten during Passover to commemorate the exodus from Egypt, when there was no time to wait for the bread to rise.

Mazel-tov Literally good luck; congratulations

Maydela "Little girl," a term of endearment

Megillah Literally "scroll," most commonly used to refer to the Scroll of Esther, which told the story of the Jewish Queen Esther and the salvation of the Jews from persecution in ancient Persia.

Mekhitzah Hebrew, the wall that divides the men's section from the women's section in a traditional synagogue.

Melamud Hebrew, teacher

Mensch Literally "person," refers to a responsible/mature person.

Mikva Ritual bath, or the bathhouse in which the ritual bath is housed.

Mitzrayim Hebrew, literally "the narrow place," the word used for Ancient Egypt.

Mitzvah/mitzvos Good deed(s), religious obligation(s)

Mordecai In the story of Purim, Mordecai is the cousin of the Jewish Queen Esther who was married to the King of Persia. Mordecai saves the king's life and then advises Esther to take action in order to save the Jews because she is close to the king, though she risks her own life in revealing her Jewish identity to the king.

Nakhes Proud pleasure

Nebekh Unfortunate(ly)

Netzakh and Hod Hebrew: in Kabbala, two of the Sefirot, the ten spheres or channels through which the Divine descends from the Endless Source to become present in the physical world. These spheres are seen as representing various Divine aspects: wisdom, love, beauty, courage, and so on. They are often diagrammed as circles connected by lines to form the shape of a person. In the diagram, Netzakh and Hod are the "legs." The right side of the diagram is seen to represent Divine compassion while the left side sets limits.

Nu Interjection like so or well as in "Nu, what do you want?"

Parev Food that can be eaten with either meat or dairy; traditional Jewish dietary laws require that eating meat be separated from eating dairy by several hours and that different dishes and utensils are used for meat and dairy.

Parsha Weekly Torah reading

Pesakh Passover, the festival commemorating the exodus from Egypt, the flight from slavery to freedom.

Pierogi Dumplings stuffed with cheese, potato or mushrooms

Pish Urinate

Pisher Literally "one who pees," term of familiarity for someone young or immature; small fry.

Potsh Slap

Pripichek There were no stoves, that is cooking ranges, above the oven. Instead, beside the oven there was a cooking grate on bricks, called the *pripichek.* A hot fire would be lit under the grate, and a pot placed on top of the grate to begin cooking, after which the pot would be put inside the oven to continue cooking slowly.

Proster A plain one; lower-class people who worked with their hands, artisans or peddlers

Purim The festival commemorating the salvation of the Jews from persecution in ancient Persia, in which there is a kind of "carnival" atmosphere. Costumes were worn, men were allowed to wear women's clothes even though it was forbidden at all other times, "lessons" in Torah and Talmud were given which made fun of religious law, humorous plays were performed; children went from house to house for a penny and treats, drinking was not only permitted but encouraged.

Ribono shel olam Master of the Universe, God

Rosh hashanah The Jewish New Year

Rosh Hodesh Hebrew, first of the Hebrew month celebrated on the New Moon, traditionally a woman's festival.

Rov Rabbi

Rusalkeh Mythical figure of a swamp-woman that lures unwary travelers to their death.

Seder Hebrew, the festive meal at Passover during which the *Haggadah* is read and the story of the exodus from Egypt told.

Sela Hebrew, forever

Sh'ma Israel, Adonai eloheinu, Adonai ekhad Hebrew, "Hear Israel, the Lord is our God, the Lord is One."

Shaalakhmonas Gifts of dried fruit, nuts, sometimes pastry given at Purim.

Shaaleh A question of ritual or ethical significance brought to the rabbi.

Shabbas The Sabbath

Shadkhen Matchmaker

Shalom ha-bayit Hebrew, peace in the home

Shammus The man that maintains the synagogue, calls the villagers to prayers, may assist at services.

Shandeh Shame, scandal

Shavuos Holiday celebrating the receiving of the Hebrew law (the Torah) at Mount Sinai; occurs seven weeks after Passover. Between Passover and Shavuos, Jewish religious law prohibits weddings except for several specified days.

Shaynela Pretty little one, a term of endearment.

Shayner A nice one, upperclass; meaning those that were wealthy and did not deal directly with peasants or those that were gifted religious scholars.

Shekhina Hebrew, God's presence in the world, the feminine aspect of God. In Kabbalistic thought, the Shekhina was understood as going into exile with the world when it became separated from God. When the world was healed, the exile would end, and the Shekhina would be reunited with the other divine aspects.

Shiddukh Match, as between prospective bride and groom.

Shivah Week of mourning for the death of a family member.

Shlemiel Loser

Shlep Carry, drag

Shmaltz Grease, fat

Shmata Rag

Shmeckel Penis; in Yiddish there are many euphemisms for penis, ranging from polite to crude. Shmeckel is the crudest and would never have been used in mixed company. *Der shvantz,* meaning the tail, was a mid-range euphemism. The politest, and the one most used by women, was *der kleiner,* the little thing. See *der kleiner.*

Shofar Hebrew, "ram's horn," the instrument blown in the synagogue on the High Holy Days.

Shoin Soon, already.

Shokhet The person whose occupation is the slaughter of animals for food according to prescribed religious ritual.

Sholom aleikhem Literally "peace be upon you," a greeting frequently responded to with *"Aleikhem sholom"*

Shtetl A Jewish town established by charter.

Shul Synagogue

Shvitz Literally "sweat," refers to a sauna.

Shvyger Mother-in-law

Simhas Torah Hebrew, literally "Joy of Torah," the festival celebrating the acceptance of the Torah. Customs include dancing with the Torah.

Talmud Hebrew, the book of Jewish religious laws written down in the first two centuries c.e. along with subsequent commentaries, parables, and moral tales.

Tashlikh Hebrew, literally "cast off," referring to the ceremony performed on the first day of Rosh Hashanah when crumbs are thrown into a river or stream to represent cast-off sins.

Tekhinas Prayers in Yiddish for women, written by both men and women, both for use at home and in the synagogue, dating from the 17th century to the 20th century. New prayers were written on an ongoing basis.

Tekiah gedolah Hebrew, literally "the great cry," spoken to signal a long blast on the ram's horn in which the sound becomes louder toward the end, a difficult feat as the person blowing the ram's horn is losing breath.

Teshuva Hebrew, repentance

Tevet Hebrew month corresponding roughly to December/January

Tishah-b'Av Hebrew, Ninth of Av, the fast day commemorating the destruction of the ancient temple in Jerusalem.

Torah Hebrew, "the law," refers to the five books of Moses in the Bible, sometimes used as a general term to refer to all religious writings of Jews.

Trayf Forbidden by Jewish dietary law; also used colloquially to mean something prohibited.

Tzena-U-Rena Hebrew, literally "come and see," refers to the weekly commentary on the Torah written in Yiddish in the 17th century for women and men illiterate in Hebrew, came to be used exclusively by women and sometimes called the Women's Bible.

Tzuris Trouble

Vestel Embroidered bodice in fashion with Jewish women at the end of the 18th century.

Vilda haya(s) Wild animal(s), a pejorative term

Vos makht a Yid Literally, "What's a Jew doing?" equivalent of "How are You?"

Yetzer-hara Literally "the evil inclination," the concept could be more accurately translated as instinctive drive.

Yikhus Honor due to family lineage of scholars, rabbis, etc.

Yingeleh Little boy

Yom Kippur Day of Atonement, a fast day in which neither food nor water are taken; begins at sunset with the Kol Nidrei prayer and continues until the next day at sunset; the most important festival of the year, also called the Great Sabbath.

Zayda Grandfather

Zetz Smack, harder than a *potsh*

Zogerin Woman who leads the women in prayer, will also say prayers for women who request them, often at the grave of someone known to be particularly pious.

THE RIVER MIDNIGHT

DISCUSSION QUESTIONS

1. Who is the strongest woman in Blaszka? Is it Misha, for her stubborn will and power to heal, or Faygela, for her ability to write and get stronger with each baby she bears? Is it Hannah-Leah or Alta-Fruma? Or are these two women too diverse in character and temperament to compare? If it were possible, which of these women would you like to befriend, and why?

2. The author structured this novel in an interesting way, recalling the same events over and over, each time from a different character's perspective. How did each version differ from the others? Did you find any one character's point of view more believable than another? Discuss why the author may have chosen this "full-circle" way of constructing her book.

3. A major turning point for Hannah-Leah is the night she eats all of the strawberries she picks, wades into the river, and throws Misha's potions away (page 53). Identify and discuss turning points experienced by other characters in *The River Midnight*. How do their personal revelations affect the way they feel about themselves, and how they are perceived by others in the village?

4. The death of Faygela's father made it impossible for her to continue her education in Warsaw. Do you think she would have had the courage to leave if she'd been given the opportunity? If she had gone away to school, would she have returned or made her life elsewhere? Discuss the significance of Faygela's visions of her dead father.

5. Discuss the notions of religion and tradition as portrayed in *The River Midnight*. What do the people of Blaszka get out of following their strict religion with its rules, songs, dances, and prayers? Do you think they spend so much time *following* these traditions that they don't have time to question them? Compare the rituals of Judaism to Misha's rituals of midwifery. Which ones help the people of Blaszka more? Which ones give them the most comfort, and why?

6. When Izzie tells his sister Emma that they, like all men and women, must distance themselves from each another, he compares

them to "milk and meat," which must always be kept apart (page 162). Discuss the different ways in which the men and women of Blaszka are divided from each other. In this community, are the women the sweet and comforting "milk," or the strong and substantial "meat?"

7. Emma's story is presented in a typhus-induced haze. Discuss why the author chose to tell her story that way. Does her dreamy state reflect the way she feels as she recalls the horror of her parents' deaths? Does she feel guilty that she survived America and they did not? Do the radical notions Emma brings from New York ill-prepare her for life in Blaszka? Or do they equip her to bring to the village the modern ideas it will need to survive in the next century? Will Emma ever really find her place in Blaszka? Or has she seen too much of the world to ever be satisfied there?

8. Do you agree with the statement that "restraint is as much of a sign of the Holy as is courage" (page 450)? If this is true, then is it possible to argue that Yarush, who exhibits courage through his aggression, is as holy as Berekh, who shows restraint through his pragmatism? Although it seems clear that Berekh is a kinder and better man than Yarush, do these men share any traits? Which characters in *The River Midnight* exhibit restraint and which ones show courage?

9. Most of the women in the village are far more interested in stories about spirits and demons than they are in Shomer's stories of royalty and heiresses. Why do you think this is so? Discuss this novel's many mystical elements: the angels and potions, the Traveler and Director, and the stories of the Demon Lilith and Manya. What impact does the belief in the supernatural have on the characters' lives? Are they frightened by it? Comforted? Fascinated?

10. Alta-Fruma was once in love with Adam Hoffmann. Yet on their last visit, she notices flaws she never saw before: his hands are clammy, and his mildness, once appealing, now seems meek and unbecoming. Do you think Adam changed, or did Alta-Fruma simply overlook his flaws in the past because she needed him in her life? If so, why doesn't she need him anymore? Does anyone else in this novel have a similar revelation, seeing someone they thought they knew for what they *really* are?

11. Most of the older characters in this book will live out their lives in the *shtetl*, relatively unaffected by the passing of time. But the younger generation's last years will be marked by the horrors of the Holocaust. Discuss how your knowledge of the dark history that looms ahead affected (or did not affect) the way you perceived this book and its characters.

12. Sweet and impressionable Ruthie seems in desperate need of finding a strong female role model. In the end, who do you think she admires the most: Misha, Emma, or her mother, Faygela? Who do you think will ultimately have the greatest impact on her life, how she lives it, and who she becomes? What effect does Ruthie's arrest and imprisonment have on her relationship with her mother and how they talk to one another?

13. Compare Misha's relationship with Hayim, the watercarrier, with her relationship with Berekh. What does Berekh give her that Hayim cannot? Do you think Misha's marriage to Hayim was doomed from the start? Why is Misha the only person Hayim cannot draw?

AUTHOR BIOGRAPHY

Born and raised in Montreal, LILIAN NATTEL now lives in Toronto. Her short stories have been anthologized, and she has been awarded grants by the Canada Council and the Ontario Arts Council.

HOW I CAME TO WRITE THIS BOOK: A NOTE TO READERS FROM LILIAN NATTEL

I was taking a course in writing and personal creativity, I imagined a large earth-mother type laughing; she was standing on a beach in prehistoric Hawaii beside a rack of drying fish. Unfortunately I don't know anything about prehistoric Hawaii, so I wondered if I could find a more familiar setting that would retain the mythical quality of my vision.

I immediately thought of the *shtetl*. I loved the incongruency: this big woman, free, independent, in a structured society in which women's roles were quite restricted. That led to a short story. People who heard me read it at a workshop were sure that I was working on a novel, but I said, "No. I'm not writing more Jewish stuff." I didn't want to be a "Jewish" writer. But the story wouldn't go away. I wrote another about the same village. But I still wasn't finished with Blaszka. So I went away for the summer to a cottage on Prince Edward Island to see what I could do with writing a novel. That summer I wrote the sketch for *The River Midnight*.

My family history was somewhat mythical to me because I never met my father's immediate family; they'd all died in the war. When I was little, I'd imagine that maybe his older sisters had survived because he hadn't actually seen them die and perhaps I'd be able to find them. So when

I came to the end of the first draft of *The River Midnight*, it occurred to me that since I knew nothing about my great-grandmother, she could have been Misha. By imaginatively reinventing my lost family history, I felt that broken threads were in some way retied.